The author lives in East Anglia with her husband and their Jack Russell terrier. Her favourite hobby is visiting churches. A DEAD MAN OUT OF MIND is her fourth novel, following APPOINTED TO DIE, A DRINK OF DEADLY WINE and THE SNARES OF DEATH.

A Dead Man
Out of Mind

I am clean forgotten, as a dead man out of mind:
I am become like a broken vessel.
Psalm 31.14

Kate Charles

HEADLINE

First published in 1994
by HEADLINE BOOK PUBLISHING

First published in paperback in 1994
by HEADLINE BOOK PUBLISHING

10 9 8 7 6 5 4 3 2 1

ISBN 0 7472 4535 5

Typeset by Keyboard Services, Luton

Printed and bound in Great Britain by
Cox & Wyman Ltd, Reading, Berks

HEADLINE BOOK PUBLISHING
A division of Hodder Headline PLC
338 Euston Road
London NW1 3BH

For Jacqui, who has demonstrated the value
of women's ministry to so many.

AUTHOR'S NOTE

As in the past, I have taken certain liberties in creating churches: St Margaret's and St Jude's, as well St Dunstan's, are as much a product of my imagination as the people inhabiting them. I have also created the post of Archdeacon of Kensington, to avoid any possible confusion with actual clerics.

Prologue

*What profit is there in my blood: when I go down to
   the pit?*

Psalm 30.9

It was a clear case of a burglary gone wrong; the police
at the scene were in no doubt about that. They'd seen
plenty of these church burglaries – an increasing
number in recent years, and not just in rich London
parishes like this one. Invariably they fell into two
categories of crime. The professional burglar knew
what he was looking for, often stealing to order; he
would be in and out of the church quickly, leaving a
minimum of mess behind. In these cases, the stolen
items – silver mostly, and antique ecclesiastical furniture – would be on a boat to the Continent before they
were even missed. The other sort of church burglary was
of the opportunistic kind, and usually left chaos in its
wake.

From the shambles in the sacristy, it was apparent
that the burglary at St Margaret's Church, Pimlico,
was in the second category. Papers and documents,
evidently from the open safe, were scattered around
the floor, a table had been overturned, an empty

1

communion wine bottle smashed, and in an act of wilful and mindless vandalism, the purple chasuble which had been laid out for the next celebration of the Mass had been slashed to ribbons. But there was one significant difference from the usual pattern: by the safe lay the body of a clergyman, the back of his head caved in.

'He must have caught them in the act, poor devil.' Detective Inspector Pierce touched the arm of the young uniformed constable who had been the first officer on the scene; the man looked distinctly green around the gills, thought Pierce with compassion. They couldn't do any more until the police pathologist arrived to certify death – not that there was any doubt about it, but procedures must be adhered to – so Pierce began talking to take both their minds off the gruesome sight before them.

'I suppose it was kids,' he said with a detachment he didn't feel. 'These sorts of crimes usually are. Unpremeditated. They break into a church looking for something they can turn into a bit of ready cash. For drugs, you know – that kind of thing.'

The PC's Adam's apple bobbed up and down as he gulped convulsively, grateful for the distraction. 'And what do they do with ... with the stuff they take, sir?'

'Oh, they flog it for a few bob. It usually turns up down the Portobello Road in a day or two.'

'And do you usually catch them?'

Pierce smiled grimly. 'Sometimes we do, and sometimes we don't. Most of them are pretty stupid, you know. At least in this kind of a crime. With the pros we don't have much chance of catching them, but the kids are a different story. The pros never leave prints, of course, but often the kids do. They wipe the obvious things and then leave a clear set of prints on a door handle. Or they wear surgical gloves and then peel the gloves off and leave them at the scene – with their prints inside.'

'So you think you'll catch whoever did ... this?' The PC's eyes returned without volition to the bloody mess that was the priest's head, and he gulped again.

'I'd say we've got a damn good chance,' Pierce reassured him. 'They're sure to have slipped up somewhere. They probably panicked after the priest surprised them, and when he ended up dead I imagine they got out in a hell of a hurry.' He fell silent for a moment, contemplating the body on the floor.

Pierce was undecided about the dead man's age; his black cassock gave no clues, and while his face was young and almost boyish, his dark hair was peppered with grey in virtually equal measure. That youthful, unlined face was turned towards Pierce, its blue eyes staring at him in a final look of sightless surprise. 'God, I wish that doctor would get here,' the inspector muttered, jamming his hands in his coat pockets.

A moment later his wish was granted. The police pathologist shoved his way into the room, made a quick examination, and nodded curtly. That was the signal for the scene-of-crime officers to begin their detailed work; as the specialists moved in to bag the hands of the corpse and gather evidence, Pierce led the PC out of the cramped and overcrowded sacristy and into the church.

'Can't you tell me what's going on in there?' The man

who hovered outside the door looked terrible, his face as bloodlessly white as that of the dead man in the sacristy. In fact, thought Pierce, he had something of the look of a death's head about him, with a cadaverously gaunt face, sunken eyes in deep sockets, a high bony forehead, and a balding crown with a few lank and lifeless strands of hair brushed across the top. 'I'm the one who found him,' he added, wringing his hands. 'When I came in this morning. He must have surprised some intruders. Thieves, robbers. Oh, it's just too terrible! That's what happened, isn't it?'

'You know just about as much as we do at this point, but it seems likely.' Pierce looked the man up and down. 'And who are you, sir, if you don't mind my asking?'

'Oh, sorry. Sorry.' The hand-wringing ceased as the man raised a hand to smooth the strands on the top of his head. 'Stanley Everitt. I'm the Parish Administrator.'

'So you work here?' It had never occurred to Pierce that people other than clergymen worked in churches.

'Some of the time.' The man's voice, with its unpleasant sibilance, took on a pedantic tone and he almost seemed to forget why the policemen were there as he explained. 'I'm actually the Administrator of St Jude's. You know, the big church up the road. St Margaret's is a satellite of St Jude's, so it comes under my jurisdiction as well. Most of the time I'm based at St Jude's, but I spend one day a week here. Fridays. I always come here on a Friday.'

'But this is Saturday,' interposed the constable, a stickler for details.

'Yes, of course, but there's a wedding today, and the

Vicar asked me to—' Everitt broke off, suddenly recollecting what had happened. 'The Vicar! Oh, how am I going to tell the Vicar?' The hand-wringing resumed with increased agitation. 'He'll be shattered. He's so over-worked already – however will he manage now?'

Pierce frowned in puzzlement. 'You mean that bloke in there isn't the Vicar?'

'Oh, good heavens no. He is ... was ... the curate. Father Julian Piper.'

'The curate?'

'Technically the curate of St Jude's *and* St Margaret's, of course,' Everitt explained. 'It's a combined benefice. Father Keble Smythe, the Vicar of St Jude's, is Priest-in-Charge at St Margaret's. But he's far too busy at St Jude's to have much time for St Margaret's, so Father Julian usually takes – or rather took – the services here. Oh, dear. I just don't know what's going to happen...'

Pierce, tiring of the man's rather prolix officiousness, interrupted the flow. 'Mr ... um ... Everitt, as soon as they're finished in there, I'd appreciate it if you'd take a look and let me know what, if anything, is missing. It will help us in our enquiries. Unless you'd rather that I asked the Vicar—'

'Oh, no, you mustn't disturb Father Keble Smythe!' Everitt pursed his lips and squared his shoulders self-importantly. 'I'll do all I can to help, of course. That's what a Parish Administrator is for.'

'Thank you.' Pierce's eyebrows lifted in unconscious irony but his voice was without inflexion.

'And I'll break the news about Father Julian's ... death ... to Father Keble Smythe,' Everitt added. 'He'll be so upset. It wouldn't do for him to hear it from a stranger.'

An hour later, the scene-of-crime officers had collected their evidence with meticulous precision, and the body had been removed to the mortuary. But the chaos remained, and Stanley Everitt flinched as he surveyed the wreckage of the normally tidy sacristy. 'Why did they have to make so much mess?' he moaned.

'Pure maliciousness, most likely,' the policeman at his side explained dispassionately. 'But this isn't bad, Mr Everitt. You should see some of the scenes of crime that we get called to. You wouldn't believe the unpleasant things some burglars do to . . . leave their mark, let's say. I won't go into details.'

Everitt turned a startled gaze on him, then opened and shut his mouth soundlessly. 'Really?' he said at last.

Pierce nodded. 'So if you wouldn't mind having a look round . . .'

The inspection didn't take long; Everitt was evidently familiar with the contents of the sacristy. 'The chalice is missing,' he proclaimed at once. 'It would have been set out ready for early Mass, so they would have seen it straightaway.'

Catching the eye of the constable, Pierce nodded meaningfully. 'Anything else?'

'I don't think so.' He stuck his head in the safe. 'The other silver is still here, all wrapped up – the alms dish, the ciborium, the candlesticks, the altar cross, the thurible, the monstrance, the ewer. I suppose they were in too much of a hurry to look any further after . . . well, you know.'

With his toe, Pierce indicated the papers which were scattered about the floor. 'What about this lot? Anything important missing?'

Everitt frowned. 'I can't imagine why there would be. These are just things like insurance forms and faculty documents – no reason to steal them. And the registers haven't been damaged – they're still in the safe.' He patted the leather-bound volumes reassuringly. 'Of course I'll have to sort through everything and get it back in order. What a lot of work!'

Patiently, Pierce tried to return his attention to the matter at hand. 'So as far as you can tell, only the chalice has been taken.'

Stanley Everitt straightened up and looked slowly around the sacristy. 'There's just one other thing . . .'

'What is that, Mr Everitt?'

'One of the brass candlesticks seems to be gone. See, there's just the one, there on the vestment chest. Its mate is missing. Why would someone steal one brass candlestick?'

Pierce smiled grimly. 'Oh, you don't have to worry about that, sir. We know exactly where that is. It's on its way to the lab, sealed in a polythene bag.'

'But . . .'

'Evidence.' He took perverse pleasure in spelling it out. 'You see, Mr Everitt, that candlestick was used recently for something other than throwing light. That candlestick was used to smash in the back of your Father Julian's head.'

Everitt closed his eyes. 'Excuse me a moment, Inspector,' he said faintly, heading for the door.

Part I

Chapter 1

*He shall call upon me, and I will hear him: yea, I am
with him in trouble; I will deliver him, and bring
him to honour.*

Psalm 91.15

Lucy Kingsley frowned thoughtfully at the letter. It
seemed a somewhat odd request for her brother to make.
Odd, too, that the letter had come from her brother,
rather than from his wife. She and her sister-in-law
corresponded intermittently, but Lucy couldn't remember ever having received a letter from Andrew.

The letter had come in the post, interrupting her
painting. Now she returned to her studio, re-reading as
she climbed the stairs the lines written in Andrew's
upright, unfamiliar hand.

'I realise that this is rather short notice, but I hope
that it will present no problems. Ruth's year at school
has to participate in a work experience project this
term, and as it is Ruth's ambition to be a solicitor, it
seems sensible that she should spend her three weeks in
a solicitor's office. Father tells me that your friend
David is a solicitor in London, and I should be very
grateful if you could arrange with him for Ruth to

"shadow" him for her work experience. It seems an ideal arrangement, as she could stay with you for the three weeks (beginning the first week of March). Although Ruth is very bright, she is in many ways a young fourteen, and I would rest more easily knowing that you were looking after her. And you know how Ruth has always adored her beautiful Aunt Lucy!'

Lucy frowned again, absently twisting a curl of strawberry blonde hair around her finger. Flattery will get you nowhere, my dear brother, she said to herself, knowing in spite of everything that she would have to say yes. But David wasn't going to like it. He wasn't going to like it at all.

David Middleton-Brown, a pleasant-looking man in his early forties, was not having a tranquil morning. A letter had been waiting on his desk from the solicitor who was dealing with an estate in which David had a personal interest: when the estate was settled, he would inherit a very valuable house near Kensington Gardens. The letter was of a routine nature, asking a few questions which needed to be cleared up before matters could proceed.

The trouble was, David didn't want matters to proceed. It wasn't that he didn't want the house, or wasn't grateful for the generous bequest. But when probate was granted, and the house was his, there were issues that would have to be faced which David was not yet ready to confront.

Would he move into the house? And if he did, would Lucy come with him? He couldn't even bring himself to discuss it with her, for fear of what she would say. The last few months, since he'd moved to London, had been the happiest time of his life. Living in Lucy's house, coming home to her every night, was almost as good as being married to her. He longed to marry Lucy, longed for the security that marriage would bring. If they were married, he told himself, the house wouldn't be important. They would be together, whether in Lucy's little mews house in South Kensington or in the grand Georgian mansion that would be his. But Lucy stubbornly refused to marry him.

He still couldn't really understand it, much as he tried. She said that she loved him, and she could be in no doubt by now that he loved her. But Lucy had been married before, years ago, and it had been a brief but painful disaster. According to her, she'd been scarred so deeply by that early failure that she was unwilling to try again; she seemed incapable of realising how different it could be this time. David had by no means given up hope, but his proposals had been offered with decreasing frequency over the past months, as he tried to avoid the hurt that inevitably came with her gentle but firm refusals.

His living at her house was meant to be a temporary measure, just until the estate was sorted out. That had been the understanding when she'd invited him to move in, and they hadn't discussed it since then. One of these days Lucy was bound to ask him, he realised, but until then...

With a grimace, David slid the letter under his 'In' tray. He wouldn't reply to it right away; perhaps that would postpone the evil day for a bit longer. He could always pretend that he hadn't received the letter, or that it had been misplaced by his secretary.

Before he'd had a chance to sort through the rest of his post, his secretary Mrs Simmons popped her head around the door to report, with a suitably solemn face, that he was wanted by no less a personage than Sir Crispin Fosdyke himself, senior partner of Fosdyke, Fosdyke & Galloway. 'Immediately,' she added unnecessarily.

The summons from on high did not come very often, especially to one with as little seniority as David had at the firm, so he approached the heavy oak door of the inner sanctum with more trepidation than anticipation. 'Come in!' was the response to his diffident knock.

Sir Crispin's office occupied the corner of the firm's suite of offices in Lincoln's Inn, so it was well lit by windows on two sides. Its furnishings were discreet but obviously expensive; the chairs were leather, the chandelier was Georgian, and unless David was very much mistaken, the Monet on the wall was no reproduction. The great man himself, seated behind his massive desk, was every bit as impressive as the room, silver-haired and with his self-assured ruddy face dominated by a pair of truly awesome silver eyebrows.

'Oh, there you are, Middleton-Brown. Come in, come in.' David edged into the room and perched on the leather chair towards which he was waved. Sir Crispin wasted no time with preliminaries. 'I have a little matter for you to see to. Do you know Henry Thymme?'

'Henry Time?' David echoed, puzzled. 'I don't think so.'

'Thymme, pronounced Time, spelled T-h-y-double m-e,' explained Sir Crispin. 'Senior partner at Barrett,

12

Peters & Co in the City. A member of my club. Known him for years.'

'Oh, yes. I *have* heard of him, but I don't believe we've met.'

Sir Crispin appraised David with ice-cold blue eyes. 'His son is in a bit of a scrape, and I'd like you to sort it out for him.' Concisely, he outlined the problem. 'And so you see, Middleton-Brown,' he concluded, 'there's no time to be lost. I'll be most grateful if you can take care of this with a minimum of fuss. I'm sure you understand me.'

Dismissed, David returned to his office, shaking his head. Young Mr Thymme had been picked up in the early hours of the morning on Hampstead Heath; he was, as official parlance would have it, engaged in an act of public indecency with another man. 'Caught with his trousers down,' David muttered to himself, bemused. 'And in the middle of winter!' The young man was now cooling his heels in the local police station, awaiting the arrival of a solicitor: David. Out of consideration for his father – or possibly in fear of his wrath – he had waited until morning to ring him, and Henry Thymme was obviously calling in a favour from his colleague Sir Crispin, thus keeping his own firm well out of it. It was clear to David why Sir Crispin had put him on to it: a case like this was distasteful in the extreme, especially for a respectable firm like Fosdyke, Fosdyke & Galloway. Under ordinary circumstances they wouldn't have touched it with a bargepole, he realised, but as a professional courtesy to a fellow senior partner, and a member of his club to boot, Sir Crispin could not very well have refused. David was the newest member of the firm, so it was only natural that the case should be shunted on to him. And perhaps, he said to himself, it was a sort of test, to see how well he acquitted himself. 'I'm afraid I've got to go out,' he said to his secretary, fetching his overcoat. 'I'll be back as soon as I can.'

David found Henry Thymme waiting for him at the police station. A large, bluff man, his thinning fair hair worn long enough to make him look younger than he probably was, he wrung David's hand gratefully. 'Awfully decent of you to come, dear chap,' he declared with feeling. 'I'm afraid the lad's got himself into a spot of trouble.'

David's manner was consciously professional. 'So Sir Crispin tells me.'

'Ah, well.' Thymme chuckled fondly. 'Boys will be boys, you know. And Justin's a good lad, really. The apple of his mother's eye.'

For a moment the professional coolness slipped. 'Justin Thymme?'

The older man laughed. 'You got it, then. Good, that, isn't it? A bit of fancy on his mother's part, and the lad has to live with it for the rest of his life! He was the last child, you see – after four girls. No more kiddies, she said. This is the end of the line. So the boy came just in time.' He laughed again with immoderate amusement, considering how many times he must have told the story.

David allowed himself a small smile. The scenario was all too clear: the spoiled young tearaway, indulged by his father and petted by his mother, and no doubt by all of those sisters as well. He was not likely to be an ideal client, and David longed to get it over with. 'I think I'd better see him now.'

'By all means, my boy, and the sooner the better. We'll have a word with the duty sergeant straightaway.'

14

Thymme gave a wink. 'Not that it's done the lad any harm to wait – quite the contrary, I should think.'

When at last David was ushered into the interview room, into the presence of the young Mr Thymme, he found him not at all what he'd expected. Far from cutting a dashing figure, his client was small and pale and prim, and not so very young either, come to that: David judged him to be about thirty, with fine fair hair receding from his high forehead. He wore oval steel-rimmed spectacles, one of the lenses of which was cracked, and above which he sported a nasty purple bruise. 'How soon can I get out of here?' he demanded; his voice was deeper than his size might have indicated, and his accent was true to his public school education.

'Good morning, Mr Thymme,' said David pleasantly, as if the other man hadn't spoken. He introduced himself, then went on, 'How did you get the black eye, if you don't mind me asking?'

Justin's hand went to the bruise. 'The chap who arrested me. He gave me a thump with his truncheon – said I was resisting arrest.'

This seemed highly unlikely to David, but he decided to let it pass. 'And were you?'

He pursed his thin mouth prissily. 'No, of course not. I'm not that stupid.'

With a thoughtful nod, David sat down, folding his hands on the table that separated them. 'You've been in here for quite a few hours now. Have you made a statement, or allowed yourself to be interviewed?'

Justin looked at him with scorn. 'I told you, I'm not stupid. And my father's a solicitor – I know how these things work. I'm not likely to have said anything to incriminate myself, am I?' He drummed his fingers on the table. 'So when are you going to get me out of here? I'm hours late for work already!'

David told Lucy about the case over supper that night, deliberately making the story as amusing as possible. 'I was expecting an eighteen-year-old in skintight jeans, an earring, and a black leather jacket, and I walk into the interview room to find someone who looks like an accountant! And do you want to know the funniest thing about it – apart from his ridiculous name, that is? That's exactly what he is – an accountant!' He shook his head with a self-deprecating grin. 'That's what I get for making assumptions.'

'An accountant?' Lucy was making a great effort to concentrate on his story, dreading what she was going to have to ask him.

'A blooming accountant. With an upper-class twit of a solicitor for a father.'

She pushed a bit of salad around on her plate. 'Did you get him out?'

David nodded. 'He's out on police bail – that's the usual thing in these cases.'

'What will happen to him now?'

'Oh, I'll be able to get him off, I think. At least if I value my job, I will,' he added wryly. 'I wouldn't want to face Sir Crispin if his friend's darling son got a fine, and his name in the papers.'

Lucy looked puzzled. 'But isn't he guilty?'

'Well, of course he is! They caught him in the act, remember.'

'I don't understand. How will you get him off, if you

know he's guilty, and the police know he's guilty?'

Choosing his words carefully, David tried to explain. 'It's all in knowing how to play the game. Now in this case, the young man tells me that the police gave him a gratuitous thump with a truncheon. I don't really believe him – these days the police are more careful than that – but that's beside the point. If I let it be known that my client is prepared to take the matter to the Police Complaints Authority ... well, let's just say that the police don't need that kind of hassle, not to mention the adverse publicity if it were leaked to the press. I think they'll be prepared to drop the charges against him, in return for keeping quiet about what he claims the police did to him. After all, he's a respectable member of society – his word would carry some weight. And don't forget his father's clout.'

Lucy's full attention had been captured at last. 'But that's dishonest!'

'Oh, no, Lucy love. It's just using the system.'

'But you're saying that because he has the right connections, and a good solicitor, he'll get off scot free, whereas if he were some poor bloke who happened to get caught...'

David laughed without amusement. 'You've got it in one, love. It may not be fair, but that's the way it works.' She looked so distressed that he reached across the table and took her hand. 'I can't pretend to have much stomach for it, myself, but it's my job, and I've got to do what's best for my client, objectionable though he may be. Not to mention that Fosdyke expects me to get the miserable little toerag off.'

'Would you say,' Lucy asked slowly, 'that Sir Crispin will owe you one after this?'

'I don't imagine that he'd put it in quite those terms, but that's the gist of it, certainly.' David's generous mouth curved in a self-deprecating smile. 'I took an unsavoury case off his hands, and if I manage it well, and get my client off without attracting any unwelcome attention to him or to Fosdyke, Fosdyke & Galloway, I should think that Sir Crispin would be suitably grateful. It won't do me any harm, anyway. But if I don't produce the goods—'

'But you will,' Lucy interrupted him urgently. 'You said that you would be able to. And then Sir Crispin will be in your debt.'

David gave her a questioning look. 'What are you getting at?'

Unable to meet his eyes, she looked first up at the ceiling and then down at their clasped hands; with her free hand she pushed back her hair. 'Well, it's just that . . .' She took a deep breath and plunged into the story of her brother's letter and her niece's proposed visit.

For a moment David just stared at her. 'You want me to ask Fosdyke if a fourteen-year-old girl can follow me around for three weeks?' he exploded at last. 'Do you have any idea what you're asking?'

'Yes, I know it's asking a lot, but you just said that he'd owe you a favour . . .'

'A favour, perhaps, but this . . . !'

Lucy's head drooped despondently, her long curly red-gold hair falling forward to shadow her face, and David's heart melted. 'Oh, all right. I'll ask him,' he relented, with much misgiving. 'I can't promise that he'll say yes, though.'

'Oh, David darling, thank you.' Her smile was radiant. 'I know that you'll do your best to convince him. And why should he object, after all? She might even be able to help you.'

'You don't know Sir Crispin Fosdyke,' he retorted darkly. 'And I very much doubt that she'd do anything but get in the way. There are issues of client confidentiality to consider – I'd have to spend all my time finding fiddly little things to keep her busy.' After a moment he had another thought. 'And she's supposed to stay here with us? In this house? Where would we put her?'

'On the sofa bed, of course.'

David frowned. 'For three weeks? It would be all right for a night or two, I'm sure, but for three weeks? Rather in the way, I'd think. And she's bound to have great quantities of clothes, and other bits and pieces – teenage girls do, don't they? She'd probably leave her things all over the place. This house just isn't big enough for three people.' Lucy looked at him quizzically, and in an instant he saw the danger in that line of reasoning: it was after all *her* house, not his, and if he wasn't careful, he'd find himself the one without a place to stay for three weeks. 'Oh, never mind,' he muttered, then effected a rapid change of subject. 'More wine, Lucy love? The bottle's almost empty.'

Chapter 2

Nevertheless, when he saw their adversity: he heard their complaint.

Psalm 106.43

For the past several minutes, the only sound in the parlour of the clergy house had been the loud ticking of the longcase clock in the corner. Seated opposite each other on expensively upholstered chairs, the two churchwardens remained silent, regarding each other uneasily.

The two men had little in common, save their office – and their high churchmanship. Martin Bairstow, the younger of the two, was a wealthy man, having made his fortune in the City. Single-minded, he had early in life directed his energies to the amassing of wealth, and that accomplished most satisfactorily, he now devoted his time outside work to being the most conscientious and hard-working churchwarden that St Margaret's Church had ever known. He was still only in his mid-forties, and was possessed of looks that most women found handsome, if somewhat stolid: he was large and well-built, his thick dark hair was only slightly threaded with grey, and his features were pleasingly even, though dominated by a heavy jaw.

Norman Topping, on the other hand, looked the part of the amiable buffoon, with his peculiar bullet-shaped head and his comical jug ears; what little hair he had was in the form of colourless stubble. He was short and slightly flabby, and his deep, somewhat nasal voice betrayed his northern origins. Topping was good-natured and amiable, but completely without imagination. Nearly sixty, and approaching retirement from his career as a mid-level civil servant, he had been churchwarden of St Margaret's for a number of years.

The clock chimed four o'clock; Norman Topping jumped somewhat, drawing a bemused and somewhat contemptuous look from his fellow warden. 'Sorry,' he mumbled. 'I thought he would have been here by now.'

Unnecessarily, Bairstow looked at his handsome gold watch. 'He's thirty minutes late,' he confirmed. 'It's not like the Vicar to be late.'

They turned expectantly as the door of the sitting room opened, but if they thought to see a contrite Father Keble Smythe, they were disappointed. Instead, the housekeeper made a diffident entrance. 'It's gone four,' she said. 'I can't think what's keeping Father, but I thought that perhaps you might like some tea.'

Used to making decisions, Bairstow agreed instantly. 'Yes, thank you, Mrs Goode. That would be very nice.'

'Yes, a cup of tea would go down a treat,' Topping seconded.

'If it's not too much trouble, Mrs Goode,' added Bairstow with his most winning smile. 'It's most kind of you to offer.'

Martin Bairstow was a particular favourite with Mrs
Goode, as he was with a great many middle-aged and
older ladies in the parishes of St Margaret and St Jude:
excellent and devout Anglican women every one, who
appreciated his consideration and his various little
kindnesses towards them, and who regularly confessed
to Father Keble Smythe the unseemly – perhaps even
sinful – envy they felt towards the fortunate Mrs
Bairstow. Flustered now by his attention, Mrs Goode
tried to cover it up with a show of efficiency. 'No trouble
at all, I'm sure. China or India?' she asked, backing out
of the room.

'China,' said Martin Bairstow.

'India,' said Norman Topping simultaneously.

'I shall make both,' Mrs Goode declared. 'And I'm sure
that Father will be here any minute.'

The tea, served in thin china cups, was delicious, and
accompanied by buttery fingers of Mrs Goode's home-
made shortbread. The Vicar had as yet failed to appear;
over their tea the men made some effort at conversation.

'Your family is well?' Bairstow enquired courteously.
'Avoiding the bugs that have been going around?'

'Oh, yes. Dolly is never ill – it's a point of pride
with her. She says that she's never been ill a day in her
life.'

Bairstow nodded. 'What is Dolly doing with herself
these days, now that Ladies Opposed to Women Priests
have lost their *raison d'être*? Has she found another
cause?'

Chuckling, Norman Topping helped himself to another shortbread finger. 'They may have lost the vote,

but they've by no means disbanded. Dolly will never give up hoping that some miracle will occur – that God will instantly strike dead all women who want to be priests, and any heretical bishop who's prepared to ordain them. But yes, she's looking to fresher pastures these days – she's getting involved with an anti-abortion campaign. And if I know Dolly, she'll be running the show within a few weeks.'

Martin Bairstow stroked his chin thoughtfully. 'The Church needs people like Dolly, who are prepared to stand up for what they believe. And she's absolutely right about women priests, of course. As we've often discussed before. Disaster for the Church of England, complete and utter disaster.'

'But as long as we don't get any of them here . . .'

Bairstow got up and went to the window. Already the days were lengthening, and it was not yet dark; he could see the austere Victorian edifice of St Jude's across the street in the deepening gloom. 'It would be out of the question – untenable,' he declared forcefully. 'I can't see it happening, quite frankly. But if it did . . . well, I'd have to re-think my position about staying in the Church of England. All of us at St Margaret's would. Dolly would be the first to—' He broke off at the sight of the Vicar's car turning into the street. 'Ah, here is Father Keble Smythe. At last. Now we can get on with this meeting.'

Father Keble Smythe, sweeping into the parlour in his great clerical cloak, was of course fulsome in his apologies for keeping his churchwardens waiting on a Saturday afternoon when they were sure to have other commitments. 'It was unavoidable,' he assured them.

'Even though I'm a bachelor myself, I am most conscious that you both have wives waiting for you at home, and I wouldn't have delayed you if it hadn't been of the utmost importance. But I'm so pleased to see that Mrs Goode has supplied you with tea. An excellent woman, Mrs Goode. The next best thing to a wife.' His voice was beautifully modulated, and his accent plummy in the extreme.

Accepting his apologies, they followed him into his study. Like the parlour, it was a well-appointed room, nicely proportioned and expensively furnished. Waving the churchwardens into chairs, the Vicar seated himself behind his desk and allowed himself a moment to glance at the silver-framed photo which had pride of place in front of him, then picked it up and handed it across the desk to Martin Bairstow. 'Have you seen this? A new portrait of Miss McKenzie, my fiancée. She had it done for me, for Christmas. Uncommonly good, don't you think?'

Bairstow studied the representation of the rather horse-faced young woman with a noncommittal expression. 'Very nice, Father.' An old-fashioned Anglo-Catholic, he disapproved of married clergy, and regretted the fact that St Margaret's affiliation with St Jude's in a united benefice had given it a vicar with rather different standards. St Margaret's had certainly never had a married vicar before, and although Miss Morag McKenzie – so often spoken of – had yet to be seen in the parish, that looked set to change at some time in the future. It was the thin end of the wedge, as far as Martin Bairstow was concerned.

Father William Keble Smythe smiled at his wardens

across the desk. Dressed in his black cassock with its thirty-nine buttons, he was everything that a young, upwardly-mobile priest should be: good-looking, personable, well-educated and evidently well-connected. He had been Vicar of St Jude's for something over five years, and in that time he had slightly, yet perceptibly, raised the churchmanship of that staid parish without alienating any of his wealthy parishioners: no mean feat. Three years ago when the benefices had been combined he had also been named Priest-in-Charge of neighbouring St Margaret's, where the churchmanship was traditionally far higher than at St Jude's; there he was admired for his avowed adherence to Catholic practices, though in actuality he rarely took a service at St Margaret's. Within the diocese of London it was acknowledged that Father William Keble Smythe had never put a foot wrong, had never rocked the boat, and was undoubtedly destined for bigger things.

'Do you know why we've asked for this meeting?' Martin Bairstow began.

The Vicar's cordial smile betrayed nothing. 'Why don't you tell me?' he invited.

Ignoring his fellow warden, Bairstow addressed the Vicar. 'You must know that the staffing situation at St Margaret's has become intolerable. To put not too fine a point on it, Father, we're absolutely desperate for a new curate.'

'You promised us a month ago that you'd do something as soon as possible,' Norman Topping put in.

'And things have got worse since then,' Bairstow continued. 'We've just about managed on Sunday mornings, with the goodwill of curates from neighbouring parishes. But the weekday Masses have been a real problem – I don't know if you realise.'

'I thought that Father Travis—'

'Father Travis means well,' said Bairstow, frowning. 'But he always was absent-minded, even when he was active. Now that he's retired – well, he just can't be relied upon. Last week he failed to turn up on three consecutive days. Three days without a Mass! You must agree, Father – that just isn't on!'

Father Keble Smythe put his fingertips together. 'No, that's not acceptable. But you must realise that I'm just as inconvenienced as you are – this is a very large parish – two parishes! – to run without the help of a curate. I've—'

'In January it's bad enough,' interrupted Norman Topping. 'But with Lent coming up soon, and then Holy Week and Easter, we just can't go on like this. Something has to be done. We've got to have a new curate, as soon as possible.'

Inclining his head, the Vicar went on in a somewhat pained voice. 'As I was about to say, gentlemen, I've made this my top priority. That is the reason I was late for this meeting – I've spent the afternoon seeing the Director of Ordinands, the Archdeacon, and then the Bishop.'

The two churchwardens' expressions changed in an instant to ones of hopeful expectation. 'And?' prompted Martin Bairstow.

Father Keble Smythe shook his head. 'I'm afraid it's all very difficult. As you would expect, curates are not that easy to come by at the moment. The next ordinations won't take place till Petertide, and we certainly can't wait until the middle of the year for a new curate.'

'But we don't want a deacon in any case,' Bairstow protested. 'We want a curate who's already been priested, one who can celebrate the Mass.'

'A second curacy,' contributed Topping.

Again the Vicar shook his head. 'Impossible, I'm afraid. There isn't anyone in the diocese who fits the bill. But as I said before, I just can't go on without a curate – I very badly need someone to help with the visiting, the sick communions, weddings, funerals, parish meetings...'

'Then what are you suggesting?' Bairstow demanded. 'You're not giving up so easily, are you?'

The Vicar waited a moment before replying, framing his words very carefully. 'I didn't say that I had been unsuccessful, only that it had been difficult.'

'You mean that you've found a curate?' The eagerness returned to Norman Topping's voice.

'Well, yes.' Now he picked his words even more carefully. 'The Director of Ordinands suggested a candidate – someone who has quite recently moved into the London diocese because of family circumstances, and who has been looking for a post.'

'Why, that's perfect!' Topping exulted. 'So he can start right away, then!'

'Within a few weeks, I hope.'

Martin Bairstow was more sensitive than his colleague to the nuances of the Vicar's announcement. 'There's a problem, though, isn't there? He's just a deacon, I suppose. That's fine for you, Father – he can help you with your parish duties with no problem. But it's not so good for us at St Margaret's, if he can't celebrate the Mass without using the Reserved Sacrament.'

Father Keble Smythe's expression was grave. 'Yes, I'm afraid that's so. Our new curate – for I've talked to the candidate, and offered the post – is a deacon, not a priest, though that will be remedied as soon as priesting is possible, with any luck in a few months' time. I've explained the circumstances – I'm sorry, but it's the best I can do at the moment.'

'Well, who is he?' Norman Topping demanded. 'I don't suppose we'll know him, but what is his name?'

For the first time that afternoon, the Vicar was not able to meet the eyes of his churchwardens; strong as were his personal reasons for the decision he'd made, he knew that they would never understand. Looking down at his hands, he spoke softly. 'Gentlemen, the name of our new curate is . . . Rachel Nightingale.'

A quarter of an hour later, after the explosion, the explanations, the threats, and the apologies, the two churchwardens stood outside on the pavement, looking at each other. At the end of the day, in spite of their protests and the Vicar's professed regrets about the matter, it was done, and it was too late to go back on it.

'A woman!' Martin Bairstow said in a dangerously quiet voice. 'I can't believe he's done this to us.'

'He said he didn't have any choice, but—'

Bairstow thought aloud. 'Someone put pressure on him, you can depend on it. Someone high up, who was trying to make a point, or do someone a favour.'

Norman Topping's concerns were closer to home. 'Whatever is Dolly going to say about this?'

'And not just Dolly, either. It might be all right at St Jude's, but St Margaret's will not stand for it!'

'But Martin! What are we going to do? What *can* we do?'

Bairstow's face was set. 'Oh, we'll do something, my friend,' he stated ominously. 'Believe me, we're not going to sit still and let him do this to us!'

Chapter 3

I stretch forth my hands unto thee: my soul gaspeth unto thee as a thirsty land.

Psalm 143.6

Late on a Friday morning at the end of January, Lucy returned home from her weekly trip around the shops, laden with bulging carrier bags of food. As she put her key in the lock, she heard the telephone ringing inside the house; she dropped her bags inside the door and made a frantic dive for the phone.

'Hello?' she gasped into the phone.

'Oh, hello,' said a tentative female voice. 'Is this Lucy Kingsley?'

'Yes, it is. I'm sorry – I've just come in from shopping, and I'm a bit breathless, getting to the phone.'

'I'm so sorry. If it's a bad time for you, I can ring back later.'

'No, not at all.' Lucy had by this time caught her breath, and she consciously warmed up her voice. 'What can I do for you?'

'My name is Vanessa Bairstow,' the other woman said. 'I'm interested in commissioning a painting, as an anniversary gift for my husband, and the Archdeacon's wife suggested that I ring you.'

For an instant, Lucy drew a blank, then remembered; even after over a year, she was unused to thinking of her friend Emily as the Archdeacon's wife. 'Oh, yes. Emily.'

'She said that you might be able to help me.'

'Of course.' Lucy never had a shortage of commissions, but she was willing to do whatever was necessary to squeeze in a friend of Emily's. 'Do you know my work at all?'

Mrs Bairstow was apologetic. 'No, I'm afraid not. But I'm sure . . .'

'Then perhaps the best thing would be for you to come by my studio and see the type of thing that I do. Before you commit yourself!' she added, laughing. 'We can talk about what you're looking for, and all the rest of it. When would you like to come?'

'Any time that's convenient for you, Miss Kingsley.' The other woman's voice had a curious yearning note. 'I don't work, so I could come any time. I wouldn't want to disturb your painting or anything.'

Lucy thought for a moment. 'Would this afternoon be too soon? I'm not actually doing any painting today, so it would be a good time for me.'

'Yes, that would be fine.'

They agreed on a time, and Lucy gave her directions. 'I'll look forward to seeing you this afternoon, Mrs Bairstow.'

'Oh, yes. Thank you so much.'

Lucy put the phone down thoughtfully and went to retrieve her abandoned shopping. She wasn't sure why, but she was looking forward to meeting Mrs Bairstow: there was something intriguing about her voice, some elusive quality that piqued Lucy's curiosity. Perhaps a bit later she'd ring Emily and ask her what she knew about Vanessa Bairstow.

Emily, in a rush to collect the children from school, didn't tell her much. Vanessa Bairstow was the wife of a churchwarden at St Margaret's Church, Pimlico, in her forties, well off, and had no children. She was a nice woman, Emily said – Lucy should get on well with her.

The woman who rang Lucy's bell some time later was very much in keeping with Emily's description, though Emily hadn't begun to convey Vanessa Bairstow's attractiveness. She was a strikingly good-looking woman, Lucy discovered, although perhaps best described as handsome rather than beautiful, with the kind of looks that improve rather than fade with age. Her wheat-coloured hair was thick, wavy and beautifully cut, and her figure, clad elegantly and expensively in the latest sophisticated fashion, was full yet firm, heavy-breasted and curvaceous. But her voice, when she spoke, had that same almost wistful note that had so intrigued Lucy on the phone. 'Hello, Miss Kingsley. It's so kind of you to see me on such short notice.'

'Please, call me Lucy. And do come in.' Lucy took her cashmere coat and hung it up carefully in the cupboard under the stairs.

'And I'd like it very much if you'd call me Vanessa.' She put a hand to her hair and took a surreptitious peek at herself in the hall mirror. 'I do hope my hair looks all right. I've just been to a new hairdresser – my old one was inconsiderate enough to move to Brighton – and you just never know, do you?'

'It looks lovely,' Lucy assured her. 'And you're right – there's nothing worse than having to find a new hairdresser!'

That shared female confidence established them on a footing of empathy immediately; after a few additional pleasantries, Lucy led Vanessa Bairstow upstairs to her studio, a small room strewn about with artists' paraphernalia and paintings in various stages of completion.

'Oh, I say, Lucy.' Vanessa looked around her with lively interest. 'Emily Neville was right – your paintings are wonderful!'

Lucy smiled modestly. 'I'm glad you think so. But Emily would say that in any case.'

'Are all of these spoken for?'

'Most of them, yes. And the ones that aren't done on commission get sent to various galleries. You said that you wanted a painting for your husband?'

'Yes, that's right. To hang in his office – as a gift for our twentieth wedding anniversary.'

They spent a quarter of an hour discussing Lucy's techniques and theories of painting as well as various details of the commission before retiring downstairs for tea. Lucy settled Vanessa in the sitting room and went to the kitchen to boil the kettle; when she returned a few minutes later, carrying a tray, she found the other woman with a cat ensconced quite firmly in her lap, curled up and purring.

'Oh, I'm sorry about Sophie,' Lucy apologised. 'She can be a bit of a pest – throw her off if she's bothering you.'

'Not at all!' Vanessa stroked the small marmalade cat lovingly, and the cat responded with a blissful yawn. 'I love cats – I have one myself. Augustine is my pride and joy.'

Lucy pictured a sleek regal Siamese, a cat worthy of this elegant woman. 'I'll look forward to meeting Augustine some time.'

'Yes, you must come to my house soon.' Her voice was almost shy in its eagerness.

'I'd like that.' Lucy poured the tea. 'I didn't ask you – Earl Grey is all right, I hope?'

'Oh, yes. My favourite.'

'With lemon?'

'Perfect.'

After a few minutes, over tea and cakes, they were chatting like old friends; Lucy's natural warmth, and the gift she always had for drawing people out, seemed to have overcome Vanessa's shyness. In short order Lucy learned that Mr Bairstow was called Martin, that he had something to do with investments in the City, that he was a churchwarden at St Margaret's, and that his wife had little more to occupy her time than volunteer work, maintaining her wardrobe, and over-seeing the running of their home. All of this was elicited without the least semblance of nosiness on Lucy's part; she was a good listener, and genuinely interested in other people. On the other hand, she was herself a very private person, and rarely revealed very much personal information.

'More tea?' Lucy lifted the pot invitingly.

'No, I mustn't. I should get home soon. Martin will be home from work early tonight – he has some church meeting this evening – and I'd better be there when he gets home. After all, this painting is meant to be a surprise, and I don't want to have to make excuses for where I've been, if I come rushing in after he's home! I'm not a very good liar, I'm afraid.'

Lucy smiled. 'He might think you were spending the afternoon with another man.'

Deposing Sophie, who departed with a displeased howl, Vanessa stood up abruptly. 'Oh, no, he mustn't think that!' She flushed and moved towards the door.

The remark had been meant to be humorous; Lucy could see instantly that it had been ill-judged. She covered over the awkwardness as best she could, fetching the cashmere coat. 'It's been such a pleasure meeting you, Vanessa. And I'll get to work on your painting as soon as I can.'

Vanessa seemed conscious that she had somehow spoiled the mood of friendly intimacy that had developed between them. At the door she turned and touched Lucy's arm. 'Thank you so much for everything. For the tea, and for ... everything.'

'It was my pleasure.' Lucy spoke with such obvious sincerity that the other woman hesitated for a moment on the doorstep.

'Lucy ...'

'Yes?'

'I wondered if I might ask you a very big favour.'

'Ask away.' She smiled. 'After all, I can always say no.'

'I just had an idea, that's all.'

'Sounds ominous!'

Vanessa was reassured by the bantering tone. 'It's

just that we have this women's group – mostly women from church, from St Margaret's, and a few from St Jude's,' she explained. 'We get together once a month, on a Wednesday afternoon, and have a speaker of some sort, then tea. Very informal.'

Lucy's heart sank. It sounded absolutely dire, she thought: a flock of well-heeled church women with nothing better to do than sit around gossiping, and listening to some boring speaker talking about gardening or some such subject of interest to the idle rich. But she supposed she'd have to grit her teeth and go. 'And you wanted me to come?'

'Well, not exactly.' Vanessa gave an apologetic half-laugh. 'Actually, I was hoping that I could talk you into speaking to us next week – the meeting is at my house. We were meant to have a woman from the Royal Horticultural Society talking to us about "Preparing Your Garden for Spring", but she's cancelled – had to go into hospital.'

Lucy was astonished. 'But I'm no public speaker!'

'Oh, but you know so much about art! I'm sure that the others would be as fascinated as I was today to hear about your paintings – where you get your ideas, how you execute them, and so forth – especially if you could bring a few examples.' Vanessa flushed with enthusiasm. 'It would be so much more interesting than our usual speakers, I assure you!'

'Oh, I don't think . . .' she protested feebly. 'Surely you can find someone else?'

Vanessa shook her head. 'Well, Dolly Topping – she's one of our members – has offered to step into the breech with a talk about the evils of abortion, but I don't think anyone wants to hear it. Anyway, she talked to us last month, about "Christmas in Other Lands", so I think we've had enough of Dolly for a while.' She gave Lucy a beseeching look. 'Won't you at least think about it? Emily Neville usually comes,' she added cunningly.

Poor Emily, thought Lucy. The things one has to endure as the Archdeacon's wife. 'Oh, all right,' she capitulated, trying not to sound ungracious, and knowing that she would probably be sorry.

Vanessa's smile was radiant. 'Thank you so much. I'll ring you on Monday with the details, if that's all right.'

'See you next week, then.' Lucy shrugged philosophically as she closed the door, realising that in spite of everything she was rather looking forward to next week. She would enjoy seeing the Bairstows' house, and her curiosity about Vanessa Bairstow was intensified rather than assuaged by their face-to-face meeting.

Absently she returned to the sitting room to clear up the tea things; as she stacked the empty cups on the tray the phone in the hall rang.

It was David, at his most apologetic. 'I hope you haven't started fixing supper, love – I'm going to be rather late. A last-minute meeting.'

'I was just going to make a pot of soup, so it won't matter. Something urgent, is it?'

'I'm not sure. I must admit that I'm rather intrigued – the chap who rang me to set up the meeting was quite mysterious about the whole thing. All I know is that the meeting is at St Margaret's, Pimlico. It was the churchwarden who rang me – a chap by the name of Martin Bairstow.'

Chapter 4

Blessed is he that considereth the poor and needy:
the Lord shall deliver him in the time of trouble.

Psalm 41.1

Martin Bairstow took out his pipe and fiddled with it, then decided it wasn't appropriate to light it in church – not even in the vestry – and put it back in his pocket. 'He should be here soon. Let me do the talking,' he instructed his fellow churchwarden, not for the first time.

'Where did you find this solicitor bloke?' queried Norman Topping.

'One of the wardens from St John's, North Kensington, recommended him. Apparently he did some work for them about a year ago, when they were threatened with closure unless they came up with the money to repair the roof,' Bairstow explained. 'He negotiated the sale of the school and the church hall to some property developers – really saved the church's bacon, apparently.'

'And we're ... you're ... going to tell him ... ?'

'What we've discussed.' Bairstow's tone was brusque. 'It should suffice for the moment. Eventually we may have to tell him the whole truth, but I don't see why that should be necessary for a while, if at all.'

Topping furrowed his brow. 'And what about the Vicar?'

'What about him?'

'What are we going to tell *him*?'

'I've already had a brief word with Father Keble Smythe, and have explained what we intend doing – at least as much as he needs to know. I don't think he'll look into it too closely – he's got enough other things on his plate at the moment, without worrying about this.'

'Is he coming to this meeting?' Topping asked.

'I've mentioned it to him, but he may be too busy preparing for the service. Perhaps he'll drop in.'

'Surely, though, the solicitor will have to be instructed by the Vicar and churchwardens, and not just...'

Bairstow's heavy jaw was thrust out farther than usual. 'Just leave it to me, Norman. And let me do the talking.'

Leaving Victoria Underground station, David looked at his watch. The church was about a ten-minute walk from the station, he reckoned, and he'd told the churchwarden that he'd be there by six. He'd allowed plenty of time for the tube journey, but it was the Friday night rush hour, and he wasn't going to have much time to spare. He walked briskly through the busy commercial area around Victoria, soon reaching the quiet streets of Pimlico, where rows of white houses gleamed with austere prosperity in the chill, misty evening.

He'd been to St Margaret's before, in the church-crawling days of his youth. Though that had been twenty or more years ago, he now found the church easily, and spent a moment or two surveying the exterior. Built of soft Kentish stone, it had weathered rather less well than other churches of a similar age. But it had evidently been well cared for, and the window tracery showed signs of having been recently renewed. Lights shone welcomingly through the stained glass; David shivered in the cold and headed for the door.

The churchwarden had mentioned during their tele-phone conversation that there would be a service that evening – hence the early starting time for their meeting – so David was not surprised to find the church unlocked and well lit. He couldn't for a moment think what festival the service was to commemorate, but as he entered the church he discovered that pride of place for the evening had been given to a large oil painting of King Charles the First. It stood near the chancel entrance, attended by an arrangement of white lilies and a votive candle stand. Of course, he said to himself. The feast of the Martyrdom of King Charles. A church like St Margaret's *would* mark that feast.

David stood for a moment, assimilating the building's interior. It was a large Victorian church, built in an uncluttered Gothic style, with exceptionally wide side aisles and a lofty roof; the overall impression was of space and light. The chancel, with its polychromed vaulting, had evidently been re-done at a later date, and was ornately gilded and decorated with Pre-Raphaelite murals. As he moved towards the chancel, David realised that he was not alone in the church: a man in a cassock was kneeling in front of the altar. He turned at David's approach.

'I'm so sorry. I didn't mean to disturb your prayers,' David apologised.

The man laughed. 'Oh, I wasn't praying.' He held up a fine-tooth comb. 'I was smartening up the altar.' Demonstrating, he began running the comb through the silk fringe of the superfrontal. 'We've put the red martyrs' set on for tonight, of course, and they do get a bit *déshabillé* with handling.' He half turned and squinted up at David. 'Can I help you with something?'

'I'm meant to be meeting the churchwardens here at six,' he explained. 'They don't seem to be here, unless I'm not looking in the right place.'

The other man jumped to his feet. He was tall, with an ugly rubbery-looking face that reminded David of a frog. 'Oh, the wardens are in the vestry. Waiting for you, I expect. It's through that door on the north side, by the organ.'

'Thanks.'

David turned to go, but the man seemed reluctant to have him leave. 'I'm the sacristan, by the way. Name's Robin West.' He thrust out his hand – the one without the comb – so David was obliged to return and shake it.

'David Middleton-Brown.'

Robin West looked him up and down, taking stock. 'Are you staying for the service?'

'I hadn't planned to,' David admitted.

'Oh, do!' He made a sweeping gesture towards the portrait of the martyred king. 'It's one of the highlights of the year at St Margaret's! No one else in London does anything like it – there will be all sorts of visiting

42

clergy, and the red copes, and lots of lace. Well worth seeing, I promise you! We're even using the 1637 Prayer Book service!'

'Sounds tempting.' While he was speaking, David looked at the altar furnishings; he was passionately interested in ecclesiastical silver, and was always interested to see what various churches possessed. The silver altar cross was disappointing, he decided: overly ornate, and not particularly well made. The six candlesticks were a mixed bag, one pair of which might be reasonably good. He wished that he could have a look at the hallmarks.

'And I shall be thurifer, of course. You really *must* stay.' Robin West smirked. 'You'll even have a chance to see the Vicar – not something that happens very often at St Margaret's, I can assure you!'

That caught David's attention. 'What do you mean?'

'Oh, our Vicar is *far* too busy at St Jude's down the road – where all the money is – to honour us with his presence very often,' the sacristan declared with an arch look. 'But tonight he'll be here – after all, this is the place to see and be seen on the Feast of King Charles the Martyr, if no other time.'

'I see.'

'Father Keble Smythe would like us all to think that he's such a good Catholic, after all.'

'And isn't he?'

Robin West twitched the skirts of his cassock. 'I really wouldn't like to say,' he stated demurely. 'Most people believe it. I suppose that's the important thing.' As David seemed about to move off, he reached out and touched his sleeve with a delicate finger. 'You *will* stay, won't you? Promise me that you'll stay?'

The man made David nervous, but he didn't know how to say no. 'All right, then. I'll stay.'

'Oh, you won't regret it. It's the best show in town. And if you're free for a drink after . . .'

David didn't stay to hear the rest of the suggestion, or to reply.

Martin Bairstow came straight to the point. 'What we're interested in, Mr Middleton-Brown, is some advice and assistance in selling a few bits and pieces. I assume that faculties will need to be applied for, and we thought that perhaps you could advise us on the best way of finding the appropriate buyers as well.'

This wasn't really what David had expected; he thought for a moment. 'Let's start at the beginning. Why do you want to sell these things, and what are they?'

'Just a few pieces of old silver,' the churchwarden explained. 'We want to raise some cash to refurbish a house in the parish.'

'Magdalen House, it's called,' Norman Topping interjected; he was quelled immediately by a look from his fellow warden.

'Magdalen House,' Bairstow repeated. 'It was founded by the Community of St Mary Magdalen, an Anglican sisterhood, back in the 1880s, as a home for what they so quaintly called "fallen women". But the last of the sisters died a few years ago, and the house is now under the jurisdiction of the parish.'

'I don't suppose there are so many fallen women these days, in any case.'

Bairstow didn't return David's smile. 'No,' he said seriously. 'In the recent past it has served as a curate's house, but it is no longer being used for that purpose.'

'Do you have another use in mind for it, then? That would require it to be refurbished?'

Bairstow's eyes flickered to Norman Topping, then back to David. 'My colleague and I feel that we have a responsibility to address the terrible problem of homelessness in London,' he stated solemnly. 'As trustees of Magdalen House, we agree that it should be converted into a shelter for the homeless.'

David nodded. 'That sounds entirely reasonable. But to sacrifice your church's silver, even for such a good cause ... ?'

'Well, it *is* lovely stuff, especially the altar cross, but we think the cause is one that's worth the sacrifice,' Bairstow said, lifting his chin in a noble look. 'I'm not sure exactly what we might expect to get for it, but we're hoping that it will fetch a few thousand pounds. And we can replace it with some nice modern pieces.'

David kept his opinion of the altar cross to himself, and decided to reserve judgement on the value of the rest until he'd seen it. 'Would it be possible for me to have a look?'

Bairstow rose. 'Yes, of course. We were hoping that you'd be able to advise us on its value. My colleague at St John's said that you knew quite a lot about church silver.'

'Not at all.' David shook his head with customary modesty. 'I'm just an amateur. But I *am* very interested in it.'

'I don't suppose any of the clergy have arrived yet, so

it's all right if we go to the sacristy,' Norman Topping contributed.

Martin Bairstow led the way. The sacristy was not, however, empty; the door was ajar, and a man with a face like a death's head was seated at a table, pen in hand. He looked up at them impatiently as they entered. 'I'm getting the service register ready for tonight,' he explained.

'We won't get in your way,' Bairstow assured him. 'We just wanted to have a look at the silver. Mr Middleton-Brown, this is Stanley Everitt, the Parish Administrator.'

The men exchanged pleasantries as Bairstow opened the safe with a long, old-fashioned key. 'Here we are.' He pulled out a cloth bag and unwrapped a chalice.

'Ah.' David assessed it in an instant: it was mass-produced, late in date, and of very little value. 'Interesting,' he said diplomatically.

'There's more.' Bairstow brought out a ciborium, an incense boat, a large alms dish, and an assortment of candlesticks. 'Then there's the altar cross, as well.'

'I see.' Searching for a tactful way to break the news, David picked up the incense boat. 'Nice.'

Norman Topping was watching him eagerly. 'Do you like it? Is it worth something, then?'

He didn't give a direct answer. 'Is this all you have? Don't you have a thurible, or a monstrance?'

'Well, the rest of the plate is only copper-gilt,' Bairstow explained with an apologetic shrug. 'There's a whole set of it, as a matter of fact. But it's really hideous Victorian stuff – not worth anything. After this is sold, we'll have to use it until we can get some new pieces.'

'Show it to him,' Topping urged.

Bairstow reached into the safe and pulled some pieces from the back. 'Here's the thurible.' He handed it to David.

'Oh, yes.' David turned the heavy thurible over in his hands with surprise and rising excitement. 'This is a lovely piece.'

The taller churchwarden straightened up and stared at him. 'It is?'

'It's very fine.' He pointed to the hallmarks. 'You see? It's not copper-gilt at all. It's silver-gilt. Very tarnished with age, but definitely silver-gilt.'

'Silver-gilt?' Topping echoed, his eyes lighting up at the implication.

'Yes. And unless I'm very much mistaken, it was designed by Pugin. The design is certainly very characteristic of his work.' David was trying to be cautious, but he couldn't help betraying a certain degree of anticipation in his voice. 'You say there's more? Could I see the rest, please?'

Bairstow lined the pieces up one by one on the counter. 'Two ciboria, flagon, monstrance, and processional cross.'

'It's a lovely set,' David stated. 'And the fact that it was probably designed by Pugin certainly adds to its value.'

'How much?' Norman Topping demanded baldly. 'What is it worth?'

'The market for ecclesiastical silver is rather depressed right now, but you should certainly get a few thousand for it. Possibly a bit more, since, as I say, it's by a prestigious designer like Pugin. And as it's a set.'

Suddenly he realised that something was missing. 'But where is the chalice?'

The two churchwardens looked at each other. 'I'm afraid it's been stolen,' Bairstow said slowly. 'There was a burglary. A month or two ago.'

'Stolen?' David was dismayed.

'I'm afraid so,' interjected Stanley Everitt, looking even more lugubrious than usual. 'The police said that it happens all the time.'

'Oh, it does. But a silver-gilt Pugin chalice! Some thief got a bit more than he bargained for, I dare say. I hope that it was insured?'

Again the churchwardens looked at each other. 'It was insured, of course, but not for very much,' Bairstow confessed. 'To tell you the truth, I've always thought that this stuff was pretty hideous.'

David shook his head, despairing at the Philistinism which, in his experience, seemed to afflict churchwardens everywhere. 'Never mind. So what do you want to do, now that you know it might be worth a bob or two?'

'Sell it, of course,' Bairstow replied promptly, without even a glance at his colleague. 'How do we go about it?'

Rubbing his chin thoughtfully, David considered the options. 'If you don't need the money immediately, the best thing would be to put it into one of the sale rooms – Christie's or Sotheby's – for auction. That would take a couple of months, to get it into the catalogue. If you're in a great hurry, I could try a few dealers, but you're not likely to get nearly as good a price from them.'

'Oh, we want as much money as we can get,' Bairstow stated.

'But as soon as possible,' Topping added.

'Don't forget, though, that you'll have to get a faculty before you can sell it,' David reminded them. 'That means that your PCC will have to agree, and then the papers will have to be filed with the Diocesan Advisory Committee, who will have to approve the sale. I don't anticipate any real problems with that, but it will take a month or two, no matter what. You can't rush the diocese.'

Wringing his hands in a thoughtful way, Everitt spoke. 'That reminds me about that question you were asking me a few days ago, Martin. Did you ring the diocesan solicitor as I suggested?'

Bairstow seemed to want to change the subject. 'Yes, I did. Now perhaps we should think about—'

'And was I right?' Everitt droned on, oblivious. 'Is it right that if a congregation leaves the Church of England, the building and everything in it remains the property of the C of E?'

The churchwarden was saved the necessity of a reply by the arrival of the Vicar. 'Father Keble Smythe! I'd like you to meet David Middleton-Brown, the solicitor who's going to help us with the sale of the silver, as I mentioned to you. And you won't believe what he's discovered! The old stuff – what we've always thought was copper-gilt – might actually be worth something!'

The Vicar made the appropriate noises, then said, 'How kind of you to turn out on such an unpleasant evening, Mr Middleton-Brown.'

For the first time, and with great interest, David shook the hand of Father William Keble Smythe. He was younger than David had expected, and very good-looking. How would he describe him to Lucy, later on?

Wavy dark hair, contrasting vividly with a pale complexion. Perhaps a bit *too* pale, he decided. In fact, everything about him seemed just a bit over the top: his hair in perfect waves and parted as if with a ruler, his accent perhaps a shade too posh, his cassock immaculate, his shoes polished to a blinding shine.

'I must begin getting ready for the service now, but I'd like to chat further with all of you after,' the Vicar said, taking in David and the churchwardens with his gesture. 'How about joining me at the clergy house for a drink after the service?'

'Sorry, Father,' Martin Bairstow demurred. 'I have to give several of the old girls a lift home.'

'And Dolly will have supper ready,' Norman Topping added. 'She wouldn't appreciate it if I were late.'

The Vicar turned back to David. 'Mr Middleton-Brown? You *are* staying for the service, I trust? How about a drink afterwards?'

David hesitated; Lucy would be expecting him, but on the other hand he felt that he ought to accept. It would help to learn as much about the set-up at St Margaret's as he could, and talking to the Vicar on his own could be a useful way of doing that. He admitted to himself as well that he was curious about Father Keble Smythe, especially in the light of Robin West's veiled remarks. And a drink with the Vicar would extricate him from the clutches of the repellent sacristan. 'A quick one, perhaps.'

'Jolly good. I'll see you after the service, then.'

The service was everything that the sacristan had promised, and more. Multiple clergy went through their paces, the proceedings obscured by copious smoke from the Pugin thurible, ably wielded by Robin West. The 1637 rite was suitably arcane for even the most hardened spiritual thrill-seekers. It was just a shame, thought David, that not more of them were present: as far as he could tell, there weren't more than a few strangers, who, like himself, joined the churchwardens, a sprinkling of devout elderly ladies, and a few others who were clearly regular members of the congregation, for an experience that was well out of the ordinary.

Some time later he found himself at the clergy house, transported there in great comfort in Father Keble Smythe's opulent car. Mrs Goode was waiting for them at the door. 'There's a nice fire going in your study, Father,' she greeted them. 'I thought you'd need it on a cold night like this.'

'Oh, excellent woman!' The Vicar removed his clerical cloak with a flourish. 'And is that your incomparable fish pie that I smell?'

The housekeeper nodded, gratified. 'It will be ready soon. Will the other gentleman be staying to supper?'

Father Keble Smythe turned to David. 'How about it, dear chap? Mrs Goode's fish pie is enough to make anyone look forward to Friday, believe me. I'd be delighted if you'd join me.'

The smell that wafted from the kitchen was enough to tempt David, and it had been a long time since he'd had a good home-made fish pie: since Lucy had become a vegetarian, nearly a year past, he'd been deprived of such fare, and at moments like this he regretted it keenly. But Lucy would be waiting for him, and her soup would be delicious, if meatless. 'I'm sorry, but I really can't.' He followed the Vicar into the study. 'I must get home, I'm afraid.'

'Are you married, Mr Middleton-Brown?'

David was instantly defensive, and not inclined to discuss his domestic arrangements with the Vicar. 'Not exactly,' he hedged.

Father Keble Smythe chuckled understandingly. 'I feel that way myself.' He swept the silver-framed photo off his desk and presented it to David. 'My fiancée, Miss Morag McKenzie,' he explained with a sentimental sigh.

'Very nice,' said David, feeling inadequate. 'She looks ... nice.'

'A lovely young woman.' The Vicar's eyes were misty. 'But I honestly don't know when our marriage will be able to take place. Her father isn't very well, you see, and she's absolutely devoted to him. So all of my pleas to her to end my bachelor state are to no avail! I have Mrs Goode to take care of me, she says, and her father has no one else.'

'Does she live in the parish?'

'Oh, goodness, no. She lives in Scotland. Her father is a professor of classics at St Andrews University.'

David could empathise with the loneliness of separation. 'That must be very difficult for you.'

'It is. It is.' Father Keble Smythe sighed again, with great feeling, and took the photo back. 'But I've invited you here for a drink, not to talk about my sad situation.' He gestured invitingly at the tray which the house-keeper had prepared. 'As you see, Mrs Goode looks after me awfully well. What would you like? Sherry? Whisky? Gin?'

'Whisky, please.' While the Vicar poured the drinks, David took a moment to appraise the room in which he found himself. The study had been furnished with a great deal of taste, he thought, and at no little expense; he wondered if the Vicar had private means, or if he were just successful in loosening the purse strings of his wealthy parishioners.

'So,' said Father Keble Smythe when they had settled comfortably by the fire with their drinks, 'you've met with the churchwardens. And you've seen the silver. Pretty good, is it?'

David nodded. 'Not the bits they wanted to sell, but the old set. I don't know how much you know about Victorian silver, but it's almost certainly designed by Pugin, and that alone makes it well above average in interest and value.'

'That's splendid. You must get on, then, with applying for a faculty to sell it.'

'I'm surprised that you can bear to part with it,' David said frankly. 'It's lovely stuff. If it were *my* church, nothing would induce me to sell it.'

'My churchwardens seem to think that it's the right thing to do.'

'The shelter for the homeless is a worthy idea, of course, but...' David tailed off at the unexpectedly ironic laugh which erupted from the Vicar.

'That's what they told you, then? And you believed it?'

He stared at Father Keble Smythe, baffled. 'Of course I believed it.'

The genial, affected manner had gone in an instant, to be replaced by an air of knowing cynicism. 'Then you haven't known as many churchwardens as I have, Mr

Middleton-Brown. Believe me, a shelter for the homeless is the *last* thing that money is intended for.'

'Then what...?'

'Oh, I'm not sure about that, though I have a fairly good idea what they've got in mind.' The Vicar's chuckle was mirthless as he held his glass up and squinted through the amber liquid, and he spoke more to himself than to David. 'But I'm a step ahead of them. I shall let them hatch their little schemes, thinking all the while that they're putting one over on me. And then ... well, my friend, I shall give them just enough rope to hang themselves!'

Chapter 5

*They are inclosed in their own fat: and their mouth
speaketh proud things.*

Psalm 17.10

'You must admit, it was rather a coincidence.' It was
Wednesday morning and Lucy was still in bed, sipping
the cup of tea that David had brought her, while he got
dressed. 'Vanessa Bairstow ringing me, the same day
that Martin Bairstow rang *you*.'

'I suppose it was, in a way.' He frowned at himself in
the mirror, which was at an awkward height for him to
see his tie properly, and straightened the knot. 'But
you've got to remember, love, that the Church of
England is a small world. Mrs Bairstow rang you
because of Emily, who happens to be the Archdeacon's
wife in addition to being your friend, and her husband
rang me because of what I'd done for St John's last year.
Not really that amazing, when you think about it. Just
one of life's funny little coincidences – the sort of thing
that happens every day.'

'I think it was very clever of you to identify the silver
as being by Pugin.'

David ran a comb through his hair – brown in colour,

with just enough silver at the temples to give him an air
of distinction. 'Not really – his stuff is quite distinctive,'
he demurred modestly. 'I've got a book on Pugin
somewhere, in one of the boxes in the loft – I'll try to find
it this evening, if you like, and show you.' He turned to
face her. 'What time are you going to the Bairstows'?'

'The meeting starts at half-past two. I'll go a few
minutes before that, I suppose.'

Abstractedly, he shrugged his suit jacket on, then
took a final glance at himself in the mirror. 'You're not
going to mention me to her – to Mrs Bairstow, are you?
About the coincidence?'

Lucy gave him an amused look. 'Good heavens, no. I
don't imagine it will come up, quite frankly. And you
know that I don't go about advertising our relationship.
But why do you ask?'

'I wouldn't want her husband to think that I'd been
talking about the case to other people. He might think it
was unprofessional.'

'Don't worry, David darling,' she laughed. 'My lips are
sealed.'

He moved close to the bed. 'That's not all they are,' he
murmured, bending to kiss her goodbye.

Laden down with paintings, Lucy took a taxi to Vanessa
Bairstow's house. It was in the exclusive heart of
Pimlico, facing a black-railed, tree-shaded square. Now,
at the beginning of February, the square was less than
inviting, its trees bare under a grey sky, but already
there were signs of life in the buds that swelled on them,
and Lucy could imagine how pleasant it would be in the
summer. The house was imposingly tall, pristinely

white, with a shiny brass doorknocker in the shape of a lion's head.

Lucy wrestled the paintings out of the taxi and up the steps to the front door. She rang the bell and waited a moment, expecting Vanessa Bairstow to answer, or possibly a servant.

The woman who opened the door was most definitely not Vanessa, but she was clearly not a servant either. To call her large would be understating the case: her massive bosom jutted out like the figurehead of a ship, and her width seemed crammed into the doorway. Her face, under a rather fussy arrangement of permed grey curls, was strong-featured and bespectacled, and seemed unnervingly familiar to Lucy, who was nevertheless unable to think where she might have encountered her in the past. 'Oh, hello,' she said uncertainly. 'I'm Lucy Kingsley.'

'Yes, of course you are.'

This reply, and the tone in which it was spoken, reinforced the impression that she should know the other woman; as she struggled into the house with her paintings, she ventured, 'Have we met?'

'No.' The woman laughed. 'You've probably seen me on television. I'm Dolly Topping, from Ladies Opposed to Women Priests.'

Lucy remembered: Mrs Topping had indeed been an ubiquitous presence on television during the General Synod debate on the ordination of women, the person who could always be counted upon to put the 'anti' point of view with force and conviction. 'A woman's place is at the kitchen table,' she had been fond of saying, 'not at the Sacred Table.' It was a good line, and it had been widely quoted at the time. 'Yes, of course,' Lucy acknowledged. 'It's nice to meet you, Mrs Topping.'

'Please, call me Dolly,' insisted the other woman. 'Everyone does. My name is really Harriet, but no one has called me that for years.' She waited for Lucy to ask her why, but when the question wasn't forthcoming she told her anyway. 'You might not believe it, but I used to be a tiny little thing. When I was first married, my husband Norman said that I was no bigger than a doll. His little Dolly, he said.'

There was no tactful response to that, so Lucy merely smiled.

'Vanessa is on the phone – it rang just as you arrived. She should be with us any minute,' Dolly went on, oblivious to the awkward silence. 'It's very kind of you to come and speak to us today, Miss Kingsley. Though as I told Vanessa, there was really no need – I could have stepped into the breach, if necessary. If I say so myself, I'm rather an expert on quite a few things – Ladies Opposed to Women Priests is by no means the only string to *my* bow,' she asserted.

Again Lucy was at a loss for an appropriate reply. 'Oh, I'm sure,' she said somewhat lamely, wondering where Vanessa Bairstow might be.

Vanessa appeared just then, carrying a cat. 'Oh, hello, Lucy,' she said with a shy smile.

'Who was on the phone?' Dolly demanded.

'Just Vera. She's not going to be able to make it this afternoon – her father isn't well.' She sighed. 'It's a real shame – she was so looking forward to it,' she said.'

'I do hope that Dr Bright isn't seriously ill,' said Dolly, frowning.

'I'm sure he's not. Probably just one of these colds that's been going around.' Vanessa turned to Lucy. 'Are you all right?'

'Yes. Mrs Topping – Dolly – has been taking care of me.'

'This is Augustine.' She held the cat up for Lucy's inspection and admiration. 'My pride and joy.'

Augustine was no sleek Siamese; Lucy saw instead an evil-looking tom, battle-scarred, with a torn ear and a single malevolent yellow eye.

Lucy once again searched frantically for a suitable response. 'How ... um ... nice.' She reached out a tentative hand to stroke him, and was regally ignored. At least, she thought, he didn't rip my hand off.

'Sweetums kitty,' crooned Vanessa, enraptured.

Dolly snorted derisively. 'That's what happens to women who don't have babies,' she muttered to Lucy. 'They go daft over their animals.'

It was a monumentally insensitive thing to say, and judging by the flush on Vanessa's cheek, the barb had gone home. But to Lucy's great relief, almost immediately the doorbell chimed, and Emily Neville joined them.

Lucy and Emily embraced with genuine pleasure and deep affection. Their friendship was of long standing, dating back more than ten years to the time when Emily first occupied the vicarage of St Anne's, Kensington Gardens, as the Vicar's brand new wife. Lucy had been on the periphery of the congregation then, largely through her interest in music and her regular attendance at the weekly organ recitals, and she had befriended the shy young woman, teaching her to cook and helping her to redecorate the forbiddingly masculine vicarage. Through the years they had met often, routinely at organ recitals, and at other times by choice, and Lucy was godmother to Viola, one of Emily's twins. Now, though, since Emily's husband had become Archdeacon – and perhaps not coincidentally since Lucy's involvement with David – their meetings were less frequent, and required more planning, though they kept in touch often by phone.

'Em! You look wonderful!' Lucy spoke only the truth: Emily did indeed look every inch the Archdeacon's wife, her dark brown hair sculptured around her heart-shaped face, her delicate and small-boned figure set off by a trim navy blue dress. But Lucy couldn't help regretting the loss of Emily's own personal style. When she had first known her, barely down from Cambridge, Emily had dressed casually; Lucy had rarely seen her in anything but a pair of jeans and an oversized jumper. It was perhaps not what most vicars' wives wore, but Emily had been loved and accepted for what she was by the parishioners of St Anne's, and there had never been a word of criticism. Now, clearly, things were different, and Emily had to conform to people's expectations of an Archdeacon's wife. Poor Emily, thought Lucy. She hoped that she didn't mind too much.

'So do you, Luce. As always. Love evidently agrees with you,' she added with a teasing smile, and was rewarded by seeing Lucy's fair skin flush. 'How is dear David?'

'Oh, fine.' Lucy went on quickly, 'How about Gabriel? And the children?'

'All very well, thanks. Gabriel is rushed off his feet, of course, but that's to be expected.'

The bell chimed again, another guest was admitted, and soon it was time for the meeting to begin.

Lucy's talk was enthusiastically received, but afterwards her efforts to reach Emily for a chat were thwarted by all the other women who wanted to speak to her.

Self-importantly, Dolly Topping pushed ahead of them all with another woman in tow. 'This is Joan Everitt, the wife of our Parish Administrator,' she announced. 'She wants to know how much you charge for your paintings, but she didn't want to ask you herself.'

'That depends, of course,' Lucy hedged delicately. 'We could discuss it, if you like.'

'I think my husband would like one, but I don't suppose we could afford it,' said Mrs Everitt. A middle-aged woman with a bland, chinless face, she wore her hair in a style inappropriate to her age, long and straight with a black velvet Alice band. Her clothes, too, were far too young for her – not, though, as with some women of mature years who wear short, tight skirts or clothes in the latest teenage fashion. Instead her garb was schoolgirlish: a round-collared white blouse, a modest pleated skirt, and black plimsolls. The effect was mildly jarring.

'We could discuss it later,' repeated Lucy, before, to the disappointment of Dolly Topping, changing the subject. 'Your husband is the Parish Administrator? That must be an interesting job.'

'Oh, yes. Stanley likes it very much.'

'And how about you?' asked Lucy, wondering how to phrase the question without giving offence, one way or the other. The women at this afternoon's gathering were not likely to have – or even want – careers of their own, but to make that assumption could be equally dangerous. 'Do you ... um ... work?'

She needn't have worried; the tone of Joan Everitt's reply was complacent rather than defensive. 'No, not me. Not since the children came along.'

'I should think not,' interjected Dolly. 'A woman's place is in the home.' She managed to say it as though it were an entirely original phrase. 'Unless,' she added with a look of pity at Lucy, 'she's unfortunate enough not to have a husband to support her.'

Lucy couldn't help herself. 'And especially if she has the temerity to want to be a priest.'

The statement was taken at face value, irony being a quality with which Dolly Topping had scant familiarity. 'Absolutely,' she agreed. 'I take it you've heard about the announcement that was made last weekend?'

'No ... ?'

Dolly seemed to swell with indignation. 'The Vicar, Father Keble Smythe, announced that there's to be a woman curate at St Jude's and St Margaret's! Can you imagine anything more ridiculous?' It was a rhetorical question; without waiting for a reply, she went on, 'I'm quite sure that it wasn't *his* idea – there must have been a great deal of pressure from higher up. After all, Father Keble Smythe is a proper Catholic – he's been a supporter of The Cause from the beginning. Many times I've heard him say that women priests are unnatural, unscriptural, completely contrary to the unbroken tradition of the Church.'

'Then why did he consent to have a woman curate?' Joan Everitt put in. 'Not that I blame him, of course.'

'As I say, he must have been under pressure,' repeated Dolly. 'Mark my words, this female was foisted on him against his will. I, for one, feel sorry for poor Father. I won't hear a word against him.'

'Stanley says that it probably won't have much effect on St Margaret's – that things will go on much as before, with priests from other churches filling in for services. After all, she's only a deacon – she can't celebrate the Mass.'

Dolly glowered. 'For the moment, that is. But she wants to be priested, Norman says. And then what will happen? It will all end in tears, I can tell you. I, for one, will not stand still to see a female desecrate the altar at St Margaret's.'

Lucy had been following the exchange with a certain detached amusement, but the vehemence of the last statement startled her. Realising that the other two women had forgotten her presence, she seized the opportunity for escape, and turned towards the corner where Emily Neville nursed a cup of tea. But almost instantly she was waylaid by several other women who had been waiting their turns to talk to her.

At long last, though, she achieved her objective; Emily beckoned her into an empty chair. 'You made it,' she observed, smiling. 'Here – I got you a cup of tea. It's probably cold by now, though.'

'Never mind. I'm so thirsty I won't even notice.' Lucy took a gulp of the tea. 'I was beginning to think I'd never get to you – and I don't think I would have agreed to do this today if Vanessa hadn't promised me that you'd be here. Don't you have to pick up the children from school this afternoon?'

Emily looked at her watch. 'Not for a while yet. They've got music today, so they won't need collecting for nearly another hour.'

'Great. Then we've got time for a natter.'

'What's all the fuss about? Any idea?' Emily indicated the knot of women around Dolly Topping; the discussion was clearly a heated one, dominated by Dolly, who seemed to be lecturing about something.

'It has something to do with their new curate, who had the misfortune to be born female,' Lucy explained wryly. 'Mrs Topping doesn't seem very keen on women in holy orders.'

'To say the least!' Emily leaned closer to Lucy, to avoid being overheard. 'As a matter of fact, I know something about the situation.'

'Because of Gabriel, you mean? I suppose the Archdeacon's wife knows all kinds of things like that.' Absently, Lucy twisted a curl around her finger.

'No, he doesn't usually discuss diocesan matters with me. But it just happens that I know the woman who is going to be their new curate – Rachel Nightingale, her name is.'

Lucy couldn't help being curious. 'How did you meet her?'

'Actually,' Emily explained, 'I've known her for years. We were friends at Cambridge – we were at the same college, and we both read English. In fact, when I married Gabriel, and turned down that graduate fellowship I'd been offered, she was the one who took it up. She's remained in Cambridge ever since, living the academic life that I would have had if it hadn't been for Gabriel.' She smiled, without regret. 'We've kept in touch with Christmas cards and so forth, but I've only seen her a few times since I came down, mostly at college functions.'

'But if she's an academic, how did she get to be a deacon? And why is she in London?'

Emily sighed. 'It's a sad story. She married a young man whom she met at Cambridge – Colin Nightingale. He was a scientist, absolutely brilliant. I knew him slightly. Several years after they were married, when they'd practically given up hope that it would happen, they had a little girl.' She looked into her empty teacup; Emily's own efforts to have children had been traumatic, though ultimately successful. 'Rachel was thrilled, though it meant a few adjustments in her academic workload.'

'And?'

'A few years ago, they were all in a car crash, on a foggy road outside Cambridge. The little girl, Rosie, was killed instantly. Colin lived, though in some ways it would have been better if he hadn't – he's virtually a cabbage, and hasn't ever regained consciousness. He's been in hospital, just kept alive, ever since the accident.' She shook her head. 'Tragic – all that scientific genius lost. Not to mention the little girl, of course.'

Lucy found that her hand was clenched around her cup. 'And Rachel?'

'She was wearing her safety belt, and was only slightly injured. But of course the experience changed her life. She'd lost her family – lost everything. Not surprisingly, she had a crisis of faith, and at the end of it she decided that she was being called into the Church, to serve other people who were hurting. To be a priest, in fact.'

'How brave of her!'

'It was difficult, especially since at that time the legislation on women priests hadn't yet been passed by the General Synod. She was no strident revolutionary with an axe to grind or a flag to wave – just a woman who felt that God was calling her to the priesthood. So she went through theological college, was ordained a deacon, and started her curacy at a church in Cambridge. Then Colin's doctors decided that they could do no more for him – that he should be transferred to a hospital in London, where they've been pioneering new treatments for brain-damaged people. It was terribly hard for Rachel to leave her church in Cambridge, but she knew that she had to put Colin's needs first, and of course she wants to be near him. She visits him every day, even though he almost certainly doesn't know that she's there.'

There were tears in Lucy's eyes and tightness in her throat. 'Oh, the poor woman!'

'Financially she has no worries, of course. The chap who was driving the lorry that hit them had just come from the pub and was well over the limit, so she was awarded substantial damages. Colin is receiving the best possible care, and now that Rachel has moved to London, she's ready to get back to work.' Emily looked over to where Dolly Topping was still holding forth on the evils of women at the altar. 'It's just her misfortune,' she added with a bittersweet smile, 'that she has to do it at St Jude's and St Margaret's, on Dolly Topping's patch.'

Chapter 6

*Who have whet their tongue like a sword: and shoot
out their arrows, even bitter words.*

Psalm 64.3

Supper had been eaten and the washing up had been
accomplished; Lucy and David had learned from experience, during their months of living together, that
unless the washing up was done immediately after
supper, it was not likely to be done until the next day.
Now, though, it was out of the way, and they were curled
up together on the sofa in front of the fire, drinking their
coffee and enjoying each other's company. Tonight Lucy
had suggested accompanying the coffee with brandy:
she felt that she needed it – and deserved it – after her
afternoon with the women's club.

Through supper she'd told David about the experience, dwelling on the dreadfulness of Dolly Topping.
He was entirely sympathetic. 'From what her husband
said,' he confirmed, 'I got the strongest feeling that she
rules him with a rod of iron.'

'I'm sure she does. She's really bossy – I found her
absolutely terrifying. And she's unwilling to accept the
existence of any point of view but her own.'

David grinned. 'And he is a bit of a wimp, I fear.'

She'd told him, as well, of Rachel Nightingale: her tragic story, and her imminent arrival in the parish. The woman's history, seen through Emily's sympathetic eyes, had touched Lucy deeply, and she found herself returning to the subject again and again. 'Poor Rachel. I can't imagine how they'll treat her at St Margaret's. Dolly Topping will be vile to her – she doesn't deserve that.'

'And I don't think that the churchwardens will be particularly gentle with her either.' David set his empty coffee cup on the table and put his arm around Lucy's shoulders. The room was cosy, the fire and the brandy were warming, and he was ready to progress to the next stage of the evening.

She twisted around to look at him. 'They didn't mention anything about her to you at all?'

'No, nothing.' He took her cup from her, putting it next to his. 'Though that isn't really surprising, if it wasn't announced till last Sunday. Presumably they were keeping it quiet until then.'

'Did they know about it, do you think?'

'Oh, probably. But I was there to talk about the silver, not the curate.' He kissed her. 'Can't we change the subject now?' he murmured. 'If I remember correctly, this is where we left off this morning.'

Lucy responded to him for a moment, then pulled away. 'The silver!' she said. 'This morning you promised to show me something about the silver, darling. A picture in a book – remember?'

David was loath to be interrupted. 'Can't it wait till later?'

But the amatory mood was broken, at least as far as Lucy was concerned; her curiosity was as aroused as David's libido. 'If you don't get up right now,' she predicted, 'there's no hope of you finding that book tonight.'

He acknowledged the truth of her statement, but failed to see it as the end of the world. 'Is that so terrible? Won't tomorrow do?' He kissed her again. 'Isn't this more fun?'

'Please? I'd really like to see it. Then we can go to bed.'

'Oh, all right,' David grumbled, sighing a martyr's sigh and disentangling himself from her. 'If it's that important to you.'

He went upstairs and pulled down the ladder to the loft, where his boxes of books were stored. When he'd moved out of his house, a few months previously, he'd put most of his books into store in Norfolk pending a more permanent arrangement, but he'd brought a few boxes of favourites with him. In the event, Lucy's tiny house, with its crowded bookshelves, couldn't absorb even these few essential volumes, and they'd been consigned to the loft.

As he looked over the boxes, his thoughts returned to their earlier conversation about Rachel Nightingale. The story interested him from a legal as well as a human point of view: he was sure that he remembered reading and hearing about the case, in which she had been awarded an astronomical amount of financial compensation, based on her husband's brilliant future in science and his subsequent reduction to a brain-dead condition. There had been something special about that case – it had set some legal precedent, or been noteworthy in some way. He wished he could remember what it was.

While his mind was thus engaged, David found the box with the books on Victorian churches, dusted it off, and in short order retrieved the book he was looking for, the catalogue from a V & A exhibition entitled *Victorian Church Art*. He took it back to the sitting room, where Lucy had put another log on the fire and was pouring out second helpings of brandy.

'That didn't take long.' She smiled and patted the sofa next to her invitingly.

Demonstrating his displeasure at her recent treatment of him, David instead took a chair. 'I knew which box it was in.' He flipped through the book, looking for the illustrations. 'As I said, Pugin's style was quite distinctive. Here, for example, is a ciborium, quite similar to the pair they've got at St Margaret's.' He began to hand the book across to her, then suddenly snatched it back and stared at the illustration. 'Good Lord,' he said.

Lucy was baffled at the look on his face as he rapidly scanned the text under the picture. 'What's the matter, darling?'

He didn't even hear her, so focused was he on the book. 'Good Lord,' he repeated softly. After a moment he looked up. 'It *is* like the set they've got,' he said with quiet assurance.

'What do you mean?'

'The silver at St Margaret's – the silver that they want to sell. I thought that it was fairly late, made to one of Pugin's designs after his death. But it says here that this set was extremely early. Lucy love, don't you see? St

Margaret's set is almost exactly like this – that means it's very rare, and much more valuable than I thought.'

'Are you sure?'

He shook his head. 'I can't be positive until I've seen it again, and taken a closer look at the hallmarks. I'll ring the Vicar,' he decided. 'Perhaps he could meet me at the church.'

'Now? At this hour?'

He glanced at his watch. 'It's not that late – barely gone nine.'

Lucy forbore to say that he was the one who was ready to go to bed a quarter of an hour before; instead she gave him an arch look. 'Shouldn't you ring the sacristan? After what you told me about him, I'm sure he'd be more than happy to drop whatever he's doing and meet you. At the church. Alone.'

'Ha. Very funny.'

'Seriously, though – shouldn't you ring the wardens? They're the ones who contacted you in the first place.'

'Technically I'm taking instructions from the Vicar *and* churchwardens.' He went to the phone. 'So at the risk of incurring the legendary wrath of Dolly Topping, I suppose I'd better ring them as well.'

David rang the Vicar first, and was restrained in what he told him – he had reason to believe, he said, that the silver might be more important than he had at first thought, and he would like a chance to examine it again at the earliest opportunity, in the light of what he now knew. That was enough, though, to make the Vicar amenable to going out on a cold night, and on very short notice.

In the end five of them gathered in the sacristy some

twenty minutes later. Both churchwardens had been only too eager to come, and the Vicar had brought along Stanley Everitt, with whom he had been having a meeting when David's call had come through.

They all watched in anticipation as the Vicar opened the safe and brought out the pieces of silver, one by one. As Martin Bairstow had done a few days earlier, he lined them up side by side on the vestment chest. 'There,' he commented. 'I always did think it was uncommonly fine silver. What are you going to tell us about it now, Mr Middleton-Brown?'

David opened the book to the page he'd marked and laid it down next to the silver; the similarity was unmistakable. 'You see? It's very like the set he designed for St Mary's Church, Clapham – comparable in quality and design.' He picked up the thurible and scrutinised the hallmarks with the magnifying glass he'd brought along for the purpose. 'Yes. John Hardman & Co., 1850. It all fits!'

'Is that good?' Norman Topping asked naïvely.

'You told us the other night that it was designed by Pugin,' Bairstow stated, looking at his watch. 'Was this really worth bringing us out tonight for? Why does it matter that it's like the set in the book?'

David took a deep breath; there was no point getting annoyed, he told himself – they really *didn't* understand. 'Don't you see?' he explained patiently. 'It means that it's extremely valuable.'

'Valuable?' echoed Stanley Everitt, his face sharpening.

'Extremely valuable.' David reached out a finger and stroked the thurible with an unconscious gesture. 'It's much earlier than I thought it was, made in Pugin's lifetime. Most of Pugin's work was done for the Roman church, of course, so for an Anglican church to have a set...'

'How much?' Bairstow asked bluntly. 'How much is it worth?'

'That's a difficult question. It always depends on how much someone is willing to pay, but I'd say that you're looking at a figure well over a hundred thousand pounds. Each piece on its own would fetch five figures, and as a set it's worth even more.'

'Cor,' breathed Norman Topping; Everitt drew in his breath, and Bairstow nodded in satisfaction.

Father Keble Smythe had been taking it all in; now he spoke thoughtfully. 'That's wonderful news, of course. But what are the implications, now that we know what it is?'

David had been thinking about that very question on his way to the church. 'Well, of course it will make the sale more difficult,' he admitted. 'For starters, the Diocesan Advisory Committee might not want you to sell it – they could quite legitimately claim that it's a unique treasure, and should stay here at St Margaret's. If the DAC throw up any obstacles, it will probably go to Consistory Court, and that will take time, and cost money – counsel will have to be briefed, and there will be other expenses. But at the end of the day, *if* you're allowed to sell it, you should have a small fortune on your hands.'

'Oh.' The Vicar stroked his chin. 'So it will take time, will it?'

'I'm afraid so.'

A significant look passed between the churchwardens. 'I think that we'd better discuss this between us before you take the matter any further,' Bairstow stated.

Everitt turned on him. 'But surely now that we know what it is, we can't just forget about it! It's unique and valuable – you heard what he said!' Wringing his hands, he pulled his normally lugubrious mouth into an approximation of a smile, revealing long teeth from which the gums had receded; this gave him an even stronger resemblance than usual to a skull. 'I don't know about you, but I think it's wonderful news!'

'What is the next step?' Father Keble Smythe put in. 'If we should decide to go ahead with the sale, that is.'

David lifted the thurible by its slender silver chains. 'In any case, whether you decide to go ahead or not, you should have it authenticated and valued. The V & A will do that for you, and they won't charge for it, but it will take a few weeks.'

'Do you have any doubt at all?' Everitt picked up the monstrance and held it protectively against his chest. 'I mean, is there a chance that they'll tell us that it's a later copy?'

'No.' David shook his head. 'I'm sure it's a very rare set of early Pugin silver. And in three or four weeks' time, that's what the V & A will tell you as well.'

The churchwardens exchanged another look. 'Then perhaps, Mr Middleton-Brown,' said Martin Bairstow, 'you would be so good as to see to that for us.'

'And I don't need to tell you all,' the Vicar added, 'that until this is settled, the matter is not to go any farther than these four walls. No one else needs to know.'

'What about the sacristan?' asked Everitt with an anxious look. 'Mr West will want to know where his silver has gone.'

'I'll deal with Mr West,' asserted the Vicar firmly. 'I'll talk to him tomorrow – leave it with me.'

Some time later, David walked home through the chill night, his hands in his pockets for warmth. It was very strange, he reflected, that the churchwardens, who had been so keen to sell the silver when they thought it was worth a relative pittance, now seemed reluctant to pursue the sale when it could bring them a very large windfall. He didn't deceive himself that they had any attachment to the silver itself – as he would have done – either for its intrinsic value, its historic interest, or its beauty. Even the Vicar had seemed subdued in the face of what David thought of as good news of the best possible sort. Only the Parish Administrator had seemed as overjoyed as he would have expected them all to be. It was most puzzling.

He wondered what Lucy, with her shrewd insights into people and their motivations, would make of it. In spite of the Vicar's injunction, he knew that he would discuss it with her: after all, she already knew what he'd discovered about the silver, so what was the point of keeping quiet about it now? And he knew that he could trust absolutely in Lucy's discretion.

The other question that fascinated him was that of the silver's origins. How had it come into the possession of St Margaret's in the first place? Who had commissioned it? And why had no one discovered it before? From what he had read, he thought he could make a fairly good guess. At the time St Margaret's Church was built, in the mid-nineteenth century, Pugin had been considered a dangerously popish designer. If an early benefactor – perhaps the first Vicar – had commissioned a set of Pugin silver for the new church, it surely would have been sailing close to the wind. No one would have publicised it; on the contrary, it would have been considered so naughty that its existence would have been kept as quiet as possible, and within a few years its origins might have been completely forgotten. It could very easily have happened that way, David realised.

Tomorrow he would collect the silver from the church safe, and deliver it to the V & A. For tonight, all he could do was talk about it with Lucy. She would have waited up for him, he knew, so it was with confident expectation and anticipation of a warm house, a warm bed, and an even warmer Lucy that he walked a little faster towards home.

Norman Topping's feet did not bear him quite so eagerly towards his house, not far from St Margaret's. He and Martin Bairstow had retired to the pub to discuss the latest development, and hadn't left till closing time, so he looked rather anxiously at his watch as he fumbled for his key and let himself into the house. He'd told Dolly that he wouldn't be more than half an hour – she wouldn't be pleased.

The house was in darkness, and she hadn't even left a light on for him. Holding his breath, Norman crept up the stairs and into the bedroom; perhaps Dolly would be asleep, and the moment of reckoning could be postponed until morning.

But as soon as he entered the room, Dolly sat up and snapped on the lamp on the table between the twin beds. Her appearance at night was even more terrifying than Lucy's daytime experience of her: her hair was wound around pink foam rollers, and covered with a loosely woven hairnet, and her face glistened with night-time potions meant to keep wrinkles at bay. 'Well?' she said; the word was invested with as much weight, as much meaning, as it was possible to squeeze into a single syllable.

'I'm really sorry, Dolly.' The coaxing propitiation of his tone didn't carry much conviction. By experience he knew that Dolly's wrath was as unpleasantly inevitable as a head cold, once the scratchy throat had manifested itself.

'You said you wouldn't be long!'

'It was important.' In a flash of inspiration he saw how he might distract her, deflect her ire away from himself and on to her pet hobbyhorse. 'Because of the woman curate, you know. I told you about Martin's plan to sell the silver.'

Dolly's fleshy jaws quivered. 'And a good plan it is, too. It's just as well that there are people who aren't prepared to stand around and see the True Church delivered over into the hands of those heretics and their female so-called priests, lock, stock, and barrel. Thank God we've got *one* churchwarden with some sense!'

Norman bowed his head meekly at the implied criticism; now was not the time to defend himself.

But in a moment she was on the offensive again. 'So what does that have to do with this evening? I thought that you had that solicitor chap all set up, and that he told you the silver should fetch a good price. What's happened?'

'Well, now he says that the silver is much more valuable than he thought. I didn't really follow the whole thing, but what it boils down to is that it might be difficult to sell it – the diocese might object – and it will take longer than we'd thought. Martin and I had to talk it over afterwards, to decide what we're going to do.'

'Hm.' Dolly narrowed her eyes, short-sighted without her spectacles. 'And what did *Martin* decide?'

'That we should wait a while and see what happens. The solicitor is going to take the stuff to the V & A to see what they say about it.'

'And in the meantime,' muttered Dolly fiercely, pulling the bedclothes around her, 'we shall have that woman foisted on us. I never thought I would live to see such an outrage in my church!'

Chapter 7

Thy wife shall be as the fruitful vine: upon the walls
of thine house.

Psalm 128.3

On the following morning, Thursday, David arrived at
St Margaret's at the prearranged time to collect the
silver. To his surprise, though, he was met not by the
Vicar as he had expected, but by the sacristan. On their
previous encounter the man had been wearing a
cassock; today he was much more colourfully arrayed in
a gaudy multi-hued jumper, adorned with a discreet
enamelled pink triangle.

The expression on Robin West's ugly, frog-like face
changed instantly from a sulk to a smile as he saw
David. 'Oh, it's you, is it? *Quelle surprise!* The Vicar
said that someone would be calling to collect the
silver, but he didn't tell me that it was going to be
you.'

David cringed inwardly, but managed to retain his
outward composure. 'Yes. I hope I haven't caused you
too much trouble.'

'Not at all. Not at all.' He turned and led the way to
the sacristy. 'Though I wouldn't admit that to the Vicar.

He expects too much of me, you know. Takes me for granted. Thinks I should be here at the drop of a hat. And he wouldn't even tell me what you're going to do with the silver.' Reaching the sacristy door, he swivelled and gave David an expectant look, tacitly inviting enlightenment on the subject.

'I'm afraid I can't really discuss that.'

The sacristan shrugged. 'Never mind. Not your fault, I'm sure.' He inserted the heavy key into the lock. 'Very hush-hush, it must be. Can't you even tell me what line of work you're in? Are you a silversmith, or an insurance valuer? Or does it have something to do with the robbery? Surely you're not a copper!'

'Oh, no. I'm a solicitor,' David admitted, somewhat reluctantly.

'A solicitor!' Robin West paused and looked David up and down. 'Curiouser and curiouser!'

'I really can't say more than that.'

'Yes, I know all about you legal types. The soul of discretion, I'm sure.' The sacristan tapped him on the arm with the safe key and favoured him with a broad wink.

David was relieved as the man turned to the safe and began fiddling with the lock, but the stream of speculation and conjecture never faltered. 'I can't imagine what a solicitor would be doing with the silver. Very interesting. There are of course other reasons why the churchwardens might employ you – to issue writs, if that's how you say it, to prevent the Vicar from bringing that woman in to this church. Now that *would* be useful.'

'Woman?' David wasn't really following the train of

thought. 'You mean his fiancée, Miss McKenzie?'

'Fiancée!' Robin West snorted in derision. 'Fiancée, I'm sure! No, I mean the so-called curate – you've heard about her, haven't you?'

'Oh, yes, of course.'

'Not that I accept the validity of her orders, of course.' The sacristan swung the heavy safe door open. 'Not even her deacon's orders. Women have no place in the Sanctuary. The very thought is a sacrilege.'

'There seem to be quite a few people at St Margaret's who agree with you about that.'

'I should think so! This is a proper *Catholic* parish, always has been!' His voice had lost its customary languor as he went on, 'I can't imagine what Father was thinking of when he agreed to her appointment! He must have known that heads would roll, that people wouldn't just sit in the pews and accept it!'

David frowned. 'But what can people do? Apart from leaving St Margaret's in protest, and finding another church? I mean, people may not like it, but...'

'Humph.' The sacristan reached into the safe and brought out a candlestick. 'I can think of a few people who would rather see that woman dead than at the altar of St Margaret's. I, for one, will not serve in the Sanctuary, or even enter it, if *she* is there.' He nodded resolutely, as though that settled the matter. 'Here – is this what you want? You'll have to tell me which pieces you're taking.'

Helping David to carry the silver to his car, Robin West continued his litany of grievances. 'I don't know how we're meant to manage without the thurible or the monstrance. Or the processional cross, for that matter. Will you have them back by the weekend? By Sunday morning?'

'I'm afraid not. It may be several weeks, in fact.'

'Then what does Father expect us to do? Though Lent will be upon us soon, and we don't have incense during Lent, so the thurible won't be so critical.'

'Perhaps you can borrow some pieces from St Jude's,' David suggested. 'I think that's probably what the Vicar has in mind.'

If he'd been wearing a cassock, Robin West would have twitched his skirts. 'Oh, I'm sure *you* know more about that than I do. After all, I'm only the sacristan,' he said cuttingly.

Having stowed the silver with great care in the boot, David was anxious to get it to the V & A before anything happened. He faced Robin West with an awkward smile. 'Well, thank you very much for your help. I won't keep you any longer.'

The sacristan waved a dismissive hand. 'Oh, that's all right. I don't have to be at work for a while yet.'

David's curiosity got the better of him. 'What sort of work do you do, Mr West?'

'Please, call me Robin,' he smirked, then explained, 'I manage a restaurant. A bistro, really. In South Ken.' With a flourish he produced a card from his pocket and handed it to David. 'As you see. *La Reine Dorée*. Lunches and dinners, seven days a week. Why don't you call in for a drink one day? On the house, of course.'

Framing his answer carefully, David replied, 'Thank you very much. Perhaps I'll come in for a meal with my ... um, girlfriend.' He realised that the word sounded faintly ridiculous coming from a man of his age, but the important thing was to establish the gender of the person involved; a more accurate term such as 'partner' could be dangerously ambiguous, and he wanted Robin West left in no doubt.

The sacristan took it well, with the equanimity of one who was used to rejection. 'Yes, of course,' he shrugged. 'But don't feel that you have to bring her if you don't want to,' he added with a grin, reaching out a hand to touch David's sleeve.

'Oh, there's the Vicar,' David said quickly.

Robin West's head swivelled to the direction David was looking, and at the same moment Father Keble Smythe saw them. He was leading a small, fair woman towards the church, gesticulating and talking, but when he spotted the two men at the kerb he changed course and started in their direction, saying something to the woman as they approached.

'It's *her*,' the sacristan hissed. 'He's actually had the nerve to bring that woman here! If he thinks I'm going to stand around and be civil to her, he's got another think coming!' And with that announcement he disappeared in the opposite direction.

In his astonishment, David had time for little more than a quick impression of the woman before they reached him. The dog collar on her light blue blouse confirmed her identity as the hated and feared Rachel Nightingale, but she wasn't what he'd expected. In the split second that he had to think about it, David realised that he wasn't sure *what* he'd been expecting her to look like – large and looming and hirsute, with feminist slogans tattooed on her forearms, or vampish and red-fingernailed? – but certainly not this. Rachel Nightingale was so slight that she seemed scarcely more than a child, though David knew that she must be approaching thirty-five. Her fine fair hair curled loosely around a china-doll face, a face without real beauty but possessed of character and great sweetness. With a small shock he recognised what it was that gave her face such character: a long, thin scar bisected her rosy cheek, running from the outside corner of her left eyebrow to her chin, the legacy and continual reminder of the accident that had robbed her of her husband and child.

'This is Mr Middleton-Brown, who is doing some legal work for us,' the Vicar told her, looking perplexedly in the direction in which his sacristan had disappeared.

She extended her small hand for a surprisingly firm handshake. 'Hello.' She smiled up at David, and her smile was friendly without being in the least bit coy. 'I'm Rachel Nightingale, the new curate.'

The Venerable Gabriel Neville, Archdeacon of Kensington, sat at his desk that Thursday morning, frowning at the telephone. A moment earlier he'd needed to place a call, but when he'd picked up the receiver he had realised that his wife was on the kitchen extension. Impatiently he tapped his pen on the foolscap sheet on which he was drafting some notes for a series of Lenten addresses which he had been asked to deliver at a prestigious Knightsbridge church. They hadn't made it clear whether there would be six addresses or seven, and he needed to know.

Gabriel Neville, at forty-one, was young for an archdeacon. He was also far better-looking than the average archdeacon, tall and slender with arresting sapphire-blue eyes and a full head of rich auburn hair. His blessings didn't stop with the purely physical, either: Gabriel was accomplished as a preacher, intellectually gifted, and possessed of a wife who adored him and who had borne him two – on the whole – delightful children. He had risen to his present eminent position largely due to his superior abilities and on the strength of his conscientious performance during ten years as the Vicar of St Anne's Church, Kensington Gardens, from which he had been promoted something over a year previously. In his more analytical moments, Gabriel realised that his wife, so very suitable, and his well-behaved and attractive children had done him no harm either when it came to promotion: a family man always makes a good impression on the powers-that-be.

At the moment, however, he was feeling slightly fed up with the demands of family life. He and Emily had argued at breakfast – though perhaps argument was too strong a word for the ongoing disagreement, or rather non-agreement, which had punctuated their life of late. Emily had mentioned that the twins were begging for a dog, and she was inclined to agree with them. At eight, she said, they were old enough to assume the responsibility for a pet. 'But what will happen when they go off to boarding school next year?' he'd asked. 'Who will look after the dog then?' Emily had been tearful, but stubborn as usual: no boarding school, she'd said. Why was it necessary to send their children away, when there were perfectly good schools in London, and when they could have places at the cathedral school? She didn't seem to understand that the Nevilles had a long tradition of Eton for boys and Cheltenham for girls; he'd put Sebastian and Viola's names down as soon as they were born. As far as Gabriel was concerned, it wasn't even an issue.

Now he sighed, looking at the telephone. Chatting on the phone, probably with Lucy Kingsley, on a morning when she knew that he had important calls to make. There were days when he entertained the fleeting notion that it would have been preferable to have remained a bachelor.

A moment later, however, Emily tapped on his study door and came in with a tray of coffee and biscuits for his mid-morning sustenance. 'I thought you'd be about ready for this,' she said.

Gabriel gave her a perfunctory smile. 'Thanks.'

Sensing his irritation, she hesitated by the door. 'Is everything all right?'

'Who were you talking to on the phone?' he replied elliptically.

It was Emily's turn to sigh. 'Dolly Topping.'

He made an involuntary face. 'Dreadful woman. Whyever were you talking to her? Didn't you talk to her yesterday, at that awful women's meeting?'

'It would be more accurate to say that *she* was talking to *me*,' Emily corrected him. 'On both occasions.'

'About the horrors of having a woman curate, no doubt.' Gabriel raised his eyebrows cynically. 'Foisted on them by some evil diocesan functionary like a bishop or even an archdeacon.'

Emily gave a dry laugh. 'The subject did come up, I believe. But that wasn't why she rang me this morning, as a matter of fact.'

Taking a sip of his coffee, he looked at her enquiringly. 'Yes?'

'It was something to do with the silver at St Margaret's,' she amplified. 'I didn't follow it very well, but apparently the churchwardens are hoping to sell some of the church silver, and they've just found out that it's very valuable.'

'Valuable?'

'Apparently so. Worth over a hundred thousand pounds, Norman told her.'

Gabriel frowned. 'They can't just sell it, you know. They'll have to apply for a faculty, and I'm not so sure they'll get it.' He put his coffee cup down with a decisive thump. 'Why haven't I been informed about this?'

Shrugging, Emily interpreted the latter as a rhetorical question. 'I thought you might be interested.'

As she slipped out of the door, Gabriel flashed her a genuine smile of gratitude. Wives could be very useful sometimes, he reflected wryly, finishing his coffee. But whatever were those churchwardens up to? The Venerable Gabriel Neville, Archdeacon of Kensington, resolved to find out.

Chapter 8

I have considered the days of old: and the years that are past.

Psalm 77.5

The voice on the loud-speaker was as muffled and incomprehensible as always, though in these days of customer service the announcements of delayed or cancelled trains were no longer stated baldly, but were couched in terms of feigned regret. 'We apologise for (crackle, spit, mumble, crackle),' David heard as he waited on the northbound Piccadilly line platform at the South Kensington tube station. He sighed; from experience he was able to decipher the garble, and the bottom line was that he would be late for work.

'Mr Middleton-Brown?' ventured a tentative voice.

David turned to see Stanley Everitt beside him on the platform. 'Oh, hello.'

'Did you understand what they said?' In his right hand he clutched a carrier bag; with his left he gestured vaguely into the air.

David's laugh was without humour. 'The usual. Security alert – that's London Transport-speak for yet another IRA bomb threat – at Gloucester Road has

caused unavoidable delays to northbound service on the
Piccadilly Line. They apologise for any inconvenience,
rhubarb, rhubarb.' He looked up at the moving light
display, which merely announced that no smoking was
permitted on the London Underground. 'They're not
even listing the next train. It could be a long wait.'

'Oh, dear.' Everitt tucked his carrier bag under his
arm to facilitate his characteristic, if unconscious,
hand-wringing. 'Did you know that there's been a bomb
at Victoria Station this morning? I went there first, and
it's all cordoned off, so I came here instead.'

In just a few months of living in London, David had
become accustomed to such things. 'Was it serious, do
you know?'

Everitt's voice dropped to a lugubrious whisper. 'I
heard that one or possibly two people had been killed.
Terrible.'

'Dreadful,' David agreed automatically. His mind
was occupied with wishing that the train would come, to
deliver him from this tiresome man. His contact with
Everitt had been slight, but the man, with his nervous
mannerisms, his peevish negativism and his cadaverous
appearance, made him uncomfortable. In fact, he
realised, the feelings elicited by the administrator were
rather similar to those he felt in the presence of the
sacristan, albeit for completely different reasons.

'Do you take this line every day?' Everitt asked after a
moment.

'Yes. My office is in the City. Lincoln's Inn.'

'I'm very lucky, really – I can walk to work. St Jude's
is just around the corner from where I live, and St
Margaret's isn't far at all. Of course I only go there one

day a week, generally. That's all it really requires to keep things ticking over there. St Margaret's used to be a much more active parish, of course, in the old days. Very high, it's always been, but that sort of thing used to be more popular than it is now. Father Keble Smythe is a proper Catholic, of course, but he knows when to trim his sails. St Jude's requires a much more moderate approach. I've always preferred St Margaret's, myself.'

David gazed at the display, willing it to flash up the next train. 'I met your new curate yesterday,' he said, without thinking.

At least it stemmed the flow of self-important stream-of-consciousness; Stanley Everitt sucked in his breath, looking as though he'd just bitten into a lemon. 'Her.'

'You've met her?'

'Yes, of course. As the Administrator I was one of the first to meet her, naturally.'

'She seems very nice,' David stated, aware that he wasn't making himself very popular.

'Oh, I have nothing against her *personally*.' Everitt raised a hand to smooth the strands of hair across the crown of his head. 'I just don't understand what the Church is about, going against two thousand years of tradition. When there are so many qualified *men* who'd like to be ordained,' he added with a significant nod.

In an instant, David understood; Everitt's objections were not so much theological as the result of hurt pride and thwarted ambition. 'You'd like to be ordained?' he hazarded.

'Well, yes,' admitted the Administrator with some reluctance. 'I have put myself forward for ordination. I do feel that I have a real call to the priesthood, a true vocation. With my administrative skills, and my interest in all things spiritual . . . Well.'

'What happened?'

The sour-lemon expression intensified. 'I was turned down by the Board of Ministry. Three times. It's all right for *some*,' he added in a burst of bitterness. 'The first batch of women – just because they're women, they don't have to go to a selection conference. Different rules apply. It's just not fair.'

With relief, David saw on the display that the next train would be arriving in two minutes. It was bound to be crowded; perhaps he'd be able to lose Stanley Everitt and be spared travelling into the City with him. 'Ah. Our train should be here soon,' he declared.

The call from Martin Bairstow came later that morning, when David had barely had a chance to catch up with his post and to deal with the inevitable consequences of his lateness by rescheduling a few missed appointments. 'The Archdeacon wants to see us,' Bairstow announced. 'This afternoon.'

His heart – or was it his stomach? – gave a quite unexpected lurch. 'The Archdeacon? But why?'

Bairstow sounded distinctly unamused. 'He's got the wind up. Someone has told him about the silver – that we want to sell it, and that it's probably worth a lot of money.'

'Who would have told him?'

'He wouldn't say, and I can't imagine who would have done it, after the Vicar specifically mentioned that we should keep it to ourselves for the time being. But he had his facts right, and I couldn't very well deny it.'

David's first guilty thought, quickly dismissed, was that Lucy might have told Emily; he digested the information in silence for a moment. 'He's asked for a meeting, you say?'

'Yes. He wants the churchwardens to come and see him this afternoon, at three.'

'Me, as well?'

'I told him that we'd be bringing our solicitor.'

'Are you sure that you wouldn't do just as well without me?' David asked faintly.

'Nonsense,' was the robust reply. 'Bringing our solicitor along will show him that we can't be intimidated, that we mean business.'

'But...'

'I'll come to your office to collect you at half-past two,' Bairstow stated in a tone that would brook no argument, a tone that he had often used to great effect in his business dealings. 'See you then.'

David put the phone down.

The Archdeacon. Gabe.

This afternoon.

He looked at his desk diary for the afternoon's entries: only one appointment, at half-past three, for a consultation about revising a will.

Gabe.

He went out to find his secretary. 'Would you mind ringing Wing Commander Fitzjames and rescheduling him for next week? Something important has just come up.'

Mrs Simmons looked disapproving, but nodded and reached for the phone.

David returned to his desk and picked up the pad on

which he was drafting a complicated brief; several times he read over what he had written, but the words didn't register.

Gabe. This afternoon. In just a few hours.

He wasn't sure that he was ready to see Gabe again. He hadn't seen him for over a year, not since before Gabe had become Archdeacon. They had parted on good terms, as friends, with their painful misunderstandings laid to rest, but they hadn't met again. David was convinced that his feelings about Gabe had been resolved – of course they had: Lucy was all that mattered to him now – but he still wasn't sure that he wanted to see him, to stir up what was for him a closed chapter of his life.

There had been occasional opportunities to see Gabe over the last year and a half, at various social occasions, but he had always managed to find some reason to avoid him. He told himself that it was out of consideration for Lucy's feelings. After all, she had never liked Gabriel Neville much, even when he was no more than the husband of her best friend. She'd been upset when David had confessed to her the history of his relationship with Gabe, which had ended suddenly and painfully almost twelve years ago when Gabe had disappeared from his life and then married Emily. Lucy's reactions had been complex, dominated by indignation at Gabriel's heartless behaviour, whatever its justification, and by compassion for David's suffering. David and Lucy hadn't really talked about it since, both of them preferring to put it behind them and to get on with building their own relationship; but by unspoken consent they had avoided social contact with the Nevilles. Lucy continued to see

Emily, if somewhat less frequently than before, and her affection for her was unchanged, but she had no desire to see Gabriel.

Neither, David realised now, did he. There was Lucy and her feelings to consider, yes, but was he also afraid of his own reactions? Was he afraid that all those years of love could not so easily be dismissed, and that seeing Gabe again would bring it all back? In spite of Lucy, and in spite of his love for her? It was unthinkable, and yet it had to be faced. How would he feel, when he saw Gabe again this afternoon?

At least David knew what was coming; Gabriel hadn't the least warning of the encounter. Before either of the churchwardens had a chance to make introductions, Gabriel blurted, 'David!'

'Oh, you've met, have you?' Martin Bairstow surmised, raising his eyebrows.

David had the advantage, but still it was perhaps surprising, given their respective characters, that he was the one who replied first. 'Yes, the Archdeacon and I go back a long way,' he said with an easy smile, stretching out his hand. 'How are you, Gabriel?'

Gabriel was grateful; it gave him an instant to regain his composure. He shook the proffered hand. 'Very well, thank you. And you?'

'Never better.'

It was true: David had never looked better, Gabriel realised with a small pang. The happiness he'd obviously found with Lucy had given him an air of contentment that became him well; the puffiness under his eyes that Gabriel remembered from their last meeting had subsided, leaving only the attractive laugh-lines at their corners, and he looked as fit and healthy as a well-fed cat.

David, returning his scrutiny, marvelled that he could do so without the least trace of self-consciousness. It was so strange, he thought in the split second as their eyes met. Once not so long ago Gabriel's very presence had had the power to reduce him to a quivering jelly. Now he saw him merely as a good-looking man, much like any other good-looking man who was past the bloom of youth. What a relief it was. 'How are Emily and the children?' he enquired calmly.

'Oh, they're fine.' Gabriel hesitated for a fraction of a second. 'And how is Lucy?'

David's smile lit his whole face. 'She's wonderful.'

And that was all. It had taken no more than a few seconds altogether, yet they both knew that the balance of power in their relationship had been altered for ever.

Gabriel turned to the churchwardens. 'Now, gentlemen. What is this that I hear about some silver?'

Chapter 9

O what great troubles and adversities hast thou shewed me! and yet didst thou turn and refresh me: yea, and broughtest me from the deep of the earth again.

Psalm 71.18

Rachel Nightingale wheeled her bicycle into the entrance hall, tucked it into a corner, and locked it just for good measure; in Cambridge she'd lost more than one bicycle by placing too much faith in the basic honesty of humankind. Then she let herself into her ground-floor flat and peeled off her coat and gloves as she headed towards the kitchen to put the kettle on.

It was still quite early on a chill Thursday morning in February, a morning on which it had taken more than the usual amount of discipline and determination to get her out of bed in the dark and launch her forth on her bicycle into the damp fog. But she'd never yet missed a morning of visiting Colin. She liked to be there early, when he woke up. Or rather when he would have woken – such terms denoting changes in state, or indeed indicating consciousness of any kind, were no longer applicable to Colin; he was in what the doctors called 'PVS', or persistent vegetative state, his bed surrounded by complicated monitors. But morning after morning Rachel ignored the medical paraphernalia and concentrated instead on the man in the bed. Invariably she sat by his side for half an hour, reading to him quietly from a scientific journal or a favourite novel, her voice low-pitched and soothing. When the half-hour was up, and the nurses began hovering about, anxious to get on with their day's routine, she would stroke his face, tell him that she loved him, and promise that she would return in the evening.

She spent up to an hour with him each evening, during which she would tell him about her day, describing all of the new people she had met. Rachel had a gift for mimicry; often, in the old days, she had made Colin roar with laughter at her spot-on impression of a fellow don, a difficult student or a well-known Cambridge eccentric. Now she included comical descriptions of her new parishioners in her monologue, believing that Colin would find them all very amusing.

The nurses told her that she was wasting her time, and wasting her breath: that Colin didn't know she was there, couldn't possibly understand her, and probably couldn't even hear her. But morning after morning and night after night she went, still trusting in spite of everything in the power of love to reach him somehow, perhaps in some manner or through some dimension that was known only to God.

Waiting for the kettle to boil, Rachel rubbed her hands together to warm them. Cycling in this weather wasn't very pleasant; though the exercise itself engendered enough heat to keep a well-clad body moderately warm, the hands and the face invariably suffered. Cycling had become a way of life for Rachel: since the accident, she had been unable to bring herself to get in a car again. Most of the time she didn't mind, but on this raw morning she was really looking forward to a cup of tea, hot and strong.

She turned on the hot-water tap and rinsed out the teapot, looking out of the window into the still-wintry garden. There had been a ground frost the night before, and the few brave daffodils which had poked swollen green heads through the grass were rimed with white. In the summer the garden would be pleasant, Rachel reflected.

She'd only been in the flat in Pimlico for about a week. She'd been lucky to find it: it was spacious and well-kept, and though it wasn't as near to Colin as she would have liked, its location mid-way between St Jude's and St Margaret's churches made it most convenient for her work. The previous curate had, she understood, lived in a house in St Margaret's parish that was owned by the church, but the churchwardens had made it clear to Rachel that the house was no longer available, and she would have to find herself a place to live. This she had done, and had moved in the week before. Already she was establishing a routine for herself: Colin first, and early Mass at St Jude's on the way home. A quick cup of tea, and perhaps a bite to eat, before a full day of parish duties. Then a simple supper – she knew that she was too thin, that she didn't eat enough, but it just wasn't a priority – and up to an hour with Colin at the end of the day. Sometimes, she knew, it would be necessary to attend parish meetings or carry out other responsibilities in the evenings, in which case she would have a shorter time with Colin. But she would never fail to go to him, even if she could spend but a few minutes at his bedside.

So far she was finding her parish work interesting. The people at St Jude's had welcomed her with a fair degree of warmth, and had made her feel that her work there was valued. St Margaret's was a different story, of course. It was ironic, she reflected: the Anglo-Catholic churchmanship at St Margaret's was actually much more to her taste than the middle-of-the-road blandness of St Jude's. Though her faith, reached through intense suffering and adversity, was deep and personal, she enjoyed the ceremonial of Anglo-Catholic liturgy and found that the appeal to the senses – incense, vestments, music – enhanced her ability to worship. It was a great shame that the people at St Margaret's seemed unable to accept her at face value, and to recognise the validity of her feeling of vocation.

Even within St Margaret's, though, she had met with a variety of reactions. Most of the parishioners were guardedly polite, in a typically English sort of way. She was learning early on which ones to avoid – though in some cases that was scarcely necessary. The sacristan, Robin West, disappeared in the opposite direction whenever he saw her coming, refusing even to speak to her, and there were a few others who behaved similarly. The churchwardens didn't have the luxury of avoiding her. Martin Bairstow treated her curtly, looking down on her from his superior height as though she were some lower life-form or perhaps a visitor from another planet. His wife, Rachel sensed, was in fact quite kindly disposed towards her; in their limited contact Vanessa Bairstow had been friendly, her manner inviting closer acquaintance. Norman Topping, too, seemed much less hostile than Rachel would have expected. On Tuesday evening at the Shrove Tuesday pancake supper, her first real introduction to parish life at St Margaret's, she had caught him more than once looking at her with something approaching a smile, and at one point she could have sworn that he winked at her.

The only person to treat her with blatant and deliberate rudeness was Dolly Topping. Rachel supposed that she shouldn't be surprised, given what she knew about Mrs Topping and her views on women clergy, but it hurt nonetheless. Her attempt at friendly conversation had been rebuffed; loudly, for all to hear, Dolly had made it clear that as far as she was concerned, Rachel was the worst thing that had happened to St Margaret's in its long history, and that once she was ordained a priest (or a 'so-called priest'), Dolly would no longer be able to worship in the church that she had loved for so many years. 'I don't know what you women are trying to prove,' she declared, 'but I hope you can live with the destruction of the Universal Church on your conscience!'

It made all the more curious the phone call which Rachel had received the previous morning, the day after the pancake supper. A tentative female voice had identified itself as belonging to Nicola Topping, and had requested a meeting at Rachel's earliest convenience.

Rachel had a vague memory of a rather large girl hovering somewhere in the background on Shrove Tuesday. 'I'm afraid today's not much good,' she had apologised. 'Ash Wednesday, you know. Father Keble Smythe has asked me to be at all the services, to assist with the ashings. How about tomorrow?'

They had agreed on a time on Thursday afternoon, after school. 'Would you like to come to my flat?' Rachel had suggested.

'Oh, yes, please. I couldn't possibly ask you to come to my house,' the girl had replied. 'I'm sure you understand.'

Now, sipping her tea at the kitchen table, Rachel wondered what Nicola Topping might want with her. At any rate, her curiosity would soon be satisfied – after a morning of calls on elderly parishioners, and lunch with her old friend from Cambridge, Emily Neville.

Her first call was on Walter Bright, a retired doctor who was recovering from a mild bout of the flu. Dr Bright hadn't felt well enough to make it to any of the Ash Wednesday services at St Margaret's, and had requested that the Sacrament be brought to him. Rachel hoped that he wouldn't mind receiving it from the hands of a woman.

Father Keble Smythe hadn't told her much about Dr Bright, other than that he had been in general practice in the area for many years, and that he was universally beloved in the community and in the parish. 'He's a splendid old chap, Dr Bright,' he'd said. 'A great character. His heyday was well before my time, of course, but there are still many people in the parish who were brought into the world by Dr Bright, or were looked after by him for much of their lives. He's a real institution in the parish, is Dr Bright.'

The door of the double-fronted house was opened by a small, spare woman with faded gingery-grey hair and a face etched deeply with lines of resignation. She was wearing a cotton housecoat and an apron; from her age, which she surmised to be around seventy, Rachel assumed that she was Dr Bright's wife, though she could possibly be his housekeeper. 'Mrs Bright?' she asked tentatively.

'*Miss* Bright, actually,' said the woman, taking in the dog collar and stepping aside for Rachel to enter. 'Vera Bright. I'm Dr Bright's daughter. And you must be the new curate.'

'Yes, I'm Rachel Nightingale. It's so nice to meet you, Miss Bright.' If this is his daughter, she thought, how old must Dr Bright be?

'My father is in the drawing room. It's so kind of you to come – he was very distressed to miss Mass yesterday. But this flu has left him rather weak – he's usually as strong as a horse, my father, but he *is* ninety-six.'

Ninety-six! thought Rachel. Born in the last century, when Queen Victoria was on the throne.

Walter Bright, dressed nattily in a tweed suit and club tie, rose to his feet without any evident effort when the two women entered the room. He was a short, wiry man, rather bird-like in appearance, with a beaky nose under small dark eyes and a round head covered with sparse downy hair. Putting his head to one side, he regarded Rachel with a welcoming grin. 'So! The Vicar has sent me his new curate instead of coming himself!'

'I'm sorry that Father Keble Smythe couldn't come,' Rachel began apologetically.

'Not at all! You're much better looking than he is, my dear. At least to my old eyes,' he twinkled. 'Come closer and let me see you.'

She moved up to him and took his hand. 'I'm Rachel Nightingale.'

'Is that Miss or Mrs? And what am I to call you, may I ask? I can't very well call you "Father", can I?'

'It's "Mrs",' she replied, keeping her voice steady as a momentary vision of Colin flashed through her mind. 'And you may call me Rachel, if you like. You don't have any objection to receiving the Sacrament from a woman?'

'Not if she's as pretty as you are, my dear,' he said with a wink. But his eyes were shrewd as he went on, 'Seriously, I don't see that it makes the slightest difference. I know there are some people at St Margaret's who get hot and bothered about it all, but I don't imagine that God cares.'

'"In Christ there is no male or female",' Rachel quoted, smiling.

'Exactly.' Dr Bright sat down and addressed his daughter, who was still standing near the door, for the first time. 'Vera, why don't you go and put the kettle on? I'm sure that Rachel would like a cup of coffee, once she's given me the Sacrament.'

Rachel turned to see the other woman's hesitation. 'Perhaps you'd like the Sacrament as well?' she suggested. 'Or were you able to make it to church yesterday?'

'No, I didn't make it to church. I can't possibly leave

106

Father when he's poorly,' Vera said. She shot her father an unreadable look. 'And I'd very much like to have the Sacrament, if you don't mind.'

'Well, come on then, girl,' Dr Bright ordered. 'Let's get this business over with first. Then you can make the coffee.'

On her long cycle ride to the Archdeacon's house, Rachel had time to think about the visits she'd paid that morning. There had been three of them altogether, but of all her jumbled impressions she found that it was Vera Bright to whom her thoughts returned again and again.

Vera had escorted her to the door. 'Thank you so much for coming,' she'd said.

Impulsively, Rachel had taken her hand. 'It was my pleasure, meeting you and your father. If there's any way I can ever be of help, please don't hesitate to let me know.'

Her sincerity must have communicated itself; for just an instant there had been such a look of yearning and hope on Vera Bright's face that Rachel had been taken aback. But then the shutters had come down again, leaving the customary lines of resignation firmly in control of her expression. The memory of that momentary slip haunted Rachel: she wondered how she could reach Vera, how she might help her. She resolved to try to meet with her alone at the earliest opportunity.

With anticipation she wheeled her bicycle up the drive to the impressive-looking stone dwelling that served as the Archdeacon's residence. She'd known Emily Neville – at that time she'd been Emily Bates –

fairly well at Cambridge and had always appreciated
her intelligence and her straightforward approach to
life. Now she looked forward to renewing the acquaintance; it would be nice to have a female friend in
London, especially one who had known Colin in happier
days.

'Rachel! You can put your bike here around the corner
if you like.' Emily came out of the house and embraced
her with affection. 'Are you hungry?'

'Starved. Cycling this far really helps build up an
appetite. Though,' she added, smiling, 'I'm fairly awash
with tea and coffee – I've just done three pastoral visits.'
She locked the bike and followed Emily into the house.

Emily laughed. 'Gabriel always says that's one of the
clergy's greatest occupational hazards. You can't very
well refuse when it's offered, can you?'

'No, though sometimes it's difficult to work up a
proper semblance of enthusiasm for yet another cup of
instant coffee or stewed tea. But offering and accepting
hospitality is a great ice-breaker sometimes,' she added
seriously.

'You must be freezing, as well. Come on into the
kitchen – it's warm in there,' Emily invited.

The kitchen was indeed warm, courtesy of the Aga. It
was also brightly lit and cheery, with a red quarry-tiled
floor, blue and white tiles on the wall, and gleaming
white counters and kitchen units. The table was set
invitingly with blue and white crockery, and delicious
smells wafted from the Aga; another woman rose from
the table as they entered.

Emily performed the introductions. 'Rachel, this is my
friend Lucy Kingsley. Lucy, this is Rachel Nightingale,

the new curate at St Jude's and St Margaret's. Gabriel is out today, so it will just be us women for lunch.'

They liked each other instantly, instinctively; by the time the food was dished up they were chatting away like old friends.

'The garlic bread isn't quite warm enough,' Emily apologised, 'but I think we'll start anyway.'

'This looks wonderful, Emily,' Rachel said as a steaming plate of pasta with a savoury-smelling mushroom sauce was put in front of her. 'I don't seem to remember that cooking was one of your accomplishments in your digs at Cambridge.'

Emily made a face. 'Your memory serves you well. Beans on toast was my chief speciality in those days.'

'Em is an excellent cook,' Lucy asserted loyally.

'But only because you taught me,' Emily reminded her, then went on to explain to Rachel. 'Lucy saved my life after I married Gabriel. She taught me everything I know about cooking. We've been friends ever since.' Lifting a bottle of Frascati, she poised it invitingly over Rachel's glass. 'Wine?'

It was Rachel's turn to make a face. 'I'm afraid not. Lent.'

'Oh, you disciplined people!' Lucy laughed. 'I'm glad to say that I'm not that holy. Yes, please, Em. Some for me.'

'I'm not that holy, either,' Emily admitted. 'Much to Gabriel's horror, I don't have to tell you. I'm giving up chocolate instead.'

Lucy groaned. 'I think that would be even worse.'

'Gabriel always gives up alcohol *and* chocolate for Lent.'

'Yes, he would.' Lucy tried to keep her voice neutral, to mask the acid hostility she felt. She must not have been particularly successful, as Emily gave her an odd look and quickly changed the subject.

'Rachel, how are you settling in to your new job?' She filled Rachel's glass with mineral water.

'It's going pretty well, actually. The most difficult thing is learning so many new names and faces all at once. Everyone expects you to remember *them*, even if you forget everyone else.'

'And how is the Vicar?' Emily queried. 'Are you getting on well with him?'

Rachel chose her words carefully. 'Father Keble Smythe is very ... agreeable. A very able man – his parishioners think the world of him. But he's quite busy, of course. He doesn't really have time to come around with me holding my hand. He gives me credit for being able and qualified to do the job, and has more or less let me get on with it. With some help from the Parish Administrator, of course.'

'Ah, yes,' Emily said. 'Mr Everitt.'

'Yes, Stanley Everitt.' Rachel gave them a conspiratorial grin. 'Within these four walls, I must admit that he's driving me completely round the twist. What a relief it is to be able to tell someone! I have to be so polite all the time.'

'What has he done?' Lucy wanted to know.

Rachel shook her head. 'Nothing, really. He's just so self-important. He never misses a chance to tell me how much the Vicar relies on him, and how everything at St Jude's and St Margaret's would grind to a complete halt without him and all of his hard work. He's as much as said that a curate – especially one who's only a deacon and can't celebrate the Mass – is really surplus to requirements with an Administrator like him around.'

'Oh, dear.' Emily, who had encountered her fair share of self-important people in the Church of England, was sympathetic.

'And he has these annoying mannerisms – he wrings his hands, just like Uriah Heep!'

'Are you sure he doesn't just patronise you because you're a woman?' Lucy asked shrewdly.

'Oh, no. He's like that with everyone.' With a deft motion of her wrist, Rachel twisted a strand of pasta around her fork and conveyed it to her mouth. 'I'll tell you who *does* patronise me because I'm a woman, though – Martin Bairstow, the churchwarden. He's very polite, but it's the sort of politeness that some people use with small children or the mentally deficient, as a thin veneer of civilisation over their contempt. It makes me uneasy. And it's strange,' she added, 'because all of the old women absolutely sing his praises. I've been to see three elderly parishioners this morning, and every one of them has told me how wonderful Martin Bairstow is, and how lucky his wife is to have such a gem for a husband.'

'I've heard that, too,' confirmed Emily. 'Apparently he gives them all lifts to church functions, and even goes round to their houses to do little odd jobs, the sort of thing that is difficult to get done without a man about the house.' Belatedly she realised that her last remark might be interpreted as insensitive, given Rachel's situation, so she hurried on. 'And what about the other churchwarden, Norman Topping?'

'He's all right,' admitted Rachel. 'It's his wife who's really rude to me.'

'Oh, Dolly.' Emily rolled her eyes.

Lucy groaned. 'That frightful woman.'

'You both know her?' They nodded. 'Then I don't have to explain.'

'Not at all,' confirmed Emily. 'And now, if the mention of Dolly Topping hasn't completely spoiled everyone's appetite, I think that the garlic bread is ready.'

It wasn't until they were drinking their coffee after lunch that Emily steeled herself to ask the question that she knew had to be asked. 'How is Colin?'

Rachel looked into her coffee cup. 'Oh, the same as he's been for some time. I visit him every morning and every evening. I talk to him and read to him, but there's no change – no indication that he knows I'm there.'

'I'm sorry, I didn't mean to . . .' Emily said awkwardly.

'No,' said Rachel, raising her hand to her scarred cheek in an unconscious, poignant gesture. 'You don't have to be afraid to mention him. He's not dead, you know.' After a moment she went on, 'It's so good to be able to talk about him. I don't, as a general rule – people are embarrassed about it, so I don't even mention him.'

Impulsively Emily leaned over and squeezed her hand. 'Well, you can talk about him to us any time you like. Can't she, Luce?'

'Any time,' echoed Lucy thoughtfully.

Rachel had scarcely had time to make herself a reviving mug of tea before the doorbell rang, heralding the arrival of Nicola Topping. 'Come in,' she greeted the girl who stood, ill at ease, at the front door. 'There's fresh tea in the pot. Would you like a cup?'

'Oh, yes, please, Miss ... Mrs ...' Nicola fumbled.

'Just call me Rachel. That will make things easier.'

Nicola followed her into the kitchen. The school uniform emphasised the girl's size, the white blouse straining across her enormous breasts. Clearly she had inherited her mother's large frame, but her face was unexpectedly pretty, especially when she smiled, which she was now doing in a nervous manner: her small, pearly teeth were flawless, and she had attractively dimpled cheeks. Her complexion was good for a girl of her age, and her long brown hair was thick and glossy.

'There's a tin of biscuits somewhere,' Rachel went on. 'Let me see if I can remember where I put it.'

'Oh, that's all right. I shouldn't really have biscuits.' Those were Nicola's words, but Rachel could read the ambivalent yearning in her voice. 'My mum would kill me if she knew I was eating biscuits.'

'Well, your mum isn't here,' Rachel stated, pulling the tin out of a cupboard. It was a commemorative Royal Wedding tin, Charles and Diana vintage, battered with age and usage. 'Hobnobs and chocolate digestives,' she analysed, peering inside. 'I thought there might be some shortbread, but I must have eaten it.'

As Rachel poured another mug of tea, Nicola pulled out a chair, sat down and shamefacedly helped herself to a chocolate digestive biscuit.

Rachel settled down across from her. 'I think it's cosier in here than in the lounge,' she said in a conversational tone, cupping her hands around her tea mug; she could sense the girl's nervousness and was

113

trying to put her at ease by behaving as naturally as possible. 'But if you'd rather, we can go in there and put the gas fire on.'

'No, this is fine.' Nicola, having polished off her first biscuit, reached for another.

Rachel waited, sipping her tea. It would all come out eventually, she knew, but she wouldn't push her. If she were a sociologist, she thought with detachment while she was waiting, she'd investigate what you could tell about people based on what they chose to drink their tea and coffee from. Cups or mugs? Bone china or stoneware? Decorated with what? Coffee at the Brights' had come in serviceable brown stoneware mugs; Emily had provided the after-lunch coffee in blue and white cups of contemporary design but impeccable English manufacture. Lucy Kingsley, Rachel was sure, would serve tea in thin bone china cups, probably antique. Her own mugs were a thoroughly mixed lot, collected over a lifetime. The one she'd given Nicola was, by coincidence, a Royal Wedding one, the two names linked forever, indissolubly, on the mug as they no longer were in life; her own tea was in a Beatrix Potter mug that had been a particular favourite of Rosie's. Rosie, now nearly four years dead. Why had she kept it?

'I suppose you're wondering why I wanted to see you,' Nicola began at last, after four biscuits and a cup of tea.

Deciding that it was safer to say nothing, Rachel inclined her head, a gesture that could mean anything Nicola wanted it to.

She interpreted it as an invitation to talk. 'I've got a problem,' she began, 'and I just didn't know who else to talk to. When I saw you the other night at the pancake supper, I could tell that you were nice. I hope you don't mind.' She gave Rachel a shy smile.

Rachel returned the smile. 'Don't mind you thinking I'm nice, or don't mind you talking to me?' *Her mother is at the bottom of this somehow*, she told herself. *Depend on it – otherwise she'd be talking to* her. 'No, of course I don't mind.'

'Well, then.' Nicola took a deep breath and another chocolate biscuit, which she held in her hand like a talisman while she talked. 'I'm in love. And Ben is in love with me, too.'

'That doesn't sound like such a problem,' Rachel said lightly.

'Oh, but it is!' Her tone was heartfelt and intense. 'You don't know my mum, or you wouldn't say that!'

Exactly. Rachel tried to keep her voice neutral. 'Your mum.'

'Yes. She's been just awful about Ben and me. We want to get married, you see. And Mum says absolutely not.'

'Well, you are quite young,' Rachel said. 'Is Ben older, then?'

'No, he's the same age as me – seventeen. He's in the sixth form with me at school. But that's not the problem!'

'It *is* a problem if your mother won't consent. You can't get married without your parents' permission until you're eighteen.'

'Don't you think I know that?' Nicola said bitterly. 'But the real problem is that Ben is ... well, his skin is darker than mine. No big deal, right? But not to my mum! She calls him ... a filthy wog!'

Just what she'd expect from the charming and tactful Mrs Topping, thought Rachel. She didn't trust herself to say anything.

'She says that he doesn't really love me – that he just wants to marry me so he can stay in this country. She's heard all these stories about people doing anything to get a British passport. But that's ridiculous – Ben is as English as I am! He was born in this country, and so were his parents. And she says that I can't possibly love him, that . . .' Here Nicola broke off, chewing her lip, as a tear escaped from each eye. She gulped and went on, 'That I'm just desperate, because I'm fat. That I think it's my only chance, and that no one else will ever want me. But I *do* love Ben,' she finished passionately. 'And he loves me. I'll always love him, no matter what my mum says!'

'What about your father? What does he think?'

Nicola's voice was scornful, dismissive. 'What he always thinks about everything – exactly what my mother tells him to.'

Rachel gave her a thoughtful nod.

'Have you ever read *Romeo and Juliet*?' Nicola asked.

She fought the urge to smile. 'English was my subject at Cambridge.'

'We did it at school, for our English GCSE,' explained Nicola. 'Well, it's just like that, isn't it? We love each other, but our parents – *my* parents – are keeping us apart. Tragic,' she sighed with melodramatic fervour. Absent-mindedly she nibbled at the biscuit she was clutching till it was gone, then licked the melted chocolate from her fingers.

'I'm not sure how I can help you,' Rachel admitted,

after careful thought. 'You do realise that it will do no good my trying to talk to your mother? I'm not exactly tops on her list,' she added in an attempt at humour.

'Yes, I know that she hates you,' Nicola said frankly. 'Maybe that's one reason I wanted to talk to you – just to get back at her for being so horrible to me.'

'Then what—'

Nicola interrupted her in a flood of emotion. 'Say that you'll marry us, as soon as we're both eighteen. Ben will be eighteen next month, and my birthday is in May. Then we can be married, whether my parents like it or not. Promise me that you'll marry us. Father Julian said that he would, and my mum wasn't half furious at him, but he's dead now so he can't. Father Keble Smythe says that he won't, because he doesn't want to upset my parents, but Mum couldn't hate you any more than she does already, so it won't matter. Please say yes, Miss . . . Rachel. Please?'

Chapter 10

Nevertheless, when he saw their adversity: he heard their complaint.
He thought upon his covenant, and pitied them, according unto the multitude of his mercies: yea, he made all those that led them away captive to pity them.

Psalm 106.43–44

Pamela Hartman rolled off Huw Meredith with a satisfied sigh. 'Brilliant,' she said, when she was ready for talking.

'Brilliant,' he echoed, meaning it.

Pamela Hartman, employed by Her Majesty as an immigration officer, had met PC Meredith about a year earlier, in the course of duty: a young man arrested by PC Meredith for being drunk and disorderly had subsequently been discovered to be an illegal immigrant. The two had hit it off immediately, and had been meeting once or twice a week since for a bit of extra-curricular fun.

He was a tall, black-bearded Welshman, just one generation removed from the coal mines. She was a sophisticated blonde, a few years older than he, and from a solidly middle-class background. Both were married, but that was irrelevant. Neither was interested in anything permanent or long-term. Their couplings were sometimes playful, sometimes rough, occasionally tender, but always enjoyable. It was an arrangement which suited them both admirably.

Usually, as now, they met on a Friday evening after work, in the flat of one of Pamela's colleagues who spent weekends in the country, thoughtfully leaving her keys behind for Pamela's use.

Pamela sat up in bed and reached for a cigarette on the bedside table with sinuous grace. She had a loose-limbed body, casually sensual in its movements, reinforcing the message of her heavy-lidded eyes, her full mouth, and her tumbled mane of honey-blonde hair.

'One for me too, love.' Huw Meredith's bass voice retained the sing-song cadence of the Welsh hills.

'Mm.' She lit two cigarettes, blew the match out with a sensuous puff, and settled back down beside him in the rumpled bed.

He took a long drag and exhaled slowly. 'Had a busy week?'

'So-so. I've got a fairly heavy caseload at the moment. How about you?'

'Just the usual sort of thing for February. A few cars pinched, and the odd burglary. Still a bit chilly for much hanky-panky on Hampstead Heath.' He grinned, displaying strong white teeth.

With her free hand she stroked the thick, curly black hair on his chest. 'Poor buggers, with no nice comfortable bed to do it in.'

120

His grin widened. 'Some people prefer it that way – adds to the thrill, you know.'

'I suppose.' She sucked on her cigarette thoughtfully. 'I can't see it, myself. I prefer all the comfort I can get.'

'Don't I know it. It's just a shame that our hosts aren't thoughtful enough to provide silk sheets for our Pam.' She tweaked his beard playfully in retribution. 'Ow,' he said, more for effect than from conviction, then gave her bare thigh a pinch that turned into a fondle.

Pamela, seeing in what direction things were moving, and regretfully conscious of the clock, searched her memory for some suitably entertaining anecdote to distract him. 'Your mum collects funny names, doesn't she? Well, I came across a good one for her this week. Justin Thymme.' She spelled it for him. 'Get it?'

'Justin Thymme.' He suddenly looked alert. 'What's he done, then?'

'Done? He hasn't done anything. Nothing except get married, that is. I had an application come across my desk this week for his wife to be granted residency status as a spouse.' She smiled, remembering. 'In fact, her name is a good one as well. May Thymme. Get it?'

Huw Meredith sat up straight. 'Justin Thymme has just got married? You're sure?'

Pamela was puzzled. 'Of course I'm sure. Why – do you know him, or something?'

'We've met.' He watched her face as he went on, 'On Hampstead Heath, as a matter of fact. A month or so ago. He had his trousers around his ankles at the time. Damn chilly, but there you are.'

Her brow furrowed. 'You mean . . . ?'

121

'Exactly. A fourteen-carat poofter.'

In spite of herself she laughed at the mental picture. 'But he can't be! It must be someone else.'

'Another Justin Thymme? Come on, Pam. Get real. It's him, all right. But it doesn't have to mean anything. You're a woman of the world – surely you must realise that even married men go cottaging.'

She narrowed her eyes at him. 'When did you say this happened?'

'Around the middle of January, I reckon.'

'But that's just about the time he was getting married, if I remember the application! I've heard of stag nights, but this is the first time I've ever heard of a man celebrating his marriage by having it off on Hampstead Heath! And in the dead of winter!'

He laughed. 'What are you going to do about it?'

In one fluid movement she stubbed out her cigarette in the bedside ashtray and got out of bed. 'I'm going to have Mr and Mrs Justin Thymme in my office first thing next week, or know the reason why,' she said crisply. 'You just can't imagine the lengths some people will go to for the right to remain in this country – including paying poofters to marry them – and I have the strangest feeling that Mrs Thymme might be one of those people.'

'Come back here. You can't do anything about it now, love.' He arranged himself to display his charms to their full advantage. 'The main course was lovely, but now I'm ready for pud.'

'Not now.' She was already beginning to get dressed, but avoided looking at him in case her resolution should fail her. 'We're going out for a meal tonight – I've got to get home.' In a few moments the transformation was complete: in prim navy-blue suit and pristine white blouse, and with her hair tied back in a modest ponytail, Pamela Hartman was once again the image of an efficient female civil servant, on her way home to her husband.

The call came through to David on the following Tuesday. It was Henry Thymme who rang him, on behalf of his son Justin. 'I'm afraid the boy needs you again,' he announced, with more amusement than chagrin.

'But the charges were dropped,' David said, confused. 'He hasn't done it again, has he?'

Thymme laughed immoderately. 'Oh, no. Not that. At least if he has, he hasn't got caught. But it seems that the immigration authorities want a word with him.'

David was more confused than ever. 'Immigration?'

'They want to see him with his wife, actually.'

'Wife?'

'Didn't I mention that the boy had a new wife?'

Unseen by the caller on the other end of the phone, David put his head in his hands in a gesture of despair. 'No, you did not.'

His tone must have communicated itself to the other man; for just a moment the persona of the amiable buffoon slipped to reveal the shrewd lawyer beneath. 'I'm sure that the immigration people must be thinking exactly what you are,' he said frankly. 'Though how they found out about it is beyond me.'

'Tell me about the wife.' David's voice was flat.

'She's Hong Kong Chinese. They married last month.

A lovely girl,' Thymme added with his usual bluffness.

David sighed. 'I don't know that much about immigration law. If you can't deal with it yourself, can't you find someone who's an expert in the field?'

'The boy wants you,' Thymme said. 'He was impressed with the way you got him off over that other business. He's your client now,' he added by way of a reminder. 'You can't abandon him.'

David could think of a few things of a more violent nature that he'd like to do to Justin Thymme, but he refrained from telling his father so. 'You'd better give me the details, then,' he said with ill-concealed resignation.

Thymme's chuckle reflected his satisfaction. 'Justin will fill you in.'

Hoping to discover just what the immigration officer knew, and how he knew it, David arranged to have a short meeting with him before his client arrived. He needed all the help he could get, he admitted to himself as he entered the Immigration Office, located at Waterloo Station: his client, Mr Justin Thymme, had been as unhelpful as he'd expected during their initial conference on the previous afternoon, insisting that theirs was a love match and indignant that anyone could think otherwise. Mrs Thymme he had not yet had the pleasure of meeting.

In the event, the immigration officer turned out to be a woman, and an attractive one at that, though her manner was businesslike to the point of being intimidating. With a firm handshake she introduced herself as Mrs Hartman and escorted David to her office.

Ensconced behind her desk, she studied a file for a moment without speaking, before raising her head to meet David's eyes. 'Well, Mr Middleton-Brown. What can I do for you?' Her voice was as crisp and as self-possessed as her appearance.

David's manner showed more assurance than he felt in the presence of this rather formidable woman. 'As you know, my client's wife has applied for a change in her residency status due to her recent marriage,' he said in what he hoped was a firm voice. 'It is my understanding that in most cases this is granted routinely, upon proof of marriage.'

Pamela Hartman nodded. 'In general, that's true.'

'Can I take it, then, that there is some problem in this particular case? Or is there some other reason that you've asked for this interview with my client and his wife?'

She assessed him for a moment. She had met her share of belligerent and demanding solicitors, but this one seemed different: there was a gentleness and a sense of integrity about him, in spite of his assured manner, and though she was determined not to show it, she warmed to him. 'Let me be honest with you, Mr Middleton-Brown,' Pamela Hartman said; it was something she said often, but this time she meant it. 'In this case there may very well be a problem.' She hesitated just a second before continuing, 'I happen to be in possession of some information that has left me in some doubt as to the validity of this marriage.'

'But I can show you the certificate,' he asserted. 'They were married last month.'

'Oh, I don't doubt that the marriage took place.' She

125

looked down at the file, afraid that her amusement would show in her eyes. 'But I do have my doubts about the ... well, let's say the motivation behind this marriage.'

David's heart misgave him, but he kept his voice steady. 'I don't understand what you mean, Mrs Hartman.'

She answered him in a roundabout way. 'Do you have any idea what some people will do to get a British passport, Mr Middleton-Brown? Entering into a marriage of convenience is one of the easier ways to do it. I've seen people in this very office whose desperation has led them to do much worse things. Lie, certainly, and steal – there is a thriving trade in stolen marriage certificates at the moment – and practically anything else short of murder. Even that wouldn't surprise me, quite frankly.'

'Are you suggesting that my client and his wife have contracted a marriage of convenience?'

'That's exactly what I'm suggesting.' Pamela Hartman's eyes met his. 'As I said, I'll be honest with you. I can't reveal my sources, but I happen to know that getting married wasn't the only thing Mr Justin Thymme did last month.' She smiled, a cool and almost mocking smile, and was unable to resist adding, 'But as you're his solicitor, you probably know that already, don't you, Mr Middleton-Brown? Hampstead Heath, remember?'

'Bloody hell!' In his shock, David was sure – almost sure – that he hadn't actually said it aloud, but given the glint of amusement in Pamela Hartman's eyes, he couldn't be positive. It was true: she was enjoying his discomposure, and even if he hadn't spoken, his thoughts were all too evident on his face. How on earth had she found out? And why had she chosen to reveal her knowledge? At least, thought David, he now knew where he – and his client – stood.

Justin Thymme and his new wife arrived a short time later. Even if he had not known what he knew about young Mr Thymme, David would have found them an oddly matched couple. He had a preconceived notion that all Chinese women were tiny; Mrs Thymme confounded that expectation by being several inches taller than her short husband, even in flat shoes. But she was slender and graceful, with a sweet, ingenuous smile and a manner that was eager to please.

And for once David could find nothing to criticise in Justin's demeanour: he was civil to David, courteous to Pamela Hartman, and showed every sign of loving devotion to his new wife, clinging to her hand and looking up at her adoringly. It was most disconcerting.

After the introductions they all sat down, the newly-weds inching their chairs closer together so they could continue to hold hands. Pamela Hartman caught David's eye and smiled in what he took to be a cynical way.

'There is something wrong?' May Thymme spoke first. Her English was good – she had entered the country on a student visa and was studying English at University College London – but heavily accented. 'Justin and I are married, since last month. We have papers. We can show you.' She seemed tense, and her dark eyes were large with worry.

Pamela Hartman studied her carefully before replying. Her instincts were usually good, but this was a difficult one to size up. Often in these cases it was all too apparent what had motivated the marriage, with the husband and wife treating each other as the virtual strangers that they were. But in spite of what she knew about Justin Thymme's sexual escapades, she wasn't so sure about this set-up. Either these two were better actors than most, or there was some genuine affection between them. It wasn't impossible, and she decided to give them the benefit of the doubt for the time being. There would be plenty of time later for getting tough, for interviewing them separately and asking them which side of the bed each slept on and how they squeezed the toothpaste tube. After all, this process of discovering the truth usually took months. If they were hiding something – and in spite of the appearances she was prepared to lay money that they were – it didn't hurt to be reassuring at this point, to lull them into a false sense of security in which they might betray themselves. 'This is only a preliminary hearing,' she said in a soothing voice. 'I'd like to see your papers, and then I'll ask you a few questions. With Mr Middleton-Brown's permission, of course,' she added with a nod of exaggerated deference in David's direction.

Chapter 11

And I lie even among the children of men, that are
set on fire: whose teeth are spears and arrows, and
their tongue a sharp sword.

Psalm 57.5

Lucy frowned, surveying her sitting room; absently she
twisted a curl around her finger. Her niece would be
arriving tomorrow. How on earth was she going to
accommodate Ruth and all her possessions? David was
right: the girl was bound to bring all sorts of things with
her. And he was right, too, that the house wasn't big
enough for three people.

Sleeping wasn't really a problem, with the sofa bed in
the sitting room. But where would she put her things?
Apart from the sitting room, the downstairs consisted of
a small dining room and a good-sized, extended kitchen
– but that was no help. Upstairs was a tiny bathroom,
the bedroom and Lucy's studio. Perfect for one person,
workable – just – for two, but three was stretching the
house beyond its limits.

Ruth was only part of the problem, of course, Lucy
realised. The other person in the equation was David.
Whatever happened, Lucy didn't want him to feel

surplus to requirements, or unwelcome in her house.
For the first time she acknowledged to herself that she
now thought of it as *their* house, hers and David's.
She loved having him there, loved sharing her life
with him. While she was working in her studio during
the day, it was wonderful to be able to look forward
to his return home, and a shared evening of good food
and conversation. Not to mention what followed: she
enjoyed the luxury of sleeping in David's arms almost
as much as she enjoyed the lovemaking that preceded
it.

Then why, she asked herself, wouldn't she marry
him? It was by no means the first time she'd wrestled
with the question. There was more to it than the
aftertaste of a bad marriage, she admitted to herself in
her more self-analytical moments. This relationship,
after all, was in no way comparable to the one she'd had
with Geoffrey, who had been so much older and had
never let her forget how superior he was to her on every
level. She and David had so much to offer each other;
they were complementary equals.

Perhaps she was afraid that marriage would somehow alter that fine balance, and spoil the relationship.
Certainly to legalise the union would endanger its
spontaneity. Their lovemaking now was both frequent
and spontaneous: would marriage make it routine and
taken-for-granted?

But she didn't want to lose him, she knew. That would
be an even greater evil. Self-sufficient though she was,
Lucy hadn't realised how much she'd hated her solitary
life until she'd found someone to share it with. Was she
being unrealistic, hoping to have her cake and eat it, to

enjoy the benefits of togetherness without the ossifying commitment of marriage? And was it fair to David, when he wanted to marry her so badly?

She dreaded the day when he would come home and tell her that he'd finally sorted out the inheritance, and could move into the house near Kensington Gardens. It would force them to talk about it, the subject that had become so painful for them both that it was now taboo. And ultimately it would propel her into some kind of decision. Until then, though, she would do everything possible to maintain the status quo.

That was what was so worrying about Ruth's visit, Lucy realised. It was a threat to the status quo. And, she asked herself, looking around, wherever would she put her things?

'The cupboard under the stairs was a great idea,' David complimented her the next morning as they waited at Euston Station.

'I had a sudden inspiration. It's always been a convenient glory hole, so I thought – why not?' She'd cleaned it out, had thrown out quite a bit of rubbish, and transferred the rest to the loft for the time being. 'It should work quite well – there's room for her to hang a few clothes, and shelves for her bits and pieces. You'll see. It won't be so bad.' She squeezed his hand, wishing that she felt as confident about it as she sounded.

'What is she like?' David squinted up at the arrivals board; her train was due at any moment. His contact with teenage girls throughout the course of his life had been minimal, and his apprehensiveness was increasing by the minute.

Lucy qualified her reply. 'I haven't seen her for nearly a year, but she actually reminds me quite a bit of myself at that age. Other people say so, too – my brother always says that it's like déjà vu.'

'Oh, well, that's all right, then.' His relief was evident.

She gave a wicked laugh. 'You don't know what I was like.'

'I know what you're like now, and you couldn't have been so very dreadful then,' David asserted loyally.

'I wouldn't be so sure about that if I were you.'

He exhaled on a sigh as the train from Northampton pulled into the station, and they waited in silence while the Saturday morning passengers trickled through the barrier. It was a different crowd from the Monday-through-Friday commuters: mostly parents with young children, coming to London for a day's outing, the children already whipped into hyperactivity by their train journey and the parents already showing signs of exhaustion. There was a sprinkling of well-dressed matrons with empty shopping bags, most likely bound for Knightsbridge, a few couples on their way to the West End for matinées at various theatres, and the inevitable rag-tag of international backpackers, young people weighed down with enormous rucksacks and large bottles of Evian water, jabbering to each other in German or Italian. David wondered inconsequentially what sights might have drawn them to Northampton; it didn't seem likely that they would be interested in shoe factories or even Eleanor Crosses.

'There's Ruth,' said Lucy, pointing. Near the end of the stream, just behind a harassed mother trying to corral three overexcited small boys, was a girl on her own, slowed down by the wobbling progress of an oversized suitcase on wheels, wearing the singularly unattractive uniform of her generation: faded jeans, a leather jacket over a T-shirt, and great clomping Doc Marten boots. At the barrier she straightened up and looked around anxiously, then spotted her aunt and waved. 'Hi, Aunt Lucy.'

David drew in his breath. To say that Ruth Kingsley resembled Lucy was not quite accurate. She was like her, yes, but in the manner of an out-of-focus photograph, or even more accurately like two paintings of the same subject executed in different media, by different artists. If Lucy was the watercolour, then her niece was the oil painting, altogether more vibrant in colouring and bolder in style. Where Lucy's hair was a pale, shimmery red-gold, the colour of ripe apricots, Ruth's was unashamedly red – almost orange – and cut short so that the curls were more pronounced, standing out around her face in an aggressive Afro. Ruth's eyes were a true green, rather than the blue-green of Lucy's; her skin was whiter than Lucy's peaches-and-cream coloration, and was demarcated by a sprinkling of freckles across her nose. Ruth's features, too, were reminiscent of Lucy's, but the overall effect was quite different: while Lucy was an attractive – some might say beautiful – woman, not even a fond parent could claim that Ruth Kingsley was other than a rather plain girl, though the charitable might add that she had the potential to grow into her looks. It was as if, thought David, she hadn't quite caught up with her face; her nose and her mouth seemed out of proportion to everything else, and the size of her mouth was only exacerbated by an awesome array of glinting hardware when she pulled back her lips in a smile. Poor kid, he found himself thinking.

Lucy stated the obvious. 'Ruthie, darling! You've got a brace on your teeth!'

The smile faded. 'Since last summer,' she admitted. 'I have to wear it for two years, probably. And please don't call me Ruthie,' she added. 'I'm not a baby any more, Aunt Lucy.'

The girl hung back awkwardly, but Lucy moved forward to embrace her. 'Darling, it's so good to see you. It's been so long!'

'Almost ten months,' Ruth stated in a voice that, even muffled in a hug, was clearly accusing. 'Not since the christening last May, remember? Aunt Lucy, why haven't you been to see us for so long?'

This evoked the very guilt it was meant to produce; Lucy had realised recently how little she had seen of her family, apart from her father, since her involvement with David. Her response was defensive. 'It hasn't really been that long,' she said, contradicting herself.

'Your Aunt Lucy is a very busy person,' David put in.

Ruth pulled away from Lucy to look at him, while Lucy performed a hurried introduction. 'Ruth darling, this is my friend Mr Middleton-Brown. David. You know, the one who's going to help you with your work experience.'

'Hi.' Ruth gave him a rather stiff nod as she tried to assess him. She didn't much like the way he was hovering around Aunt Lucy, and she definitely didn't like the way he'd spoken to her in Aunt Lucy's defence.

She hadn't been talking to *him*, after all – who did he think he was? And why did he have to be here, anyway, when she wouldn't start her work experience until Monday morning? She'd been looking forward to having Aunt Lucy all to herself this weekend, without her parents or her brothers around to share the attention.

David could feel the hostility radiating from the girl, but was at a loss to understand the reason for it. Bewildered, he overcompensated with a false smile and a jolly manner. 'We're really pleased to have you, aren't we, Lucy? Now, let me take your case. It must be awfully heavy for a girl like you.'

Ruth pressed her lips together – a painful thing to do given the quantity of hardware in her mouth – and made a lunge for the handle of her case. In a complete contrast to Lucy's natural grace, her movements were gawky and graceless. 'No, thank you. I can do it myself. It's got wheels.' With a determined grunt, she pulled it into motion.

Before David could protest and take it from her, Lucy caught his eye and shook her head slightly. 'Well, at least I've brought the car,' said David ruefully, as they followed Ruth and the wobbling behemoth in a slow, awkward procession through Euston Station.

After Ruth had unpacked and settled her possessions in the cupboard under the stairs, and after they'd had some lunch, they moved into the sitting room to discuss the plans for the afternoon. Ruth scooped up a somewhat reluctant Sophie and claimed the spot next to Lucy on the sofa, relegating David to a chair. 'Nice kitty,' she crooned, ignoring Sophie's squirms.

'We wondered, darling, what you'd like to do this afternoon,' Lucy began. She and David had discussed it at length, and had a few ideas, but had decided to leave the final decision up to Ruth.

'I don't know,' Ruth said unhelpfully, her head bent over the cat.

'We thought that you might like to go to one of the museums – the Science Museum or the Natural History Museum,' David put in. 'They're not far from here, you know.'

Ruth looked up at him and wrinkled her nose. 'That sounds dead boring. I hate science, and I can't think of anything more boring than a load of old dinosaur bones.'

'Well, how about the Tower of London, then?' suggested Lucy.

'We went there on a school outing. Boring. Full of naff American tourists, all saying that they want to take the Crown Jewels home for a souvenir.'

'There's always the zoo, though it's still a bit chilly for that,' said David.

'Zoos are for little kids,' Ruth stated with an indignant scowl at him. 'I told you, I'm not a baby.'

'Of course you're not,' Lucy said quickly, giving David a warning look. 'He didn't mean to imply that you were. Lots of grown-ups enjoy the zoo, too.' Before Ruth could express her opinion of the sort of grown-ups who enjoyed the zoo, she went on, 'There's Madame Tussaud's, or any of the art museums. Or we could even go shopping at Covent Garden, or Harrod's, or the General Trading Company.'

'Him too?' she nodded her head in David's direction.

'Yes, of course.'

'I'd rather wait and go shopping with just you, Aunt Lucy. Shopping's much more fun without men around. Dad goes spare when he has to take me and Mum shopping.'

Lucy, fighting to curb her own rising irritation, didn't dare to look at David. 'Well, where would you like to go then, Ruth darling?' she asked sweetly, thinking to herself, Oh God, it's going to be a long three weeks.

Clutching Sophie to her chest, Ruth thought hard. 'How about Westminster Abbey?' she said at last. 'We've been doing Elizabeth I at school, and I'd like to see her tomb. I think she was pretty cool. And I'd like to go to Evensong.'

'Well, that's settled, then.' Relief and exasperation were mingled on David's face as he rose from the chair. The fact that the girl wanted to visit a church was something in her favour at last as far as David was concerned, and it redeemed her slightly in his mind. Though her affinity for Elizabeth I was no accident, he told himself wryly: it takes one imperious redhead to appreciate another.

They passed a few hours in Westminster Abbey, taking one of the supertours and then poking around the chapels on their own, paying homage to Elizabeth I. Ruth deigned to do a rubbing of a lady with a horned headdress and a supercilious expression in the brass rubbing centre, while Lucy and David strolled around the cloister, and then it was time for Evensong.

A well-sung cathedral-style Choral Evensong was one of the chief pleasures of David's life; by closing his eyes and losing himself in the music and the liturgy – the beautiful, time-honoured cadences of the Book of Common Prayer – he was able to forget for a few moments what a trial the next three weeks were likely to be. Thus Lucy was the first to notice a fellow worshipper on the opposite side of the stalls. During the first reading she nudged him gently. 'Look,' she whispered, 'there's Rachel Nightingale over there.'

Immersed in the tranquillity of the service, Rachel didn't see them until the very end, as the verger led the choir and clergy out of the stalls and the congregation stood. After the organ voluntary had finished, she crossed the chancel with a smile. 'Hello, Lucy. How are you?'

'Oh, very well. And you?'

'Not bad.' Rachel looked curiously at David, sure that she'd seen him before, but equally sure that it had had nothing to do with Lucy. 'Haven't we met?'

'Yes,' he said, smiling. 'At St Margaret's. Father Keble Smythe introduced us. David Middleton-Brown.'

'Yes, of course. I'm sorry, but you were out of context. The solicitor, wasn't it?'

'That's right.'

'Rachel, this is my niece, Ruth Kingsley,' Lucy interposed. 'She's visiting me for a few weeks.'

Rachel favoured Ruth with her sweetest smile. 'Hello, Ruth. How lovely for you, Lucy. You *are* lucky.'

'Hi,' said Ruth, returning the smile.

'Where are you from, Ruth?'

'Northampton. A boring town,' she stated dismissively. 'But I'll leave there as soon as I can. I want to live in London, when I'm qualified.'

'Ruth wants to be a solicitor,' Lucy explained. 'That's why she's here – she's doing a work experience project with David.'

'I see. And what about university?'

'That's a few years off,' Ruth admitted. 'But I'd like to go to Cambridge.'

Rachel looked off into the distance. 'Cambridge,' she said reflectively. 'You'll love it there. I spent over fifteen years of my life in Cambridge, and I think it's the most wonderful place on earth. Let me know when you're going up,' she added on impulse, 'and I'll come up to meet you and show you around, introduce you to a few people, that sort of thing. I'd love to show you around Cambridge.'

'Oh, yes!' Enchanted, Ruth studied her avidly, noticing the discreet dog collar that she wore with her sprigged blouse. 'Are you a woman vicar?' she asked.

Rachel laughed lightly. 'Not yet. But I will be one day soon, God willing. I'm only a deacon at the moment. Just an overworked curate.'

'And they let you off long enough to come to Westminster Abbey?' asked Lucy.

Lucy's tone may have been facetious, but Rachel's reply was serious. 'I don't have much free time, but Saturday is supposed to be my day off. I had a wedding this afternoon and two hospital visits in spite of that, so I felt entitled to take a little time to treat myself to Evensong. It's something I love, so I come here whenever I can – they do it so beautifully.'

'They let you do weddings, even if you're not a vicar?' Ruth wanted to know.

'Oh, yes, that's one of the things a deacon is allowed to

139

do, and one of the things that curates often get stuck with – I've got one next week as well.' She looked at her watch. 'And that reminds me – one of the other things a deacon is allowed to do is preach, and I've got a sermon to finish up for tomorrow morning's 10.30 service at St Jude's, so if you'll excuse me . . .'

Ruth was fairly quiet through supper, but afterwards, when David retired to the sitting room to leave her alone with Lucy, she became animated. As they did the washing up, she began talking about Rachel Nightingale. 'I think she's wonderful,' Ruth pronounced. 'Where is her church, anyway? Didn't she say it was called St Jude's?'

'That's right. It's in Pimlico. Not too far away. She's got two churches, actually – St Jude's and St Margaret's.'

'Well, can we go to St Jude's tomorrow, Aunt Lucy? I'd really like to hear her sermon. I'll bet it will be great.'

Lucy looked bemused. 'Yes, I suppose so, darling. If you really want to.'

'Of course I want to.' Then she started asking Lucy questions about Rachel; Lucy told her what she knew about Rachel's tragic life and how she had managed to rise above her pain and eventually to bring good out of it. At the end of the story Ruth had tears in her eyes. 'I think that's the saddest thing I've ever heard,' she said with feeling. 'The most romantic story, with the saddest ending. Poor Rachel. And poor Colin. And poor Rosie. Oh, she must have loved them both very much. And now, to see him like he is . . . Oh, poor Rachel.'

Lucy nodded. 'And she's such a lovely person.'

'Oh, she is, Aunt Lucy! She's wonderful!' Ruth declared passionately. She fell silent for a moment, rubbing the tea towel round and round on a plate until it squeaked. 'I wonder . . .' she said in a thoughtful voice. 'I wonder if I could be a solicitor *and* a woman priest?'

Lucy stifled her desire to laugh, and replied seriously, 'I don't know why not, Ruth darling. But it does seem rather a lot to take on, doesn't it? They're two very demanding jobs, and with a family as well . . .'

'Oh, I shan't have a family,' Ruth stated. 'I'm never getting married.' Her expression was fiercely determined. 'Never.'

'I see.'

'No, I mean it. It may start out all right, but after a while you just start fighting, and then you end up hating each other,' she asserted with authority. 'You're much better off on your own. I mean, look at *you*, Aunt Lucy.'

A wet plate slipped in Lucy's hand and she caught it just in time. Ruth's statement had surprised her: her short-lived marriage had preceded in its entirety her niece's birth, and she wasn't sure whether Ruth even knew that it had happened – certainly she had never told her. Her cynical description of the course of a marriage described with devastating accuracy the few months that Lucy had spent as Geoffrey's wife, but how would Ruth know about that? And if not her, to whom was she referring? 'Yes?' she said neutrally, hoping that Ruth would elaborate.

'You're not married, and you have a wonderful life – living in London, in your own house, and with a successful career.' Her voice dropped. 'I've always wanted to be like you, Aunt Lucy,' she confided, almost shyly. 'You're proof that a woman can live life on her own terms, without some man telling her what to do all the time.'

Lucy realised that she didn't have the courage to disillusion her niece, either about the past or about her present situation. 'Well, you've got plenty of time before you have to decide about anything like that,' she said in a falsely jolly voice, hating her own cowardice as she said it; at Ruth's age, she had despised grown-ups who patronised her in that way. Seeing the disappointment on Ruth's face, she went on quickly, 'It looks like the washing up is just about finished. What would you like to do for the rest of the evening, darling? I've got a brand-new Cluedo set – how about a game or two?' In a moment of inspiration earlier in the week, Lucy had recalled the favoured activity on visits to her brother's family, long afternoons around the kitchen table with Ruth and her two younger brothers, punctuated with triumphant cries of 'Miss Scarlet in the library with the lead pipe!' or 'Colonel Mustard in the conservatory with the rope!' The idea had sent her off to the shops to buy a new set, in the hopes that it would help to keep her niece occupied for at least part of the three weeks.

Ruth frowned. 'I don't play Cluedo much any more – it's kind of babyish, I think. And it doesn't work very well with just two people. I like Scrabble better. But I've got a better idea – why don't we go out and get a video to watch?'

'I'm afraid I haven't got a video machine,' Lucy apologised. 'I don't watch much television. And I don't have Scrabble. But there are three of us for Cluedo – that would be all right, wouldn't it?'

Ruth's frown deepened, and she lowered her head. 'When is *he* going home?' she said quietly. 'He doesn't need to stay all evening, does he? Can he take a hint, or will you have to tell him to go?'

Lucy felt as though the breath had been knocked out of her; she put a hand on the counter to steady herself. The emphasis that the girl had put on the word 'he' made Lucy realise that Ruth had not once, since she'd arrived, called or referred to David by name. Taking a deep breath, she forced herself to look at her niece. 'Ruth darling,' she said in a remarkably calm voice, 'David *is* at home. He lives here.'

The girl's mouth dropped open, and a scarlet flush spread up her neck to suffuse her face. 'He lives *here*?' she gasped. 'Do you mean that he sleeps in your bed, with *you*?'

Lucy took another deep breath. 'That's right. You're old enough to understand about things like that. As you keep reminding me, you're not a baby.'

'But that's immoral! It's . . . disgusting!' Her lower lip trembled.

Feeling sick, Lucy turned her head away. It hadn't occurred to her that a fourteen-year-old, growing up in a sexually aware and morally ambivalent society, would find such an arrangement unusual or blameworthy. But Ruth *was* a young fourteen, as Andrew had said, and she had probably led a fairly sheltered life. 'We love each other,' she said. 'One day you'll understand. I'm sorry if you don't approve, if it upsets you . . .'

'Does Grandad know that you're living in sin?'

If Ruth had tried, thought Lucy, she couldn't have hit a sorer spot: she wasn't ashamed of her relationship

with David, but somehow she didn't expect her un-
worldly father to understand it. 'No, he doesn't,' she
admitted. 'And I'd be very grateful, darling, if you didn't
mention it to him.'

'And Rachel – I bet you haven't told her, either.
Rachel would never approve of anything so horrible,'
Ruth went on with deliberate cruelty. But there were
tears in her eyes as she added, 'Oh, Aunt Lucy – how
could you?'

Much later, behind the closed door of the bedroom, with
Ruth safely tucked up on the sofa bed at last, Lucy and
David talked into the night. 'She hates me,' David
stated, with as much bewilderment as resentment, as he
got into bed. 'How on earth am I supposed to work with
her, when she treats me like some lower life-form?'

Lucy, brushing her hair in front of the mirror, was
determined not to tell him about Ruth's strong disapproval of their living arrangements, though she was
afraid that it was already all too evident to him. 'She'll
get used to you,' she tried to convince him. 'She just
wasn't expecting to have to share me with you, if you
know what I mean.'

'She thought that she and her Aunt Lucy would have
a cosy time together, you mean? Just the girls, doing
girlish things?'

'That's it exactly,' Lucy confirmed. 'She has two
younger brothers at home, you know, and I think she
was looking forward to getting lots of attention from
me.'

'Well, too bad.' He didn't care if it sounded callous; he
wasn't particularly in the mood to be charitable.

She slid in beside him. 'David darling, you've got to make allowances for her,' she said coaxingly, snuggling up against him. 'She's at a very difficult age.'

David gave a self-deprecating laugh. 'Then what's *my* excuse? I don't like sharing you, either.'

Things weren't so bad if David could still laugh at himself, Lucy decided. 'I'm serious, darling. I remember being fourteen, and I was absolutely frightful.'

'Not you.'

'Oh, yes I was.' She turned on her back and looked up at the ceiling, reflecting. 'It was an awful age to be. I remember when I was around that age, grown-ups were always telling me how lucky I was to be young, and I knew that it was a lie – that being fourteen is horrible, and that either they were lying, or they didn't remember. I said to myself then that I would never forget how absolutely awful it was to be fourteen.'

'And?'

'Oh, you *do* forget,' she said with a thoughtful sigh. 'Of course you do. It's like any kind of pain, a toothache or a stubbed toe – you can remember that it hurt, but not really how much. At least, though, I'll never underestimate the agony of being fourteen. That much I've held on to.'

'You're more charitable than I am, my love.'

'And of course,' she added in a matter-of-fact voice that masked great depths of unresolved pain, 'when I was about her age, my mother died. At least Ruth is lucky enough to have two parents to help her through being fourteen.'

David had his doubts that Ruth would be any less objectionable at forty than she was at fourteen, but he refrained from saying so. 'And lucky to have her Aunt Lucy as well.' He turned and put his arms around her. 'Just don't forget that *I* need you, too.'

'Oh, darling. It's only three weeks,' Lucy protested against his chest.

David's response was rhetorical but heartfelt. 'Why do I have the feeling that it will be the longest three weeks of my life?'

Chapter 12

The law of thy mouth is dearer unto me: than
thousands of gold and silver.

Psalm 119.72

Vanessa Bairstow spread her toast with marmalade,
looked at it without seeing it, then put it down on her
plate untouched. 'I wonder where he could be?' she
asked rhetorically, her normally tranquil forehead
creased with concern.

Her husband sighed. That damned cat, he thought. If
Vanessa spent half as much time worrying about the
important things in life... But he made the dutiful, if
impatient, reply. 'I'm sure he'll turn up soon. When he's
good and ready. You know that cat has a mind of his
own.'

'But Augustine has never stayed away *this* long
before.' Absently she brushed toast crumbs off the table
cloth.

Augustine's non-appearance was not affecting Martin
Bairstow's appetite; he always declared that breakfast
was the most important meal of the day, and he practised
what he preached, deploring the fact that his wife limited
herself to toast.

'Perhaps I'll stay at home today, just in case.'

Bairstow looked at his wife in surprise. As far as he was aware, she rarely left the house anyway, excepting the occasional shopping trip. 'Why, where were you going?'

'Oh, this afternoon is the monthly women's club. First Wednesday of the month, you know.'

'Hm.' That information was enough to satisfy his perfunctory curiosity on the subject; he put down his fork for a moment and picked up the copy of the *Financial Times* from the table to scrutinise a story on the front page which had caught his eye.

Desperate to retain her husband's attention, Vanessa went on, 'It's at Joan Everitt's house this month. Rachel Nightingale is the speaker – she's going to give a sort of travelogue about Cambridge, I believe.'

She had succeeded in capturing his attention. He looked up quickly, frowning. 'You weren't planning to go, were you?'

'Why, yes. Until Augustine went missing, anyway. Now I don't know.'

Martin Bairstow put his newspaper on the table for emphasis and leaned across the table to look his wife in the eye. 'I'd really rather you didn't. The more that woman is encouraged ... well, let's just say I don't think it's a good idea. Surely Dolly isn't going?'

'Well, no,' Vanessa admitted. 'Dolly said that under no circumstances would she have any social contact with her.'

'Very wise, too. I certainly hope that you'll follow her example.'

Vanessa didn't dare tell him that in her limited

contact she had found Rachel Nightingale to be a warm and sympathetic person, and was looking forward to seeing her that afternoon, and possibly even intended to encourage further meetings. 'Well, we'll see,' she prevaricated.

Her husband merely raised his heavy eyebrows in a way that conveyed his disapproval more clearly than words. Rolling up his napkin and restoring it to its silver ring, he rose from the table. 'I'll be a bit late tonight,' he announced. 'Norman and I have a meeting with the Vicar at six. So I should be home shortly after seven.'

'I'll ring you if there's any news about Augustine,' Vanessa promised to his indifferent back. 'I'm sure he's all right,' she added, more to herself than to him. 'He *must* be all right.'

'It's dead boring,' Ruth protested to David. 'Nothing but photocopying. Why can't you give me something interesting to do?'

He didn't try very hard to conceal his irritation. 'If you'd rather, you can collate and staple those reports. Or make me a cup of tea,' he added, knowing that the suggestion would infuriate her.

'I didn't come all this way to spend three weeks running the photocopier, or making tea!' she flared. 'I want to learn to be a solicitor, not a secretary!'

David took a deep breath, on the verge of retorting, 'Then I suggest that you begin acting less like a spoiled brat and more like the bright young lady that everyone tells me you are,' but he caught himself in time. It was only the third morning of the first week, and already he'd had ample cause, both personal and professional, to regret giving in to Lucy in the matter of Ruth's work experience. He'd tried, several times, to explain to the girl that client confidentiality prevented her becoming involved in any meaningful way in his work, but she seemed unable to accept the limitations, and resented the menial work to which she was relegated. He had known it would happen, and he had been right. Looking down at his desk in an effort to control himself, he saw the notes he'd been making during his last telephone conversation, and had an inspiration. 'Then you can go downstairs to the library, and see what you can find out about Canon Law and Consistory Courts,' he said in a mild voice. 'Take as long as you like.'

'Oh.' He had caught her by surprise, and it took her a little while to recover. 'All right. But don't forget that you said I could have the afternoon off,' she added. She was going to hear Rachel Nightingale speaking to the women's club. Lucy had been invited by Vanessa Bairstow, and had reluctantly agreed to go, along with Emily, to support Rachel; when Ruth had found out about it, she had insisted on going along, and David was only too willing to accede to her request for a few hours off.

'I haven't forgotten.'

'Well, I'm off to the library, then.'

As soon as she had gone, David picked up the phone and dialled Martin Bairstow's business number, passing through several layers of secretaries before reaching the man himself. 'I have some news about the silver,' he told Bairstow.

The other man's voice was eager. 'Yes?'

'It's not good news, I'm afraid,' David cautioned belatedly. 'I've just been talking to the secretary of the Diocesan Advisory Committee. He says that the DAC have turned down our application for permission to sell it. In view of its singular importance and great value, he said.'

'Oh.' Bairstow was silent for a moment, assimilating the information. 'What recourse do we have?'

'Well, Mr Bairstow, there's the Consistory Court, but as I explained to you before, that will take time and cost money. Counsel will have to be briefed, and it might take months.' He scanned his notes. 'And, to be perfectly honest, the DAC secretary said that he didn't think we stood a chance of overturning the DAC's decision. In similar matters, the Consistory Court has always backed the DAC – they're the experts, after all. Of course, it's up to you,' he added. 'And Mr Topping and Father Keble Smythe. I'm prepared to fight it, if that's what you decide you want to do.'

There was another, shorter silence. 'Thank you, Mr Middleton-Brown,' Bairstow said at last. 'I'll have to get back to you. As it happens, I'm meeting this evening with the Vicar and Norman Topping, and I promise you that this will be top of the agenda. I'll ring you as soon as I can.'

'No hurry,' said David. 'And I'm awfully sorry to have been the bearer of bad news.' As he put the phone down, he realised that in fact he was quite cheerful: the DAC's decision had affirmed his faith in the system. He had been uneasy all along about the sale of the silver, especially after the Vicar's veiled hints about the churchwardens' hidden agenda. In consequence he'd

been feeling faintly guilty about his own role in doing
something he didn't believe in, though he never would
have admitted it even to Lucy. Now he hoped that the
churchwardens and the Vicar would have the good
sense to leave it, even if it meant that his fees would be
considerably less than they might have been if it went to
Consistory Court.

The Everitts' house was, compared to Vanessa Bairstow's
mansion, a modest dwelling, perhaps a bit too near
Victoria to be strictly considered Pimlico. But Joan had
spared no trouble, or at least expense, in preparing for
the meeting, offering her guests an impressive array of
delicacies that had obviously come from the food hall of
a famous Knightsbridge emporium.

For Rachel's sake, if not her hostess's, Lucy was glad
she'd come: the turnout was embarrassingly small. She
and Emily and Ruth made up nearly half the audience
for Rachel's talk, in the absence of both churchwardens'
wives as well as quite a number of the other women who
had been at the previous month's meeting. Lucy could
only assume that the snub was deliberate and possibly
even organised, and hoped that Rachel didn't realise it.

Joan Everitt had no such compunction, as she
circulated after the talk with cups of tea for her guests,
looking more than ever like an ingenuous schoolgirl.
'I'm sorry about the poor turnout,' she said to Rachel,
who had been cornered by an enraptured Ruth as soon
as she'd finished speaking. 'We usually have loads more
than this. Dolly wouldn't come, of course, and Vanessa
rang earlier to say that her cat had gone missing, and
she wanted to stay home in case he turned up.'

'Oh, dear. That will have upset her. Perhaps I should call by her house later to make sure everything is all right,' Rachel thought aloud.

'And Vera Bright had wanted to come,' Joan went on, 'but she didn't feel that she should leave her father alone. Then, of course, there are the rest of Dolly's crowd, who wouldn't come because of you.' Seemingly oblivious to the possible hurt she had caused, she passed on to her other guests, leaving Rachel bemused and Ruth indignant.

'Of all the insensitive . . . !' Ruth spluttered furiously.

Rachel, undecided whether it had been deliberate or merely naïve, gave her a philosophic smile. 'Don't worry, my dear. I'm used to it.'

'What do you mean?'

'I'm afraid that there are still quite a few people who haven't accepted the reality of women clergy in the Church of England – that's the problem with being the first generation. I don't consider myself a trailblazer, but somehow it's ended up that way. By the time that *you're* grown up, no one will think anything about it.'

'I'd like to be a priest,' Ruth confided on impulse.

Rachel was surprised. 'I thought you wanted to be a solicitor.'

The girl's face flamed, but she set her mouth in a determined line. 'I thought I did, but I'm not so sure any more,' she admitted. 'My work experience so far has been boring – dead boring. Your job seems *much* more interesting, even if there are people who don't appreciate you. I wish that I could do my work experience with *you*.'

Recognising the elements of hero-worship, and the

153

unrealistic expectations that were driving the girl's new, as well as her former, career aspirations, Rachel had an idea. 'I wouldn't want to interfere with what you're doing with Mr Middleton-Brown. But you're free in the evenings, aren't you?'

Ruth looked at her eagerly. 'Yes.'

'Perhaps you'd like to come out with me one evening when I'm on duty, as it were.' That would disabuse her of any notions of glamour in the quickest possible way.

The prospect beckoned, infinitely more appealing than yet another endless evening of telly and Cluedo with Aunt Lucy and her awful boyfriend. 'Oh, yes, please.'

'Well, then...'

'Can't it be tonight?' Ruth suggested, unwilling to wait any longer than necessary. Her mind leapt ahead: perhaps it could even become a regular thing, for what was left of the three weeks.

Rachel took a sip of her tea and considered the idea. She had already decided to call on Vera Bright that evening, in view of her non-appearance at the meeting. Perhaps it would do both Vera and Ruth good to meet, across the generations. 'All right,' she said. 'But I'm afraid that it will have to be on foot – I don't have a car, and I don't think you'll fit on the back of my bicycle!'

'I don't mind,' Ruth assured her. 'Honestly, I don't.' For Rachel, no inconvenience was too great.

Chapter 13

Who say, Let us take to ourselves: the houses of God
  in possession.

Psalm 83.12

The Vicar hadn't yet returned home from saying Evensong, for which Martin Bairstow was grateful: it gave him an opportunity to discuss matters with his fellow warden before Father Keble Smythe became involved, as they waited in the vicarage study.

'Middleton-Brown says that the DAC have turned us down,' he stated baldly. 'And that he doesn't think a Consistory Court would take a more ... liberal view of our request to sell the silver.'

Norman Topping thought of what Dolly would say, and he frowned. Though perhaps, he reflected, with all this business about Nicola to occupy her, Dolly wouldn't be so bothered. 'Then what can we do? Is there anything else we can flog off?' He began taking a mental inventory of the church's treasures.

'I've thought about that, and I don't think there's anything else that would raise the sort of ready cash that we'd need.'

'To refurbish Magdalen House, you mean?' Topping

155

whispered. 'But how else will we manage when we go over to Rome? We've got to have a place to hold services, and since we can't take the building with us...'

Looking at his watch, Bairstow spoke urgently. 'Listen, Norman, there's not much time. Father Keble Smythe will be here any minute. I've been thinking about this all afternoon, and I'll tell you what I think we should do.'

'I'm all ears.'

'I think that we should forget about our original idea of going over to Rome, and consider opting out of the diocese instead. They've made some rather generous provisions for congregations that remain in the Anglican communion with alternative episcopal oversight, you know. Then we could keep our building – no compromises like Magdalen House.'

'But that was such a brilliant idea of yours, Martin – to fix up Magdalen House, and then as trustees to hand it over to Rome, so we could use it as our church when we went over. Dolly thought that it was a wonderful idea.'

Bairstow fought to keep his impatience out of his voice. 'I'm telling you, Norman, it isn't going to work. Without the cash from the silver to refurbish it, Magdalen House is just a house. It's not suitable for use as a church. Rome wouldn't want it.'

Dolly's not going to be happy about this, thought Norman Topping. 'But how can we opt out of the diocese over the ordination of women, when we've got ... her? The curate? She rather buggers things up, doesn't she?'

The door opened and Bairstow gave the other man a

warning look. It was Mrs Goode, bringing in the drinks tray. 'Are you gentlemen all right?' she asked, ostensibly addressing both of them but fixing her attention on Bairstow. 'Father should be home any minute. But I'm sure he'd want you to help yourself to a drink.'

Bairstow favoured her with one of his patented charming smiles. 'Thank you so much, Mrs Goode. It's so kind of you to bother with us.' He was glad of the interruption: Topping had raised a point for which he had no easy answer. The existence of Rachel Nightingale as their curate was rather a challenge to their claim of doctrinal purity, even if she had not yet been ordained as a priest. If only the Vicar hadn't been conned into having her, he reflected, they would have so many more options. If only there were a tidy way of getting rid of her...

As Mrs Goode set the tray down, the phone rang; having been well trained not to pick up the extension in the study, she hurried off into the hall to answer it. Bairstow busied himself pouring drinks to avoid addressing Topping's question, and within a moment Mrs Goode was back. 'It was a message for you,' she said to Bairstow. 'Your wife. She said to tell you that the cat has just come home – she thought you'd want to know.'

He tried to summon some enthusiasm but failed. 'Thank you, Mrs Goode. Sorry for the bother.'

'Oh, no bother. No bother at all, Mr Bairstow.' She smiled at him and hesitated by the door, hoping for a little chat. 'I had a cat myself once. A fine black tom he was. Mr Goode used to say that I had more time for that cat than I had for *him*.'

He was once again spared the necessity of a reply by

Mrs Goode's prompt reaction to the faint sound of a key in the front door. 'Oh, there's Father now,' she stated, making a quick exit from the study. 'I'll tell him you're here.'

Bairstow had time only for a whispered warning to Norman Topping before the Vicar entered, rubbing his hands together briskly. 'Chilly out there, isn't it? I see that the excellent Mrs Goode has taken care of your needs, with drinks and a nice cheery fire.'

'Oh, yes,' Norman Topping assured him with a chuckle. 'This whisky goes down a treat, all right. Keeps the chill out better than the fire.'

Pouring himself a drink, the Vicar sat down across from them. 'To your good health,' he said, lifting his glass.

Bairstow was in no mood for pleasantries. 'The DAC have said no,' he announced bluntly. 'We can't sell the silver.'

'Ah.' The Vicar's smile didn't falter, but he put his glass down and pressed his fingertips together in a thoughtful way. Unwilling to commit himself to further comment, he regarded his wardens and waited for them to speak.

Although Bairstow understood what game was being played, and would have preferred a more cautious approach, he was afraid of what Norman Topping might say if the silence continued too long, so he rushed to forestall him. 'It requires that we ... re-think certain plans we'd made,' he said as circumspectly as possible.

'About the shelter for the homeless, you mean.' The Vicar managed to say it without a hint of irony in his voice or on his face.

158

Silently Bairstow cursed him; he was making it damnably difficult. He knew that they all knew exactly what was at stake, but he wasn't about to let the Vicar force him into spelling it out. Changing tack, he replied. 'Yes, that's right – it's a great shame, isn't it? The need is so great, even in this affluent part of London.'

'The solicitor said that a Consistory Court wouldn't go against the DAC,' Topping contributed. 'I was wondering if there was anything else we could sell instead. But Martin said—'

Bairstow interrupted him. 'I said that perhaps we'll have to put that idea on the back burner for the time being, and look at other priorities in the parish instead.'

'Yes?' The Vicar raised his eyebrows, inviting him to go on.

Taking a deep breath, Bairstow plunged in. 'It's that ... the curate. She's got to go, Father.'

'Rachel?' The look of surprise on his face raised deliberate obtuseness to a fine art. 'But she's doing a good job. Works jolly hard, she does. It's been a great help to me in my parish work. And she's bright, as well – she's only been on the job a few weeks, but already she's picked up so much about the people involved, and the setup in the two parishes. Give her a few more months, Martin. It's early days yet. She'll shape up – you'll see.'

'Only if she's capable of changing her gender!' Bairstow exploded. 'Bloody hell, Father! I have nothing against the woman personally, but this is an Anglo-Catholic parish! Don't you read the papers? Don't you know what's happening in the Church of England?'

Long after the wardens had gone, Father Keble Smythe

sat in his study, cradling an empty glass and staring into the dying embers of the fire. It didn't require a Martin Bairstow to tell him that he'd made a mistake in appointing Rachel Nightingale as his curate. But his concern was not for the parish, nor for the delicate sensibilities of Dolly Topping and her cronies. From his point of view the mistake was personal, with consequences that might damage his own prospects.

His piloting of his own career to date had been characterised by an unerring instinct for those things that would best enhance his image, and a certain amount of caution; together with good connections and a fair degree of ability those qualities had served him well, and had advanced him to a position where preferment seemed assured. But now he had made a potentially fatal error: he had allowed his short-term needs to overshadow his long-term goals. The loss of Father Julian as his curate had left him hopelessly swamped with parish work, and that, along with the desire to curry favour with those who had suggested it, had blinded him to the dangers inherent in Rachel Nightingale's appointment. His instincts had let him down, and that in itself depressed him almost as much as the consequences of his misstep.

Now that it was too late, now that he had tacitly allied himself with the pro-women camp, it had become evident that the Church of England was prepared to be more than generous with opponents of women's ordination who were willing to stay within the Anglican Church rather than joining the exodus to Rome. Fast-streaming promotion opportunities were available – deanships, archdeaconries and suffragan bishoprics were being offered to the best and brightest of the anti-women clergy. Bribes, perhaps, if one were being cynical, but those who were beneficiaries of such largesse were not about to put too fine a point on it.

It might have been him. William Keble Smythe groaned unconsciously, thinking about what might have been. He could have been a suffragan bishop, or even a London area bishop.

Then what was he to do? Going over to Rome, as he'd been aware all along was his churchwardens' intention, wasn't really an option for him. He had no illusions that a horde – or even a trickle – of rogue Anglican clergy would be received by Rome with open arms, bags of money, or opportunities for career advancement. Rome was a dead end. Even without the complications of a wife, he knew that it wasn't for him.

But what was left?

If only . . .

She had to go.

With a surge of resolution, Father Keble Smythe reached for the whisky decanter and refilled his long-empty glass. He didn't know how it was to be accomplished, but Martin Bairstow was right. Rachel Nightingale had to go. Changing horses in mid-stream could be a dangerous activity, but sometimes it was the only alternative to drowning. Somehow, some day soon, she had to go.

Walking along beside Ruth Kingsley, Rachel was glad that the girl was in an ebullient, talkative mood: it gave her time for reflection, and masked the fact that she was less than her usual cheerful self.

Her impromptu visit to Vanessa Bairstow had been cut short by Martin Bairstow's return home, and the resulting scene had not been a pleasant one. Accustomed as she was to rudeness, both subtle and direct, Rachel had still not been prepared for what the churchwarden had said to her. The experience had left her badly shaken.

But Ruth seemed unaware of her disquiet, chattering on about her boredom with her work experience. 'Dead boring,' she said yet again. 'Nothing but running the photocopier and making tea, although today he sent me to the library to look up some information. About Canon Law and Consistory Courts. Don't ask me why. It wasn't really much more interesting than photocopying, but at least it got me out of that boring office.'

'Canon Law?' For a moment Rachel's interest was caught, but soon Ruth was off on another variation of her complaint. 'And the evenings are just as bad. Sitting around playing Cluedo, just like I was eight years old. Aunt Lucy just doesn't seem to realise that I'm nearly grown up. And *him*.' She shuddered melodramatically. 'He's *awful*. I just don't know what Aunt Lucy sees in him.'

'Mr Middleton-Brown, you mean?'

Ruth nodded. 'Yes, *him*. He's so soppy about Aunt Lucy – it just makes me sick.' With a few gagging noises to demonstrate her disgust, she went on, 'Last night, I went into the kitchen before dinner and found them *kissing*. Ugh – it was nauseating! Before dinner, even!' She gagged again. 'Gross.'

In spite of herself, Rachel smiled in amusement. Poor Lucy, she thought. And poor Ruth, to have her delicate sensibilities so offended. 'Aren't you being a little hard on your aunt?' she suggested gently.

'Oh, no. Aunt Lucy used to be so ... sensible. Before she met *him*,' Ruth declared, adding maliciously, 'they're living in sin, you know. And she doesn't want Grandad to find out. I told her that you wouldn't approve.'

Rachel decided that the situation wasn't really so amusing; she thought carefully about how to respond. 'It's not up to me to approve or disapprove,' she said as mildly as possible. 'And it's not up to you, either. Your aunt is a grown woman, responsible for her own decisions.'

'But it's so hypocritical,' Ruth declared with fierce intensity. 'If she wasn't ashamed of it, she wouldn't mind Grandad knowing about it.'

'Oh, Ruth.' Rachel shook her head. 'I'm afraid that people are often a lot more complicated than we'd like them to be. That's one thing I've learned in my job. There are so often conflicting motivations, and so many factors that someone on the outside can't possibly understand. When I realised that, I knew that I was halfway towards accepting people as they are, not as I wish they were.'

She wouldn't have listened to anyone else, but Rachel's words carried a great deal of weight with Ruth. 'Oh,' she said thoughtfully. 'Well, maybe. But still...'

'Now, here we are at Vera Bright's house,' Rachel interrupted in a brisk voice. 'She lives with her father, who is very old – nearly a hundred.'

That had the desired effect; Ruth turned to her with wide eyes. 'A hundred!'

'Well, nearly. Ninety-six,' she amended.

To Ruth, it was much the same; as far as she was concerned, anyone over thirty, even Aunt Lucy though perhaps not Rachel Nightingale, was terminally old. The woman who answered the door, with her wrinkled face and stringy body, looked to her young eyes as though she might have been a hundred as well, but common sense told her that if she was the daughter of the ninety-six-year-old man, she probably wasn't much over seventy.

'Hello, Miss Bright,' said Rachel with a smile. 'Have we called at an inconvenient time?'

The older woman's face lit up. 'No, not at all. Father and I were just watching the television. We do most evenings.'

'I wouldn't want to interrupt anything important.'

'Oh, no,' Vera Bright assured her. 'It's only a programme about the life cycle of the bee that Father wanted to see. He likes the nature programmes, though I'd sometimes prefer to watch a film. Or listen to the wireless. Please come in.' She looked curiously at Ruth as they stepped into the hall, but was too polite to say anything.

'This is my young friend, Ruth Kingsley,' Rachel introduced her. 'Ruth, this is Miss Bright.'

Vera Bright smiled at Ruth. 'How nice to meet you. You might not believe this, but you remind me a great deal of myself when I was a girl. My hair was just that colour.'

Ruth hoped that her face didn't betray her amazement. It was difficult enough to believe that this faded, drained-looking woman had ever been young at all, but that she should have been like her was beyond comprehension. 'Oh, really?' she managed.

The older woman gave a quick look over her shoulder in the direction of the room from which issued a barrage of sound, loud buzzing with an even louder voice-over. 'Come upstairs for a minute,' she whispered conspiratorially. 'I'll show you.'

Rachel and Ruth followed her up the stairs and into a room that was surprisingly small and claustrophobic for a house of that size. It wasn't that the room was cluttered – it was in fact almost bare in its simplicity – but it had an airless quality about it that both Ruth and Rachel found oppressive. 'Here,' said Vera, picking up a silver-framed photo from the table beside the bed and handing it to Ruth. 'See what I mean?'

The girl who laughed up at Ruth was young, probably in her late teens or early twenties. Though the photo was in black and white, the camera had captured the girl's essence: a face bursting with vitality and happiness, framed with vigorous curls that might have been red, her head held on a proud neck above a lithe, lively body.

'Oh!' said Ruth.

'She *is* like you,' Rachel declared, looking over her shoulder. She smiled at the older woman. 'Miss Bright, you were lovely.'

After a moment of staring at the girl in the photo, Ruth's attention shifted to the other inhabitant of the frame. Next to the young Vera Bright, his arm draped around her shoulders casually but possessively, was a good-looking young man in uniform. He had an open, guileless face with liquid dark eyes and a wide smiling mouth, under cropped hair that looked as if it might have been dark blond in colour. 'Who is he?' she asked with curiosity.

To her own amazement, Vera Bright's voice was steady; she hadn't spoken his name in years. 'Sergeant Gerald Hansen, his name was. Gerry. He was an American airman, in the war. We were going to be married. But he ... he was killed.'

'Oh!' Stricken, Ruth looked up at her. 'Oh, I'm so sorry. How sad.'

'It was a long time ago,' Vera Bright said quickly, embarrassed. She reached for the photo.

Over the cacophony of the television below, a querulous, imperious voice made itself heard. 'Vera? Where have you disappeared to, girl? Who was it at the door?'

Chapter 14

*Teach me thy way, O Lord: and lead me in the right
way, because of mine enemies.*

Psalm 27.13

The next two days were busy ones for Rachel, as Ruth
returned to the tedium of the photocopier. In addition to
her regular parish duties, there were several things
that she needed to follow up on.

It was on Thursday afternoon that she paid another
call on Vera Bright. The older woman had been much on
her mind lately, but she'd found it extremely difficult to
get to know her in any meaningful way with the old
doctor always present. On Thursday, however, she was
in luck: Dr Bright was taking a nap when she called,
and she was able to have nearly an hour alone with his
daughter before he returned to consciousness and began
demanding his tea.

Afterwards, cycling home, Rachel wasn't sure whether
it had been a good thing or not. Vera Bright had clearly
needed someone to talk to, someone to listen to her, but
it had been an emotionally draining – and troubling –
experience for Rachel. Vera Bright had poured out her
soul to her: where should she take it from there?

Obviously some action was needed. It was the second time in as many days that she'd felt pastorally out of her depth, and it made her realise how inadequate her theological college training had been in preparing her to minister to people in the real world. Her knowledge of tidy textbook cases was extensive, but it was only now that she was becoming aware of how insufficient that was. People, and the lives they lived, *weren't* tidy – they were messy and complicated. She had a lot to learn, Rachel thought ruefully, and the realisation was both depressing and dispiriting.

The problem was, she didn't know quite where to turn for help. Father Keble Smythe wasn't the answer, she decided: he was far too busy with his own parish responsibilities. He might even think she was interfering, overstepping her brief as a curate, by getting involved with the parishioners in this way.

Father Desmond! she thought suddenly, as she came around the corner near her flat, wondering why she hadn't thought of him sooner. Father Desmond, her mentor, who had seen her through that terrible time after the accident, and had set her feet on the road to healing, faith, commitment and finally vocation. He had been her spiritual director through her time at theological college, a wise and holy man as well as an experienced parish priest. Dear Father Desmond – he would know what to do. Letting herself into the flat, she was overwhelmed with the need to see him, to draw on his compassion, his wisdom, and above all his experience.

She went straight to the phone and rang his Cambridge vicarage. He wasn't there. 'I'll have him ring you as soon as he gets in,' his housekeeper promised. She knew that she could have expected no more, but Rachel couldn't help feeling vaguely disappointed as she put the kettle on for a cup of tea.

Father Desmond rang back later. 'Come up and see me, my dear,' he said promptly. 'Come tonight, if you like.'

'I can't do that,' she protested. 'I have to visit Colin tonight.'

'Then come in the morning, on the train. You can be here in an hour. Name the time, Rachel dear – I'll meet you at the station.'

Frantically she reviewed her schedule for the following day. It would be tight, but if she put off one or two non-essential things she just might be able to manage it and still be back in time for her weekly late afternoon staff meeting with Father Keble Smythe, the Administrator, and the Director of Music at St Jude's. 'All right,' she said, making her mind up. 'But I'm not sure about the time – why don't I ring you when I get to King's Cross?'

Her visit to Colin the next morning was necessarily a brief one. She had to get to St Margaret's well before early Mass to prepare the register for Saturday's wedding, a task she'd meant to do later in the afternoon; now, given the uncertain timing of this trip to Cambridge, she decided that she'd better get it out of the way before she left. As soon as Mass was over she was on her way to the Victoria tube station to get the Underground to King's Cross.

* * *

When she returned home, a little after three, her answerphone was flashing. She filled the kettle and switched it on, then pushed the button to listen to her messages while the kettle boiled.

There were two messages. The first was from an almost incoherent Nicola Topping. The girl's voice was frantic, desperate: 'Rachel,' she gasped tearfully, 'I've got to see you. This afternoon. It's a matter of life or death. You can't reach me, but I'll come to your flat at four. Please don't let me down.' There followed a few seconds of uncontrolled sobs before the phone was put down.

Rachel barely had time to react before the second message began playing. It was, surprisingly, from Colin's brother Francis; Colin and his brother had never been particularly close, and Rachel's contact with him since the accident had been minimal. 'This is Francis Nightingale,' the brisk voice informed her. 'Please ring me at my office. I don't think it's anything to be alarmed about, but Colin's doctors weren't able to reach you so they've just rung me instead.'

Rachel wasn't alarmed. She might have been, but this sort of thing had happened before: periodically, Colin developed infections, and the doctors had to check with her before they started treatment. The only difference was that Francis had never before been involved; these new London doctors were evidently being ultra-conscientious.

She'd better ring Francis first, and reassure him, she decided, before worrying about Nicola and the staff meeting. Automatically she went about the soothing routine of making tea, pouring the boiling water on to the bags in the teapot, releasing their fragrance.

While the tea steeped she set about locating the number for Francis's London office; it wasn't one she had often required. Eventually she found an old address book in the bureau. She poured herself a large mug of tea and took a reviving sip; she hadn't realised until that moment how tiring her flying trip to Cambridge had been.

The secretary who answered put her on to Francis almost immediately. 'Hello?' he queried.

'Francis?'

'Oh, hello, Rachel.'

'Colin's doctors rang?' she prompted him.

'Yes. They couldn't reach you, and they had me down on their list as next-of-kin after you. It seems that he's developed a kidney infection, and they wanted to talk to you about treatment.'

'But the answerphone was on,' she said. 'Why didn't they just leave a message?'

'I suppose they thought that a message on your answerphone might alarm you.'

'Oh, I'm not alarmed,' Rachel reassured her brother-in-law. 'This sort of thing has happened before, when he was in Cambridge.'

'They don't just automatically start treatment, then?' he asked curiously.

Rachel laughed. 'It's all terribly discreet – they'd never come out and say so – but what it's all about is . . . well, you know. Letting people die.'

'What do you mean?'

She took a sip of her tea. 'Sometimes, family members . . . well, I suppose they find it difficult having someone

171

like Colin to worry about. They might even consider it a burden in some ways. And when the person gets an infection, it's easy for the doctors to give them minimal treatment, in effect just to let them die of the infection. It happens all the time. The doctors always like to give the next-of-kin the chance to opt for that.'

'And what about you?' he probed.

'Oh, there's no question about it,' Rachel stated. 'The doctors in Cambridge stopped asking, after a while, because they knew I would always want them to do everything they could.'

There was a pause on the other end of the phone. 'Haven't you ever been tempted? I mean, it must be very difficult for you . . . ?'

Rachel might have been angry, but she realised that her brother-in-law didn't know her very well. 'Good heavens, no,' she responded mildly. 'I love Colin. I've never considered him a burden.'

'Then what will you do?'

'Well, if you'll give me the number, I'll ring the doctors straightaway and tell them to go ahead with the treatment. And tonight I'll go and see him as usual.'

Francis gave her the number; there was another brief pause. 'Do you think that I might visit him some time?'

He had never before expressed any interest in seeing his brother, so Rachel was surprised and touched. 'Yes, of course. It would be lovely if you did.'

'When do you usually go?'

'Early in the morning, and again at night, at about half-past nine.'

'Every day?' Francis asked incredulously.

'Of course.'

After yet another thoughtful pause, Francis said, 'Well, perhaps I'll see you there one day soon.'

As she put down the phone, and before she rang the doctors, Rachel acknowledged an unhappy truth to herself: it wasn't quite as simple as she'd made it sound to Francis. One day the treatment wouldn't work; one day she would lose him. She said a silent prayer that it would be far in the future, and that when the time came, she would have the grace to let him go.

The doctors dealt with, Rachel looked at her watch. It was clear to her that she'd have to be here when Nicola arrived at four, but that would mean missing the staff meeting. She picked the phone up again and rang the vicarage.

Father Keble Smythe answered himself. 'Stanley's just arrived,' he said. 'I thought you'd be on your way by now.'

'I'm so sorry, Father, but I won't be able to make it this afternoon,' she apologised. 'Something very important has come up – an emergency with a parishioner.'

He masked his irritation quite well. 'Ah, well. Can't be helped, I suppose. Anything I should know about?'

'Not really, Father. Perhaps later.' Rachel hesitated. 'There is something else, though. Something I really need to talk to you about, and as soon as possible. I was wondering if you might have a few moments this evening, after the service...?'

The Vicar gave a short laugh. 'Actually, that's one thing I wanted to speak to you about. I've got some problems about tonight, and I'd like you to take the service for me.'

He wasn't really offering her a choice, but Rachel thought carefully just the same. The service wasn't a Mass – it was St Margaret's Friday night Lenten observance of Exposition of the Blessed Sacrament and Devotions – so there was theoretically no reason why she shouldn't take it, but it seemed to her that there were a number of factors that made it not a very good idea. Her detractors at St Margaret's – how would they accept it? And she'd never done it before, so she was unsure about how well she would manage it. 'I don't know, Father,' she equivocated. 'Isn't there anyone else? I'm not so sure...'

'Nonsense,' he declared heartily. 'You've been there every week – you know the form. Just a few prayers, the usual stuff. You'll do just fine. Didn't you do that sort of thing at Cambridge?'

'Well, no,' she admitted. 'But that reminds me, Father. I had to make a quick trip to Cambridge earlier today, and while I was there I called in at my old theological college, and met someone who said he knew you at St Andrews – his name was Douglas. Hamish Douglas. He said to say hello to you.'

There was a brief silence on the other end of the phone. Oh God, thought William Keble Smythe. Not that. He felt a trickle of sweat on his brow that had nothing to do with the warmth of the fire which Mrs Goode had so efficiently provided in his study. 'So you'll take the service,' he said at last, in a jolly voice that sounded false to his own ears. 'Good girl. And I'll see you on Sunday.'

* * *

Aimlessly Rachel rearranged a few things on her kitchen counter, then looked at her watch again. There was still nearly a quarter of an hour to go before Nicola was due, enough time to make another phone call, this time to the Archdeacon.

Emily Neville answered the phone. 'Oh, hello, Emily,' said Rachel. 'This is Rachel. I'd hoped for a word with the Archdeacon.'

Returning her greeting, Emily went on, 'I'm sorry, but Gabriel's not here. I don't expect him back much before supper time. Was it something urgent?'

Rachel, half regretting the impulse that had made her ring, hardly knew how to articulate it. 'Well, no, I wouldn't say urgent. But it's important, I think. I'm not even sure that he's the person I need to talk to, but there's something that's bothering me, something not quite right, and I thought perhaps I ought to tell him about it.'

'If you'll hold on a minute, I'll check the diary in his study,' Emily offered. After a brief pause she came back on the line. 'It looks as though he should be able to see you first thing on Monday,' she said. 'Say about nine. Will that be good enough?'

'Oh, that's fine.' Rachel was relieved; that would give her time to think out what she wanted to say to him, and perhaps to have a word with the Vicar as well. She switched gears. 'So, how are you, Emily?'

'Fine. We're all fine. How about you? Is the job getting to you?'

'Oh, it's not so bad,' Rachel said charitably.

'Even Dolly?'

Rachel laughed. 'Even Dolly. I stay out of her way,

and she seems to be trying equally hard to stay out of mine.'

'I'm sure that's just as well.'

'We're both much happier that way, I'm sure,' Rachel agreed.

'And how is Colin?'

'Well, not so good at the moment, as a matter of fact. He's got a kidney infection.'

'Oh, dear.' Emily sounded genuinely concerned, prompting Rachel to go into more detail.

'He'll be fine,' she assured her friend. 'Once they get him pumped full of antibiotics. I was in Cambridge earlier today – I made a quick trip up to see Father Desmond – and when I got back I had a message that the doctors had contacted Colin's brother.'

'I didn't know that Colin had a brother,' said Emily curiously. 'And why did they contact him?'

'Yes, just the one brother, but we've never seen much of him. Francis is some sort of high-powered businessman in London, and Colin has never felt that they had much in common. Anyway,' she went on, 'the doctors needed permission from the family so that they could begin treating his infection.' She then explained matter-of-factly to Emily, as she had to Francis earlier, that some families might wish to have treatment withheld, and the reason why.

Emily was horrified. 'But that's terrible! How could anyone do that – just let someone die?'

'I used to feel that way about it,' Rachel said with a small sigh. 'I certainly couldn't do it, myself. But now I realise that other people's circumstances are different. For instance, I'm very fortunate – the financial side of it isn't a problem for me. But nursing care of the type Colin needs doesn't come cheap, and might be devastatingly expensive for someone who didn't have the money and who wanted something beyond the level of care that the NHS provides.'

'Colin is lucky that he has you,' Emily declared staunchly, then realised how it might sound to define as lucky a person who was doomed to spend the rest of his life in a hospital bed, completely unaware of his surroundings – especially to the person who seemed likely to spend the rest of *her* life looking after him in one way or another.

But Rachel didn't take it amiss. 'Well, yes,' she said in a facetious tone. 'If he didn't have me, Francis would be his next-of-kin, and he might decide to pull the plug!'

Chapter 15

*When my spirit was in heaviness thou knewest my
path: in the way wherein I walked have they
privily laid a snare for me.*

Psalm 142.3

At St Margaret's it would be remembered as one of the
all-time great rows in the church's history, its causes
and its aftermath discussed endlessly afterwards. Oddly
enough, in all the postmortem analysis, no one ever
thought to accuse Father Keble Smythe of deliberate
maliciousness in sending his curate to take the service
in his place, or indeed to attribute to him any base
motivation or blame for what ensued from his opting
out. And though the question of his whereabouts might
have come up at the time, such minor matters were
swept away by what happened, and later no one gave it
a thought. Suffice it to say that Father Keble Smythe
was not present at St Margaret's that evening, and
never claimed to be; no one else would have admitted
missing it.

Robin West, the sacristan, took credit for having seen
her first. He was in the chancel when she came in
through the church, and though the sole fact of her

presence in the church was not a great shock, he was alarmed to see her heading towards the sacristy, his own domain.

His natural impulse, whenever he saw Rachel Nightingale, was to flee, but on this instance, for whatever reason, he decided to stand and fight. Moving in the direction of the sacristy, he intercepted her near the door, just under the stained glass window depicting the stoning of St Stephen. 'Where do you think you're going?' he demanded.

As it was the first time he'd ever spoken to her, she was understandably startled. 'To the sacristy, to vest,' she explained. 'The Vicar has asked me to take the service.'

The sacristan bristled in outraged indignation. 'That doesn't seem very likely. I'm sure that *Father* would never do such a thing.'

It was just the sort of reaction that Rachel had expected; she took a deep breath and stood her ground, and her voice sounded remarkably calm. 'Nevertheless, it's quite true.'

Robin West sputtered ineffectually for a moment and paused as Rachel continued on her way into the sacristy. Uncertain, he turned to find that Martin Bairstow, Stanley Everitt and the Toppings had arrived more or less simultaneously at the back of the church; he rushed to intercept them. 'It's that woman!' he announced dramatically. 'She claims that Father has sent her to take the service She's gone into the sacristy!'

In spite of her considerable bulk, Dolly was the first to reach the sacristy door, followed closely by the others.

They met Rachel coming out, her face set in determination, carrying the veiled monstrance. 'Oh no, you don't,' Dolly bellowed. 'Not here. Not at St Margaret's. You're not ruining *our* church. Can't you see that you're not wanted here? Why don't you just go away and leave us alone?'

Stanley Everitt wrung his hands in an even more agitated manner than usual and begged everyone to stay calm, but his voice was scarcely heard in the fracas. Bairstow raised his voice in support of Dolly; Norman Topping nodded vigorously and emitted the occasional squeak of encouragement. In the midst of it all, Rachel Nightingale stood with her eyes closed, her scar standing out in angry relief on her pale cheek. She clutched the base of the monstrance, willing it all to end. I didn't ask for this, she said to herself, trying to think of a way to escape. It was clear that no service would be held that night: no matter the outcome of the battle, these people were in no fit state to worship God, to bow their knees and their heads before the presence of the Sacrament.

Incensed beyond rational thought, Dolly made a grab for the monstrance. She hadn't counted on Rachel's firm grasp; for a moment the two women seemed locked in a stalemate. Then, with a superhuman wrench, Dolly tore it away from Rachel, and the veil, dislodged by the violence of the gesture, floated downwards between them like a silent scream of protest.

It was only a short time later, though it seemed an age, that Rachel was on her bicycle, traversing the familiar streets that led her, every morning and every evening, to the nursing home and Colin. She made a very great effort not to dwell on the horrific scene that had just taken place, thinking instead about Father Desmond, about Colin, and about the unfortunate and unhappy Nicola Topping.

I do hope that I've done the right thing about Nicola, Rachel thought. Sending her to talk to Vera Bright – it could well be a great help for both of them. Then again, it could backfire, and make things even worse.

She was an experienced bicyclist; no matter how preoccupied she was with other concerns, or how familiar she was with the quiet backstreets, she rode cautiously and didn't take foolish risks. But she never saw the car coming. It caught her broadside, sent her flying, and the pavement rushing up to meet her was the last thing that Rachel Nightingale saw.

Quiet as the street was, it was only moments later that the off-duty PC Huw Meredith strolled along, feeling sated and more than a little pleased with himself after one of his regular Friday evening interludes with Pamela Hartman. This evening's encounter had been exceptionally satisfying, and Pam had promised to try to make some excuse to her husband and meet him on Saturday as well. Even after tonight, or perhaps especially after tonight, that was something to look forward to: a whole Saturday afternoon in bed – or on the sofa, or in the shower, or on the hearth rug in front of the fire – with the delectable Pam.

What caught his eye was the spinning bicycle wheel. Its rapid revolutions had slowed considerably, but still it turned with the click-click-click sound of a roulette wheel. Huw Meredith paused to investigate, wrenching his mind away from Pam.

The sight was not a pretty one: apart from the spinning front wheel, the bicycle was a mangled and twisted metal sculpture with no resemblance to its former state. With a small shock, PC Meredith saw that its rider had been a blonde, like Pam, and that she had probably been an attractive young woman. Probably – with the injuries she had sustained, it was difficult to tell. He was an experienced policeman, whose beat included some rather unsavoury areas of London, and he had seen hit-and-run accidents before. 'Bloody kids,' he muttered savagely as he looked around for a phone box, furious to have his enjoyable evening spoilt by a bit of juvenile tomfoolery gone wrong. 'Bloody joy-riding kids.' He would ring the nearest police station; it was clearly too late for an ambulance.

Part II

Chapter 16

*Out of the mouth of very babes and sucklings hast
thou ordained strength, because of thine enemies:
that thou mightest still the enemy, and the
avenger.*

Psalm 8.2

Few people in London truly mourned for Rachel
Nightingale, but of those who did, Ruth Kingsley was
inconsolable.

From the beginning – from the first shattering
moment – she'd insisted that it had been no accident;
nothing that anyone said could convince her to the
contrary.

'But darling,' said Lucy in her most reasonable voice,
one which she'd been called upon to employ consciously
with increasing frequency since Ruth's arrival. It was a
raw March Sunday afternoon, the day after they'd
learned about Rachel's death; with no real will to do
anything else, the three of them were in the sitting room
of Lucy's house, waiting for the day to end. 'Darling, the
police know about these things. They say that it was a
hit-and-run driver who killed her. Another person was
badly hurt in almost the same spot, just a few weeks

earlier. By young kids, probably in a stolen car. It happens more often than you'd think in London.' David had checked with a policeman he knew, and he'd been quite definite.

'That's what they *say*.' Ruth's tear-stained face had a mulish expression. 'Maybe they believe that, or maybe they're just saying it. But I *know*. I know that someone at that church – at St Margaret's – did it, on purpose. They wanted to get rid of her, and they did. They ran her down in cold blood.'

'Aren't you being just a wee bit melodramatic?' David's patience with Ruth, always tenuous, had worn a bit thin of late.

The girl seemed even more gawky than usual, wrapping her thin arms around her body as she glared at him with undisguised hostility. 'I don't care what you say. I don't care what the police say. I know that they did her in, one of them.'

They'd been through it all before, endlessly, but Lucy, who was keeping a firm lid on her own emotional reaction, hoped that there might be something cathartic for Ruth in the process, and that it was better for the girl to talk about it than to bottle it up inside. 'But why, darling? They're church people. Church people don't go around murdering one another just because they don't like them.'

'Because she was a woman, of course. They were horrible to her. She told me so.'

Lucy lifted the lid of the teapot and peered inside. They'd been through a great deal of tea, but it looked like this pot might stretch to one more cup for someone, before she had to get up and boil the kettle again.

Unselfishly she offered it to Ruth. 'More tea, darling?'

The girl shook her head in a listless negative, but Lucy poured the remaining tea into her cup anyway, then took the empty pot to the kitchen. Not touching the tea, Ruth sat very still, tears trickling down her cheeks. After a moment, she gulped, wiped at her eyes with the back of her hand, and said in a bitter voice, 'The police won't do anything, will they?'

David sighed. 'They'll try to find the hit-and-run driver, if they can. After all, it was more than the usual hit-and-run – someone was killed. The driver could be charged with causing death by reckless driving, and that's a criminal offence, with a prison sentence involved.'

'But how could they find them?'

He picked up his teacup and looked at the dregs in the bottom. 'Oh, the police have ways. If the car was stolen, it may be abandoned later, and it might have prints in it. And they check body shops for cars that have been brought in for repairs to damaged wings. I mean, unless someone was driving a tank, that sort of impact would have to do some sort of damage to their car,' he explained, with a feeble smile at the mental picture of a tank on the streets of Pimlico.

'If that's supposed to be funny,' snapped Ruth, 'I don't think much of your sense of humour.'

Deciding that defending himself would be counter-productive, David lapsed into silence. He wished that Lucy would come back with more tea; he wished that it weren't too early for something stronger. In his opinion it was by no means too early, but he was sure that the *enfant terrible* would disagree. *Enfant terrible*: that was how he had come to think of Ruth. Once or twice it had slipped out when talking to Lucy, who didn't appear to find it very amusing.

The intrusive chirp of the telephone interrupted his reverie, as it rang just once; obviously Lucy had been near enough to pick it up right away. It meant, though, that she might be a while in returning. Clearing his throat, he tried again with Ruth, who had withdrawn into a bleak stillness. 'I know that you're upset about Rachel, but...'

'Upset?' She startled David with the intensity of her reply. 'Of course I'm upset! She was the most wonderful person I've ever known, and now she's dead, and the person who murdered her is going to get away with it, because no one believes me!'

'Murder is an easy word to throw around,' he said carefully. 'But I think you'll find that people don't very often murder each other because of their gender. There are plenty of reasons I've heard for murder, but that's not one of them.'

In spite of herself, Ruth was interested. 'Like what?' she demanded. 'What sort of reasons?'

'Money, for a start. If there were someone who was going to benefit financially from Rachel's death, I'd want to take a closer look at it myself. Or sometimes people commit murder to conceal a secret, something that they wouldn't want anyone else to find out. If Rachel had found out something like that...'

'Maybe that's it,' Ruth interrupted him excitedly. 'People confided in her, you know – she was that kind of person. Maybe someone told her something, and later regretted it. And then they murdered her so she wouldn't tell anyone else. I'm going to find out what it was,' she added with resolution. 'If the police won't do it, I'll have to investigate myself. *I'll* find out who murdered her.'

The vehemence of David's reaction surprised him almost as much as it did Ruth. 'Don't be so bloody stupid,' he said with quiet force. 'You can't just go around asking people questions, as though it were a game of Cluedo! You're not dealing with Mrs Peacock or the Reverend Green here – we're talking about real people, with real lives and real secrets. You could get yourself into a hell of a lot of trouble prying into things that aren't your business, murder or no murder.'

Shocked but stubborn, Ruth didn't deign to answer, pulling her lips over her mouthful of metal and withdrawing back into herself. She turned away from David and bit her lip as the trickle of tears started again.

Why did I do that? David asked himself. I've only antagonised her, and she's going to go ahead and do whatever she damn well pleases anyway.

He was comforted when, a moment later, Sophie appeared and jumped on his lap. And so Lucy found them – sitting in silence, Ruth with her tears and David with the cat – when she returned, bearing a fresh pot of tea and looking thoughtful.

'Who was on the phone, love?' David held his cup out.

'Emily.' She took the cup, filled it and handed it back to him.

He sniffed the steaming liquid gratefully, waiting a moment for it to cool. 'Anything important?'

She shook her head, but gave him a look which he

rightly interpreted to mean that she'd tell him about it later.

Although David and Lucy generally favoured a rather leisurely approach to lovemaking, that night they made love with an unaccustomed urgency, fuelled by the inevitable sense of mortality in the aftermath of the death of someone they knew, someone younger than either of them. Afterwards, too keyed up to sleep, they talked for a long time.

'You don't think that Ruth could be right – that Rachel's death wasn't really an accident?' Lucy suggested tentatively.

David laughed. 'I know that our recent experiences have suggested otherwise, love, but sometimes people really *do* die by accident. Just because your charming niece has a fixation about Rachel Nightingale . . .'

'That's not really being fair to Ruth,' she protested. 'There *were* people who hated Rachel, who wanted to get rid of her. If it weren't Ruth who was saying it, you'd be the first one to agree that her death is a little too convenient.'

He thought about that for a moment, then admitted with a self-deprecating chuckle, 'Well, you may be right about that. I *am* inclined to take a contrary position where the *enfant terrible* is concerned. But that aside, Lucy love, I just can't see that anyone had a strong enough motive to . . . well, you know. Just because she was a woman who wanted to be a priest, I mean. I'd have to be convinced that there was some other motive before I even considered the possibility seriously. Like money, as I said to Ruth earlier.'

'According to what Emily told me,' Lucy thought aloud, 'Rachel must have had a lot of money. From the settlement after the accident, you know.'

'Not necessarily,' he cautioned. 'In the first place, the money might only just be enough to pay for her husband's personal care, assuming he lives for a good many years yet. And secondly, who would benefit financially from Rachel's death? Presumably only her husband, so that doesn't really lead us anywhere.'

The heat generated by their lovemaking had begun to dissipate; Lucy shivered slightly and pulled the duvet up under her chin. 'Colin has a brother, Emily tells me. Couldn't he benefit somehow?'

'I don't see how, as long as Colin is alive. Why – what does he have to do with anything?'

'Well,' Lucy explained, 'when Emily rang me this afternoon she told me that she talked to Rachel on the phone on Friday, just a few hours before . . . you know.'

'And?' he prompted.

'Rachel told her that Colin had a kidney infection, and that somehow his brother had got involved. Emily said that she made a little joke that she hoped nothing happened to her, or Colin's brother might decide to pull the plug. And a few hours later . . .'

'H'm. Just a coincidence, I'm sure,' David stated as he drifted off to sleep. 'And not a very funny joke, as it turned out.'

But two days later, when he opened his morning paper to the obituary page, David read that Colin Nightingale had died at the age of thirty-five, of complications from a kidney infection.

Chapter 17

Thou hast turned my heaviness into joy: thou hast put off my sackcloth, and girded me with gladness.

Psalm 30.12

David read the obituary out to Lucy over their after-breakfast coffee, while Ruth was taking her customary extended shower. ' "The young scientist, whose brilliant career was cut so tragically short by a road accident nearly four years ago, had survived in a vegetative state since then. By sad coincidence, his wife Rachel, a Deacon in the Church of England, was killed in another accident just last week in London." And then it goes on about his career, and the research he was involved in before the accident. Don't ask me to read it – I can't even pronounce most of the words.'

Lucy, still in shock at the news but fully aware of the implications, put her finger on the cogent point. 'But it doesn't say anything about the money? Or about any survivors or other family members?'

'Nothing. These things usually don't.'

'Is there any way you can find out?'

He shook his head, still unwilling to admit that there

was anything in it. 'Not really. Why don't you ring Emily and see if she knows? If you're really that curious, that is.'

Lucy gave him a warning look as Ruth came into the kitchen, her face almost as white as her towelling dressing gown, the freckles standing out in sharp relief and her short, damp, copper curls providing a shocking contrast to her pallor; two days and nights of crying had taken their toll. 'I don't really feel like going to work today,' she announced. 'I think I'll just stay here.'

David was quick to agree. 'If you don't feel well, then you must stay home. Your Aunt Lucy will take good care of you.'

The look Lucy gave him this time mingled understanding with annoyance – now *she* was the one whose work would suffer – though her voice betrayed nothing but concern. 'Of course you must stay home, darling. I'm sure that David will manage without you somehow.'

He smiled wryly. 'Yes, I'll manage.'

'You'll just have to find some other flunky to make your tea,' the girl muttered, sitting down at the table in expectation of being waited on by her aunt.

Lucy did what was expected. 'Would you like some tea now, darling?' She got up and went to fill the kettle.

'Yes, please.'

'And how about something to eat?'

Ruth considered the options. 'I think I might be able to eat a poached egg. And some dry toast, perhaps.'

'And I'd better be off,' David stated, anxious now to escape in spite of feeling vaguely guilty about lumbering Lucy with the burden of Ruth for the day. But it was

194

Lucy's own fault that the girl was here in the first place, he justified to himself.

Lucy walked him to the front door. 'Have a good day, David darling, and if you have a chance to find out anything about Colin Nightingale . . .'

'Not likely, my love.' He kissed her lightly. 'And you take good care of the *enfant terrible* for me.'

In spite of his scepticism, though, David found himself, during the course of the morning, thinking about Colin Nightingale and the unlikely coincidence of his demise just a few days after his wife's untimely death. Once again he remembered the feeling that had nagged him when Lucy had first told him about Rachel: there was something about that settlement that had been important.

Restlessly he left his desk in the late morning and wandered downstairs to the firm's library. From the shelves he pulled a few volumes of cases and precedents; based on the date of the accident, he could judge with a fair degree of accuracy when the legal aftermath was likely to have occurred. He settled down at a table with the weighty books and began flipping through them.

It didn't take him long to find what he was looking for. He read through it twice, just to make sure that he hadn't misunderstood; his eyebrows went up and his mouth rounded in a soundless whistle.

Lucy had been right about one thing: there was a great deal of money involved. Although the settlement that Rachel had been given in compensation for her own rather minor injuries was not large, nor was the amount awarded for the death of her daughter, that was only the beginning. She had also been awarded a generous settlement – much more generous than was usual – in compensation for the loss of companionship and financial support of her husband. That was in addition to the even larger sum bestowed on Colin, based on the curtailment of his brilliant future as a scientist and the likely cost of his medical care over his expected lifetime. All told it added up to an astronomical sum, in excess of a million pounds.

It sounded like a lot of money, but David realised that it was not over-generous: private medical care for brain-damaged people was cripplingly expensive, and over a number of years the money would be eaten away, even if the capital was carefully invested. But the settlement had been made less than a year ago, so little of the money would have been spent. That meant, thought David, that at the time of her death Rachel Nightingale had been in possession of a tidy fortune. On her death it would have gone to Colin, but now Colin was dead as well. Someone, he thought, has done very well indeed out of the two deaths, occurring as they had in that particular order and with such convenient proximity in time.

It was nearly time for lunch. During the past week, David had been encumbered with Ruth at lunchtime; in spite of his contention that the girl was perfectly capable of going around the corner for a sandwich on her own, Lucy had been firm. It was a part of her over-cautious reaction to her position *in loco parentis* that had led Lucy to insist that Ruth was not to travel anywhere in London on her own, a restriction that Ruth resented every bit as much as David did. And so David had been reduced to eating his lunch in Ruth's company at a sandwich bar in High Holborn, thus missing out on the legal gossip on offer at the various pubs and wine bars clustered around the Inns of Court which catered to members of the bar, solicitors, and assorted hangers-on in the profession. Indulging in a bit of professional gossip over a drink at lunch was one of the things he most enjoyed about working in London, and after a week of bland sandwiches and even blander con-versation – if you could call Ruth's peevish and non-communicative noises that – he felt out of touch; today, without her, he could catch up. He headed for El Vino's, perhaps the most venerable of the establishments frequented by lawyers, vowing to treat himself to a smoked salmon sandwich and a half-bottle of the house champagne in celebration of his unexpected freedom from the *enfant terrible*.

In the five or so months that he'd been in London, David had made quite a few contacts over lunchtime drinks. Entering El Vino's, he scanned the crowd for a likely source of gossip; to his disappointment, the only familiar face he saw belonged to none other than Henry Thymme. That was one person he definitely *didn't* want to talk to, he decided. He found a seat at a table with a view of the bar, ordered the champagne and sandwich, and retreated behind his newspaper, noting with interest an item about a forthcoming sale at Christie's, featuring ecclesiastical silver and other bits and pieces. It would be worth stopping by one day when he was in that area and picking up a catalogue – not because he was likely to buy anything, but just from general interest.

When his lunch arrived he put his paper down and glanced in the direction of Henry Thymme, curious to see what he was up to. Thymme seemed to be enjoying an uproarious drinking session with another man at the bar; his face was even redder than usual, and his voice boomed out across the room. 'Time for another, dear chap?'

His companion nodded, turning to the bar. He didn't look familiar to David; in fact, there was something about him – about the cut of his suit, perhaps, or the cut of his hair – that seemed to indicate that he wasn't a lawyer. Not that there weren't impeccably dressed and coiffured barristers and even solicitors, especially in this part of Fleet Street, but somehow David didn't think that this man was one of them. He was tall and thin, sharp-featured, with an artistic swoop of grey hair and a trim grey moustache to match, though he didn't look much over forty.

His curiosity satisfied, David returned to his newspaper as he sipped his champagne and ate his sandwich, becoming engrossed in an article about a church treasurer who had managed to embezzle a mind-boggling sum of money over a period of some twenty-three years before being found out when the new incumbent decided to have a look at the books. 'Ah, the good old C of E,' he muttered, shaking his head. But his cynical ruminations were interrupted by a cry of delighted recognition at his elbow.

'Middleton-Brown, my good man!' Henry Thymme hailed him. 'Why are you hiding behind your newspaper? Come and join me for a drink!'

'But . . .' David protested feebly.

'No buts, my friend. You're all alone, and that's not a good thing to be. In fact, it's not allowed at El Vino's, is it?' he insisted, addressing the last query to the waitress, who shook her head obligingly, mindful of a good customer. 'What are you drinking, my boy?' he went on, pulling up a chair across from David.

David swiftly calculated his intake. He'd finished off a half-bottle of champagne; he could safely have another glass or two and still be able to function in the afternoon. Realising that there was no escape, he capitulated. 'Well, I was having champagne.'

Thymme snapped his fingers at the waitress; he seemed to have trouble making them work properly. 'A bottle of your best champagne,' he ordered.

It arrived promptly, on ice, and was poured out with ceremony. David, whose budget didn't usually run to that particular brand, took an appreciative sip. 'Lovely stuff. Thanks.'

'I like a man who knows his champagne.' Leaning across the table, Thymme confided loudly, 'That's one of my disappointments with the lad. Young Justin. Never has developed a taste for good wine. Says he prefers lager, like some football lout. Or sweet sherry – even worse. A great disappointment.'

The subject of Justin Thymme was one to be avoided at all costs. Casting about wildly for a neutral topic of conversation, David observed, 'Are you alone? I thought you were with someone else.'

'*Was*, dear boy. He's gone now. Client of mine, just had some good news. Wanted to buy me a drink.'

'Yes?' David wasn't particularly interested, but any

alternative subject was to be encouraged.

Thymme shook his head ruminatively. 'Just goes to show you how quickly things can change. You know what I mean?' David nodded his encouragement, and Thymme lowered his voice to a volume more appropriate for the delivery of confidential information. 'When I saw him a week ago, he was ready to cut his throat. Not literally, of course, but the man was pretty damn low. Lost a packet with Lloyd's. Not the only one, of course – hell, plenty have. But that wasn't all, poor sod. Rich wife. American. She's just left him. Left him or chucked him out, I'm not sure which. Found out he's been screwing his secretary. Found out how much money he'd lost. Can't really blame him about Lloyd's, of course. But between you and me, my friend, he's got a weakness for the ponies, as well. He's in rather deep to a few unsavoury types. When his wife left him, he didn't know how he was going to raise the cash.' He shook his head again. 'Life's funny, isn't it?'

David was fascinated in spite of himself. 'What happened?'

'Oh, didn't I tell you?' Thymme's voice dropped to a whisper. 'He's come into an absolute fortune. A million at least. His brother died, and he'll get everything. Even after death duties, it's a hell of a lot of money. Now it's up to me to get the divorce settlement pushed through before the will is settled, so his bitch of a wife can't get her filthy little hands on any of the dosh.'

'Francis Nightingale?' whispered Lucy in amazement; they had to keep their voices low so that Ruth, languishing in the sitting room, wouldn't hear them. 'But how clever of you, darling!'

'Not clever at all,' David replied with a self-deprecating but pleased smile. 'You might say that it was handed to me on a plate – or more accurately, in a glass. Thymme was so legless by that point that he didn't care how indiscreet he was being. He told me everything I ever wanted to know about Francis Nightingale, including the fact that he's due to get all of his brother's money. And that he needed it pretty badly.'

They were in the kitchen, preparing supper. David related the gist of Thymme's revelations under the cover of running water as he washed the lettuce.

Lucy's verdict was swift and succinct. 'He sounds like a complete sod.'

'Absolutely,' he agreed. 'Just like his solicitor. But the point is, Lucy love, that I should have trusted your instincts. Francis Nightingale had a hell of a motive to run his sister-in-law down and make it look like a random hit-and-run. Rachel dying when she did, before Colin, saved his bacon – if Colin had died first, Francis would presumably not have seen a penny of all that money.'

'But how could he have known that Colin was going to die? If, like Emily said, he'd had these infections before, why should anyone think that this one would kill him?'

David turned the water off and shook the lettuce vigorously. 'You're forgetting the other thing that Emily said. That after Rachel was dead, it was up to Francis whether he pulled the plug or not – whether Colin received treatment for the infection.'

'And you think ...?'

'I think,' said David, 'that if the police aren't going to take a closer look at Francis Nightingale, someone else is going to have to do it.'

Chapter 18

*Plead thou my cause, O Lord, with them that strive
with me: and fight thou against them that fight
against me.*

Psalm 35.1

The next morning, David sat unproductively at his
desk, trying to think through the puzzle of Rachel
Nightingale's death. He was by no means convinced,
even yet, that it had been anything but accidental, but
he admitted to himself that there were some cir-
cumstantial grounds for suspicion. It certainly would
have been possible, in any case, for her brother-in-law to
have been involved. Rachel went to see her husband
every night, presumably at a regular time. From that
supposition it took only a small leap for David to arrive
at the conclusion that anyone who knew of her routine,
and that surely included her brother-in-law, would
have been able to lie in wait for her to cycle past. It
really had nothing to do with him, he acknowledged,
though he was curious nonetheless. Would it be possible
to make some discreet enquiries, just to satisfy himself?
If so, how might he go about it? Before he'd had time to
formulate a plan, a call came through from Henry

Thymme. It was an occurrence that David had come to dread, heralding as it always did some further problem with 'young Justin', so he picked up the phone with trepidation.

Thymme sounded unusually subdued; perhaps, thought David, he was just hung over. He certainly deserved to be, given the quantity of alcohol he'd consumed in the early part of the previous day, let alone what he'd probably drunk later. 'I've realised, my dear boy, that I might have been just a touch ... ah ... indiscreet in our conversation yesterday. From what I can remember, anyway,' he added with a more characteristic chuckle.

'Think nothing of it,' David assured him.

'The thing is, old chap, I could use your help.'

'Oh?' He tried to keep his voice noncommittal, but he was afraid that it sounded as dismayed as he felt. Here it comes, he thought. The latest escapade of Justin Thymme. The immigration office's investigation into the validity of the younger Thymme's marriage was still in progress; had the fool done something idiotic to jeopardise that? Surely he hadn't been back to Hampstead Heath ...

'I think I mentioned that I was handling my client's divorce, and that I wanted to expedite it as much as possible.'

'Yes, you did mention that.'

Thymme cleared his throat thoughtfully. 'Well, I've remembered that the wife's solicitor is a partner at your firm – Russell Galloway.'

'One of the senior partners,' David amplified.

'Yes, of course. The thing is, I was rather hoping that

you might do me a great favour and have a word with him.'

'Oh, yes? About what, exactly?'

Thymme's voice took on a wheedling tone. 'About this divorce settlement. Try to get him to speed it up at his end. Without telling him what I mentioned to you yesterday about the money, needless to say.'

David was astonished at the man's effrontery. 'And why should I do that? Why should I want to do something against the best interests of a client of one of the partners in my firm?'

There was a pause on the other end of the phone as Thymme chose his words carefully. 'I like you, my boy. You've done well by me and the lad so far, and I think you're a damned good solicitor. And with all due respect to Sir Crispin and Fosdyke, Fosdyke and Galloway, I also think that you could do better for yourself. I could use a smart chap like you in my firm. I could offer you a partnership straightaway, with a substantial financial incentive, and unlimited potential for advancement. What do you say, Middleton-Brown?'

'I say,' David stated quietly, 'that I'm going to forget that we ever had this conversation, and I suggest that you do likewise. And that I wouldn't work for you, Mr Thymme, if you were the last solicitor in London.' Before Thymme could reply or even react, he put the phone down, gently but with great satisfaction.

Mastering his fury, after a few minutes he was able to think coherently about what Thymme had said to him, and about its implications. Mrs Francis Nightingale, a client of his own firm: this might be an avenue to explore. Perhaps he should have a word with Russell Galloway.

It was Russell Galloway who had been instrumental in David's move to Fosdyke, Fosdyke & Galloway. David had met the senior partner the previous year when acting in a volunteer capacity on behalf of a London church, in a successful effort to save it from redundancy and possible demolition; Galloway had been impressed with David and the job offer had resulted. David liked and respected Russell Galloway, finding him more approachable and less intimidating than Sir Crispin.

Now he went through the corridors to Galloway's office, pondering how best to handle the matter. If he told Russell Galloway what he'd learned, Thymme would certainly know where the information had come from, and would undoubtedly be prepared to make David's life difficult in future. Since 'young Justin' was still his client, whether he wanted him or not, and was currently under investigation by the immigration office, that could be awkward. But his first loyalty was to his firm; he'd have to find a subtle way to let Galloway know about Thymme's interest in the case.

Russell Galloway was behind his desk, which as usual looked as though it had a life of its own, piled high with papers, briefs, files, empty crockery and other assorted items. David had learned, though, that the impression of chaos was illusory: Galloway knew exactly where everything was, and could instantly put his hands on anything required. Russell Galloway's own appearance was equally deceptive. He had none of Sir Crispin's polished elegance, instead possessing a distinct resemblance to an unmade bed: his suit was always rumpled, and his tie was always askew. With his lack of sartorial style and his broken nose he looked more like a prize fighter than a highly-paid solicitor, and though he also lacked Sir Crispin's underlying ruthlessness, he was a pragmatic man with a great deal of integrity; David had learned early on that it would be a mistake to underestimate him.

Looking up to see David hovering at the door, Russell Galloway grinned. 'Come in, my friend.' He returned David's liking and esteem, perhaps recognising in him some of his own qualities of gentleness underlaid with strength and integrity.

'Are you busy?'

Galloway laughed and ran his fingers through his greying hair, short and as crisply waved as corrugated cardboard. 'I'm always busy. But always ready for an excuse for a break. Pull up a chair and tell me something I don't know.'

Deciding that the direct approach was best with a forthright man such as Galloway, David plunged straight in. 'The grapevine tells me that you're handling a divorce for a Mrs Nightingale.'

Galloway groaned. 'Yes, for my sins.'

'Difficult?' David probed.

'God, yes,' was the heartfelt reply. 'She's a twenty-two carat bitch, that one, and she knows exactly what she wants.'

'What *does* she want?'

'She wants to get shot of her worthless philandering

spendthrift husband as quickly as possible, before he can spend any more of her money,' he said succinctly.

'But won't he be entitled to some of it when they divorce?' asked David.

Galloway shook his head. 'She's been far too clever for that. Or rather Daddy's smart American lawyers have been. It's her father's money, really – he owns a chain of supermarkets in the southern United States. So he's got the money all tied up for her in neat little legal knots. Prenuptial agreements and all that. The husband can't touch it.'

'Interesting,' David commented. 'So where do you come in?'

'My job, pure and simple, is to produce the divorce. Nothing more, nothing less. Fortunately it shouldn't be too complicated – no kids involved, and clear evidence of his adultery. His wife found letters from the secretary, and they didn't leave much doubt, or much to the imagination. I don't think he's contesting – he'd like to get his hands on some of Daddy's American bucks, I'm sure, but if he's got any sense he'll realise that there's no hope – so it should go through on the nod.' He turned curious eyes on David. 'Why do you ask?'

David shrugged. 'I just wondered.'

Galloway scratched his head with an elaborate display of nonchalance, then said casually, 'I don't suppose I could talk you into standing in for me at a meeting with her?'

This was better than David could have hoped for, but he matched Galloway's casual disinterest in the tone of his reply. 'Why?'

'Oh, it's nothing really. But I'm supposed to see her

on Friday morning, and the wife is giving me hell about missing some school play that I promised a long time ago that I'd go to. The kid has a starring role, apparently.' Russell Galloway produced the half-embarrassed smile of a proud father. Though he was some years older than David, with grown children, he was in a second marriage to a younger woman and was raising a young family, with the generally successful intention of doing a better job of it than the first time around; complications like this one caused him more mental anguish than he'd care to admit.

'Why can't you just see her another time, then?'

'Not that simple, I'm afraid. She's been in Paris for the last few weeks, and is only stopping over in London on Friday, on her way back to the States, and presumably the comfort of Daddy's loving arms. Not to mention his bank account.' Galloway rummaged around on his desk and came up with his diary, then checked the entry for Friday. 'Here it is. I'm supposed to meet her in the Concorde lounge at Terminal 4, Heathrow. Friday morning at half-past nine.'

David had no intention of missing out on this opportunity, but he didn't want to appear too eager. 'Well, Russell, I don't know. What is the meeting supposed to be about? Won't she mind if you don't come yourself?'

'It's really just to get her to sign some papers – nothing more complicated than that. And believe me – as long as she gets her divorce, Cindy Lou Nightingale won't give a damn who turns up! If you could see your way clear to helping me out, I'd be more than grateful.'

There was such pleading in his eyes that David could

hold out no longer. 'Well, all right. After all, I wouldn't want to disappoint your wife.'

Russell Galloway sighed gratefully. 'Thanks, David. You're a real friend.'

Chapter 19

Or ever your pots be made hot with thorns: so let
indignation vex him, even as a thing that is raw.
Psalm 58.8

Rachel Nightingale's funeral was to be held at St Jude's
Church on Friday morning. Incongruously, the day had
dawned clear and sunny and almost warm, after nearly
a month of chill grey skies. David thought about the
irony of it as he drove along the A4 at the end of the
morning rush hour. He had expected Lucy to be
disappointed that he couldn't go with her to the funeral,
but she had taken altogether a more pragmatic view.
'It's more important for you to take advantage of
this opportunity,' she'd said. 'Besides, you didn't
know Rachel as well as I did, so it won't really matter
if you miss it. Ruth will go with me. And maybe
it's even better this way,' she'd reflected. 'The people
at St Margaret's still don't know that there's a connection between us, and perhaps it's not a bad thing to
keep it that way. Some of them may well be at the
funeral.'

So while Lucy was putting on her best black dress, he
was on his way to Heathrow Airport. Perhaps it was just

as well, he reflected. Ruth had shown signs of incipient hysteria before he'd left, and he felt unequal to dealing with her.

In his briefcase were the papers for Cindy Lou Nightingale to sign, papers that would set into motion the machinery of law that would ultimately result in her divorce. Signing the papers wouldn't take long, but David hoped that the soon-to-be-former Mrs Nightingale would be inclined to chat with him, in spite of the impression he had formed of her as being difficult and temperamental. His plans hadn't been formulated beyond that: meeting Mrs Nightingale, and encouraging her to talk. Anything that she might add to the picture he was building up of her husband could be helpful.

He'd never been to Terminal 4 before, so he followed the signs carefully to the multi-storey car park. There was plenty of time, he noted on his watch. But it took more time than he'd planned to find the Concorde lounge, tucked away discreetly in a corner of the terminal, and he had to do some fast talking – and to submit to repeated and thorough inspections of his briefcase – to get through the security checks without a ticket or a boarding pass in order to gain entry to an area of the terminal which was intended for departing passengers only. That he hadn't anticipated, so it was just about half-past nine when he finally arrived at his destination.

David sank nearly up to his ankles in thick carpet as he looked around the lounge for Mrs Nightingale. It wasn't difficult to spot her; most of the passengers were businessmen, in a hurry to get to New York for morning meetings, beavering away on their lap-top computers or reading the *Financial Times*, and there were one or two wealthy dowager-types, be-ringed and bejewelled. Only one inhabitant of the lounge looked a possible candidate. She sat alone in the centre of a luxuriously upholstered blue sofa, sipping a glass of champagne: a stunning brunette clad in a flame-red and lime-green ensemble that had obviously just come out of the door of one of the more famous Paris fashion houses, tailored to fit her statuesque form to perfection. Her jewellery was not, like that of the dowagers, flashy or ostentatious, but instead was discreet in the extreme: gold button earrings and a thin gold chain. No wedding ring, David noted with interest − not even for the purpose of discouraging unwanted attention from her travelling companions. Then he realised that such help was scarcely needed; her demeanour was such that not even the dimmest businessman could fail to get the message that she was not available, and not to be approached.

It was all he could do to approach her himself. She looked up as he neared and frowned, a small crease of displeasure between her perfectly plucked brows. 'Mrs Nightingale?' he said in a voice that sounded more confident than he felt. 'I'm David Middleton-Brown from Fosdyke, Fosdyke and Galloway. Mr Galloway sent me to see you.'

'Why didn't he come himself? I've always dealt with Mr Galloway in the past.' Her southern drawl was as thick as a slab of shoo-fly pie and as viscous as blackstrap molasses.

Good Lord, David thought. She thinks she's Scarlett

O'Hara. 'I'm afraid that Mr Galloway had a ... family
emergency,' he exaggerated, summoning up his most
appealing smile. 'He's briefed me on your case, and I'll
do my best to look after you as well as he would have
done.'

Cindy Lou took in his appearance with practised
rapidity: not exactly a heart-stopper, but more than
presentable, and an improvement on the unprepossess-
ing Russell Galloway in any case. She decided that
there was nothing to be gained by being difficult, so she
may as well be as charming as only the flower of
southern womanhood could be. She dimpled fetchingly
and indicated the chair across from her. 'Oh, I'm sure
you'll do just fine, Mr Middleton-Brown. Why don't you
sit down over there?' (She pronounced it 'ovah theyah'.)
He sat, and she added, 'Wouldn't you like some
champagne?'

Having prepared himself for at least some degree of
hostility, David was taken aback. Oh, why not, he
decided. It was never really too early for champagne,
and the *enfant terrible* wasn't around to disapprove.
'Yes, please.'

As another glass materialised, he took the papers
from his briefcase. 'Do you want to go ahead and sign
these papers now?' he asked. 'Get it out of the way? Or is
there anything you'd like to discuss first?'

She waved a languid hand in the air. 'All in good time.
There's no hurry, is there? My plane doesn't leave for
another hour.'

'Fine.' Uneasily David settled back in his chair and
took a sip of champagne. Now that he was here with
Francis Nightingale's wife – and she was behaving

much more pleasantly than he'd expected – he hardly knew where to begin. 'You've been in Paris, I understand?' he ventured.

'Yes. Buying a few new clothes, trying to cheer myself up.' She assumed a tragic expression and sighed deeply. 'But I think it was a mistake. Paris is no place to be on your own, Mr Middleton-Brown. Don't you agree?' She didn't really expect an answer, continuing with the trembling lower lip of an ill-done-by faithful wife, 'Frankie and I went to Paris on our honeymoon. It's full of such bittersweet memories for me.'

David, whose only trip to Paris had been on his own but who now entertained fantasies of taking Lucy there one day, nodded sympathetically. 'If you feel that way,' he said, 'perhaps you ought not to rush into this divorce. Give it a little more time, perhaps. You might be able to work things out between you.' That sort of advice would infuriate Henry Thymme, he realised with satisfaction.

Abruptly her mood and her demeanour shifted. 'Frankie is a worthless, no-good piece of shit,' she snapped. 'A dog turd. Lower than a rattlesnake's belly. I wouldn't have him back if he were the last man on earth, and came crawling to me on his hands and knees. The way that man treated me . . .' Then the tears welled up in her luminous dark eyes, demanding more sympathy. At a loss for words, David produced a clean handkerchief and leaned across to put it in her hand.

Cindy Lou's manicured fingers lingered on his for a moment as she took it from him; she dabbed at her eyes in a delicate way so as not to smudge her make-up, and gave him a watery smile of gratitude. 'Oh, you're very kind,' she murmured. 'I'm sorry. I don't know what's come over me. But Frankie hurt me so bad that sometimes I just can't help myself.'

'He did?'

'I gave that man everything. Everything I had! And how did he repay me?'

David shook his head.

'By sleeping with his slut of a secretary.' Her anger flashed again for an instant as she thought about it, her Frankie and that unspeakable girl who, apart from her youth, could surely have nothing to offer a man like Frankie, who was used to the better things of life. The letters that she'd found had been written in a childish scrawl and were badly spelled, if sexually explicit; it was an unforgiveable insult to *her*, his wife, that he should have transgressed with someone so unworthy. This time a tear actually did spill over; she let it roll down her cheek for effect and said in a piteous voice, 'And she's not even pretty! I just don't understand how Frankie could do it. It wasn't a gentlemanly thing to do. Oh, Mr Middleton-Brown – you'd never do anything like that to your wife, would you?' She regarded him searchingly.

Disconcerted, he tried to pass it off as a joke. 'My secretary is sixty-two,' he mumbled with an unconvincing smile.

She looked hurt, as if she had expected a more gallant reply. 'You know what I mean, Mr Middleton-Brown.'

He gazed into his champagne, hoping to be forgiven for his gaucherie. He had expected Mrs Nightingale to be indifferent towards her husband, or possibly even vindictive, but from what Russell Galloway had said he hadn't anticipated this combination of outrage and misery.

'I gave that man everything,' Cindy Lou repeated bitterly. 'Frankie was happy enough to have my money – my daddy's money – to spend. And he was glad enough for the lifestyle that money gave him, and the doors it opened. Do you think he ever would have made it as far as he has in business without my money behind him?'

'But I thought that the money wasn't at issue,' said David, glad to be back on firm ground. 'Mr Galloway said that your husband wasn't seeking any sort of financial settlement...'

She gave a scathing laugh. 'He'd better not even try it, the rat. My daddy's got lawyers who can run circles around Frankie's lawyers. Daddy never did like Frankie. He made sure before we got married that there was no way Frankie would ever be able to touch my money if we split up, or if I didn't want him to have it.' Downing the rest of her champagne in one gulp, she held out her glass for David to refill it, adding, 'Now let's see how he likes being poor again, like he was before he met me.'

At last the conversation was beginning to go the way David had hoped. 'You mean he doesn't have any money of his own?' he probed.

'Hardly a red cent,' she declared with satisfaction. 'In fact, between his gambling debts, and all the money he's lost with Lloyd's, he's so far in the hole that he'll *never* dig himself out. Not unless he manages to figure out a way to kill off his sister-in-law and his brother, in that order, and get away with it!' she added facetiously. 'Not that I'd put it past him, mind you!'

David was stunned; he stared at Cindy Lou Nightingale

for a moment as he realised that she'd been abroad and wouldn't have known about the two deaths. She misunderstood his reaction, and went on to explain, 'His brother has millions, but it's not doing him any good, poor guy. He was in an accident, and will be a vegetable for the rest of his life. But even if he dies, Frankie won't get any of his money unless the wife dies first – otherwise she'll get it all. Poor old Frankie – two inconvenient people in between him and all that money.'

'But it's been in all the papers,' David blurted out. 'You wouldn't have seen it. They're both dead. Rachel Nightingale was killed in a traffic accident last week – a hit-and-run driver. And her husband died a few days later.'

Cindy Lou's laughter was tinged with hysteria. 'Then he's done it, the greedy little bastard. He's finished them off somehow. I know him, better than anyone, and I know what he's capable of, especially when that much money is involved. Mark my words – those deaths may have looked accidental, but Frankie was behind them.' She raised her glass with a smile of grudging admiration. 'Here's to Frankie. May all that money bring him nothing but misery. And I hope he gets caught.'

Chapter 20

*Their throat is an open sepulchre: they flatter with
their tongue.*

Psalm 5.10

St Jude's Church was full for Rachel Nightingale's
funeral, as two congregations of parishioners turned out
to pay tribute to their curate; now that she was no
longer a threat to them in any way, they were prepared
to be generous to her in death as they never would have
been in her life, and to mourn her with every evidence of
sincerity.

Father Keble Smythe delivered an eulogy that was
both stirring and profoundly touching in its evocation of
a Godly life cut short by cruel fate. That, combined with
the beautiful singing of the choir and the heart-rending
words of the Order for the Burial of the Dead from the
Book of Common Prayer, ensured that Ruth Kingsley
was not the only person in the congregation to shed
tears that morning.

Ruth wept noisily; beside her, Lucy's tears trickled in
silence as she clutched Ruth's hand. In her own quiet
way, Lucy mourned as deeply as Ruth: in the short time
she'd known Rachel, the other woman had made a great

219

impression on her, chiefly for the manner in which she had managed to transcend unspeakable tragedy and rebuild her life so positively. Lucy had looked forward to getting to know her better, to discovering the secret of her inner strength. Now she would never have that opportunity.

After the funeral there was no interment, or even a committal; in due time there would be another service in Cambridge, in the church where Rachel had begun her clerical career, and afterwards she and Colin would both be laid to rest beside their young daughter, in a Cambridge churchyard. So the proceedings rather fizzled out at the end, and the mourners adjourned to the vicarage, where, in the absence of a close family to do the honours, Mrs Goode had surpassed herself in providing a plentiful cold feast for anyone who chose to come. Needless to say, no one stayed away, and soon the vicarage was crammed full of those who had come to mourn, to eat, or to gossip – or any combination of the three. They filled the sitting room, then spilled over into the dining room, where the food and drink were on offer, and even eventually took over the kitchen and the Vicar's study.

In a remarkably short time, and by virtue of her untimely death, Rachel Nightingale had seemingly achieved the status of sainthood. So Lucy surmised from the conversation in the kitchen, where Dolly Topping and her cadre of women gathered. 'I, for one, won't hear a thing said against her,' Dolly pontificated. 'We may not have always seen eye to eye, Rachel and I, but she was a lovely young woman. And so devoted to her poor husband.'

'Oh, she was,' Joan Everitt agreed. 'You remember, Dolly? – I always did say so. Last week, when the meeting was at my house – you didn't come, Dolly, remember? – I was so impressed with the way she spoke. Afterwards I asked her about her husband, and it nearly made me cry, the way she talked about him.'

'Terribly sad,' confirmed Dolly, who insisted on having the last word on all matters. 'And I'm so sorry that I had to miss that meeting. I heard that her talk was fascinating.'

Sickened, Lucy turned away. Ruth had already disappeared; Lucy was very much afraid that the girl, who held doggedly to her belief that Rachel had been murdered, might be engaged on a misguided fact-finding mission. Before she found her niece, though, she ran into Emily. 'Oh, there you are, Luce. I've been looking for you,' Emily greeted her.

Lucy looked around for Emily's husband. 'Gabriel's not here?' The Archdeacon had assisted with the funeral service and might have been expected to attend the post-funeral reception.

'He's around somewhere,' confirmed Emily. 'The last time I saw him, that creepy Administrator was dragging him off into a corner for a chat about something. That's when I decided to leave him to his own devices and find you instead.'

'Have you seen Ruth?'

'I did, a little while ago. She seemed to be coping all right.'

'Poor kid.' Lucy sighed. 'She's taken it very hard, you know. She didn't know Rachel long, but she really got attached to her. How are *you* coping, Em?' she added.

Emily shook her head reflectively. 'I thought I was doing all right, until today. But I just can't deal with all these endless eulogies by people who would have gone a mile out of their way to avoid her a fortnight ago.'

'Horrible, isn't it?'

'Obscene,' Emily stated with force. 'Apparently there was a huge row at St Margaret's, everyone ganging up on Rachel, last Friday evening just before her ... accident. And now no one will admit that they took part in it – just innocent bystanders, they all claim.' Her voice sounded bitter.

'Well,' said Lucy, who hadn't heard about the row before, 'at least it may explain some of what's going on now – all the denial and so forth. Though no one would ever say it, I'm sure they feel guilty about it. I mean, it's possible that she was so badly upset about the row that she wasn't being as careful as she might have been on her bicycle – and in that case, all the people who were involved might feel a little bit responsible for her death. Does that make sense?'

'There might be more to it than that.' Emily lowered her voice cautiously. 'Listen, Luce. Gabriel thinks that there's something funny going on. I can't really explain it now, but he has reason for thinking it. And we wondered ... well, you and David have had experience with this sort of thing before. I know it's short notice, but could the two of you come to supper tomorrow night, just to talk about it?'

Lucy hesitated. She was reluctant to speak for David, especially given the situation. And she wasn't particularly keen on an evening with Gabriel herself; in the best of circumstances it would be awkward, and this was far from the best of circumstances. But Emily's dark eyes were fixed on her with a pleading look, and the demands of friendship prohibited a negative answer. Besides, she said to herself, they owed it to Rachel. David might not be very happy about it, but he would agree that it had to be done. 'Yes, all right,' she said. 'What time would you like us to come?'

In an effort to redirect her grief over Rachel's death, Ruth resolved to carry through with her intention to do a bit of investigation. To that end she had slipped away from her aunt, and tried to make herself inconspicuous on the edges of various groups of people, eavesdropping on conversations. But she heard little more than the sort of valedictory comments about the dead curate that had so upset Lucy.

'Oh, hello,' said a tentative voice at Ruth's shoulder; she turned to find Vera Bright, her face splotchy and her eyelids swollen. Recognising the signs of a fellow sufferer from genuine bereavement, Ruth gave the older woman a quick, impulsive hug.

'Hello, Miss Bright. I was looking for you at the church, but I didn't see you.'

Vera Bright clutched Ruth's hand. 'How nice. We were a little late, I'm afraid.'

'Your father came too?'

'Yes. He's gone off into the other room to talk to the men, and I just didn't feel like being on my own, so I thought I'd have a word with you.' She fumbled in her pocket for a handkerchief, which she produced to dab ineffectually at her eyes. 'I'm sorry, my dear. I can't help myself. This has been such a shock.'

'Oh, I know.' Ruth looked around and spotted a pair of vacant chairs against the wall of the sitting room. 'Why don't we go over there and sit down?' she suggested.

Vera complied readily. 'This is very nice, my dear. And it's most kind of you to keep an old lady company.'

'Not at all,' Ruth protested. 'Can I get you anything? A cup of tea, or something to eat?'

'Oh, no. I don't feel that I could eat a thing. I haven't really eaten properly since ... well, you know. Since it happened,' she confided.

'Me neither,' admitted Ruth. 'I haven't had any appetite at all. I just can't believe it. I can't believe that she's really ... gone. It's too horrible to contemplate.'

Vera sighed. 'You're the first person I've talked to who really understands. There are a lot of people here saying nice things about Rachel, but somehow they don't sound as if they really mean it. I believe that you do.'

'Oh, yes,' Ruth declared passionately. 'I loved her – she was the most wonderful person. I've been devastated. Shattered. And I just can't stand listening to all those hypocrites who were so horrible to her when she was alive.'

'There was *one* other person who cared about Rachel,' said Vera. 'But I haven't seen her here today. Nicola Topping – do you know her? She was very fond of Rachel – I can't imagine why she's not here.'

'Topping? Is she related to Dolly Topping?' demanded Ruth with an incredulous look.

'Her daughter. She's a few years older than you, my dear. But you can take my word for it that she never shared her mother's opinion of Rachel. In fact, I don't think her mother ever knew how much she relied on

224

Rachel's advice, or how much time she spent with her.'

Ruth was still suspicious. 'How do *you* know?'

For the first time in their conversation, Vera looked uncomfortable. 'I'm not really at liberty to say. But I promise you that it's true. I hope her mother didn't find out and keep Nicola away today.'

'Is Dolly Topping around?' asked Ruth. 'I've never met her. I'd like to know who she is.'

'I think she's in the kitchen. I'll let you know if I see her.'

Ruth folded her arms across her chest and regarded the room full of chattering people with something approaching loathing. 'I wish I knew which one of them killed her,' she muttered, almost to herself.

'What did you say?' Vera turned a startled face on the girl.

'I said I wish I knew which one of them killed her,' Ruth repeated defiantly. 'One of them did, you know. I'm sure of it. They said it was an accident, but I don't believe that for a minute.'

'Oh, my dear!' Her voice fluttered with dismay.

'Don't you believe me? There's no reason why you should, I suppose – no one else does. Not my aunt, or anyone else.'

'Oh, if it were true . . .' Vera faltered, looking down at her hands.

Standing near the food table in the dining room, Emily introduced Lucy to the churchwarden Martin Bairstow. 'A sad occasion to bring us all together today,' Bairstow said with lugubrious gravity. 'And a great loss for us at St Margaret's.'

Father Keble Smythe chimed in, 'She gave of herself so unstintingly to all of us. Rachel Nightingale was a rare young woman. Not that the principle of women clergy is one we can all subscribe to, of course. But Rachel was different.'

'Different,' echoed Norman Topping. 'Even Dolly always said so.'

Stanley Everitt wrung his hands. 'The Church of England is the poorer for the loss of such a one.'

'And she was a pretty little thing, as well,' twinkled old Dr Bright, drawing horrified looks from the others. 'Well, she was,' he insisted, unrepentant. 'Pretty as a little rose. And always as charming as could be to me, when she came to bring me the Sacrament or to see my Vera.'

Lucy edged away from them and over towards the food table, where she contemplated the array on offer. As a vegetarian, her choices were necessarily limited, but there were cocktail sticks with cheese and pineapple, and what looked like a cheese and onion quiche, as well as a number of salads. She had just picked up a plate and begun to help herself, giving the sausage rolls a wide berth, when Ruth flew up to her in a state of high excitement. 'Aunt Lucy!' she hailed her in a shrill voice that carried much more penetratingly than she realised. 'I'm not the only one who thinks that Rachel was murdered! Miss Bright thinks so too, but that's not all! She won't tell me, but I'm sure she knows who did it!'

Chapter 21

*I am wiser than the aged: because I keep thy
commandments.*

Psalm 119.100

'But I don't see why I can't go!' Ruth whined. 'It's not fair
for you to go off and leave me by myself – you're
supposed to be looking after me, Aunt Lucy. I don't
think my parents would be very happy if they knew that
you were abandoning me.'

'Ruth, darling.' Lucy struggled to keep her voice even.
'You're continually telling us how grown-up you are,
and keep reminding us that you're not a baby. This is
your chance to prove it. It's only for a few hours – I think
you're quite capable of amusing yourself for one
evening. Surely you can read a book, or watch the
telly.'

'But I don't *want* to stay here by myself! You're going
to talk about Rachel, and I should be there! After all,
I've said all along that someone did her in, but no one
believed me.'

Lucy looked at David, hoping for moral and verbal
support, but he was too busy counting to ten –
repeatedly – to notice her unspoken plea for help. Going

227

to Emily and Gabriel's for supper was the last thing he wanted to do that evening; Ruth's intractable whingeing only deepened his gloom.

In the end the grown-ups prevailed and Ruth, protesting to the end, was left behind. They were able to talk more freely in the car en route than they had at home. 'I still don't see what this is all about,' David stated. 'I can't see that it has anything to do with the church. *If* Rachel's death was something other than an accident, I think it's fairly clear that her brother-in-law was behind it. He was the one who had everything to gain.'

'You're being as stubborn about this as Ruth,' Lucy pointed out. 'Don't you think you should keep an open mind until you hear what Gabriel has to say?'

David bristled at the comparison, while acknowledging to himself that there might be truth in it. 'I'll listen to what he has to say,' he conceded grudgingly.

His underlying apprehension about the evening was dispelled somewhat by the spontaneous warmth of Emily's greeting, as she embraced him unreservedly. He had always got on well with Emily, in spite of factors that should have made them adversaries; the fact that he hadn't seen much of her during the course of his relationship with Lucy didn't seem to make any practical difference, and she seemed willing to pick up their friendship where they'd left off.

Gabriel's greeting was slightly less enthusiastic, if only in comparison. He kissed Lucy's cheek and shook David's hand, masking any discomfort in a way that a clergyman well practised in such social niceties should find well within his powers. He asked the time-honoured question for smoothing over social awkwardnesses. 'What can I get you to drink?'

'I'll have a glass of white wine, if that's on offer,' said Lucy, taking a seat in their handsome sitting room.

'Gin and tonic, I think,' David replied, perching next to her on the sofa.

Gabriel poured generous measures of gin into two glasses while Emily went to the kitchen for the wine. There was a fractional moment of silence, then the three of them began talking at once.

'My niece wasn't very happy about being left at home tonight,' said Lucy.

'Have you had this room redecorated?' was David's contribution.

Gabriel said, 'We missed you at the funeral yesterday, David.'

They all laughed, the ice was broken, and Emily returned a moment later to find the atmosphere considerably eased. Over their drinks they settled down to inconsequential small talk about the weather (improving), the twins (thriving, though the vexed topic of their schooling was assiduously avoided), Lucy's paintings (selling well), David's new job (challenging) and Ruth's visit (trying).

It wasn't until they had moved to the dining room and were into the first course that Gabriel broached the subject on all of their minds. 'I apologise for having brought you here at such short notice,' he said, 'but I thought that it might be a good idea for us to put our heads together.' He flashed an ingratiating smile at Lucy, then at David. 'The two of you have had some experience at this sort of thing, I believe.'

'*What* sort of thing?' David asked with deliberate obtuseness.

'Informal investigation, if you'd like to call it that.'

'Gabriel thinks that Rachel's death might not have been as accidental as it's been made out to be,' Emily intervened. 'And from what Ruth said yesterday at the vicarage, he's not the only one to feel that way.'

Mentioning Ruth was not a good move in trying to enlist David's support. 'And why should I believe the fantasies of a hysterical, hero-worshipping teenager?' he snapped. 'Why should *you*, Archdeacon? I would have thought you'd have more common sense.'

Gabriel took it with a smile, including the almost insulting use of his title. 'I was about to tell you that,' he said gently.

David, unwilling to admit or to share the basis of his own suspicions of the dead woman's brother-in-law, subsided into silence.

'Rachel talked to Emily on the phone just a few hours before she died,' Gabriel began.

'Yes, Emily told me,' said Lucy. 'Rachel was telling her about Colin's illness.'

'But that wasn't the reason why Rachel rang. She didn't ring to talk to Emily – she wanted to talk to *me*.'

That announcement took David by surprise; he raised his head from contemplation of his avocado vinaigrette.

'To *me*,' Gabriel repeated for emphasis. 'Not personally, but in my official capacity. She said that she wanted to discuss something with me. What were her exact words, darling?'

Emily's brow furrowed as she called on her excellent

memory. 'She said that she wanted a word with Gabriel – the Archdeacon, she said. I asked her if it was urgent, since he wasn't at home, and she said something like, "No, not urgent, but it's important, I think. I'm not even sure that he's the person I need to talk to, but there's something that's bothering me, something not quite right, and I thought perhaps I should tell him about it.'

' "Something not quite right",' echoed Gabriel. 'And a few hours later she was dead.'

'What are you implying?' David asked slowly.

'That she might have uncovered some funny business at St Margaret's – something she wanted to discuss with me – and that someone was sufficiently concerned about the consequences of discovery to want to stop her. With a convenient accident.'

'It could have happened, quite easily,' Emily added earnestly; evidently the two of them had discussed the possibility at some length. 'David, did you hear about the row at St Margaret's just before the accident? I mentioned it to Lucy yesterday.'

'What row?' He took a fortifying gulp of wine and tried to concentrate on what was being said. 'I don't know about any row. What happened?'

Concisely, Emily described the circumstances of the unfortunate encounter in St Margaret's, as gleaned from the accounts of several who had been present. 'And so Rachel left early, and apparently was on her way to see Colin when the accident happened. Anyone who'd been at the church that night could have followed her by car and knocked her off her bike.'

'She went early?' David picked out the relevant fact and caught Lucy's eye with a slight grimace; his *de facto*

231

case against Francis Nightingale was based entirely on the supposition that Rachel's nightly visit to her husband took place every night at a regular and verifiable time. This new piece of information seemed to make that impossible: her brother-in-law couldn't conceivably have known that she'd go early that night.

But anyone who had been at St Margaret's would have known. David pressed his fingers to his temples and admitted to himself that he'd been on the wrong track all along.

'Quite early, as a matter of fact. The service didn't take place, so she was probably an hour and a half earlier than usual,' said Emily, demonstrating that she had thought it through.

David made one last attempt to preserve his neutrality. 'But perhaps you're overreacting to what she said on the phone, in the light of what happened afterwards. It might have been just some small incident – Dolly Topping being rude to her or something else minor. Archdeacons must get curates complaining to them all the time about trivial things like that.'

'Rachel wasn't like that,' Emily defended her friend. 'She was sensible, and she was used to being badly treated. I'm sure she wouldn't have even thought of bothering Gabriel unless it was something really important.'

Lucy, who had been absorbing the unfolding story in silence, nodded her agreement. 'Emily's right. I'm sure it's relevant. It's certainly consistent with what we know about Rachel.'

'And about St Margaret's,' added Gabriel.

'What do you mean?' queried David.

'I was concerned about that church well before Rachel died. As I said, there are some rather peculiar things going on there.'

'Do you mean Dolly Topping and her opposition to women priests?' David challenged. 'It's not the only church in the diocese to have outspoken opponents of the ordination of women in the congregation. I really don't see how that can be turned into a motive for murder.'

'That's not really what I meant.' Gabriel looked thoughtful as he framed his words carefully. 'You've been involved with them – with the churchwardens and the Vicar – on this proposed selling of the silver.'

'Yes?'

'Well, you must admit that it doesn't add up. All that holy claptrap about providing housing for homeless people. Does that square with what you know about those two churchwardens? Or the Vicar either, for that matter?'

For the first time that evening, David laughed. 'Not at all,' he admitted. 'I never believed that that was their true intent – in fact, the Vicar hinted as much, the first time I met him.'

'He didn't happen to say what they were *really* up to?'

'No.' David picked up his wine glass and twirled it by the stem. 'He wasn't in on it, that much I know. It was the churchwardens who were scheming, and he was trying to out-guess them.'

'A nice little setup.' The Archdeacon gave an un-amused laugh.

Emily hopped up. 'Just a minute. The casserole will be all dried out if we don't eat it soon.' There was a pause while she cleared the plates and served the main course.

'So,' said David as they resumed eating. 'The church-wardens were playing a little game with the Vicar and the diocese, and had something to hide. But they'd given up on the plan to sell the silver, once the DAC ruled against them.'

'That doesn't mean that they didn't have something else up their sleeves,' Gabriel pointed out.

'No...'

'And then there's the Vicar, our friend Father Keble Smythe himself,' Gabriel went on. 'I don't think he's exactly as pure as the driven snow, either.' Automatically he lowered his voice. 'This isn't to go beyond these four walls, of course, but he's written me a most peculiar letter. When he came to see me a while ago, absolutely desperate to have a replacement for his curate, I told him that there was no one available but Rachel. A woman. I expected him to refuse outright, given the presence of people like Dolly in his congregation. And the fact that he likes to be known in the diocese as a Catholic, albeit a fairly moderate one.'

'But he didn't refuse?' Lucy put in.

'No, he didn't. He was desperate, of course, but he actually seemed rather keen to give it a try. Don't ask me why. I was surprised at his position – I even tried to talk him out of it. I pointed out that a parish like St Margaret's would probably not take very kindly to a woman curate, that it wouldn't be fair on her. But he insisted.'

'What about this letter?' David prompted.

'Yes. The letter. It came last week, just about the time that Rachel died. In it he said that the appointment *I'd* insisted on had been a mistake, and he wondered if anything could be done to rectify it.'

'Don't you see?' Emily interrupted her husband. 'In the first place, he must have known that nothing could be done to *un*-appoint Rachel at that point. And Gabriel *hadn't* insisted on their having her.'

'Curiouser and curiouser,' said Lucy, pushing her hair back from her face.

David added a comment in a somewhat flippant tone. 'I don't understand why he was so desperate in the first place. Didn't he know that he was going to lose his previous curate? Why hadn't he made arrangements for a replacement before the old curate left? That doesn't sound like our friend Father Keble Smythe at all!'

Gabriel looked at him as though he'd just told a joke in rather bad taste. 'That's not really very funny.'

'Why? What happened to him?' David asked idly.

'You don't know?'

'Don't know what?'

'You don't know what happened to Father Julian? Honestly?'

David was baffled at his tone. 'I'd rather supposed he'd got his own parish somewhere. Not that I'd given it all that much thought.'

'Father Julian was killed in the burglary at St Margaret's last December,' Gabriel said with appropriate gravity. 'The burglary in the sacristy. Surely you've heard about that.'

'Killed?' David stared at him for a moment, trying to absorb it. 'Good Lord.'

Lucy stopped with a forkful of food halfway to her mouth. 'You mean he was murdered?'

Gabriel shrugged. 'Accidentally. It would seem that he was unlucky enough to surprise the burglars, and had his head smashed in for his pains.'

That horrific fact, so casually delivered, made Lucy wince. 'But have they caught the people who did it? Surely the police have tracked them down somehow.'

'No, they haven't, as a matter of fact. He was under my jurisdiction, of course, so they've kept me informed. And so far they haven't managed to find anything – no prints at the scene of the crime, so they didn't really have much to go on.' He shrugged again. 'I think that after a few weeks they just gave up and shoved it into the files. A sad thing, but I'm sure it happens all the time.'

While he was speaking, David was engaged in serious re-evaluation of the situation, in the light of this second death. 'It just doesn't wash, you know,' he interjected suddenly. 'Two curates at the same church, dead within four months. Accidentally. It's statistically impossible.'

'Oscar Wilde might have said that to lose one curate could be counted as unfortunate...' said Gabriel, waiting for David to complete his thought as he had done so many times in the past.

'But to lose two is careless,' David finished. 'I think that in this case it's gone a bit beyond careless. Don't you agree?'

It was the previously undisclosed fact of Father Julian's murder – for surely it could be called nothing short of murder – that finally turned the tide in David's mind, and convinced him, in spite of his prejudice against Ruth and her intuition, that Rachel Nightingale's death could not have been an accident. Nothing else would have persuaded him to agree to Gabriel's request for his – and Lucy's – help with a discreet investigation into the circumstances of a death on which the police had closed the book, apart from a desultory search for the driver of the hit-and-run car.

Once that agreement had been obtained, they proceeded to make more detailed plans. 'It must have been someone who was at St Margaret's that night, when they had the row,' David thought aloud. 'No one else would have known that she would be going at that particular time.'

'That doesn't really narrow things down too much,' Emily pointed out. 'From what I've heard, everyone was there.'

'Except Father Keble Smythe,' Gabriel added slowly.

'Well, that lets the Vicar out, then,' David stated. 'The one person with an alibi.'

'But it leaves us with quite a few others as possibilities,' said Lucy. 'I should think that the churchwardens would have to come top of the list.'

'Martin Bairstow, yes,' David agreed. 'But not Norman Topping. He wouldn't have the bottle.'

Lucy smiled. 'Unless Dolly told him to.'

'Lady Macbeth, handing her wimpy husband the dagger,' said Emily the English scholar. 'Or Dolly might have done it herself,' she added. 'Let's not be sexist here – a woman could have done it just as easily as a man.'

By this time they had moved back to the sitting room for their coffee; Gabriel added a dollop of cream to his and stirred it thoughtfully. 'It seems to me,' he said, 'that the first thing you need to do, David, is to talk to the churchwardens. With or without the Vicar – I don't think it makes much difference, unless you think he might be able to shed any light.'

'But how can I do that?' David protested. 'I don't have a credible excuse. As far as they're concerned, my usefulness is over. I discovered that their silver was valuable, but I wasn't able to persuade the diocese to let them sell it. I can't just ring them up . . .'

'Oh, but you can,' Gabriel interrupted smoothly. 'What if you were to ring Martin Bairstow and tell him that your old friend the Archdeacon – and you made a point of our long-standing friendship, if you'll remember – has had a change of heart about the silver? That he's willing to consider recommending to the DAC that since there are two ciboria, one of them might be sold to the V & A?'

David sighed. 'Yes, I suppose that would work. I could ask them to come to my office to see me, to talk about the details.'

'It would be better to see them at the church, surely?'

'Yes, all right,' David gave in. 'I'll talk to them.'

Gabriel got up and went to the drinks tray. 'Can I offer you a drink with your coffee? Cognac, or a liqueur, Lucy?'

'I'll have a Cointreau, thanks.'

He dispensed it, then lifted a bottle of single-malt whisky. 'And is this still your favourite tipple, David?'

'Yes, thanks. How kind of you to remember.'

No one in the room, least of all Gabriel, could have been unaware of the irony in his tone, but he poured the drink and passed it to David without further comment.

Lucy put down her coffee cup with an abrupt

movement and a clatter of spoon and saucer. 'I think there's something we're overlooking,' she stated. 'You may be disinclined to believe anything that Ruth says, David darling, but don't forget what she said about Vera Bright.'

Gabriel turned towards her. 'Oh, yes. That business at the vicarage yesterday. What was that all about? Who *is* Vera Bright?'

'Vera Bright is a member of the congregation at St Margaret's,' Lucy explained. 'Ruth met her through Rachel. Yesterday at the vicarage Ruth was talking to her, and she said something that made Ruth think that she not only believed Rachel had been murdered, but that she knew who was behind it. Based on something that Rachel had said to her, apparently – though she wouldn't tell Ruth what it was, or whom she suspects.'

'Just another of Ruth's fantasies, I expect.' David waved his hand dismissively.

Gabriel, however, got up and paced across the room. 'I don't think we can afford to ignore it out of hand, David. There may be something in it. Does anyone know this Vera Bright? Besides Ruth, that is?'

Lucy nodded. 'Well, I've met her, anyway, though I don't really know her. Do you think I should have a word with her?'

'If you would,' said Gabriel. 'At least you might be able to get some feeling about whether she really knows anything, or if it's all in Ruth's mind.'

'All right. I'll go on Monday.'

'Shouldn't someone talk to the churchwardens' wives?' suggested Emily. 'To Dolly Topping, anyway?'

'I've got a good excuse to see Vanessa,' Lucy admitted.

'The painting she commissioned is just about finished, and I could deliver it to her this week. But I can't really think of any plausible way that I could talk to Dolly.'

Emily sighed. 'I suppose it's my turn to be noble. Much as I loathe the woman, I'll invite her round for a cup of tea this week, and get her talking about Rachel.'

'Will she come?' David wanted to know.

'Oh, she'll come.' Emily smiled smugly. 'In her circle, one doesn't turn down invitations from the Archdeacon's wife. If you understand me.'

'Yes, of course.' David lifted his glass and squinted through the pale straw-coloured liquid. 'I'm thinking,' he said slowly, 'that it might be a mistake to concentrate on Rachel, without considering this Father Julian as well. Perhaps the two deaths are actually connected in some way.'

Gabriel gave him a sharp look. 'What do you mean?'

'Well, maybe they both died because of something they had in common. And as far as I can tell, that's only one thing.'

'Yes?' With one raised eyebrow, Gabriel invited him to continue.

'I mean, it doesn't seem that there was much commonality there. He was a man and she was a woman. She was married, and he was...?'

'Not.' Gabriel's voice might have conveyed a trace of disapproval or even distaste.

'She was a deacon, and he was a priest. But...' David looked around at the three of them. 'They were both curates of St Jude's and St Margaret's. That's the link, and that may be important.'

'So what are you implying?'

David continued with some reluctance. 'That we won't really be doing everything we can to discover the truth about Rachel's death unless we find out something about Father Julian as well. About who he was, first of all, and then about how he died, and why. And there's only one person I can think of who could almost certainly tell us the answer to at least the first of those questions.' He paused, and forced himself to say it. 'Robin West. The sacristan at St Margaret's.'

'Ah.' Gabriel's mouth twitched in what might have been a suppressed smile; clearly he had run across him in the course of his official duties. 'I think that talking to him is just the job for you, David.'

'Can't someone else do it?' he pleaded without much hope. 'Gabriel, how about you?'

'Oh, no. That wouldn't be the done thing at all. I'm afraid it's got to be you, David.' He smirked. 'Pull up your socks and take your medicine like a man.'

'That's the whole problem,' David muttered miserably.

'Well, then.' Gabriel rubbed his hands together in a brisk manner. 'We all know what we have to do within the next week or so. I suggest that we meet again next weekend to compare notes and see where we've got. Emily, you're to chat with Dolly Topping. Lucy, you've got Vera Bright and Mrs Bairstow to talk to. And David, you need to see the churchwardens and the sacristan.'

'Wait a minute,' said David. 'What about *you*?'

'Oh, I'm the Archdeacon. It wouldn't be proper for me to get involved directly. But,' Gabriel added, 'let me know if there's anything at all that I can do to back you up. That's what I'm here for.'

Chapter 22

Let his posterity be destroyed: and in the next
generation let his name be clean put out.

                                        Psalm 109.12

Lucy rang Vera Bright on Monday morning, reminding
the older woman that she was Ruth's aunt, and asking if
it might be convenient for her to call and see her a bit
later. Vera agreed readily; any visitor was a welcome
change from her father's sole company.

'What time would be best for you?' Lucy asked,
mindful of the intrusion.

'Any time. Any time at all. It's such a nice morning that I thought I might venture out into the
garden for a bit, but I'd be happy to see you whenever you can make it. For coffee, perhaps? Around
eleven?'

'If that's not putting you out.'

'Not at all. I'll look forward to seeing you later, Miss
Kingsley. And may I say,' she added shyly, 'that I find
your niece a delightful young lady. Absolutely delightful. A credit to you and your family.'

'Oh. Thank you.' Nonplussed, Lucy put the phone
down; it was the first time since Ruth's arrival that

anyone other than Rachel had said a good word about her.

It was indeed a beautiful morning, the air mild and fresh and promising real warmth as the day progressed. So spring has come at long last, Lucy reflected as she walked the short distance to Vera's house. On a day like this she could almost believe that somehow, one day soon when Ruth had gone, things would return to normal, in spite of the trauma of Rachel's death.

She found the Brights' house without difficulty. It was in a street that was respectable rather than prestigious, but it was freshly painted and beautifully maintained on the outside. Lucy rang the bell. There was no reply, so after a few minutes she pushed it again, holding it in for a rather longer time; Vera might be in the garden, she realised, and might not have heard the bell.

After a delay, Lucy heard sounds from inside the house: heavy footsteps and a querulous old voice. 'Vera!' said an old man's scratchy grumble. 'Are you deaf, girl? Can't you hear the bell?' Then, as he got nearer, 'Hold your horses, out there. I'm coming.' The door flew open, and the old man from the post-funeral gathering peered out at Lucy. Ever-susceptible to a pretty face, Walter Bright transformed his scowl into an approximation of a smile, baring a mouth full of surprisingly sound teeth. 'Oh, it's you! I saw you at the vicarage, didn't I?'

'That's right. I'm so sorry to bother you, Dr Bright. I'm Lucy Kingsley, and Vera is expecting me.'

'Well, you'd better come in then, hadn't you?' The old

man stepped aside to let her in. 'I don't know where the damnfool girl has got to, though.'

'She said that she was going to do some gardening,' Lucy suggested. 'Perhaps she's out in the back and didn't hear the bell.'

'I was taking my nap. I always have a nap in the mornings, and then Vera brings me my coffee.'

'I'm so sorry to have disturbed your nap,' Lucy apologised again.

The old man grinned. 'I don't mind being disturbed by someone as pretty as you.' Walter Bright's eyes dropped to Lucy's chest and seemed fixated there. Embarrassed, Lucy spared a moment of empathetic pity for generations of his women patients. She was not to know that during his many years of practice, Dr Bright had been the model of rectitude and upright behaviour; it was only in his dotage that he had begun to ogle young women, to his daughter's immense mortification.

'Should we look for her in the garden?' Lucy suggested.

'I'll go. You stay here.' He tore his eyes away from her chest and shuffled off towards the back of the house.

His shriek, a moment later, was unearthly in quality, a banshee's wail that struck Lucy to the bone with intuitive terror. Without any volition or conscious thought she followed the sound, and found herself standing next to the old man in the kitchen. Out of some primitive instinct of self-preservation, her eyes looked everywhere but in the direction of the old man's trembling finger. In some corner of her brain she took in the cheery sprigged wallpaper, the angle of the sun streaming through the window on to the counter, the serviceable brown coffee mugs – three in number – set on a tray near the old-fashioned metallic electric kettle along with a plate of biscuits, the two identical brown mugs on the draining board, the muddy-fingered gardening gloves thrown carelessly on the table, the open door into the garden. Then she could avoid it no longer; her eyes followed his finger.

It was a strangely peaceful sight, with no blood and no signs of violence, but it was all the more horrible for that. Vera Bright was sitting in a chair, slumped over the table. One thin arm was flung across the table, palm up, in a beseeching gesture. And over her head was a green plastic bag with an unmistakeable gold logo, tied around her neck with a piece of garden twine.

Somehow Lucy managed to do the right things. She removed the old man from the kitchen, rang the police, told them the facts in a concise manner, then calmed Dr Bright down with a mug of strong, sweet tea, being careful while making it not to touch anything that might be important.

Ensconced in his customary armchair in the sitting room with his tea, the old man talked incessantly and seemingly at random as they waited for the police to arrive. 'It's the bag I don't understand,' he said over and over. 'My Vera didn't give herself airs. She never set foot in a shop like that in her life. She wasn't that kind of girl. But who would have done such a thing? To my Vera? She may have been useless, that girl, but she

246

never hurt a fly. Who would want to harm her?' He wrapped his arms around himself and rocked back and forth. 'And what am I going to do without her? I'm not going into some home, where they'll tie me down and leave me to die. I don't understand about the bag. Why would anyone want to hurt Vera?' He repeated it over and over, in various permutations, like some kind of litany of misery. Lucy let him talk, realising that he wasn't really asking for answers.

The police arrived, a uniformed PC first and then a number of plainclothes officers and the police doctor. Lucy could hear them in the kitchen, going about their choreographed routine, but she blocked out any conscious speculation about what they were doing. For some little while they left her alone with the old man, who continued to ramble in the same vein. After a time, though, a neatly-dressed man with kind dark eyes and a large square jaw joined them in the sitting room and introduced himself. 'I'm Inspector Shepherd.' He looked at Lucy expectantly.

In a few words she told him who she was and why she was there, then indicated Dr Bright. 'This is Miss Bright's father. I'm afraid he's a bit incoherent at the moment – as you can imagine, Inspector, this has been a great shock for him.'

The policeman leaned over and addressed the old man. 'I'm very sorry about your daughter, sir.'

'Oh, my poor Vera. She was a good girl. Careful with her money. Not like some of these young things who go off shopping all the time. She never was like that, my Vera. Never been inside that shop in her life. And why should she be?' The last was said on a belligerent note.

'No reason at all, sir,' said the policeman soothingly; he was used to dealing with people in shock, and the irrelevant things they often said. He turned back to Lucy. 'He found her, did he?'

She nodded. 'But I was right behind him. I'm sure he didn't touch anything. And I tried not to disturb anything either, though I didn't think it would hurt if I made a pot of tea. I thought he could use it.'

'No problem. We'll need to take your fingerprints, of course. And his as well, just for purposes of elimination.' He took out his notebook. 'Do you mind if I ask you a few questions, Miss Kingsley?'

'Not at all.'

'Did anything in the kitchen look out of place, or unusual?'

Regretfully she shook her head. 'I'm afraid I can't really help you. This is the first time I've been here, so I wouldn't know.'

'So you also wouldn't know if anything in the house were missing?'

'No. Sorry. You'll have to ask Dr Bright.'

The policeman looked at the old man without much hope. 'Sir,' he said, 'it looks like your daughter might have surprised a burglar. At some point, when you're feeling like it, I'd like you to have a look round and tell me if anything is missing. Silver, jewellery, appliances like video recorders or tellies.'

Walter Bright gestured scornfully at the box across from him. 'There's the television. Still there. No modern do-dads like video recorders in this house. And none of that other rot – I told you, my Vera was a simple girl.' He fixed the policeman with a belligerent glare. 'Don't you dare say otherwise. She might have been useless, but at least she was no spendthrift.'

Hastily Inspector Shepherd turned back to Lucy. 'You'll be wanting to get on, I expect. I don't think there's anything else we need from you at the moment. If you'll just let me know how we can get in touch with you, if necessary...'

'Dr Bright shouldn't be left alone,' she protested. 'He's very upset.'

'Don't worry about him – I'll get a WPC to sit with him,' the policeman assured her.

'Yes, just go off and leave me. Just like my Vera,' moaned the old man. 'How could she desert me like this? All alone. I'm all alone.'

Suddenly the horror of the situation – and the reality of it – descended on Lucy like a black curtain; she put her hands over her face and sobbed. 'I'm sorry. I know I shouldn't be like this. But it's just so ... awful. Poor Vera.'

The policeman, who had seen far too many scenes like this, let her cry for a moment. 'Do you have a car, Miss Kingsley, or can we take you somewhere? I know that this has been upsetting for you.'

After a time Lucy regained control and lifted her chin. 'I'll be all right. If I could just use the phone and ring someone to collect me ...?'

'Yes, of course.'

Fortunately the phone was in the hall rather than in the kitchen. It was the old-fashioned sort with a dial; somehow she forced her fingers to push the dial around.

'Fosdyke, Fosdyke and Galloway,' announced a solemn female voice. 'May I help you?'

Lucy's voice sounded remarkably calm. 'Mr Middleton-Brown, please.'

'I'm sorry, but Mr Middleton-Brown is not in his office. Would you like to speak to his secretary, or can someone else help you?'

She took a deep breath as she felt the panic rising again. 'No, thank you. But if you could tell him that Lucy rang...'

The receptionist did not feel that conveying personal messages was part of her job. 'Very well,' she said repressively. 'I'll tell him.'

Putting the phone down, Lucy leaned her head against the wall and thought about what to do next. Emily, she decided gratefully. Emily would come for her. She dialled again.

'I'll be there in a few minutes,' Emily promised, when she'd had a brief outline of what had happened. 'Just hang on, Luce.'

'Thanks, Em.'

Before she left, Lucy had her fingerprints taken, efficiently and without fuss, then returned to the sitting room to say goodbye to the old man. She took his hand and leaned over him. 'I'm going soon, Dr Bright. But I'm sure they'll take good care of you.'

He raised his eyes, glanced over at the placid form of the WPC on the sofa, then beckoned Lucy closer. She bent down, and he cupped his hand over her ear to whisper, 'Those damned police don't believe me. They think I'm daft. But I know it was no burglar that killed my Vera. She would never go to that shop. And what about those two cups on the draining board? How do they explain those, hey?' For an instant the belligerence left him and his eyes were those of a vulnerable, pleading old man. 'Please,' he said softly. 'You're a good girl. Please find out who killed my Vera. Don't let them get away with it.'

Chapter 23

Their priests were slain with the sword: and there were no widows to make lamentation.

Psalm 78.65

Monday morning seemed to go very slowly for David. Ruth was being more than usually stroppy with him, causing him to reflect that five days was after all a very long time – time enough for God to create a fair chunk of the world. And hanging over the sunny morning like a black cloud was the prospect of his visit to Robin West. Having made up his mind of the necessity to interview the sacristan, he had determined to do it straightaway – that very lunchtime, in fact. It would be less suspicious – and undoubtedly safer – to meet him at his restaurant, as if by accident, and to have an informal chat. After all, he *had* been invited to stop by for a drink. He was sure that West would take his visit at face value, and that with the sacristan's penchant for gossip, there would be no difficulty in getting him to talk.

First, though, he wanted to ring Martin Bairstow. The younger churchwarden, ruthless in his business dealings and temperamentally suited to eliminating his opponents, seemed to David to be the most logical suspect, though a clear-cut motive eluded him. Perhaps it was as Gabriel had suggested, and Rachel had found out what the wardens had hoped to accomplish by the sale of the church's silver. Was there any way that the two of them could collude to skim off some of the money? But Bairstow didn't seem in any need of money, so there must be something else in the equation that David didn't know about.

Consulting his files for the number, he rang Bairstow's office. 'I'm sorry,' said his secretary, 'but Mr Bairstow isn't in at the moment. I expect him back at any time – can I have him return your call?'

'It's not urgent,' David said, but he gave his name and number to the secretary, and towards the end of the morning Mrs Simmons put through a call from the churchwarden.

'How can I help you, Mr Middleton-Brown?' Bairstow sounded slightly more brusque than usual.

David adopted an apologetic tone. 'I don't know how you feel about this,' he said, 'but if you're still interested in selling some of your silver, the Archdeacon has indicated to me that he would support the sale of one of the ciboria to the V & A. A privately negotiated sale, to keep it in the national collection. I realise that's far short of what you originally had in mind, but it would still bring in a tidy sum. Fifteen or twenty thousand, at a guess.'

There was a pause on the other end. 'I'll have to think about it,' was the eventual cautious reply. 'And speak to Norman Topping and Father Keble Smythe, of course. Can I get back to you in a few days?'

'I thought that perhaps we might meet to discuss

it. At St Margaret's, if that's more convenient for you.'

Bairstow, who had seen his share of inflated solicitors' bills, wasn't so easily convinced. 'I'll get back to you as soon as I can,' he repeated. 'By the end of the week, if possible.'

David had to be satisfied with that. 'Very well, Mr Bairstow. I'll look forward to hearing from you.'

He looked at his watch; it was getting on for lunchtime. Realising that there was at least one advantage to his visit to *La Reine Dorée*, he went out to Mrs Simmons's desk to ask her if she'd mind very much taking Ruth to lunch with her, as he had an urgent lunchtime meeting.

Having been subjected to Ruth for the last fortnight, Mrs Simmons inevitably *did* mind very much, but she couldn't very well say so. 'No problem at all, Mr Middleton-Brown,' she replied bravely.

Good woman, he said to himself, resolving to pick up some flowers for her on his way back from lunch.

La Reine Dorée was located in South Kensington, not far from the tube station but in the opposite direction from Lucy's house. It was much as David had expected it to be: rather dimly lit, its walls adorned with a mixture of old French cigarette posters and framed black-and-white glossy photos of 1930s' screen goddesses, and patronised by a glittering array of decorative young people exemplifying various permutations of sexual preference but with a predominance of men.

Robin West, who was leaning in a cultivatedly

insouciant pose near the door, stood to attention when he spotted David's entrance. 'My dear chap!' he beamed, putting out both hands. 'So you've finally come! I knew that you wouldn't be able to stay away for ever.' He gave David an exaggerated wink. 'Where's the girlfriend?'

'Oh, she ... couldn't come today,' David said lamely.

West turned down the corners of his mouth. '*Quel dommage!*'

Overcoming his distaste, David forced a smile. 'Yes, well. How about that drink you promised me?'

'Absolutely, my dear. What will you have?'

For a split second David considered whether he would be better off staying sober and keeping his wits about him, or blotting out the pain of this ordeal with as much alcohol as possible. Prudence prevailed, and he chose the first option. 'Just mineral water, thanks. With ice and lemon.'

'How *boring*. Wouldn't you rather have a G & T? Or even champagne? It's on the house, remember?'

It was tempting, but not tempting enough. 'Sorry, no. I've got to go back to work this afternoon,' David explained, adding, 'I'll have to come back another time for the champagne.'

'Promise that you'll leave the girlfriend behind again and it's a deal,' West smirked, going behind the bar for the mineral water. He poured it out with a flourish, added an artistic twist of lemon, then concocted a gin and tonic for himself, before leading the way to a corner table. 'Are you having some lunch?' he asked.

'I thought I might.'

West went off for a moment and returned with a

menu. 'The breast of *poussin* in cream and Kirsch sauce is quite nice,' he advised. 'Or if that's too rich for you, I recommend the warm salad with *goujons* of duck and rocket in balsamic vinaigrette.'

David studied the menu. 'Actually, I fancy the steak sandwich,' he said firmly. And he wouldn't tell Lucy about it afterwards, either; although he of course ate no meat at home, her attempts to woo him into committed vegetarianism had thus far failed, but he didn't go out of his way to confess to her his occasional and enjoyable lapses into meat eating. 'And some chips, if you do anything so plebeian,' he added in a defiant tone.

West looked shocked, but refrained from voicing his disillusionment with David's taste. 'If that's what you want, then that's what you shall have.' He flagged down a waiter and gave the order, choosing the *poussin* for himself, then settled back and grinned at David. 'I suppose you've heard about all the excitement at St Margaret's,' he said with relish.

'You mean about your curate's death?'

'That woman, yes. I never acknowledged her as the curate, as you know. Her orders were invalid.'

'You're not one of the people who's praising her to the heavens now that she's dead?'

West snorted in derision. 'Not I. I didn't want her at St Margaret's, and I'm not sorry that she's gone, though I might have settled for a less drastic method of removal. I wasn't alone in either of those sentiments, as I'm sure you're aware, but you'd never know it from the way people are talking now. Even Dolly Topping. That particular brand of hypocrisy doesn't appeal to me, my dear. No, I'm not ashamed to admit that I'm glad she's gone.'

'Still, it must have come as rather a shock, so soon after Father Julian's death,' David ventured.

'Father Julian.' Robin West sighed gustily and shook his head. 'Now that was a great loss to the church. Not just to St Margaret's, but to the Holy Catholic Church. He was a true Catholic. With a brilliant feel for liturgy, as well.'

'Did you know him well, then?'

'Oh, quite well. He used to come in here often in the evenings with Alistair. I'd usually have a drink with them if we weren't too busy.'

'Alistair?'

'He always called Alistair his "lodger", of course.' West gave him a knowing wink.

'You're telling me that this Alistair was Father Julian's ... lover?'

'Of course. What else? You know and I know that it goes on all over this diocese. I think that there are more priests with "lodgers" than without, my dear. But our blessed Archdeacon takes a dim view of such things,' West said cuttingly. 'A good family man, our Archdeacon. So it has to be "lodgers" and "friends".'

Gabriel? thought David in astonishment. That was rich. To cover his confusion, he asked quickly, 'This Alistair chap. He lived with Father Julian in ... what's it called? Magdalen House?'

'That's right. They'd been together for quite a while – he came to London with Julian.' If Robin West thought David's questions were odd, he gave no indication.

Obviously David had not misjudged his voracious appetite for gossip.

'And where is he now? I mean, surely he had to move out of the house? Does he still come in here?'

Robin West shook his head. 'He's left London, I'm afraid. Gone to Brighton. Gone off with one of my other regular customers, as a matter of fact. Father Gilbert, who was at St Benedict's, Earl's Court – he's just moved to a church in Brighton. St Dunstan's – do you know it?'

'Yes,' said David. 'Yes, I do.'

'It's supposed to be a real spike shop,' West declared with a certain amount of envy. 'No nonsense about women in a place like that.'

Suddenly David knew that he had to go to Brighton, to talk to this Alistair. He needed to find out as much as he could about Father Julian, and Alistair was the obvious person to talk to. 'But St Dunstan's has a clergy house,' he thought aloud. 'Father Gilbert can't have a lodger there.'

'Why not, dear?' West waved a careless hand and giggled. 'He's turfed the curate out, I hear. But the curate didn't mind. Now he can go into digs with his boyfriend.'

The food arrived, and David ate his sandwich with enjoyment. The sacristan chattered on through the meal, mainly about Father Keble Smythe and the ludicrous charade of his fiancée Miss Morag McKenzie, but David was no longer interested in the gossip. He had found out about the existence and the whereabouts of Alistair; that was enough.

Refusing a sweet, he made his escape with as much

speed as was possible – with promises to return in the near future for that champagne. There was still time to get to Brighton that afternoon, if he hurried. He stopped at a call box and rang Lucy's house to let her know his plans, but there was no reply; knowing that she'd planned to visit Vera Bright that day, he wasn't unduly worried at her absence. He could ring her again later, he decided, hurrying to the tube station to catch the Circle Line to Blackfriars, where he transferred to the Thameslink train to Brighton.

It was a relatively quick journey; David arrived in Brighton by mid-afternoon. From the station he made another unsuccessful attempt to reach Lucy, then hailed a taxi; 'St Dunstan's clergy house,' he instructed. In the taxi he reflected upon the possible folly of his precipitate journey: there was no guarantee that this Alistair would be there. In fact, given that it was a Monday afternoon, the chances were good that Alistair would be elsewhere, most likely at his place of employment.

This line of thought, distressing as it was, kept him from brooding on the irony of returning to St Dunstan's clergy house in these circumstances. He hadn't been back there since Gabriel's days as curate of St Dunstan's, years ago. It was inevitable that there should be memories associated with the place, even now. Not that he had ever lived there with Gabe – there had never been any question of that. They had always been painstakingly discreet about their relationship. And in those long-ago days, neither curates nor incumbents seemed to flaunt their 'lodgers' more or less openly, as they clearly did now.

Arriving at the clergy house, he paid the cab driver, then took a deep breath, went to the door, and rang the bell.

In the old days, it would have been the dragon of a housekeeper who answered the door. Now it was a thin young man in his late twenties, casually dressed, with fine straight sandy hair which hung nearly to his shoulders and grazed his eyebrows in a sideswept fringe. 'Hello?' he said questioningly, his open face displaying no suspicion.

'Are you by any chance called Alistair?'

'That's right. Alistair Duncan.' His voice had a heavy but pleasing Scots burr.

David produced the story he'd decided upon during his train journey – one that was very nearly the truth. 'My name is David Middleton-Brown. I'm a solicitor, acting for St Margaret's Church in London. I understand that you ... knew ... Father Julian, their former curate, and I wondered if you'd mind my asking you a few questions.'

A guarded, tense expression clamped down on his face. 'Have they caught the bastards that killed him yet?'

'No,' said David seriously. 'That's why I'm here, really. There are several people who are interested in finding out the truth about what happened to Father Julian, and they don't think that the police are doing enough. They've asked me to come along and see you – if you're prepared to talk to me, of course. You might be able to tell us something important, something that we don't know, that will help us find the killer.'

The young man relaxed, shrugged, and smiled an attractive lopsided smile. 'Why not?' He waved his arm. 'Come on in, why don't you?'

They went into the drawing room. Amazingly, it had altered hardly at all in the years since David had last been there; the ancient and massive furniture was a bit more frayed around the edges, and the oriental carpet was rather more threadbare. But the gloomy wallpaper, of indeterminate pattern and colour, was the same, with its even darker rectangles hinting at long-departed pictures that once must have occupied the walls. Those walls sported the same dreary engravings that David remembered: ugly continental churches, and the odd simpering saint. He couldn't understand why someone hadn't got rid of them years ago.

The drawing room was definitely dustier than it had been in the regime of the dragon-housekeeper (whatever had her name been?), the windows admitted the light through a film of grime, and the vast fireplace showed signs of a recent fire. *She* would never have allowed such a thing, he was sure, not even in the dead of winter – let alone on the cusp of spring.

'Could I get you a cup of tea?' Alistair offered hospitably.

That sounded wonderful, but David made the polite response. 'I don't want to put you to any trouble.'

'No trouble. I was about to have one myself.'

'Then I'd love a cup.'

Tea was produced in short order, and properly: on a tray with a cloth, poured from a silver teapot into bone china cups, and served with thin triangles of bread and butter. David, having expected somehow to be presented with a mug of tea, was glad to see that standards at the clergy house had not entirely slipped. 'How nice,' he said.

The young man grinned engagingly. 'It's the one thing I've been well trained to do. Jules wasn't particularly bothered, but Gil likes his tea done properly.' He waved his hand around at the room. 'I may not be much of a housekeeper, but at least I can serve up a proper tea.'

'You're the housekeeper, then?'

'In a manner of speaking.' He grinned again. 'As you can see.'

David found himself liking this open and honest young man very much. 'That doesn't seem like a very exciting career,' he remarked, smiling.

'It's all I've got at the moment,' Alistair explained. 'Since I came to Brighton, I haven't been very successful in finding work in my own profession.'

'Which is . . . ?'

'I'm a hairdresser. And if you know anything at all about Brighton, you'll realise that hairdressers are quite thick on the ground here.'

David laughed: yes, they would be.

'So until something comes up, Gil has said I can be his housekeeper. The patience of a saint, that man has, to put up with me and my slovenly ways.'

'You weren't Father Julian's housekeeper, then?'

'Oh, Lord, no.' Alistair laughed at the idea. 'Jules had a woman who came in twice a week. He was a bit fussier than Gil. And I was just the lodger. In a manner of speaking.'

David leaned forward. 'I hope you don't mind talking about Father Julian. After all, it must be rather painful for you.'

The young man looked out of the window and brushed the fringe from his forehead absently. 'A wee bit,' he confessed. 'Jules and I were together for a long time, you know. He was my first real love, and that's always special.'

'Yes,' said David.

'And of course I never had any official status in his life, which made it more difficult. His lodger, that's all I was.' His voice had become bitter.

'You weren't a member of the congregation, then?'

'Me? You've got to be joking! I have no use for the bloody Church of England.' His face was as congested with pain as his voice. 'A church that put up so many barriers between me and the man I loved, that forced us to live a lie just so a load of old biddies wouldn't have their delicate sensibilities offended! It's mad – a church that would rather turn a blind eye to its priests cottaging in public loos than encourage them to form stable, loving relationships like the one that Jules and I had.' He shook his head. 'Most of the people in Jules's churches didn't know that I existed. And it had to be that way. Not because I wanted it to be a secret, but because of their own bloody hypocrisy.'

David was stunned; he framed his next question carefully. 'If you feel so strongly about the Church, then why have you become involved with another priest?' And so soon, was the unspoken corollary.

Alistair pressed his lips together, then twisted them into a semblance of a smile. 'It must seem hardhearted to you, and even calculating. After what I've told you about what Jules and I meant to each other. That I could take up with Gil so quickly, I mean. But I didn't really have much choice.' He ran his long fingers through his fringe. 'I don't know why I'm telling you all this,' he confessed, 'but somehow it seems like you understand. And I haven't really had anyone to talk to about Jules. Gil doesn't like it when I go on about him all the time.'

'What did you mean, that you didn't have much choice?'

The young man shrugged, and answered baldly. 'I had to move out of Magdalen House after Jules died, didn't I? I was having trouble finding new digs that I could afford. Gil had been offered this new post here in Brighton. He'd always fancied me, even when I was with Jules, so he said I could come along and be his housekeeper.' He shrugged again, looking down into his tea cup. 'It's not so bad. Gil's all right. We rub along well together. But it's not like it was with Jules...'

'Why don't you tell me about Jules, if you feel that you can,' David suggested gently.

Alistair's voice changed as he talked about him. 'Oh, Jules was special, he was. Ask anyone at that bloody church and they'll tell you the same. A caring man – he got involved with people. He really cared about them, and their problems. And he was good at his job. Conscientious. All that bloody paperwork that some priests can't be bothered with – he did all that, too. It seemed like he spent half his time doing things that that useless bugger of a vicar didn't want to deal with.'

'Father Keble Smythe?' asked David, smiling at the description.

'Him.' His dismissively scornful tone indicated what he thought of the Vicar of St Jude's and St Margaret's. 'Jules wouldn't hear a word against him, but I thought he was a waste of space. And I know a few things about him, through the Scottish grapevine, that I don't think he'd want his precious congregation to know. They think he's some bloody saint or something.'

'Did Father Julian get on with the churchwardens?' David probed, mindful of his mission.

'Oh, aye. Jules got on with everyone. There wasn't a soul who didn't like Jules.' A small smile twitched at the corner of his mouth. 'And I know what you're thinking – that I'm just saying that because I loved him. But it's true. Jules was a grand lad, with a heart as big as a house. Or a church. He loved all those people, just like they loved him.'

And one of them had killed him. The thought popped unbidden into David's head, but as he articulated it to himself he knew that it was true. One of them had killed him, and made it look like a bungled burglary. The same person who had cut Rachel Nightingale's life short. What dangerous knowledge had the two curates of St Margaret's shared? Knowledge so deadly that it had cost both of those loving and gentle people their lives...

'Do you by any chance have a photo of Father Julian that you could show me?' requested David.

'Oh, aye. I have to keep them well hidden from Gil, you understand.' The young man left the room for a minute or two, after providing David with a fresh cup of tea; he returned bearing a heavy photograph album. 'This goes back a long time,' he explained, sitting next to David on the sofa. He opened it to the first page and pointed. 'Here's Jules. Years ago, when we first met.' A fresh-faced, happy young man, little more than a youth, grinned at the camera. He had straight dark hair, worn rather long, and honest blue eyes. 'And here I am.' A younger version of Alistair, with the same lopsided smile, inhabited the next photo, equally young and equally happy as his friend.

Alistair flipped through the pages of the album, lingering over some pages with nostalgic melancholy, providing occasional explanations or commentary for David when it seemed called for. Most of the photos were of the two young men, separately as they turned the camera on each other, formally posed or candid, and sometimes together when they found a third party to press the shutter. Some of the most hilarious were, Alistair explained, experiments with the camera's self-timer: the two young men together in absurd and antic poses, with various humorous props. 'Oh, we did have a grand time,' he said, and David could believe it.

As the pages progressed, the young men matured. Julian's face lost some of its fresh innocence, but none of its gentle good humour. Premature threads of grey emerged in his dark hair even before the dog collar appeared. Eventually the grey replaced the dark in almost equal measure, adding a certain air of gravitas that was not at all unattractive.

Then, suddenly, they were at the last page, or at least the last page with pictures on it; a number of blank sheets followed, poignant testimony to holidays never to be taken and occasions never to be shared. 'Last summer, on our holiday in Scotland,' Alistair said, his voice bleak. 'There may be a few more in the camera, as a matter of fact. I haven't used it since ... since Jules died.' No antic snapshot sessions with Father Gilbert, then, David thought. He was moved: Julian Piper looked like a man who would have been worth knowing.

'Your Jules looks like a lovely man,' he offered inadequately, but it was enough.

'I have some other things I could show you, if you were interested,' Alistair suggested in a tentative way.

David turned to him with eagerness. 'Yes, of course. I'd like to see anything you've got.'

'Actually, I've got all of his things. Most, anyway. His family took a few things, but the house had to be cleared, so I took what was left.'

'And you have it? Here?' He tried to control his excitement.

'In a chest in the loft.' Father Gilbert again. 'Most of it wouldn't mean much to anyone but me, but there are a few bits you might find of interest.'

He disappeared for a few more minutes, returning with an armload of scrapbooks and other ephemera of a life, left behind like a butterfly's discarded cocoon. Perched on top was an item of even less use than most in the next life, but one upon which David's attention was immediately fixed. 'Can I see that?' he asked eagerly.

'Oh, aye. I thought you might like to look at his diary.' Alistair put down his burden and handed David the diary, the date of the previous year stamped in gold on the cover.

As David took it, the clock chimed six. 'Good Lord, is that really the time?' he said with a start.

'I'm afraid so. Gil will be back from saying Evensong soon, so we don't have long to look at Jules's bits and pieces. Would you like to join us for supper?' he added diffidently but sincerely. 'It won't be much, but you're welcome to stay.'

'Thanks, but I really can't.' David checked his watch in disbelief. 'Listen, would you mind awfully if I used your phone to make an important call? It's to London, I'm afraid. But my girlfriend doesn't know where I am.' It was amazing how easily the word tripped from his tongue once he was used to it.

'No problem.' Alistair grinned. 'Talk as long as you like. The diocese pays the phone bill.' He led David to the phone in the hall, then withdrew discreetly.

Whatever would Lucy be thinking? David worried as he dialled the number. She would be expecting him home by now. He prepared his apologies as it started to ring. The phone was picked up on the third ring, but it wasn't Lucy's voice which answered.

'Hello?' said Ruth.

Ruth. Good Lord, thought David, stricken. He'd forgotten all about the *enfant terrible*. 'Oh, hello,' he said casually, deciding to bluff it out. 'Can I have a word with Lucy?'

'She's not here.' Ruth's voice was outraged. 'And I don't know where she is, either. What's going on around here? What's happened to everybody? First you go off and leave me without a word, and then Aunt Lucy disappears. It's just a good thing that I've got a key to this place. My parents aren't going

269

to be very impressed when I tell them how you've neglected me. I waited for you,' she added accusingly. 'I waited until half-past five at the office, and then I had to come back here by myself. Anything could have happened to me. I could have been mugged on the Underground, or even murdered, and you wouldn't have cared.'

No, I *wouldn't* have cared, he thought savagely. All he cared about at the moment was Lucy. Where the hell was she?

'And the cat is starving as well,' she went on in an excess of gratuitous malice. 'I'm sure that the RSPCA would like to hear about that.'

'Just stay there,' he told her with as much civility as he could muster, which wasn't a great deal. 'Fix yourself something to eat. I'll be home eventually.'

He took a deep breath and tried to apply logic to the situation. Who would know where Lucy was? Emily, he apprehended in a flash of inspiration. If anyone knew where Lucy was, it would be Emily.

Of course he didn't have the number. But that was one advantage to being in a clergy house: on the desk in the hall, sticking out from under the Brighton phone directory, was a copy of the Church of England Yearbook. He pulled it out, opened it to the section on the London diocese, and found the number for the Archdeacon of Kensington.

Emily answered the phone on the second ring. 'David, thank God,' she said in a heartfelt voice when he'd identified himself.

His heart rose to his throat. 'Lucy?' he choked.

'Oh, she'll be all right. But we've been trying to reach

you all afternoon. Something terrible has happened. I won't go into it on the phone – I'll tell you all about it when you get here. But hurry, David. Lucy needs you.'

Chapter 24

*Why art thou so heavy, O my soul: and why art thou
   so disquieted within me?*

                                              Psalm 43.5

The trip between Brighton and London had never
seemed longer, as David's fevered imagination ran riot
over all the lurid possibilities. Lucy injured, or ill.
Perhaps she'd been attacked by someone who knew that
she was getting close to the truth about Rachel's death.
That possibility couldn't be underestimated, he realised:
after all, two people had already died to protect
whatever secret someone was hiding. Emily had said
that it was something terrible. Oh God, what could it
be?

   He didn't have much recollection of getting from the
clergy house to the station, or indeed of anything after
the phone call, but after a time he became aware, sitting
on the train, that Father Julian Piper's diary was still
clutched in his hand. Either Alistair had given him
permission to take it, or hadn't realised that he still had
it – David couldn't remember which.

   To take his mind off his painful but ultimately
fruitless speculations, he opened the diary and flipped

through it. It was the sort with a week to a page, so there was little space for detailed annotation. Father Julian, with the busy life that he had obviously led, had developed a kind of shorthand to squeeze as much information as possible into each daily square. David applied his brain to cracking the code.

Some of it was easy. A single 'M' quite clearly stood for Mass, as there was one noted for each day, with a time and either 'SJ' or 'SM': St Jude's and St Margaret's, and far more of the latter than the former. A single 'S', usually on a Sunday, most likely indicated a sermon. On Saturdays there often appeared a 'W' – weddings, thought David. And there were 'F's as well, sprinkled throughout. Funerals, both at SJ and SM. Other double letters were probably initials, indicating people with whom he was meeting for pastoral counselling or various other reasons.

Interested in spite of himself, David turned through the months to December. What had Father Julian been doing around the time of his death? He tried to remember the exact day that the priest had died, deciding that perhaps Gabriel hadn't told him more than that it had been at the beginning of December.

Advent, the start of the Church's year. The season of penitence as much as of anticipation. 'Lo, he comes with clouds descending', but also 'deeply wailing', and 'That day of wrath, that dreadful day'. In the diary, the usual daily 'M', an 'AP' on the first Sunday – Advent Procession, translated David – and a 'W' on the following Saturday. Unusual to have a wedding during Advent, since flowers were not normally allowed in the church, but it wasn't unknown.

Then his attention was truly caught by a notation on the Friday of that week. 'VB, 2', it said, and right under it, 'NT, 4'. 'Vera Bright,' he said aloud, drawing a dubious look from the woman across from him. Father Julian had seen Vera Bright right around the time he had been killed, as Rachel Nightingale had done just before her death. And then, seemingly, he had seen Norman Topping on the same day, before Solemn Evensong.

If he hadn't been so worried about Lucy, he would have been jubilant. He wondered, though, if Lucy had managed to talk to Vera Bright, and if so what she had found out. This was convincing evidence, if such had been necessary, that Vera Bright might well hold the key to the two curates' deaths. Galling as it was to admit it, Ruth might have been right in her belief that Vera knew who had killed Rachel. And Father Julian, David added to himself, tucking the diary into his pocket for safekeeping.

Emily met him at the door. 'She's all right, really she is,' she assured him. 'Just a bit shaken up. But she was in no fit state to be on her own, so I brought her here.'

'But what happened? Has she been hurt? You said something terrible ...'

'Nothing like that. Vera Bright is dead, and Lucy found her body,' Emily told him bluntly.

David experienced a jumble of conflicting emotions: relief that Lucy wasn't hurt, dismay about Vera Bright, and a great sense of powerlessness and frustration. 'Dead?!'

'Murdered.'

'Oh, God. Where's Lucy?'

'In the drawing room.'

With two strides he was at the door to the room. In the back of his mind David registered the fact that Gabriel was there, and somehow Ruth had appeared as well – presumably Lucy had remembered her and someone had fetched her. But Lucy was the only one he saw. She rose from the sofa as he appeared at the door, her eyes huge in a white face. 'David,' she said as he crossed the room to her and crushed her against his chest.

'Oh, my love,' he murmured with great tenderness. 'Lucy, my poor love.' He didn't care what Gabriel thought; he didn't care what Ruth thought. Lucy was all that mattered.

'Vera's dead.'

'Emily said.'

'Oh, David. It was so horrible. I can't tell you how awful it was.' Her body trembled in a convulsive spasm as she remembered the scene vividly once again in every dreadful detail.

He held her tighter. 'Oh, love. Don't think about it.'

'How can I forget it?' Lucy raised her eyes to his face. 'I'll *never* forget it.'

Emily had held the meal until David's arrival, so after a while, the twins tucked into bed, they adjourned to the dining room for a simple, subdued meal.

It was inevitable that there should be one primary topic of conversation: Vera Bright's murder, and the light that it cast on the previous deaths.

There was no question this time of excluding Ruth. She was very much a part of the discussion; in fact, wallowing in guilt, she very nearly stole the limelight from Lucy.

She'd been very quiet for a few minutes before her initial outburst. 'It's all my fault,' she wailed suddenly. 'I practically killed her myself!'

'Don't be ridiculous,' David snapped, being in no mood for her histrionics.

'But don't you see? She'd still be alive now if I hadn't said what I did after the funeral!'

'What do you mean?' Gabriel asked slowly.

'You were there – you heard me. I told Aunt Lucy that Miss Bright knew who killed Rachel.'

Lucy nodded. 'I'm afraid that nearly everyone heard you.'

'That's just the point! I was so excited that I didn't realise how loud my voice was, and everyone heard me. Including the murderer, and then he knew that he had to kill her, too. To stop her telling anyone what she knew.'

There was an appalled silence around the table, as everyone acknowledged the probable truth of her reasoning.

'How could I have been so stupid?' Ruth said shrilly. 'I should have known that the murderer would have been there, and would have heard what I said. But I thought it was Dolly Topping, and she wasn't in the dining room.'

'Her husband was,' Emily pointed out. 'He could have told her quite easily, or so could a number of other people. As you said, you didn't exactly lower your voice.'

'Oh, I'll never forgive myself. Poor Miss Bright – she didn't deserve to die. She didn't deserve what I did to her.'

David looked across the table and saw Lucy's expression of distress. 'Stop it!' he said sharply to Ruth. 'Can't you see that you're upsetting your aunt?'

Ruth wasn't about to let up. 'At least now everyone will believe that Rachel was murdered,' she stated. 'I mean, Miss Bright's death wasn't exactly an accident, and no one could say that it was. Now maybe the police will start looking for the murderer.'

Lucy shook her head suddenly. 'No,' she said. 'The police think that Vera Bright was killed by a burglar who'd broken into her house. That's all they'll be looking for – a burglar like the one who supposedly killed Father Julian.'

'Father Julian?' Ruth hadn't yet heard about the previous curate. Between them, they explained.

The girl was incensed. 'You mean that *three* people have been murdered, and the police still aren't doing anything?'

'That's about the extent of it,' said Emily.

David stood up. 'I'm going to ring my contact on the police,' he announced. 'I want to see what they have to say about what happened today. Surely they *can't* think that it was a burglar.'

He returned a few minutes later. 'You were right,' he told Lucy. 'Her father, the old doctor, insists that it couldn't have been a burglar, but they've dismissed him as a senile old man. The way they reckon it, the burglar came through the back door into the kitchen. Either she was there when he came in, or else she came in from the garden a few minutes later and caught him red-handed. He panicked, grabbed a plastic bag that was lying in the kitchen, popped it over her head, and, as he so colourfully said, "Bob's your uncle". Sorry, love,' he added contritely at the look on her face.

'It's all right.' She gave a brave smile. 'We have to talk about it, don't we? It's clear that the police aren't going to do anything.'

'No, they're not,' he confirmed. 'No more than they did for Father Julian.'

'Or Rachel,' put in a loyal Ruth.

'They didn't really listen to Dr Bright, but what he said made perfect sense,' Lucy said. 'He told me – just like he told the police – that Vera never shopped at any of those smart Knightsbridge shops. That may have sounded like an old man's nonsensical ramblings, but what he was trying to say was that whoever killed her came into the house armed with that carrier bag.'

'What do you mean?' Emily asked.

Lucy gulped as she visualised the green bag. 'The bag that suffocated her came from a shop she never went to, so the murderer must have brought the bag with him.'

'Or her,' David amended.

'Or her. And there was other evidence that she knew the murderer, and probably let him, or her, in herself.'

She had their undivided attention.

'Her father was taking a nap, so someone might have even rung the bell and come in through the front. Apparently he takes a nap every morning, and probably everyone at the church knows that, so it wouldn't really be taking any chances to come quite openly while he was asleep. And I believe he's a bit deaf as well.'

'But what's the other evidence?' demanded Ruth impatiently.

'The mugs. There were three mugs on a tray, ready for morning coffee – one for me as well, since she was expecting me. But there were also two mugs on the draining board, rinsed out but recently used. I saw them myself, and Dr Bright mentioned it to me later.'

'Couldn't they have been left over from their breakfast?' Gabriel asked.

'Apparently not, according to Dr Bright. He told me that she always washed up and put away the breakfast dishes straightaway. He'd watched her do it this morning, as usual, so those mugs had been used since then.'

'By Vera and the murderer,' said Emily slowly. 'But didn't he tell the police about the mugs?'

'Yes, of course he did. More than once, probably. But again, they didn't understand the significance. They thought that he was just rambling.'

'So,' David summed up. 'It looks as though it's down to us.'

It was odd that no one had thought to ask before, but in the drama surrounding Vera's death it scarcely seemed to matter. Not until they were eating the fresh fruit that served for a dessert did Gabriel enquire, 'And where were *you* today, David, by the way?'

'Brighton,' David said deliberately, watching Gabriel's face.

With an effort Gabriel controlled his expression, betraying emotion only with a flicker of his eyelids. 'Oh?'

'But that's the end of the story, really, rather than the beginning,' David went on. 'I had lunch at Robin West's restaurant, and had a little chat with him about Father Julian. He told me, with great relish, that Father Julian had had a lodger at Magdalen House.'

'Oh?' This time it was Lucy, giving David a warning look as she kicked him under the table and indicated Ruth with a slight inclination of her head.

But Ruth, peeling a banana, was oblivious both to her aunt's concern and to the subtext of David's statement. David looked at Ruth and the banana with equal distaste, but resolved to couch his story in terms that would not offend or corrupt innocent young ears. 'It turns out that this lodger, a chap by the name of Alistair Duncan, is an unemployed hairdresser, currently living in Brighton and acting as housekeeper for the new Vicar of St Dunstan's.'

'A man housekeeper – that's funny,' Ruth said scornfully. 'I don't suppose he's very good at it.'

Her comment covered the sound of Gabriel dropping his fruit knife. He picked it up again, hoping that no one had noticed. 'St Dunstan's? What a coincidence,' he remarked in a hearty voice. Turning to Ruth, he explained genially, 'I was a curate at St Dunstan's, a long time ago.'

'Oh, yes?' She didn't try very hard to sound interested. It must have been a *very* long time ago, she thought, since the Archdeacon was now so elderly. Forty, at least. As old as her father.

'And your Uncle David was there at the same time, as a server.'

'Don't call him my uncle,' she muttered fiercely. 'He's

not my uncle. He's living in sin with my aunt, not married to her!'

There was a long, embarrassed silence, then Gabriel turned back to David. 'So you actually went to St Dunstan's, then?'

'To the clergy house.'

'And how was it?' Gabriel would have given anything at that moment if he and David could have been alone having this conversation, launching into a reminiscence of old times, reaffirming the ties that had never completely disappeared. As it was, he fought to keep the yearning and the enthusiasm from his voice.

'Very much the same.' David's tone was dry. 'Though Ruth is right – Alistair Duncan *isn't* a very good housekeeper. Everything was a bit dusty and grimy.'

Gabriel produced a chuckle. 'Wouldn't old Mrs Ellison turn over in her grave, then?'

That was her name, thought David. 'I dare say she's spinning even as we speak.'

Emily was growing impatient with all this nostalgic chat, from which she rightly felt excluded. 'So what about this Alistair Duncan? Did he tell you anything useful about Father Julian?'

'Oh, yes. He gave me a great deal of background information, which I won't go into now,' he said; the flick of his eyes in Ruth's direction was immediately understood by the others. 'And,' he went on, 'he gave me Father Julian's diary for last year.' With a flourish he produced it from his pocket.

'His diary!' Lucy looked up at last from the extended examination of some satsuma peel to which Gabriel and David's exchange had driven her.

He opened it up to the first week in December. 'Did you ever tell us, Gabriel, exactly what day he was killed?'

'It was on a Friday night or Saturday morning at the beginning of December, that first week. He was found in the sacristy on Saturday morning, but they're not sure exactly what time he died, because of the effect of the cold temperature of the church in delaying rigor mortis,' the Archdeacon explained with technical precision.

'Well, that makes it the fourth or the fifth. And look,' David stated triumphantly, pointing to the entry in the diary. 'This is what I think is significant. On Friday the fourth of December, Father Julian had an appointment with VB at 2 o'clock. That must be Vera Bright! Don't you see? Rachel talked to Vera Bright the day before she died, and so did Father Julian!'

Ruth practically bounced up and down in her seat with excitement. 'So I was right! They both told her something, didn't they? She *did* know who killed them!'

'It certainly looks that way,' David agreed. 'And look what else I think is interesting. Right after he saw Vera Bright, he had a meeting with NT. Norman Topping – what do you think of that?'

Not surprisingly, Lucy didn't sleep very well that night. Vera's death, and the circumstances surrounding it, had hit her hard, intensifying the distress that Rachel's death had aroused in her. She tossed and turned, dozing intermittently, but every time she dropped off it was to a gut-wrenching dream of that outstretched, pathetic hand, a slumped body with a green bag where a head should be, or alternatively the pleading eyes of an old man who begged her, 'Find out who killed my Vera.'

Vera Bright. Vera Bright. Vera Bright. The name pounded in her head like an unwelcome mantra, impossible to exorcise. In a desperate effort to counteract it, she tried to project her thoughts into the future rather than the past. After all, they were a long way from knowing who had murdered Vera Bright, even if they did know why. And the motive for the other two deaths was still unclear.

What could they do – *she* do – to find out? She had failed signally, it must be admitted, in the task assigned to her, to talk to Vera Bright. She had been just a little too late, and because of that, Vera had died, and her knowledge with her.

Was there anything else she could do? She had intended, she remembered, to deliver the finished painting to Vanessa Bairstow, and have a chat with her. Vanessa Bairstow, as different as could be imagined from Vera Bright, beautifully coiffed and elegant. Vanessa Bairstow. Vera Bright.

She sat up in bed and shook David's shoulder urgently. 'David darling, wake up!'

He had been sleeping rather better than she – he, after all, had not found a dead body that day, but had done some fairly tiring travelling – so it was surprising how quickly he came to life. 'What's wrong, love?'

'Vanessa Bairstow. It might have been Vanessa Bairstow.'

'What are you talking about?'

'Listen, darling. It was natural that you should have thought that Father Julian went to see Vera Bright on the day before he died, since we know that Rachel did.

But it could have been Vanessa Bairstow. VB – don't
you see?'

He grasped her point. 'Oh. But I don't...'

'And that's not all. I just remembered something that
she said, the first time I met her. She said that she had a
new hairdresser, because her old one had just moved to
Brighton.'

'But...'

'We've thought about her husband as someone who
might be involved in the deaths. But what if *she* has
something to do with it, directly or indirectly?'

'It's possible, I suppose,' David admitted sleepily.

'I'm not sure how it all fits together, but there could be
some connection. I'll go and see her tomorrow.' She
thought for a moment, then added, 'But there's something you can do, as well – you can ring your friend
Alistair, and see if he knows anything about Vanessa
Bairstow.'

'All right,' he agreed, yawning. 'If you'll promise to
stop worrying about it for now, and try to get some sleep.
On second thoughts,' he amended as she lay back down
beside him, 'I think we could both use a cuddle. Come
here, Lucy love.'

She allowed him to take her in his arms, and didn't
resist when his caresses became more insistent, but for
the first time in the history of their lovemaking she was
just going through the motions; though her body was
engaged most pleasurably, her mind was elsewhere,
and her heart was gripped in a chill ache that was
beyond comfort.

Chapter 25

There is no health in my flesh, because of thy
displeasure: neither is there any rest in my bones,
by reason of my sin.
For my wickednesses are gone over my head: and are
like a sore burden, too heavy for me to bear.

Psalm 38.3–4

After seeing David and Ruth off to work on Tuesday
morning, Lucy washed up the breakfast dishes, fed
Sophie, then moved about the house restlessly, feeling
that she should be doing something of a constructive
nature. The sitting room was a mess: Ruth had left the
sofa bed unfolded, so Lucy removed the bedding, folded
it up and stashed it in the cupboard under the stairs,
then restored the innards to their hidden state inside
the sofa. Her niece had also left an assortment of sweet
wrappers and empty crisp packets on the table and even
the floor. With an unconscious sigh she collected them
all up and transported them to the bin in the kitchen,
then took a cookery book off the shelf and located a
recipe for that evening's meal.

She went upstairs, took a leisurely hot bubble bath,
washed her hair and dried it, got dressed, then went into

her studio. Vanessa's painting was on the easel, completed and ready to be wrapped up and delivered. Lucy was pleased with the painting, and thought that Vanessa would be as well; in keeping with the importance of the occasion which it was to mark, it had been executed on an ambitious scale, and it had worked. She had used Christian motifs, including a variety of crosses, repeated and combined in innovative ways, and the result was pleasing to the eye, devotional without being in any way sentimental.

Lucy looked at her watch. It was late enough to ring Vanessa, so she went into the bedroom to use the phone there.

Vanessa answered promptly, and seemed eager to see both Lucy and the painting. 'Do you want me to come and fetch it?' she offered.

'Oh, no. That's not necessary. I'll bring it to you. I can come by taxi.'

'I can't wait to see it. And I can't wait to give it to Martin.'

'Your anniversary is this weekend?'

'That's right. Twenty years.' Vanessa sighed. 'It doesn't seem possible that it's been that long.'

'Well, I hope that you'll both like the painting. Is this afternoon convenient for you?'

'Of course. Do you want to come around teatime?'

'That would be nice,' agreed Lucy. 'I'll see you then.'

David rang a short time later, his voice conveying suppressed excitement. 'You may well be on to something with this Vanessa Bairstow business, love,' he informed her. 'I've just had a chat with Alistair, and Vanessa *was* one of his hairdressing clients.'

'And where does that take us?'

'He told me something very interesting. He said that women tell their hairdressers things that they'd never tell anyone else, except maybe a psychiatrist or a priest. Do you think that's true?'

'Yes,' said Lucy thoughtfully. 'Yes, it's true, in a sense. There's something impersonal about a hairdresser – they just listen, and don't really engage with you like a priest would, or a psychiatrist. But I suppose that's the attraction for a lot of women. A nonjudgemental, listening ear. Something they don't get anywhere else.'

'Especially not from their husbands,' David added with a dry chuckle.

'Well, exactly. That's just the point. I've heard women sitting in the next chair to me, and whilst the scissors are snipping away they're chatting on in the most astonishingly intimate detail. The hairdressers never bat an eye. They'll just say, once in a while, in a bored voice, "Oh, yes, dear? And what did he do then?" It's amazing. Don't men do that too, at the barbers'?'

'You've got to be joking, love. The barbers are the ones who do all the talking – every one of them is a self-proclaimed expert on cricket, football, and politics. In fact,' he said, 'I think that this country would be in much better shape if we sacked the government and put the barbers in charge.'

Lucy laughed, then recalled the purpose of the call. 'But what about Vanessa? Does she have a deep dark secret that she confided to her hairdresser?'

'You've got it in one, you clever girl. Did I ever tell you that I adore you?'

'Once or twice. But what was it?' she demanded. 'Did he tell you what it was?'

'No,' David admitted. 'He said that as far as he's concerned, he's in the same position as a priest. The sacredness of the confessional, you know. He listens, but he won't repeat anything that a client tells him. He'd like to help us, he said, but if we want to know, we'll have to find out some other way. You've got to admire his integrity, though it's as annoying as hell.'

Thoughtfully Lucy twisted a red-gold curl around her finger. 'But what about Father Julian?' she asked after a moment. 'Did *he* know Vanessa's secret?'

'It would seem so,' David confirmed. 'Alistair admitted that she'd been to talk to Father Julian – she'd actually come to the house to see him. That's how Alistair knew the connection, that one of his clients was also one of Julian's parishioners.'

'Ah,' said Lucy. 'It's all beginning to make some sense. I think. Anyway,' she continued briskly, 'I'm going to deliver her painting this afternoon. So we'll see what I can find out.'

'You're good at getting people to tell you things,' David encouraged her, adding with a chuckle, 'And if all other methods fail, can't you offer to cut her hair?'

Later that afternoon, Lucy balanced the unwieldy painting on the top step and pushed Vanessa's bell, with a terrible sense of *déjà vu* from the day before.

Vanessa opened the door a little way, then swung it wide. 'Oh, hello, Lucy. Come in,' Her voice, normally deep-pitched and rich, sounded flat.

'Where would you like me to put the painting? Somewhere in the light, where you can look at it properly?'

She gave an indifferent shrug. 'It doesn't matter. Put it anywhere. I'll look at it later.' Vanessa turned and walked towards the drawing room, moving woodenly.

Puzzled, Lucy followed her. There was something wrong, she realised quickly: gone was the enthusiasm that Vanessa had shown on the phone that morning. And though Vanessa was dressed as elegantly as always, her face, under its layer of perfect make-up, seemed almost *too* perfectly arranged.

But whatever was wrong, she remembered her manners, gesturing to a chair. 'Please, sit down, Lucy. Can I offer you some tea?'

'If you're having some.'

Without another word, Vanessa went off to the kitchen, coming back a few minutes later with a tea tray. She set it down carefully on the table, her movements controlled in an unnatural way. 'Lemon or milk?' she asked.

Concerned, Lucy stood up and went to her, putting a hand on her arm. 'Listen, Vanessa. Something's wrong, isn't it? Can't you tell me what it is?'

The other woman tensed, then consciously relaxed. 'I'll show you,' she said in a lifeless voice. Again she turned, and, moving almost like an automaton, led Lucy up the stairs and into a beautifully appointed bedroom – the sort of bedroom that she would have expected

Vanessa to have, with lovely Georgian furniture, Colefax and Fowler wallpaper, and coordinating quilted spreads on the twin beds.

'There,' said Vanessa, pointing to one of the beds.

Again Lucy experienced a painful sense of *déjà vu* at the pointing finger, but she forced herself to look. There, stretched on the bed, was a large yellow cat, with no apparent injuries but unmistakeably dead, its limbs extended stiffly and its mouth slightly open. As unmistakeably dead as Vera Bright, thought Lucy with an involuntary shudder.

Vanessa sensed the shudder, and turned to face her. 'It's Augustine,' she said unnecessarily and with studied calm. 'I found him a little while ago. He's dead. It looks like poison.'

'Oh, Vanessa, I'm so sorry!' With impulsive but genuine empathy and pity, Lucy put her arms around the other woman, feeling her as rigid as the dead cat in her embrace.

This unexpected evidence of human warmth was all it took; in an instant Vanessa was wracked with tearing dry sobs of agony. 'Oh,' she gasped. 'Oh, he's dead! My baby – he's dead!'

Lucy knew that it was better for her to cry, healthier to express her grief than to suppress it. 'Yes, yes,' she murmured.

Vanessa cried for a long time, clinging to Lucy, the dry sobs giving way to tears which thoroughly soaked Lucy's shoulder and wrecked her own perfect make-up. Eventually, with an effort, she controlled her sobs and pulled away from Lucy, revealing a face all the more human for the runnels of mascara and the smears of iridescent eye shadow. She reached for a tissue from the bedside table, then sat abruptly on the edge of the other bed, dabbing at her eyes.

'Who could have done such a thing?' she said almost to herself.

'Do you think that someone did it on purpose?' Lucy asked, horrified. 'Put down poison?'

'Oh, yes, I'm sure of it. The neighbours didn't like Augustine much, you know. They didn't like the way he killed birds, or ... you know ... in their gardens.' Vanessa wrapped her arms around her body and began rocking, forward and back, on the edge of the bed. 'But how could they have done it?' she said softly. 'The neighbours all have children. But he was all that I had. My darling Augustine, my beautiful cat. He was all that I had to love.'

Lucy knelt beside her. 'That's not true,' she protested. 'You might not have any children, but you have Martin.'

'Martin.' Her laugh was low and without humour as she continued her rhythmic rocking. After a moment she began speaking, softly and quickly, almost as if to herself. 'He's never loved me, you know. Not even at the beginning. If he had, surely he would have wanted me to be a true wife to him. It didn't matter so much to me at first – I loved him so much, and thought that the other would come in time. But later I wanted it – not just because I wanted children, but because I needed to know that he loved me. I wanted to be held, I wanted to be loved.' She bit her lip, choked, and went on. 'He never even wanted to try. Whenever I suggested it, he would turn away from me, as if I were something ... filthy. Unclean. Sometimes I was so desperate that I even got into his bed with him. Usually he just pushed me out. Once or twice he ... tried. That was the worst.' She squeezed her eyes shut; tears trickled from their corners. 'He just couldn't do it. He didn't find me attractive, he said. It was my fault.' Lowering her head, she whispered, 'I've tried so hard to be attractive for him, to make him proud of me, to make him love me, to make him ... want me. But it's no good. Now he can't even bear to touch me.'

Lucy took her hand and pressed it comfortingly; there was nothing she could say.

'They all think he's the ideal husband, of course,' Vanessa went on in a noticeably more bitter tone. 'All those old women at St Margaret's. They all envy me – can you believe it? But why shouldn't they? In public he always treats me like a cherished possession. And why shouldn't they think he's wonderful? There's nothing he wouldn't do for them – he gives them lifts to church, wires their plugs, prunes their hedges, helps them balance their chequebooks. He has more time for them than he's ever had for me. Sometimes I wonder what they'd say if they knew what he was really like.' Her mouth twisted in a sour smile. 'Sometimes I just feel like standing up in the middle of church and shouting it out: "This man is a fraud – twenty years of marriage and he can scarcely bring himself to touch his wife, or even look at her, let alone make love to her!" What a fine churchwarden he is.'

Then she raised her head and looked at Lucy as though she were seeing her for the first time. 'Oh, God, what have I done?' she breathed in an appalled whisper. 'Please, you mustn't say anything, and you must never let Martin know that I've told you. There's no telling what he'd do if he found out.'

'But this isn't something that you should have to deal with alone. Haven't you ever talked about it with anyone before?' Lucy asked, knowing the answer even as the question was spoken.

Vanessa sighed and looked down at her clasped hands. 'Sometimes I feel desperate, as though I have to tell someone or I'll burst. Once I tried to say something to Father Keble Smythe, but he didn't want to know. So I talked to Father Julian. He was wonderful. He made me realise for the first time that Martin is the one with the problem, and that I'm not really as repulsive and . . . unnatural . . . as he always tells me I am, just because I want a normal married life. But then he died. And Rachel. She stopped by to see me a couple of weeks ago. Augustine had disappeared, and I was so upset. I said more than I should, and Martin came home in the middle of it and went mad. He loves playing the part of the perfect husband in front of everyone at St Margaret's – it would kill him if people knew the truth. Please,' she repeated with unmistakeable urgency. 'Please forget that this ever happened. Promise me that you'll never tell a soul!'

Lucy hadn't been home long when David and Ruth returned from work. 'Hello, my love,' David greeted her, and was pleasantly surprised at the warmth of her welcoming kiss; she'd been more shaken by the day's events than she was willing to admit.

'Ugh – gross,' gagged Ruth, but they'd learned by now to ignore her.

He lifted the lid of the casserole on the hob, sniffed and nodded in approval, then said, 'How about a drink while you tell us what happened at Vanessa's this afternoon?'

'Alcoholic,' muttered Ruth, but this too they'd learned to ignore.

'The drink sounds good – supper won't be ready for a bit. But I'm afraid that I don't have anything to tell you.' She flicked her eyes in Ruth's direction.

'You mean that you don't want me to know, don't you?' the girl challenged her in a shrill voice. 'Well, I think that stinks. I'm not a baby – there's no reason why I shouldn't know what's going on! Emily would tell me – I know she would. You're just being horrible to me on purpose, Aunt Lucy.'

Lucy sighed but said nothing. There was no way that she was going to be bullied into telling Ruth, and by now she'd discovered that arguing with the girl didn't work – a dignified silence was by far the best approach. At first David had automatically jumped to Lucy's defence in these encounters, but he too had finally realised that it only made matters worse.

So David had to contain his curiosity throughout supper, and afterwards, when he would have expected Ruth to disappear and leave him to help Lucy with the washing up, the girl stubbornly refused to leave.

While they were washing up – David washing, Lucy drying, Ruth spectating – the phone rang. 'I'll get it,' offered Ruth in a moment of unusual helpfulness.

She was only gone for a few seconds, afraid that they'd say something important in her absence. 'It's Emily,' she announced. 'She wants to talk to you, Aunt Lucy.'

'Thanks, Ruth darling.' Lucy went to the phone in the hall, leaving Ruth looking thoughtful.

With studied nonchalance she said, 'I think I'm going to go up and take a bath now. Is that all right?'

'Fine,' David responded in amazement; it was the first time that he could remember her asking his permission for anything. 'But there won't be much hot water at the moment, while we're washing up.'

'Oh, it doesn't matter. I like cold baths,' she said over her shoulder. Her progress up the stairs was stately, but once out of Lucy's vision she made a dash for the bedroom and lifted the receiver of the extension phone silently, with the expertise born of long practice.

She was in luck: they were still exchanging pleasantries. 'Well, I'm glad that you're feeling better today, at any rate,' said Emily in a concerned voice. 'That really was a dreadful shock for you, Luce.'

'I didn't sleep very well last night,' Lucy admitted. 'But the person I really feel sorry for is her father. He's a bit of a selfish old man, but that's what makes it so difficult for him. He'll miss having a live-in slave, I expect.'

They chatted in that vein for a few minutes. 'Have you made any progress today?' Emily asked at last.

'As a matter of fact I have. I realised last night that David was jumping to conclusions when he assumed that "VB" had to be Vera Bright – it might have been Vanessa Bairstow instead.'

'That was clever of you,' Emily said approvingly.

'So today I went to see her – Vanessa. It was pretty horrific. Not on the same scale as yesterday, of course, but I got more than I bargained for.'

'Well, tell me!'

Lucy paused and Ruth held her breath. 'I can't, Em. Not on the phone. It's not the sort of thing you can talk about on the phone. I'll see you later in the week and tell you about it.'

'All right, then.' Emily accepted it equably. 'I'm afraid that I don't have much to report from this end. I decided to get the martyrdom bit out of the way as quickly as possible, so I had Dolly over for coffee, but she didn't tell me anything that I hadn't heard from her a dozen times before.'

'Such as?'

'Oh, just all the usual twaddle about women priests, and about poor dear Father Keble Smythe, and what a saint he is. Somehow, though, it almost seemed as if she were just going through the motions, as if her heart wasn't really in it. She seemed almost distracted.'

'That doesn't sound like Dolly.'

'I think,' said Emily, 'that she may have family problems of some sort. She said that she couldn't stay long as she had to get home to her daughter.'

'I didn't know that Dolly had a daughter.'

'Just the one – she's a teenager, I think.'

'Oh, well,' Lucy said with heartfelt conviction. 'Say no more. Family problems is probably putting it mildly, if that's the case.'

Ruth scowled and put her tongue out at the phone. But as she scurried to the bathroom to run the taps, she was already beginning to make plans of her own.

It wasn't until they were in bed that Lucy was able to tell David about her visit to Vanessa. He listened in silence and a large measure of disbelief as she outlined the nub of the Bairstows' problem.

'You're telling me, love,' he said at last, when she'd finished, 'that they've been married for twenty years, and have never consummated their marriage?'

'That's exactly what I'm telling you. Vanessa Bairstow is a virgin – her husband has never laid a finger on her. Won't, can't – I don't know. I don't really understand the psychology of it. All I know is that it's ruined her life.'

'But surely such a thing isn't possible!'

Lucy shook her head. 'It seems almost impossible to believe, but I've heard about such cases before. Apparently it's a lot more common than you'd ever think.'

David put his arm around her and drew her head on to his shoulder, stroking her hair absently. 'The poor woman.'

'From what she said, I think that the worst part of it is the damage it's done to her ego, to her self-esteem. I mean, people can live without sex, even without plain simple human contact. But to have a person – the person that you loved – telling you for years that you weren't attractive, that you repulsed them, and that there was something wrong with you for wanting a normal sex life – it's a wonder that she's managed to keep her sanity.'

David's mind leapt to the next conclusion before Lucy could tell him. 'She talked to Father Julian and Rachel about it, didn't she?'

She nodded. 'Yes. And now she's in a real state. Not just because her cat is dead. Not just because her husband won't touch her.' Lucy paused to give her next words their full impact. 'Darling, I'm sure that Vanessa Bairstow is terrified because she thinks that her husband killed them. So that they'd never be able to tell.'

'Good Lord,' said David, stunned.

Chapter 26

Behold, I was shapen in wickedness: and in sin hath my mother conceived me.

Psalm 51.5

Ruth worked her plan out carefully, taking into account all variables. The first problem, of course, was getting away from work without arousing anyone's suspicions. That meant acting in character, so it wouldn't very well do to try to appear helpful – to offer to run an errand for David's secretary, for instance. Nor could she pretend to feel ill – they would never send her back to Aunt Lucy's on her own. In the end she decided that the simplest solution was probably the best: she would just walk out and hope that no one would miss her or raise the alarm.

The second problem was finding Nicola Topping. That proved to be not at all difficult. While Mrs Simmons was away from her desk for a few minutes, Ruth borrowed her phone; ringing Directory Enquiries, she asked for a number for Norman Topping, which was readily supplied. All that was then required was to ring the number, and when Dolly answered, to ask for Nicola. For effect, and to be on the safe side, Ruth altered her voice by lowering it to what she reckoned to be an unrecognisable pitch.

In the event, Dolly was a more formidable obstacle than she'd anticipated, protecting her daughter from unwanted attentions. 'I'm afraid that Nicola's not very well. It's not convenient for her to come to the phone just now,' she asserted.

'It's very important,' Ruth insisted. 'I'm in her form at school,' she added in a burst of inspiration. 'I know that she's missed a few days lately, and I need to tell her something about ... exams. Something she needs to know.'

Dolly paused. 'What did you say your name was?'

'It's ... Sophie. Sophie King,' she improvised, thinking of Aunt Lucy's cat.

'I don't remember hearing Nicola mention your name before. You haven't been to the house with her, have you?'

'I don't really know Nicola very well, Mrs Topping,' Ruth replied ingratiatingly. 'But I admire her very much.'

'I'll call her to the phone, then,' Dolly relented.

Ruth was elated. This was easy – and fun.

'Hello?' came a cautious, expectant voice a moment later.

'Can your mother hear you? Is she right there?'

'Yes...'

'Then pretend that you know me. My name is Sophie. I'll explain as much as I can, if you'll just go along with me.'

Nicola was a natural. 'Oh, thanks for ringing, Sophie.'

'I need to see you. You don't know me, but it's about somebody important to you.'

'I'm not sure. When I'll be back to school, that is.'

'When can I see you? Some time today? It's important,' Ruth stressed.

'This afternoon? You're sure that there's an exam this afternoon?'

'I don't suppose it's any good me coming to your house, is it? With your mum there?'

'Well, if you'd like to stop by after school for a few minutes with the revision notes, I'm sure that it would be all right.'

Ruth looked over her shoulder to make sure that Mrs Simmons wasn't coming back; this was taking longer than she'd expected. 'And we can talk in private? Would three o'clock be all right?'

'No problem.' Displaying considerable ingenuity herself, Nicola went on, 'You've never been to my house before, have you, Sophie? Do you know the address?' She proceeded to give it. 'Just a little way along from St Margaret's Church,' she added for good measure. 'I'll see you later, Sophie. Thanks for thinking about me.'

Nicola was smiling as she put the phone down. 'Why haven't you ever mentioned this girl Sophie before?' Dolly interrogated her suspiciously.

'Oh, she's rather new. But she's really nice, Mum. You'll like her.'

'Is she coming round, then?'

'She offered to bring me some notes that I need for revision, after school this afternoon.' Nicola said it innocently, as though her mother hadn't been listening to every word.

'Well, then. You'd better go and lie down for a while, hadn't you? Before your friend gets here.'

'All right, Mum.' Docilely she went back to her room, hugging her secret knowledge to herself. This time she scarcely minded the sound of the key in the lock as she pulled the covers up to her chin. In a few hours Sophie would be here, bringing a message from Ben. She'd known all along that Ben hadn't forgotten her, and would manage somehow to get a message through to her, even though she was a virtual prisoner in her own house. The ingenuity of his method, using a girl who pretended to be from her school, surprised and delighted her. She couldn't wait to meet this Sophie, and to hear Ben's message of continuing love and support.

At half-past two, Ruth left her pile of documents for photocopying on the machine, extracting a few to serve as dummy revision notes, and calmly walked out of Fosdyke, Fosdyke & Galloway into Lincoln's Inn, and in a matter of minutes she was on the Piccadilly Line en route to South Kensington. After a short walk from the Tube at the other end, she rang the bell at three precisely, composing her face into an ingratiating smile for Dolly Topping. 'Hello, Mrs Topping,' she said sweetly. 'I'm Sophie King. Nicola is expecting me.'

Dolly looked her up and down. 'Haven't you just come from school? Why aren't you wearing a uniform?'

Ruth's dismay didn't register on her face, and she thought quickly. 'We don't have to wear uniforms on the days that we have exams. Didn't Nicola tell you?'

'I've never heard that rule before, I must say.'

Waving the papers in her hand – Dolly would have

been surprised, had she inspected them, to discover that they were the middle section of a conveyancing document – Ruth gave a bright, perky smile. 'Here are the revision notes that I promised to bring for Nicola.' She held on to them tightly, lest Dolly should offer to take them.

'Well, all right,' Dolly capitulated. 'Nicola is in her room. I suppose you can go and see her there for a few minutes.'

'Thank you, Mrs Topping. I'll try not to tire her out.' Neither Lucy nor David would have recognised this mannerly and considerate child.

Dolly led the way upstairs to Nicola's room, tapped on the door, and turned the key in the lock on the outside. 'Your friend Sophie is here,' she announced. 'Not too long, now,' she cautioned Ruth. 'Remember, Nicola isn't very well.'

Then she was in the room, and she could hear the key turning in the lock on the other side.

The room was dark, with the curtains pulled and the lights out; it took a moment for her eyes to adjust to the dimness. She could just make out the bed, with a large form under the duvet.

'Come over here,' Nicola whispered in a state of high excitement, heaving herself up in bed.

Ruth moved closer. She could see Nicola now, and was surprised at her size, though perhaps she shouldn't have been, having met her mother.

Nicola seized her hands and pulled her down to her level. 'Tell me what he said,' she said urgently but quietly. 'Give me the message.'

The other girl's intensity startled Ruth as much as

the unexpected demand. 'What message?' she blurted out stupidly.

'Ben's message, of course.'

'Who is Ben?'

'You don't have to pretend,' Nicola assured her. 'She can't hear, even if she presses her ear against the door. But if this will make you feel better . . .' She switched on her bedside radio, which was tuned to Radio 1, and turned the volume up. 'Now we can talk. Tell me what Ben said.'

'But I don't know any Ben,' insisted Ruth.

'If you don't know Ben,' Nicola said slowly, fixing her with feverish and rather beautiful eyes, 'then who are you? And what are you doing here?'

Ruth knelt down beside the bed; her voice matched the other girl's in intensity. 'I'm here because of Rachel – Rachel Nightingale. Miss Bright told me that you cared about Rachel.'

Nicola's eyes grew wider, and her mouth opened in a soundless 'O'. 'But she's dead,' she whispered. 'Rachel is dead.'

'Yes, and I'm trying to find out who killed her!' Ruth blurted out passionately. 'Rachel was wonderful, and I don't want them to get away with it! The police don't care. She didn't die by accident. I've got to find out who killed her!'

Nicola flung herself down on the bed and turned her back to Ruth. 'No,' she said, her voice muffled in her pillow. 'Just leave it.'

'I can't leave it, and neither can you. Not if you cared about Rachel.' There was no response, so Ruth leaned over the recumbent girl and added a little more loudly,

'And there was Father Julian, as well. Did you know Father Julian? Did you know that someone murdered him?'

Covering her ears with her hands, Nicola spoke stonily. 'Just go away. I won't listen to you.'

Roughly Ruth pulled a hand away and spoke close to the other girl's ear. 'And now someone has killed Miss Bright.'

'No!' Nicola turned to face her, her eyes huge in her paper-white face. 'You're making that up!'

'On Monday morning,' Ruth said deliberately. 'Someone went to her house, and killed her. So that she wouldn't tell what she knew about who murdered Rachel and Father Julian.'

'Oh my God.' Tears brimmed in the luminous eyes, spilling over and running down the full cheeks. 'It's true, isn't it? Mum didn't tell me.'

'It's true, all right.' For emphasis, or out of wilful cruelty, she told her, 'They went into her house and smothered her with a carrier bag.'

'Oh God.' Nicola covered her face with her hands. 'I liked Miss Bright.'

'So did I. Don't you see, then, that you've got to help me? You've got to tell me what you know!'

'Don't *you* see – you've got to get out of here, and don't ever come back.' Nicola's voice dropped to a whisper in volume but lost none of its vehemence. 'I'm cursed,' she said, with the extraordinary egocentricity of the young. 'All the people I talk to end up dead. Don't you see – it's all my fault! They'd all still be alive if it weren't for me!'

Ruth tried to take it in. 'What on earth are you saying?'

'It's God's punishment on me for disobeying my parents.' The tears trickled faster; she reached for a tissue.

'What a load of rubbish!' declared Ruth in a robust whisper.

'No – I promise you it's true! I talked to Father Julian, and he died. Then I talked to Rachel and *she* died. And now Miss Bright!'

'They didn't just die – they were murdered!'

Nicola gave her head a hopeless shake. 'It doesn't matter.'

'Of course it matters!' Ruth leaned down so that her face was only an inch or two from the other girl's. 'You've got to tell me what you know – you've *got* to. You owe it to Rachel.'

For a moment it hung in the balance, as Nicola stared into Ruth's eyes. Then she made up her mind. 'Yes, all right,' she said quietly. 'If you really want to know, I'll tell you.'

She did just that, concisely and unemotionally, over the next quarter of an hour, until the sound of the key turning cut her off in mid-sentence. Instantly she composed her face into a smile, which she turned towards the door as her mother entered.

'Don't you think that this gossip session has gone on long enough?' Dolly Topping said in a jolly voice. 'I, for one, think that it has.'

'Sophie's just been telling me about everything that's been happening at school while I've been ... sick,' Nicola explained lightly. 'You wouldn't believe some of her stories.'

'Would you girls like a cup of tea?'

Ruth looked at her watch. 'Thanks awfully, Mrs Topping, but I really must be going. My mum will be expecting me.'

Dolly saw her to the door, then returned to Nicola's room with her daughter's tea. 'What a nice, polite girl,' she commented. 'You must have her round again, when you're feeling better.'

Bursting with her news, Ruth went straight to Lucy's house. She let herself in with her key, to find her aunt in the sitting room curled up on the sofa, feet up, sipping a cup of tea.

Lucy, who had been listening to Choral Evensong on Radio 3, looked up, startled at the girl's precipitate arrival. 'Ruth! Whatever are you doing here? What's wrong? Where's David?'

'Oh, never mind him,' the girl said impatiently. 'He's still at work, for all I know. Or care. But, Aunt Lucy – wait till you hear what I've found out!'

'Does he know that you've come home by yourself?' Lucy persisted.

'No, I just walked out. But that doesn't matter. I've just been—'

'He'll be worried sick, then. I'd better ring him and tell him that you're home safely.'

'All you care about is *him*.' Ruth's voice lost its excitement, became shrill and aggrieved. 'I've got something important to tell you, and you won't even listen to me.'

For once Lucy was firm. 'Whatever it is, it can wait until David gets home. I'm going to ring him now. And you'd better have a jolly good reason for doing what you've done, young lady!' she added with unaccustomed severity.

Unchastened and unrepentant, Ruth helped herself to Lucy's biscuits while her aunt went out to use the phone.

David *hadn't* missed her, he was chagrined to admit – to himself if not to Lucy. If he had been aware of the unusual tranquillity around the offices, he had accepted it gratefully – after all, if you went looking for trouble, you usually found it. So he'd stayed at his desk and enjoyed the brief if unexplained respite from Ruth's astringent presence.

After Lucy's call he came home straightaway, though; partly to propitiate his guilt and partly to assuage his curiosity. She had said that Ruth had found out something important: what on earth could it be?

The girl was in a fever of impatience by the time they'd all gathered in the sitting room. 'I've been to see Nicola Topping,' she burst out.

'Nicola Topping? Who on earth is she?' demanded David.

'Dolly Topping's daughter, of course.' She glared at him scornfully. If she'd dared, she would have added 'stupid', as she would have done with her brothers.

'How did you know that Dolly Topping had a daughter?' Lucy asked.

'Miss Bright told me. And she told me that she'd been close to Rachel, though her mum didn't know it. So when you said that Father Julian had had an appointment with someone called NT, I thought that it might have been Nicola instead of her father.'

David, though secretly impressed by her deductive powers, was not amused. 'Why on earth didn't you say?'

'Because,' she muttered rebelliously, 'you were keeping things from *me*. So I decided to investigate it on my own. Then you'd be sorry that you didn't tell me everything. *And*,' she went on, her level of excitement rising again, 'I managed to see her. I was really clever – I pretended that I was a friend from school, so that her mother would let me in the house to see her. And she talked to me! She told me everything!' Ruth paused momentously. 'So now I know who killed Ruth. And Father Julian, and Miss Bright.'

It was a poignant story, all the more heartrending for being narrated by someone who was still almost a child, as told to her by another who was very little older. Lucy and David listened, appalled yet fascinated, as Ruth related Nicola's tale.

In love with a boy of another race, against her mother's implacable – though not unexpected – opposition, Nicola Topping had confided in Father Julian Piper. Father Julian had been sympathetic, even to the extent of promising to marry the two young people when they reached eighteen and no longer needed their parents' consent. But after Father Julian's death, the girl had been without a confidante until the new curate had arrived at St Margaret's.

She'd lost no time in baring her soul to Rachel Nightingale. Rachel, too, had been sympathetic but cautious of becoming involved, given the virulence of Dolly's hatred for her. 'Wait until you're eighteen,' she had advised with prudence.

Desperate to take some sort of action, to seize the initiative from her mother, Nicola had deliberately become pregnant, believing that her parents would then have to allow her marriage. She had underestimated her mother. 'You're not marrying that wog,' Dolly had declared implacably. 'And you're not presenting me with a half-breed grandchild. It's out of the question.'

On the last afternoon of Rachel's life, a frantic Nicola had gone straight from school to see her, pouring out her fearful dilemma. Her parents hadn't relented, the marriage would not be allowed, and now there was the added complication of the baby to consider. What should she do? Her mother – that highly principled woman whose latest ideological involvement was with an anti-abortion group – was insisting that the pregnancy be terminated, secretly and at once. Nicola was resisting, and seeking support for her resistance. Rachel, feeling that her support would be counterproductive as far as the girl's parents were concerned, advised her to talk to Vera Bright, a woman to whom the senior Toppings might listen. On Nicola's return home from Rachel's there had been a terrible scene – the worst yet. She'd admitted her visit to Rachel; her mother had been livid.

And then Rachel was dead. Nicola, overcome with grief and guilt, had taken Rachel's final advice and had gone to see Vera Bright a few days later. There, in an emotional encounter, she had discovered why Rachel had sent her to that particular person.

She'd poured out her dilemma to the older woman, and had begged her to tell her what to do. 'Don't let them bully you,' Vera had insisted forcefully. 'Don't let them ruin your life.' Then, amidst tears on both sides, she had revealed her own story.

The Romeo to Vera's Juliet had been an American airman, in those long-ago wartime years. They had wanted to be married; her parents had been adamant in their opposition. 'No daughter of ours is going to marry a foreigner and go off to some foreign country to live,' Dr Bright had stated immovably. Like Nicola, young Vera had seen pregnancy as an escape route. It had seemed foolproof: in those days, unwed motherhood was a stigma too terrible to contemplate, and abortion was illegal. Her parents would have to consent to the marriage, or face public shame.

Vera had underestimated her father, as Nicola had underestimated her mother. Fate had played a role, as well: tragically, Gerry Hansen had been shot out of the sky before he even knew that he was to become a father. And Dr Bright had performed the abortion himself.

In the long years following, he had never let his daughter forget how she had disgraced him, or missed an opportunity to remind her of her indebtedness to him. 'You've made your bed, girl, and now you'll lie in it,' he'd been fond of saying, whenever making some particularly unreasonable demand. But the life had gone out of Vera with Gerry Hansen's death, and the loss of her baby. Her mother had died not long after – of shame, Dr Bright had insisted – and Vera had almost willingly embraced the life of servitude to a selfish old man's whims.

But she hadn't wanted to see Nicola take the same path; it was almost as if, in Nicola, she was being given a second chance to redeem her own folly. 'I've ruined my life. You mustn't ruin yours,' she'd insisted, adding, 'And that baby's.'

Galvanised into strength by Vera's support, Nicola had returned home to do battle for her baby's life. But over the nightmarish days that followed, locked in her room and on starvation rations, she'd been gradually worn down until, at last, crushed into submission by her mother's iron will, she'd had the abortion. Quickly, quietly. In a private clinic in the country, where the Toppings weren't known. Then back to her locked room for recuperation, insulated by her mother from the outside world, from news of Vera's death, from Ben. From everything, until a persistent girl who called herself Sophie had managed to penetrate the fortress and reach her in her misery and her guilt. Guilt upon guilt. Guilt about the baby, about Father Julian, about Rachel. And now about Vera Bright as well.

As Ruth drew near the end of the story, Lucy found that she'd been holding her breath. She let it out consciously in a sigh, then bowed her head, her hands still clenched.

'So did she actually tell you that her mother had killed them?' David demanded when she'd finished. 'Rachel, Father Julian, and Vera Bright?'

'Well, no,' Ruth admitted. 'She didn't have a chance to tell me – her mother came in the room before we got that far. She was just telling me that she'd heard her mother go out on Monday morning, when Miss Bright was murdered. And that her mother shops in Knightsbridge. But I'm sure that it was Dolly Topping who killed them, because they'd tried to help Nicola. And I know that

Nicola thinks so, too – otherwise why would she feel so guilty?'

There were dimensions of guilt and variations of guilt that Ruth, in her youth and arrogance, couldn't begin to comprehend, David realised, feeling tremendously old. He took Lucy's hand and squeezed it, then addressed himself to her rather than to Ruth. 'Well, love. What do we do now?'

Ruth was furious. 'What about *me*? I'm the one who's done all the work! Why are you always trying to leave me out?'

Chapter 27

I will receive the cup of salvation: and call upon the Name of the Lord.

Psalm 116.12

'Two more days,' was the first thing that David said on Thursday morning, even before he'd opened his eyes. 'I think we're going to make it, love.'

Lucy wasn't quite awake yet. 'Hm?'

'I said that I think we're going to make it. We only have two days in which to restrain ourselves from wringing her neck. Forty-eight hours and a bit.'

'What a lovely thought.' She turned over and burrowed her face into her pillow, then remembered the day before and was suddenly wide awake. 'Seriously, darling,' she said in a completely different tone of voice. 'What *are* we going to do now? About the things that we've found out?'

'I'm not sure,' David confessed. 'We've never been in quite this position before, have we? We can't just go marching up to the police and tell them that we've solved three murders for them.'

'We haven't exactly solved them,' she protested. 'And

317

anyway, I think that we should take it slowly and carefully, don't you?'

'There's no hurry, as far as I can see,' he agreed. 'I think we should definitely wait until Ruth is gone before we do anything at all.'

'That will make her furious.'

He smiled. 'I know.'

'You're terrible,' she giggled.

'I know that too, and you love me for it.'

'Or in spite of it.' There followed a few undignified moments in which tickling played a prominent part, but after they settled down and stopped laughing David returned to the subject again.

'At any rate, Lucy love, we're meant to be seeing Gabriel and Emily again on Saturday. Ruth will be safely out of the way by then, so that should be time enough to decide where we take it from here. After all, it was Gabriel who got us into this in the first place. So I think we'd be justified in throwing it back into his lap. Just tell him what we've learned, and let him deal with it. He's the Archdeacon, as he's so fond of reminding us.'

'Yes . . .' Lucy turned her back to him. 'Do we have to go?' she said quietly into her pillow. 'To see them on Saturday, I mean?'

'But why ever not, love?'

He had to strain to hear her answer. 'I hated it the other night. I hated the way that you were flirting with Gabriel.'

David was astonished. 'Me? Flirting with Gabriel? That's absurd!'

'All right, then. *He* was flirting with *you*, and you let him.'

'Don't be ridiculous!' He wasn't defensive, only puzzled. 'Why on earth would you think such a thing?'

'All that talk about old times, about Brighton and St
Dunstan's. How was I supposed to feel, David?'

He leaned over so that he could see her face. 'I
honestly don't know what you're going on about, my
love. There was absolutely nothing in it, as far as I was
concerned. And as far as Gabriel was concerned as well,
I'm quite sure. He's a happily married man, and I'm a . . .
well, what *would* you call me? Since you refuse to make
an honest man of me?' He put on such a comically
mournful expression that Lucy couldn't help giggling,
and it soon degenerated into further tickling and other
forms of intimate activity.

David had an idea over breakfast; he broached it to
Lucy while Ruth was still in the shower. 'Were you
doing anything special this afternoon?' he asked as a
preliminary.

'Nothing in particular. I've got a commission that I
should be getting on with, for Joan Everitt, but it's not
pressing. Why? Did you have something in mind?'

'Well, I thought that it might be nice for you to take
the *enfant terrible* out to lunch, on her nearly-last
day.'

'Oh, yes?' Lucy sounded sceptical. 'In other words, you
want to get rid of her.'

He gave her a shamefaced grin. 'Well, that *is* part of
it, of course. And I've got an important client to see at
lunchtime, which means that I'll have to lumber my
secretary with her again, otherwise. But I *did* think
that it would be a good idea – after all, love, you and

Ruth haven't had much time together, just the two of you, since she's been here.'

'That's true,' Lucy admitted. 'She'd probably like to have me to herself for an hour or two.'

The idea developed further. 'You could take her shopping afterwards, if you liked.'

'So you'd be rid of her for even longer.'

'Well, yes. But she'd enjoy it, more than what she'd be doing at the office. Take her to Covent Garden and buy her something. I'll give you some money.'

'Oh, so now you're offering me bribes to take my niece off your hands.' Lucy tried to look cross, but a smile twitched at the corner of her mouth.

David was beginning to get enthusiastic about the plan. 'She should really buy something to take home to her parents,' he went on, developing it further. 'Something from F & M would be nice. Some special tea, or perhaps chocolates. I could meet you there at teatime, give the two of you a nice Fortnum's tea.'

'You've talked me into it,' Lucy laughed. 'I can never resist a Fortnum's tea.'

Lucy came by Fosdyke, Fosdyke & Galloway to collect Ruth as arranged, at about half-past twelve, stopping in only long enough to say hello to David. Things augured well for a less stressful afternoon than might have been expected: Ruth had actually expressed enthusiasm for the plan, and seemed to be looking forward to an afternoon of having her aunt to herself, at least until teatime. She had been almost pleasant that morning, perhaps still savouring her clever triumphs of the previous day.

Still, David wasn't sorry to see her go. His afternoon passed quickly, with two important meetings and a great deal of paperwork to be got through.

He took the Central Line to Bond Street and walked down towards Piccadilly; having allowed plenty of time to get through the early rush-hour traffic, he found himself in Old Bond Street with several minutes to spare. Suddenly he remembered his intention to call into Christie's to look at the catalogue for their sale of ecclesiastical items; it seemed a good time to do that.

There was only time to flick through it cursorily, but it looked interesting, so David bought a copy for a later, more detailed perusal, then progressed on towards Fortnum & Mason.

Lucy and her niece, laden down with carrier bags, were already waiting for him in the tearoom. They both seemed in high good humour; evidently their afternoon together had been a great success, and had gone a long way towards re-establishing the bond between them.

They were seated; David said grandly, 'I think we'll have the lot, don't you? Sandwiches, scones, and cakes.'

'Oh, yes,' agreed Ruth.

'Of course.' Lucy nodded. 'Now this is what I call civilised,' she added, indicating the string quartet.

'We've had such fun,' Ruth told him. 'We went to the Hard Rock Cafe for lunch — it was brilliant.'

'Oh, was it?' David glanced at Lucy; she resolutely refused to catch his eye. 'Had hamburgers, did you?'

Oblivious, Ruth rattled on. '*I* did. Aunt Lucy had a salad. And then we went to Covent Garden. That was super. There was a bloke there who was walking on his hands. And another one who was standing like a statue, dead still, and people tried to get him to move.'

'Did you buy anything?'

'Oh, yes. Aunt Lucy bought me some earrings, and then I found this wonderful hat. Didn't you notice?' She indicated the floppy black velvet which was perched atop her red curls.

'Very nice,' David acknowledged, realising to his shock that she was almost pretty when she smiled, in spite of the flashing hardware; it wasn't a phenomenon that he'd had very much chance to observe.

'And there was a cute teddy bear, but I decided against it. I thought that it was probably too babyish. But I bought some things for my brothers – some wooden toys. And in one of the shops I got some pipe tobacco for my father. And when we got here, I bought some special tea for my mum.'

The food arrived, and Ruth tucked in happily – appropriating all of the smoked salmon sandwiches, to David's secret sorrow.

'Aunt Lucy,' she said, 'I want your opinion about this hat. Now honestly, does it look better with the flower in the front, like this, or on the side, like that? What do you think?'

While Lucy gave careful consideration to the question and its ramifications, David picked up the Christie's catalogue and leafed through it casually. He turned a page, stopped, and went back. 'Good Lord,' he said. His voice was calm, but his mind was racing nearly as fast as his heart.

'What is it?' Lucy looked across the table.

'Here.' He held it up for her to see. 'For sale at Christie's. It's the chalice from St Margaret's.'

It was the one thing that they'd forgotten, David admitted to Gabriel later: the missing chalice. That it was no small omission he also admitted, with some chagrin. The chalice, it was to be assumed, had been taken at the time of Father Julian's murder to give the appearance of a burglary; it followed that the person who had taken the chalice had also killed Father Julian. And two other people as well. The chalice was the evidence they needed to catch the murderer – suspicions were all very well and good, but they needed something more concrete than suspicions to take to the police. They needed the chalice, or at least the name of the person who had taken it.

Admittedly, the police hadn't looked very hard for the chalice either. They had checked the usual outlets for stolen goods, Bermondsey Market and Portobello Road; they had circulated a vague description which might have applied just as well to a thousand other chalices.

Who would have thought that it would have turned up at Christie's? The catalogue description was admirably accurate. 'Silver gilt. Hallmarked John Hardman & Co., 1850. Thought to be a very early design by A. W. Pugin,' it said. The reserve price was £15,000.

Of course David raced back to Christie's as soon as they'd finished their tea. Not surprisingly, at the end of the day, there was no one there who could give him any information about the person who had put the chalice into the sale. 'I'm very sorry, sir, but you'll have to come back in the morning,' said a very junior functionary.

'You can check with our sales desk at that time. They may be able to help you.' He didn't sound very hopeful about the prospect.

Chapter 28

*With the holy thou shalt be holy : and with a perfect
man thou shalt be perfect.*
*With the clean thou shalt be clean : and with the
froward thou shalt learn frowardness.*

Psalm 18.25–26

'I'm going with you,' Lucy said at breakfast on Friday
morning, in a tone that would admit no argument.
'You're not leaving me behind.'

'Me, too.' Ruth's jaw stuck out at a pugnacious angle.

David wasn't sure that it was a good idea, but he could
tell when he was outnumbered, and surrendered grace-
fully. 'Suit yourselves.'

They arrived at Christie's shortly after its opening,
and went straight to the sales desk. An officious-
mannered young man with more teeth than chin came
forward to peer down his nose at them through horn-
rimmed spectacles. 'Can I be of help?' he enunciated in
the most exaggeratedly self-conscious public school
accent that David had ever heard.

David produced the catalogue along with his most
imperious manner; this was not the time or the place for
diffidence, he'd decided instantly. 'I do hope so. I'd like to

know the name of the person who placed this item – the chalice – into your sale, please.'

'Out of the question,' the young man said with satisfaction. Saying no, and finding pretentious ways of saying it, afforded him his greatest pleasure in life. 'That information is of course classified.'

Briefly and fancifully considering whether he might not invite Ruth to sink her armoured teeth into the young man's tweedy leg, like the red-headed Rottweiler that she was, he decided to pull rank instead. 'We'll see what Sir Crispin Fosdyke has to say about that,' David stated, matching supercilious for supercilious. 'He *is* on your Board of Directors, I believe?' From his pocket he produced a business card and extended it with the 'Fosdyke, Fosdyke and Galloway' logo in prominent view.

It was the right thing to say. Instantly the young man's manner changed; he became almost fawningly obsequious. 'Oh, well of course if it's for Sir Crispin, that puts an entirely different light on things. I'm so sorry. You should have said.' He nearly bowed, backing off into the nether regions. 'I won't be a moment, sir.'

And indeed he was back quickly, with a card. 'Here's the information you require, sir. I've written it down for you.'

He'd been thorough. It was the name of an antique dealer, along with the address of his shop in Kensington Church Street. David knew the shop, though he didn't think he'd ever been inside: it was small but reputable, and not given, so far as he knew, to dealing in items of stolen church plate.

'Thank you very much indeed,' he said magnanimously. 'Sir Crispin will be pleased to hear that you've been so helpful. And so cooperative.'

'My pleasure, sir. And do convey my very warmest regards to Sir Crispin.' He ducked his head.

In a moment they were back in Bond Street; David thought hard as he hailed a taxi. 'Lincoln's Inn,' he told the taxi driver.

Ruth insisted on sitting backwards on the little fold-down seat. 'Why are we going to the office?'

'*You* are going to the office,' he stated firmly. 'Out of harm's way.'

Her face became a thundercloud. 'But I don't *want* to. I want to go with you and Aunt Lucy. You can't leave me out of this now. Now that it's getting exciting!'

David refused to discuss it. He folded his arms and leaned back, ignoring her tirade. When they reached Lincoln's Inn, he instructed the taxi driver to wait. 'You stay here,' he told Lucy. 'I'll be back in a minute.'

'You can't do this to me!' Ruth howled as he seized her arm and marched her into the offices.

'Don't make a scene,' he ordered; perhaps the rarefied atmosphere of Fosdyke, Fosdyke & Galloway had something to do with it, but for once she obeyed him. She clamped her lips together to suppress an outraged sob, pulled her arm away from his grasp, and stalked in front of him with her head held high.

'Keep an eye on her,' he instructed Mrs Simmons, who quailed inwardly at the assignment. 'Give her something to do. I've been called away on a matter of urgent business, but I'll be back as soon as possible.'

'You don't need to worry about me,' Ruth called after him with bitter dignity. 'I'll be just fine.'

At the tail end of the morning rush hour their progress was reasonable, but in David's impatient state it seemed to take an age to get to Kensington Church Street. Watching the meter, he had the money ready, paid the driver quickly, grabbed Lucy's hand and hurried to the shop.

He pushed the buzzer and the door opened in response by some remote-controlled magic, but it was some time before anyone appeared. Lucy inspected a tray of Victorian jewellery in a case, while David tapped his foot by the small desk in the corner. It was an old-fashioned sort of shop, with none of the appurtenances of modern commerce such as fax machines and cash tills – computerised or otherwise – and it contained an amazing quantity of items in a very small space. The shop specialised in decorative items, silver and jewellery rather than furniture. But everything in the shop, David apprehended quickly, was of the very highest quality, with prices to match. No junk, no knick-knacks, no jumble of dusty white elephants. Just a great many beautiful things displayed lovingly, if cheek-by-jowl. It told him something about the proprietor of the shop, and he realised even before the man appeared that the approach he'd taken with the young man at Christie's would not work here. Nor would the alternative approach that he'd considered during the taxi journey: veiled threats to report him for dealing in stolen goods if he refused to cooperate. A far more subtle touch would be required here. He slipped the Christie's catalogue back into his briefcase.

The William Morris tapestry curtains at the back of the shop parted and a face peered out, followed by a body. David expected it to be one of the dim-witted young twits usually employed in such places, seemingly with the sole function of screening out and dealing with casual browsers so that the proprietor could concentrate on the serious customers. But the man who appeared was on the verge of – though not quite – being elderly, small with a trim grey beard, and dragged one leg with a pronounced stiff-legged limp: clearly the proprietor himself. 'Oh, good morning. I'm sorry to have kept you waiting, but I was on the phone, and my assistant isn't in today.' His voice was courteous and precise, and he sized them up expertly without seeming to do so. 'Are you looking for something in particular? Some jewellery for the lady, perhaps?'

'Yes,' said David, inspired. Just the thing, he thought. 'I'd like to buy something special for her.'

'I can see that she's a very special lady,' the man said with a gallant little bow. He moved towards the case that Lucy was inspecting. 'I'm Mr Atkins, by the way. I like to be on a personal basis with my customers. And you're . . . ?'

'Mr Middleton-Brown, and this is Miss Kingsley.'

'Ah. Perhaps you were looking for a ring, Mr Middleton-Brown?' He raised his eyebrows in a sig-nificant way.

David looked at Lucy questioningly: not daring to ask, not daring to hope.

She didn't meet his eyes, but gave her head an infinitesimal shake.

'No, not this time,' he told Mr Atkins, unable to keep the disappointment from his voice. 'Could you suggest something else?'

The little man put his head to one side and gave Lucy the benefit of his professional consideration. 'With her beautiful colouring, and that lovely hair, I think that a nice cameo would be just the ticket.'

She smiled. 'I love cameos.'

'Then you shall have one, my love. Do you see any here that you fancy?'

Mr Atkins leaned forward and spoke in a confidential tone. 'I have something quite special in the back. Would you like to see it?'

David assented, and with painful slowness the man limped off to his curtained hideaway; he was away for several minutes, during which David had leisure to reflect on the advantages of cultivating patience. 'I can see that this is going to take all morning,' he muttered to Lucy.

'Here it is. I've found it.' The cultured voice preceded the corporal being in issuing from behind the curtain. 'I think, Mr Middleton-Brown, that you'll agree this was worth waiting for. I had it tucked away, waiting for just the right person to come along.' Eventually he reached the case, spread out a black velvet cloth, and arranged the cameo on it so that David and Lucy could see it to full effect. 'What do you think? Isn't it exquisite?'

It wasn't large or ostentatious, but it was beautifully carved, and surrounded by an intricate filigree of fine gold wires, suspended from a delicate gold chain. 'Oh, yes,' said Lucy. 'It's lovely.'

'Would you like to try it on?' Mr Atkins limped off in pursuit of a mirror, Lucy lifted her hair out of the way, and David carefully fastened the clasp at the back of her neck. 'Oh, it suits you very well,' Mr Atkins declared, nodding his approval. 'Just the thing, with your long neck, and that beautiful hair.' He held the mirror up for her.

Lucy smiled her pleasure, and David caught the other man's eye. 'Thank you, Mr Atkins. It's perfect.'

With admirable discretion Mr Atkins presented him with a slip of paper on which he'd written the price. David nodded and reached in his pocket for his cheque-book.

'Is there anything else I can do for you today, Mr Middleton-Brown? Something for yourself, perhaps? I have a very nice set of cuff links that came in just yesterday.'

Uncapping his pen, David said casually, 'Actually, I'm rather interested in ecclesiastical silver. Do you have anything like that, perhaps in the back room? I don't see any pieces on display.'

Mr Atkins scratched his head and gave the matter some thought. 'I don't think I *do* have anything at the moment, actually. It's a rather specialised market, you know. There's never any problem selling candlesticks, of course – they walk out of the door as soon as I put them on display. And occasionally people buy incense boats to use as sugar bowls, if you can believe it. But things like thuribles and chalices have a very limited appeal to the average man in the street. I don't very often buy that sort of thing.' He lowered his voice to a confidential tone, though there was no one else in the shop. 'I *did* have a beautiful piece, not long ago. A Pugin chalice. Very rare. Quite early. Silver gilt.'

David effected to look just a bit more than politely interested. 'I would have liked to have seen that.'

'Actually,' said Mr Atkins, 'I've put it into Christie's. Perhaps you've seen the catalogue – the sale is coming up soon.'

'No, I haven't been into Christie's for a while.'

'I've got a copy of the catalogue here somewhere.' There followed another frustratingly extended interval wherein Mr Atkins disappeared behind the curtains and conducted a search. 'Yes, here it is.' Slowly he returned and held it open for David to see the photograph.

All of David's acting skills were called upon now. He looked, then started and moved in for a closer look. 'Do you mind?' he said, taking the catalogue from Mr Atkins and carrying it to the light.

'It's beautiful, isn't it?' the shop's proprietor asked rhetorically.

'Mr Atkins.' David looked up at the other man, a puzzled frown creasing his brow. 'Might I ask you where you obtained this chalice?'

Mr Atkins cleared his throat. 'I'm afraid I can't tell you that. My business depends on my absolute discretion in matters like this – I'm sure you understand.'

'What would you say,' David pressed him, 'if I told you that this chalice was stolen property?'

The other man choked; his voice came out in an

uncharacteristic squeak. 'Stolen? But that's impossible.' He drew himself up to his full height. 'I can assure
you, Mr Middleton-Brown, that this is *not* that sort of a
shop!'

'Nevertheless, I'm afraid that this chalice is stolen
property. It was stolen from St Margaret's Church,
Pimlico, last December.' He paused to allow the full
impact of his words. 'I know that you're an honest man,
Mr Atkins, and I'm sure that you acquired this chalice
in good faith. But I'm afraid that the police may not take
that view.'

'Police!' It was the most feared word in Mr Atkins's
vocabulary. 'This isn't that sort of a shop,' he repeated,
but less forcefully, and beads of sweat had appeared on
his forehead.

'Perhaps I might be of some help,' offered David. 'I'm a
solicitor, and I've done some work for the Vicar and
churchwardens of St Margaret's. That's how I happen to
know about the stolen chalice. Perhaps this could be
managed discreetly.'

He seized on the hope of reprieve with touching
eagerness. 'You mean that the police might be kept out
of it?'

'I'm afraid that the police will have to be told.
But if I had a word with them, it could be done
with no discredit to you. And no publicity,' he
added.

'Oh, Mr Middleton-Brown! If you could!' He almost
trembled in his relief. 'I'd be so very grateful if you could
manage it. I can't have the police coming in here, with
their great feet, knocking things about. This is a
respectable shop – above reproach. I've never had any

trouble before. I don't...' He was descending into incoherence.

'I'll deal with the police,' promised David. 'But you must tell me everything. How did you obtain the chalice, Mr Atkins?'

He pressed his fingers to his temples to calm himself; after a moment he spoke. 'A chap brought it in to the shop one day,' he said. 'A respectable chap – I can tell the other sort a mile off.'

'I'm sure you can.'

'He said that the chalice was a family heirloom – his grandfather had been a bishop, he said, and it had belonged to him.'

'Did he have any idea how valuable the chalice was?'

'Oh, yes. He knew that it was Pugin, and worth a great deal of money. I didn't try to cheat him,' Mr Atkins insisted, defending his professional integrity. 'I told him, quite honestly, that he'd do better putting it in the sale room himself. But he was in a hurry for a sale.'

'A hurry?'

'Yes, he said that his wife needed an operation, and he had to have the money right away. He couldn't wait to put it through Christie's himself. I felt sorry for the chap. It was hard luck for him, having to sell a family treasure for a reason like that. I was more generous with him than I might have been.'

'I'll need to tell the police how much you paid him.'

'I gave him £7000,' Mr Atkins said reluctantly. 'In cash. It was rather a lot of cash, I know. I don't usually have that much right to hand, but I'd just had an American – a Texan – in that morning who bought several things. Pulled a roll of notes out of his pocket and paid in cash.'

'That doesn't happen very often, I imagine.'

'Not often enough! It was one of those lucky coincidences,' the man reflected. 'The American said that he wouldn't have even come down Kensington Church Street that morning, but an IRA bomb scare had closed the tube station – someone had been killed by a bomb at Victoria, I seem to remember. He walked past and saw something in the window that caught his eye. So he popped in, and ended up spending nearly ten thousand pounds.'

'What is it they say about an ill wind?' David remarked idly.

'Exactly. And so when the gentleman brought in the chalice, I was glad to be able to get rid of the cash – saved me closing the shop to go and bank it.'

It was time for the crucial question. 'You *did* get this man's name, I assume?'

'Of course,' said Mr Atkins indignantly. 'I always do things properly. I had him sign the book, just as the tax man requires me to do.'

'And may I see the book?'

David held his breath as the retreat behind the curtain was repeated for a third time. 'Yes, here it is.' He made his slow return, carrying a large book. He opened it on the desk, fumbled in his pocket for a pair of spectacles, which he settled on his nose with care, then flipped through the pages of the book. 'June, September, December. That's last year. I'm sure it was early this year. Yes, here. February. The eighth of February, this year.' He peered at the entry. 'That's right, I remember that he was a clergyman. So of course I dealt with him in good faith.' He paused to decipher the writing, then read it aloud. 'The Reverend William Keble Smythe, St Jude's Vicarage, Pimlico, SW1.'

'But what does it mean?' Lucy shook her head, baffled, as they took yet another taxi ride to Pimlico. 'I was expecting him to say Martin Bairstow, or Norman Topping. Not William Keble Smythe.'

'The Vicar.' David was rapidly readjusting his conceptions about their investigation. 'I can't believe that it was the Vicar all along.'

'We eliminated him because he had an alibi,' Lucy pointed out. 'Remember? He was the one person who wasn't at the church that night, when they had the row.'

'That's not really an alibi, if you think about it. We know where he *wasn't*, but that doesn't mean that we know where he *was*. If you understand me.'

'You mean that he could have been in his car, waiting for her to ride past?'

'Well,' David thought aloud, 'after all, he had asked her to take the service. He must have known what a kerfuffle it would cause.'

'He might have done it on purpose,' Lucy concluded slowly, touching her new cameo in an absent gesture. 'Asked her to take the service, knowing that there would be a row. And then waited for her to ride past. But why? Why would he want to kill Rachel?'

'The same reason that anyone else would, I reckon.

What if she'd found out something about him that was a threat to him in some way?'

'But I thought that Father Keble Smythe led a blameless life. That's what Dolly says, anyway.'

Something niggled at the corner of David's mind. 'I'm not so sure. I've heard hints that he may not be all that he seems. I wish I could remember.'

'Or maybe she found out somehow that he'd killed Father Julian,' Lucy suggested. 'That would be reason enough, I'd think.'

The taxi pulled up in front of the vicarage. 'Here you are, mate,' said the driver.

David paid him. 'I hope he's in,' he remarked as they marched up to the door.

Mrs Goode answered; she recognised David from his first visit, though to her chagrin she couldn't remember his name, and Lucy looked vaguely familiar to her as well. She looked back and forth between them, hoping for some clue.

'Hello, Mrs Goode,' David said smilingly, thereby endearing himself. 'I don't expect you to remember me, but I'm David Middleton-Brown. This is Miss Kingsley. I wondered if we might have a word with Father Keble Smythe.'

She returned his smile. 'Is Father expecting you?'

'No, but we'd be most awfully grateful if you could persuade him to spare us a few minutes. It's important.'

'I'll see what I can do,' she promised, and withdrew in the direction of the Vicar's study, chuckling to herself. How romantic, she thought. They've just decided to get married, and they can't wait to talk to Father to set the date. What a lovely couple they make.

Mrs Goode returned more speedily than Mr Atkins had managed. 'Father is very busy,' she said, 'but I've persuaded him to see you.' She gave them a conspiratorial wink. 'I told him it was important.'

Father Keble Smythe was seated at his desk; he rose as they entered. 'Do come in,' he said courteously.

Lucy looked around with interest; it was her first visit to the Vicar's study. In a glance she took in the discreetly expensive furniture, the thick carpet, the silver-framed photo of the famed Miss Morag McKenzie.

'I apologise for the intrusion, Father,' David began, 'but it really is rather important.'

'So Mrs Goode said.' He gave them a genial smile. 'How much did you have to bribe her?' A modest chuckle at his own wit, then, 'Please, do sit down.'

David remained standing and wasted no time with preliminary chitchat. 'I've located your stolen chalice,' he announced, watching carefully for the other man's response.

'My dear chap! How very splendid of you!' It was either genuine, or the man was a very good actor indeed. But Lucy remembered his star performance at Rachel's funeral, and determined to keep an open mind on the matter. 'But where is it? How did you find it? And when can we have it back?'

'At the moment,' said David, 'it's in Christie's sale room. But I expect you know that.'

The Vicar looked puzzled. 'I don't know what you mean. This is the first I've heard of it.'

'Or perhaps you thought that it was still in Mr Atkins's shop in Kensington Church Street.'

'What are you talking about?' The puzzlement was

beginning to transmute into annoyance.

The room was still. For a long moment David sized up William Keble Smythe, then spoke deliberately into the silence, his words falling like stones between them. 'I'm talking about theft, Father. And murder. How else can you explain your signature in Mr Atkins's sales book?'

Chapter 29

As soon as they hear of me, they shall obey me: but
the strange children shall dissemble with me.
The strange children shall fail: and be afraid out of
their prisons.

Psalm 18.45–46

David sat at his desk, staring at without seeing the
rather splendid view from his window. Spring was truly
upon them, the yellow trumpets of the daffodils playing
a symphony of their own in the newly verdant grass of
Lincoln's Inn. For all that David appreciated it, though,
it might still have been the dead of winter.

Father Keble Smythe had denied everything. All
knowledge, all involvement. He had professed himself
as baffled as they as to how his signature had appeared
in Mr Atkins's book. And to say that he had not been
amused at the accusation that David had levelled
against him was something of an understatement. To
call a man in holy orders – and the incumbent of a
prestigious London parish to boot – a triple murderer
was no small thing.

The worst of it was, David still wasn't sure whether
the Vicar was telling the truth or not. If he *had*

committed three murders to protect some secret, he certainly wouldn't admit it just because some solicitor strolled into his study and suggested that he might have done it. And he *was* a good actor, demonstrably so, with Rachel's funeral eulogy as an example.

In retrospect, David realised that their action in rushing straight to the vicarage to confront Father Keble Smythe might have been considered foolhardy. But at the time it hadn't crossed his mind, trusting instinctively in the proximity of the excellent Mrs Goode.

He'd realised, as well, that in their haste to get to the vicarage, they'd failed to ask Mr Atkins for a description of the man who had sold him the chalice – that might have gone a long way towards establishing Father Keble Smythe's guilt or innocence. An attempt to rectify their omission had failed: on their return to the shop, they'd been greeted with a notice on the door that the proprietor had gone for the weekend.

Frustrated, David put his mind to the problem. What could the Vicar be hiding? Ambition was one thing, and it was clear that Father Keble Smythe had that in abundance, but was there something else? What secret could he have that was worth killing to keep?

Suddenly he recalled the memory that had been on the edge of his consciousness: Alistair Duncan, in the musty, dusty sitting room of the clergy house in Brighton, suggesting that perhaps Father Keble Smythe might have one or two skeletons in his cupboard. At the time it had scarcely registerez, but now it seemed overwhelmingly important.

He found the number quickly and dialled, holding his breath until the distinctive Scots burr said, 'Hello?'

'Oh, hello. This is David Middleton-Brown.' His mind worked rapidly. 'I've just realised that I walked off with Father Julian's diary when I saw you the other day, and wondered how desperate you were to have it back.'

'Not desperate.' Alistair's laugh was bittersweet. 'I don't think I've got much use for it at the moment. Keep it if you think it will help.'

'It just might.'

'You haven't found out yet who killed Jules?' The young man's voice held little hope.

'Not yet,' David admitted, 'but I may be getting close. And you might be able to get me a little further along, if you wouldn't mind telling me something.'

'Anything,' Alistair said promptly and without reservation. 'Anything that will help you catch the sodding bastard.'

David hesitated as he framed his next statement. 'When I saw you on Monday you mentioned Father Keble Smythe. You said that you knew a few things about him that you didn't think he would want his congregation to know.'

'Oh, aye.' Alistair laughed again, but without a great deal of amusement. 'He spent some time in Scotland, you see. At St Andrews, where he did his degree. He had rather a reputation north of the border.'

'What sort of a reputation?' David was afraid that he knew the answer already.

'Oh, you know. Wild parties. Men. There was a chap called Hamish Douglas that he was involved with for a while. But he put all that behind him when he came down south, or so it would seem.' He chuckled. 'Jules said that he was even claiming a fiancée nowadays. That's a pretty good one, given some of the stories I've heard about William Keble Smythe. Or Wendy, as he was known in those days. Wendy Smythe – he seems to have picked up the "Keble" somewhere along the line.'

'So you mean,' David said slowly, 'that Father Julian knew about Father Keble Smythe's past.'

'Of course he did. There wasn't any reason for me not to tell him, was there?' Alistair sounded slightly defensive.

David couldn't say what he was thinking: that perhaps that knowledge had led to Julian Piper's death. He adopted a reassuring tone, hoping that Alistair wouldn't make the connection. 'No. Of course not. But thanks for telling me, and for all your help. And,' he added before ringing off, 'I'll let you know as soon as there's anything to tell. I promise.'

It could have been, David said to himself, looking blankly at the phone. Father Keble Smythe. He could have done it – he certainly had motive enough, at least to kill Father Julian. And Rachel could have found out as well about his unsavoury past. If only he'd remembered to get the description from Mr Atkins. Nothing could be proved until they had that.

So much had happened in just a few hours – it was now only early afternoon. So much, but had it accomplished anything? They were still no closer to knowing the truth of the chalice than they'd been the day before.

The chalice. David was certain that its importance, ignored until so recently, could not be overestimated. For, as he had postulated earlier, the person who had taken the chalice had also killed three people.

The chalice. It had all begun with the chalice, and now it had come full circle. One chalice, three lives. David picked up a pencil and began doodling, sketching a chalice. One chalice, and then one more. And another.

He realised with a start that he was defacing a letter that he hadn't even read yet, part of the morning's post which had been opened by his efficient secretary and stacked on his desk for his attention.

A letter from the immigration office. Damn, he thought. Justin Thymme. Am I to be plagued forever by Justin Thymme?

The letter, from Mrs Hartman the immigration officer, was straightforward: a formal interview of his client, Mr Justin Thymme, had been scheduled for a date a fortnight hence, and he was being notified as a matter of course, since it was assumed that he would want to be in attendance. That was all, but it sparked something in his brain, something that had been there all along lying dormant. Something that Pamela Hartman had said to him on the occasion of their initial interview.

Suddenly the pieces came together, like bits of coloured glass in a stained glass window: Pamela Hartman's offhand remark; something that Rachel Nightingale had said to Ruth after Evensong at Westminster Abbey; an entry in Father Julian's diary. In the space of time no longer than it took to draw breath, David knew why three people had died. There was only one piece missing: he didn't know who had killed them. Thinking rapidly, he reckoned that it almost certainly must have been one of two people. Two possibilities.

When Gabriel had told him about Father Julian, the death that had started it all, David had theorised that he and Rachel had both died because of the one thing that they had in common: the fact that they were both curates at St Margaret's Church. Now he realised how true that assumption had been, and how easily he and Lucy had been sidetracked – with Ruth's help – into quite the wrong conclusion, based on that assumption. They had thought that the significant thing about curates was that, as counsellors and recipients of confidences, they knew people's secrets – secrets that people would kill to keep that way. The truth was both simpler and more complicated than that.

The answer lay where the whole thing had begun: in the sacristy of St Margaret's Church. David was convinced of that. All he had to do was to get into that sacristy, on his own, and he would find the answer. The proof he needed was certainly there, and, with any luck, a pointer to the guilty person.

He thought for a moment more, then picked up the phone. But before he could dial the number, Ruth popped her head round the door. 'Would you like some tea?' she offered sullenly; she still hadn't forgiven him for excluding her that morning, but this was her own way of offering an olive branch.

'Yes, thanks. In a minute. I need to make an important phone call now – if you wouldn't mind shutting the door, please.'

Ruth didn't like being dismissed so peremptorily, especially when she'd been prepared to be nice to him. Then, with rising excitement, she realised that he'd said an important phone call. She was in luck – Mrs

Simmons was still at lunch, so Ruth picked up the phone on her desk in time to hear Emily calling the Archdeacon to the phone.

'Gabriel,' said David after a moment, 'I've got a favour to ask you.'

'What's that?'

'Remember the other night, when you said that you would be available if we needed you to do something? Feel free to call on you, is what you said.' David paused. 'Well, you're about to be called upon.'

'What can I do for you, then?'

'I need the keys to the sacristy of St Margaret's. And to the safe.'

'You need what?' He sounded incredulous.

'Yes, I know that it's a strange request. But you'll have to trust me – it's important. And I need them as soon as possible,' he added.

There was a long pause. 'And how do you expect me to produce these keys?'

'I've thought it all out,' David explained. 'You're the Archdeacon. You have the right to make a visitation to any church at any time, don't you? Just ring the Vicar, or the Administrator, or one of the churchwardens, and say that you're coming this afternoon, to inspect the terrier. It's within your rights, Gabriel. They may think it's odd, but they can't really say no.'

'That's true,' Gabriel admitted cautiously. 'And then what am I supposed to do?'

'Pocket the keys somehow, when they're not looking. I know that you can do it,' he wheedled. 'And if you can get me those keys this afternoon – and a key to the church itself would be a great help, by the way – by tomorrow I ought to be able to tell you who killed the two curates and Vera Bright, and why.'

'Can't you tell me *now*?'

'I'm afraid that I won't know until I've been able to get into that sacristy. That's where the answer is to be found.'

'Well,' Gabriel capitulated. 'If it's that important, I'll see what I can do. I'll ring you later.'

'I won't leave my desk until I hear from you.' He gave Gabriel the number, adding, 'You promised, remember?'

As soon as she heard the click to show that the connection had been broken, Ruth put down the phone. Her mind worked furiously as she made the promised tea for David; she tapped on his closed door and, when he invited her to enter, delivered the tea with a smile.

'Thanks, Ruth,' he said abstractedly, then looked up at her. 'Do you have anything to do? I know that it's your last afternoon here – you could leave early, if you wanted. I could ring and ask your Aunt Lucy to come for you. I may have to stay a bit late today.'

'Oh, no. That's all right,' she assured him. 'Since it's my last day, everyone has come up with plenty of photocopying for me to do. Next week there won't be anyone here to do it!'

She was taking it in remarkably good spirit, he grudgingly admitted to himself. 'Well, if you'll be all right...'

'Yes. Don't worry about me. I'll be in the photocopier room.'

She went back to Mrs Simmons's desk, picked up the

348

phone, and rang Directory Enquiries, asking for the number for St Margaret's Church. She wasn't sure whether there would even be a phone, and if there was, who might be there to answer it, but in due course it was answered. 'St Margaret's Church,' came a voice down the phone.

'Is this the Vicar?' she asked.

'No, this is the Administrator.'

'Oh, well, you'll do just as well,' she said sweetly. 'My name is Ruth Kingsley – I think that you know my aunt, Lucy Kingsley. You see, I'm doing a project at school for RE. We have to visit a church, and write something about it. And I'm afraid I've left it rather late. It has to be handed in next week. So I was wondering if it would be all right if I came to your church this afternoon.'

'Well, I don't know. I'm awfully busy. Isn't there any other church you could visit instead?'

'But your church is so beautiful,' Ruth said, though she'd never been inside it. 'I can't think of any other church that I like nearly so well as yours.'

The flattery was not without effect. 'What, in particular, would you like to see?'

She tried to think what was kept in the sacristy. 'The ... um ... silver,' she said. 'I'm sure that you could tell me some interesting things about it. My aunt says that you know ever so much about everything in the church.'

He sighed heavily. 'I'm a very busy man, young lady. The Archdeacon has just rung to say that he's coming by later to inspect the silver.'

'But if you have to get it out for him anyway,' she coaxed, 'it won't be any trouble for me to have a look at it as well.'

'All right, then,' he gave in. 'Perhaps the sacristan will be in a bit later, to change the frontals for the weekend, and he might be able to spare rather more time than I can. Will you be coming soon?'

'Oh, yes. Right away. I'll see you in a little while, then.'

Ruth put the phone down and turned to find Mrs Simmons looking at her, hands on ample hips. 'What do you think you're doing?' she demanded.

'Oh, I was just talking to Aunt Lucy.' Ruth gave her an innocent smile. 'Uncle David has said that I can go home early, as it's my last day, and I just wanted to tell her that I was coming.'

'By yourself?'

'Oh, yes.' Ruth waved her hand dismissively. 'He doesn't mind. He knows that I'm not a baby. I'm perfectly capable of getting to South Kensington by myself.'

'Well, if you're sure...'

She was already on her way. 'It's been nice knowing you,' she said over her shoulder. 'And remember – he's busy. Don't bother him.'

Half an hour later, Lucy rang David. As Mrs Simmons put the call through, she asked, 'Has Ruth made it home safely, then?'

Lucy was puzzled. 'Ruth? Why, no. She wouldn't come home on her own.'

'But she set off about thirty minutes ago. She said that Mr Middleton-Brown had told her to go home early. And she rang you to tell you that she was coming – I heard the end of the conversation.'

350

'No,' said Lucy, beginning to be alarmed. 'She *didn't* ring me. You'd better put me through to David right away.'

He sent for Mrs Simmons a minute later. 'Would you mind telling me what this is all about?' he asked. 'Where is Ruth?'

'She's gone home,' she repeated. 'She said that you told her to go.'

David frowned. 'Can you remember her exact words?'

'She said, "Uncle David said that I can go home early, as it's my last day." Or something quite close to that.'

He groaned. 'Are you sure that she said "Uncle David"?'

'Oh, yes. I remember that, because I've never heard her call you that before.'

Into the phone he said, 'Now I *know* that she's up to something, love.'

'You mean that you didn't tell her to go home?' queried Mrs Simmons, only beginning to understand.

'No, I didn't.'

'Then perhaps I should tell you that I thought it was a little strange. She said that she was talking to her Aunt Lucy on the phone, but part of the conversation was about churches and silver. She mentioned St Margaret's Church.'

'Good Lord.' David spoke into the phone again. 'I think that she's gone to St Margaret's. I'll go after her, Lucy. She'll be all right.'

'I'll meet you there,' she said immediately.

'I'd rather you didn't,' he protested, knowing that it would make no difference.

It should be all right, he thought as he walked rapidly

to High Holborn and the tube station. Ruth wouldn't really be in danger, no matter how idiotically she had behaved. She didn't really know anything, and surely no one would harm her in a church, in daylight. There would be people around. Then he remembered who those people might be, and he quickened his pace. For a moment he considered whether it might not be faster to take a taxi, but decided that afternoon traffic in London would make the Underground the wiser choice, if speed were important. It wasn't just Ruth – Lucy was on her way as well, and no matter how quickly he managed to travel she would get there before he did. And he hadn't had the opportunity to tell her of his conclusions about the murderer. She'd be arriving at St Margaret's with only slightly more knowledge, and more wariness, than Ruth.

Would the Vicar be going to St Margaret's later to say Evensong? Or would he go to St Jude's, which was nearer the vicarage? And what time was Evensong, anyway? It could be important. David thought about the notation in Father Julian's diary, and he went suddenly cold as the last piece fell into place. He knew with a grim certainty who had killed three people – Father Julian had told him.

Would it be enough to convict? Probably not: they would need the evidence from the sacristy as well. And of course the testimony of Mr Atkins, who should be able to identify the seller of the chalice. As he hurried down the steps into the tube station, he remembered something that Mr Atkins had told him only that morning. It hadn't registered as significant at the time, but now it provided all the confirmation he needed to be sure that the information in Father Julian's diary was relevant. And that he didn't have any time to lose.

After her visit to the Toppings, Ruth had no difficulty in locating the neighbouring St Margaret's Church. The church was unlocked and seemingly empty, but after a brief exploration of the building Ruth found Stanley Everitt waiting for her in the sacristy. She had never met Stanley Everitt, though she'd seen him at Rachel's funeral – his death's head face was unmistakeable – but she wasn't sure whether he remembered her or not. 'Hello, Mr Everitt. I'm Ruth Kingsley,' she said with the ingratiating smile that she'd used to such good effect on Dolly Topping. 'I really do appreciate you taking the time to show me your silver.'

His peeved expression softened a fraction, and he unbent sufficiently to say, 'You're very fortunate that you came today. Friday is the only day I'm at St Margaret's – the rest of the week I'm at St Jude's.'

'Oh, what a lucky coincidence,' she gushed.

Everitt cleared his throat. 'Yes. Well.'

She saw that he had already taken the silver from the safe and set it out on the top of a vestment chest. That was a disappointment; she'd hoped to get a peek inside the safe when he opened it, but he had forestalled her. But she injected great eagerness into her voice as she said, 'So is this your silver, then?'

'Yes. I assume that what you're interested in for your school project is its liturgical use rather than its artistic qualities.' His tone was schoolmasterish, and indeed he had been an RE teacher himself before being made redundant and taking on the Administrator's job. 'This, of course, is a chalice. It is used to hold the wine during the Mass, referring to Our Lord's last supper.'

'Oh, so you have another chalice,' Ruth blurted out without thinking.

Everitt looked at her. 'What do you mean?'

'Oh, um,' she faltered. 'I just meant that of course everyone knows that the chalice was stolen in a robbery, when Father Julian was killed.'

'That was a terrible thing,' he intoned, furrowing his brow and wringing his hands. 'I was the one who found his body, you know. On the Saturday morning when I came in to prepare for a wedding. A great shock, it was.'

'Oh, it must have been.' She gained confidence in her information-gathering techniques. 'And an even greater shock to have another curate killed so soon after,' she added boldly.

The Administrator put the chalice down and took a closer look at Ruth. 'You were at the funeral.'

'Yes.'

'And at the vicarage after.' He leaned down and brought his face close to hers. 'You were a friend of Miss Bright, were you?'

'That's right.'

His voice was soft; it had lost its customary pedantic, self-important edge. 'You said that she knew who had killed Rachel. She didn't happen to tell you who it was, did she?'

Ruth decided to be cagy. 'Maybe she did, and maybe she didn't.'

He stared at her for a moment, as if weighing up her words, and she returned his stare coolly. It was at that moment that she saw, out of the corner of her eye, a green and gold carrier bag on the table in the corner, and she knew that she was confronting a murderer. 'It was you, wasn't it?' she said slowly. 'You killed Miss Bright. You killed them all.'

Things happened very quickly after that. Stanley Everitt reached for a penknife, left carelessly behind by the sacristan after cleaning the lumps of melted incense out of the thurible. Lucy appeared at the door, and Ruth screamed. 'Run, Aunt Lucy,' she shrilled. 'He killed them. Go and tell David. Tell him—'

Her shout was cut off by a hand over her mouth, and the knife blade was pressed to her throat. 'I don't think you'll want to do that, Miss Kingsley. Not unless you relish seeing your niece's throat cut.' His voice was chillingly calm; Lucy was transfixed with horror just inside the door.

It was only a few seconds later that David arrived, winded, having run from the tube station. He took in the situation instantly, pushing Lucy behind him and bursting into the sacristy.

'Stop right there,' Everitt warned. 'Don't come any closer, or I promise you that I'll kill her.'

All other circumstances aside, David was at a physical disadvantage, his heart pounding as he gasped for breath.

They were at an impasse. Everitt and his hostage, frozen in terror, faced David across the sacristy. 'Come inside away from the door,' Everitt commanded. 'You and the girl's aunt both. I don't want either one of you thinking that you're going to go for help. Over there.' He gestured with his head to the corner farthest from the door.

David knew that they had to obey. He took Lucy's hand and moved slowly around the circumference of the sacristy; Everitt backed around towards the door, continuing to watch them warily. 'Don't try anything, or I'll kill her,' he repeated.

'You would, too, wouldn't you?' David spoke at last. 'Just like you killed the others.'

Ruth gasped in pain as he nicked her throat with the knife. 'What do you know about that?' Everitt asked softly.

'I know that you killed them, and I know why.' David's voice sounded calm. 'But I'd like to know one thing. Why did you steal the marriage certificates? Was it just for the money?'

'Just for the money?' Everitt laughed. 'It was a great deal of money. More money than *you'll* ever see.'

'How did you get involved in it, then?'

'Do you really want to know?'

'Why don't you tell me,' David invited.

Everitt decided that there was nothing to lose; it was obvious that David knew something about it already, and he was actually quite proud of his own cleverness, welcoming a chance to share it. 'I was approached,' he said. 'The first time, it was just one that they wanted. One marriage certificate. A chap approached me and asked if I could get it for them. They offered me a thousand pounds for it. So I said yes.'

'They asked you because you were the Administrator?'

'Yes, of course. They knew that I'd have access to the certificates. It was no problem,' he boasted. 'Father Keble Smythe never checks the registers. He's always allowed me to fill them out and to do the reports for the registrar, so it couldn't have been simpler.'

'Then they wanted more?'

'As many as I could get for them, they said. They'd pay me a thousand pounds apiece for as many blank marriage certificates as I could supply.'

David knew that he had to keep him talking as long as possible. 'Then Father Julian stumbled on to your little ... sideline?'

Everitt laughed. 'He was too conscientious by half. He decided that he wanted to fill out the register for the weddings he took, and he discovered that the numbers didn't match up. Fortunately he came to me instead of going to Father Keble Smythe.'

'So you killed him.'

'I had no choice – he would have exposed me. And there was an added benefit. Two, actually.' He chuckled softly to himself. 'I was able to take a whole book of certificates, as though it were part of the burglary. Later I reported them as stolen to the registrar, and was sent a whole new book. And of course there was the chalice.'

'But you didn't know how valuable it was when you took it, did you?'

'No, of course not. No one knew that the silver was worth anything. I took it just to add authenticity to the burglary, and put it at the back of my wardrobe at home. And then you came along and told me that it was worth thousands. I couldn't resist selling it.'

Lucy spoke for the first time. 'What about Rachel? Why did you have to kill *her*?'

Everitt frowned. 'They came back to me later, and

wanted more certificates, only a few this time. She had weddings two Saturdays in a row. I'd taken the certificates during that week, and she noticed that the numbers were off. She was going to tell the Vicar – I was with him when she rang to say that she wanted to talk to him. I knew that she'd found out, so I took my chance.'

'And Miss Bright,' Lucy said. 'Did she really know that you'd killed them?'

His laugh was unpleasant. 'I don't know if she knew anything or not. But I couldn't chance it, could I? I don't think that she *did* know anything – she let me into her house quite happily, and made me a cup of coffee.'

Lucy shuddered; David squeezed her hand.

'What is the meaning of this?' The authoritative and outraged tones of the Archdeacon were heard at the sacristy door, triggering another rapid sequence of events.

Everitt turned his head sharply towards the door, for an instant slackening the pressure of the knife on Ruth's throat. She sensed her opportunity and sank her metal-encrusted teeth into the hand that covered her mouth; he shrieked in agony. And David, with a well-judged movement of his foot, kicked the silver choir cross which leaned against the wall, unbalancing it and causing it to topple over on to Everitt. It was over six feet tall and extremely heavy; the top of the cross caught him on the side of the head as it fell and sent him sprawling, unconscious. Ruth sprang clear, to be grabbed by Lucy with fierce protectiveness.

It had all happened so quickly, in a matter of seconds. Gabriel stood at the door, astonished.

Weak with relief, David grinned. 'Hello, Archdeacon,'

he drawled. 'Well timed, though I confess I was beginning to think that you'd never get here. Why don't you make yourself useful and go ring 999?'

'Let me do it,' Ruth demanded, resilient as ever. 'Let *me* ring 999 – after all, I'm the one who discovered him.'

A few hours later they were all in the Archdeacon's drawing room. The ambulance had been and gone, and of course the police as well, who had taken their statements, collected certain evidence from the sacristy in consequence, and sent them home.

The shock was beginning to wear off, though Lucy still looked pale and was unusually subdued. Emily, the only one who had missed out on the excitement first-hand, cossetted her with cups of strong tea and, when that didn't seem to have the desired effect, with brandy instead.

Of course David had to relate to Emily and to Gabriel the substance of Everitt's admissions of guilt, aided ably by Ruth's interjections. 'I still don't understand why he did it,' Emily said at the end, shaking her head in bafflement. 'Was there some reason that he needed the money?'

'I was just about to ask him, when your husband got around to rescuing us,' David put in with a wry grin.

Gabriel, who had been on the phone with the police, ignored David's jibe. 'He made a full statement to the police after he regained consciousness. They didn't want to tell me what he said, of course, but I threw my weight around a bit. Said that as Archdeacon I had a right to know, so they told me. It seems that his wife's a bit of a social climber. Keeping up with the Bairstows seems to be the chief concern – and that's where the problems began. Martin Bairstow is a successful businessman with more money than he and his wife between them know what to do with, and Stanley Everitt is – was – a parish administrator, making barely enough to survive. His wife doesn't work, and they have no additional income. So he thought that this would give him a little extra cash so that his wife would stop nagging him.'

'Everything she served at that meeting at her house a few weeks back came from Knightsbridge,' recalled Emily. 'I thought at the time that she seemed to be trying to out-do Vanessa.'

'And hence the carrier bag,' David added with a grim smile.

Lucy nodded. 'When she found out that Vanessa had commissioned a painting from me, she said that she wanted one as well. I wondered how on earth she could afford it, but at that meeting she said that she definitely wanted to go ahead with it.'

'Presumably,' David deduced, 'that was about the time that her husband went back to the well again, and stole the last few marriage certificates – the ones that made Rachel suspicious.'

'I think,' said Emily slowly, 'that there was more to it than that. More than just his wife, I mean. I think that, if anything, that was just an excuse for what he did.'

'What do you mean?' queried Gabriel.

'I think that it was his way of getting revenge on the Church. He was turned down by the Board of Ministry, wasn't he?'

'Yes,' Gabriel confirmed. 'Three times.'

'He wanted to be a priest,' remembered David. 'He

told me so – and he was really bitter that the Church
didn't want him, didn't value his talents.'

Emily nodded. 'That's what I mean. He had to be
satisfied with being Administrator, always telling
people how important he was. And surely it's significant
that two of the people that he killed were curates.
Something he'd never be, no matter how much he
wanted it.'

'But what about Miss Bright?' Ruth put in. 'Why did
he have to kill her too? When he wasn't even sure that
she knew anything?'

'I think that by that time he'd got to like killing
people,' Emily analysed shrewdly. 'I think he enjoyed
the feeling of power that it gave him.' She shook her
head. 'I think he's a real psychopath.'

Gabriel sighed. 'If only I'd been here that day when
Rachel phoned. It was too late for Julian Piper, but two
other deaths might have been prevented.'

'You mustn't think that.' Emily went to him, perching
on the edge of his chair and putting a protective arm
around his shoulders.

'Yes, well,' David put in quickly, in an attempt to
forestall Ruth's breastbeating routine over Vera Bright.
'For a while I had the wrong end of the stick altogether. I
was running around after Francis Nightingale.'

True to form, Ruth favoured him with an accusing
glare. 'You never said.'

'Francis Nightingale?' Emily turned to him blankly.
'Colin's brother, you mean?'

'Yes.' David ignored Ruth. 'I don't think I ever told
you about him. I was convinced that if anyone had killed
Rachel, it had been him, because he was the one who

benefited financially from her death. He needed money badly, I found out.'

'And after what Rachel said to me about him pulling the plug on Colin . . .' Emily surmised.

'Exactly. I think that he *did* pull the plug on Colin in the end, as it happens, but that's neither here nor there.'

Emily looked thoughtful. 'David, you still haven't told us how you figured it out about the marriage certificates. And how you knew that Stanley Everitt was the one who'd taken them.'

His mouth twisted in a self-deprecating smile. 'I should have known much sooner, actually. All of the evidence about the marriage certificates had been staring me in the face all along.'

'What do you mean?' Emily pressed him.

'I have a client called Justin Thymme,' he began, then paused at Emily and Gabriel's disbelieving looks to assure them, 'Yes, that's really his name. He's run into some trouble with the immigration office because he's married a Hong Kong Chinese woman. I won't bore you with the details, but for various reasons the immigration officer in charge of the case feels that the marriage might be a fraudulent one, entered into so that the wife can claim residency in this country, and eventually be eligible for a British passport, so that she can then bring all of her family in.' He took a sip of his whisky and went on. 'I happen to believe that she's right, but that's also neither here nor there. When I met the immigration officer, she was quite frank with me. She explained that some people will stop at nothing to get a British passport, and mentioned that there was a thriving trade in stolen marriage certificates going on. And where else would one steal marriage certificates, if not from a church? But I didn't make the connection, not then, and not till much later.'

Emily tried to make him feel better. 'But why should you have made the connection?'

'I knew about the burglary at St Margaret's, but as far as I was aware, nothing but the chalice had been stolen,' he acknowledged. 'I didn't even know, until you told me less than a week ago, that Father Julian had been killed in the burglary. But I *did* know that Rachel Nightingale performed a wedding on the Saturday before her death, because she told us so when we ran into her later that day at Westminster Abbey, and she mentioned that she had one the following week as well. And when I obtained Father Julian's diary, I also knew that he was to have performed a wedding on the Saturday after his death. But when I was looking for links, for connections, the weddings never occurred to me. And after Rachel had made a point of telling us that weddings were something that even deacons could perform!' He shook his head. 'I had a feeling all along that those two deaths had something to do with the fact that both of them were curates, but I was on completely the wrong track.'

Gabriel leaned forward. 'But once you'd figured out about the marriage certificates, how did you know that it was Stanley Everitt who had taken them?'

'Before I tell you that, why don't you explain to Lucy how the whole business of marriage certificates works?' David suggested, aware of her silence and mindful that she might be confused.

The Archdeacon nodded. 'Ordinarily,' he explained, 'the vicar is the one who fills out the register when a

marriage takes place. Or the curate, of course. There are
very strict rules about it, and it has to be done very
carefully. Each entry is numbered, and the numbers in
the register correspond to the numbers on the certificate
which is given to the couple. Every quarter, each
incumbent is required to fill out a form for the registrar,
copying the information from the registers and supply-
ing the numbers. A bit of a fiddle, because it has to be
done just right, but one of those things that most clergy
just get on with as part of the job. Apparently, though,
Father Keble Smythe thought that it was a job which
could safely be left to his Administrator.'

David took up the tale. 'So it seemed to me that it
almost certainly had to be either the Administrator or
the Vicar, as they were the only two people, apart from
the curates, who would have had access to the marriage
registers and the certificates. An inside job, in the
vernacular,' he grinned. 'But which one? I had reason to
suspect Father Keble Smythe, but I had no proof in
either direction. And then, as I was on my way to St
Margaret's, I remembered two things. I remembered
that I'd run into Stanley Everitt in South Ken tube
station, the day that there'd been an IRA bomb scare.
And that, according to Mr Atkins the antique dealer,
was the day that a man purporting to be Father William
Keble Smythe had sold him a valuable chalice. Someone
had been killed by a bomb – Mr Atkins and I both
recalled it. And that was the day after I told the
churchwardens and Everitt that the silver was worth a
small fortune.'

'Hardly conclusive evidence,' Gabriel commented
neutrally. 'But you said two things?'

'Oh, yes. The other thing that I remembered was Father Julian's diary.'

'You already mentioned that,' Emily pointed out. 'About the weddings.'

David shook his head. 'Not the weddings. Something else. You know that Father Julian's diary was in a sort of shorthand, so that he could fit everything in? Initials, and so forth?' He gave a dry laugh. 'That shorthand misled us more than once already, when we jumped to certain conclusions – remember VB and NT? Well, the mistake I made was even more unforgivable than that, for one who professes to know something about churches.'

Gabriel looked intrigued. 'What on earth are you getting at?'

Again David laughed. 'SE,' he said succinctly. 'The diary said SE on that last evening of his life. It meant Stanley Everitt, of course – he had planned to see him, to confront him with the discrepancies in the registers. Everitt always spent Fridays at St Margaret's, apparently. But – fool that I was – I just assumed that it meant Solemn Evensong!'

'Solemn Evensong – on a Friday evening in Advent?' Gabriel's laugh was rich and genuine. 'You must be joking! David, you do disappoint me!'

David shared in the general laughter at his own expense, knowing that he deserved it. But one voice that should have been the first to condemn his folly was strangely silent. He looked towards the chair which Ruth had appropriated – the most comfortable in the room, by virtue of her great ordeal. The girl's head had fallen to one side, her mouth was slightly open, and her eyes were closed. In sleep she looked peaceful, almost angelic, her red hair forming a halo around her serene face. Appearances can be deceiving, David said to himself.

Chapter 30

For in the hand of the Lord there is a cup, and the
wine is red: it is full mixed, and he poureth out of
the same.
As for the dregs thereof: all the ungodly of the earth
shall drink them, and suck them out.

Psalm 75.9–10

'Well, I suppose this is it.' They were all thinking it, but
it was Ruth who spoke the words as they stood on the
platform at Euston Station. It hardly seemed possible,
reflected David, that it had only been three weeks since
the three of them had come together in this spot. Three
of the longest weeks of his life – just as he had predicted
that first night, he thought with a wry smile.

The train to Northampton would be leaving in just a
few minutes. Ruth had allowed David to carry her case –
now even heavier than it had been three weeks ago,
with the addition of her Covent Garden purchases – and
to heft it on to the train for her. Now it only remained to
say goodbye.

Ruth stood squarely in front of David and thrust her
hand out. 'Thank you for helping me with my work experience,' she said formally, almost as if on remembered

instructions from her parents. 'And for everything else, too,' she added with a near-smile.

He took her hand and shook it. 'Have a safe journey.'

Lucy held out her arms to her niece; the girl went into them and hugged her aunt with an affection that even she couldn't hide. And she whispered something in her ear that made Lucy smile.

Then she clambered on to the train. Her face appeared by the window for a last wave and a moment later the train pulled out.

They stood for a moment as it receded into the distance. 'The poor kid,' said Lucy on a sigh.

'What do you mean, poor kid? Her parents are the ones to feel sorry for now, getting her back.'

Lucy shook her head. 'The other day when we had lunch together, she told me that her parents are having real problems with their marriage. That's why they packed her off here, instead of arranging for her to do her work experience in Northampton. She said that they row all the time, that life at home is pretty grim. It's no wonder she's mixed up, David. Being fourteen is quite bad enough without having to deal with hell at home.'

'Or maybe it's the other way around. Maybe *she's* the reason *they're* having problems.'

'Give the kid a break, David.' Lucy smiled. 'Don't you want to know what she whispered before she left?'

'I wait with bated breath.'

'She said that you're not too bad.'

'High praise indeed from the *enfant terrible*.' But he was touched in spite of himself. 'Just do me a favour,' he added.

'What's that?'

'If I ever suggest, in a moment of insanity, that we should have a child, just say "Ruth" to me. Or better yet, put a bullet through my head and put me out of my misery.'

Laughing, Lucy turned to him and put both hands over her abdomen. 'David,' she said, 'I'm afraid I have something to tell you.' For an instant she watched the welter of conflicting emotions struggling for supremacy on his face before she relented. 'Only joking, darling.'

David clutched his heart and gasped. 'Don't ever do that to me again.'

They walked back down the platform and into the station. 'Should we have coffee?' Lucy suggested, indicating the station café.

'Here? Surely we can do better than Travellers' Fare, love. Why don't we just go home?'

She turned her head away. 'There's something I need to say to you, and I'd rather do it here, on neutral territory.'

David had no presentiment of approaching disaster; he was merely puzzled. 'All right,' he agreed.

They went in and ordered coffee; it came in polystyrene cups, and they drank it sitting on red plastic chairs.

'So what did you want to say?' David prompted her.

Lucy took a deep breath. 'Something came in the post for you this morning. I opened it by mistake.'

'And what was it?' he grinned. 'Something terrible out of my past that's finally caught up with me?'

'Well, in a way it was. It was about Lady Constance's house. The will has been proved, and you can take possession at the beginning of April.' She added, 'The letter said that they'd sent some correspondence to you at the office but you hadn't replied, so they were writing to you at your home address instead.'

So the evil moment had come. 'Well?' he said cautiously. 'Does it have to make any difference?'

'I think that you should move into the house.' Lucy spoke rapidly in a voice that didn't sound anything like her. 'I think that perhaps it's time for us to live apart.'

It hit him like a painful blow to the solar plexus; for a moment he couldn't speak – couldn't even breathe. 'What are you saying?' he gulped finally.

Lucy cupped her hands around the polystyrene container and looked down. 'I'll tell you,' she said. 'Please don't interrupt me, or try to argue – this is hard enough already. I just want to tell you and have done with it.'

'Go on.' David couldn't believe how calm he sounded, but now that the initial blow had fallen, he felt almost detached, as though this were happening to someone else.

She said it all quickly, without looking at him. 'I don't like what's been happening to us lately. It has nothing to do with Ruth – it has to do with me. And it's not that I don't love you, David – quite the contrary. Recently I've come to realise how much I *do* love you – much more than I've ever loved anyone before.'

He couldn't help himself. 'Surely that's good?'

'No, it's not. I don't like what it's doing to me. The other night at Emily and Gabriel's, I suddenly realised that I was jealous – jealous of you and Gabriel. I've never been a jealous person. I've never minded before –

about what happened between you. But now I do mind – not because he's a man, but because you loved him – and I don't like that. And the other morning when I nagged you about it, I just couldn't help myself. I hated myself for it, but I couldn't stop.' She swirled the murky dregs around in the cup. 'I suppose what I'm saying is that I'm afraid of loving you too much.'

'But what is there to be afraid of?'

Lucy bit her lip. 'I suppose it's a sort of superstitious fear,' she confessed. 'That if I love you too much – invest too much of myself in you – you'll be taken away from me somehow. And I'd rather have that happen on my own terms.'

'You're going to try to stop loving me, then?' David's voice seemed to him to come from a long distance.

She replied obliquely. 'All of the things that have happened over the past few weeks, all of the misery that we've encountered, all of the unhappy people; when you think about it, it's all been about love. Casualties of love, every one of them. People who have loved too much, and look what it's done to them. Alistair Duncan loving Father Julian. Nicola Topping and her Ben. Vera Bright and her American. Vanessa. Rachel, too, in her way. And Ruth – damaged in the second generation by love that's gone wrong. And of course there was you and Gabriel.' She sighed softly. 'I don't want to be one of those casualties, David.'

David realised that what he said next could well determine the course of the rest of his life, and he'd better get it right. He fought the desire to reach across and touch her. Instinctively he knew that this was not the time for tears or impassioned argument, or for any

371

sort of emotional blackmail; when he spoke his voice was calm and reasonable. 'Lucy, my own dear love, don't you realise that it's not possible to love too much – only too little? It's true that we've seen a lot of pain in other people, caused by love. Casualties of love, you called them, and that may be true. But I think that our love is something different from that – something strong and good, not constricting or limiting.'

He tore a piece of polystyrene from his cup. 'I'd rather think of it in terms of redemption, to use a Christian term. Redemption of the past. What we feel for each other doesn't cancel out what happened to either one of us before. But it can redeem it, if we let it. And in a sense it can redeem what's happened to all of those other unhappy people, if we can make it work. Our love is the only thing that makes it all worthwhile.' Unconsciously he was shredding the cup, reducing it to bits of polystyrene all over the table. 'I remember what it was like to be alone, before I met you,' he said. 'And nothing could be worse than that. I don't want to go back to that, and I don't really think that you do either. It seems to me that taking the risk of loving – loving too much, as you call it – is far better than not loving at all.'

At last she lifted her eyes to meet his; hers were swimming with unshed tears. That unnerved him at last. 'Please don't cry,' he said brokenly. 'I can't bear to see you cry, my love.'

She reached across the table and took his hand. 'Well,' she said, with a watery smile, 'it's still over a week until the first of April. It looks as though you've got a week to convince me.'

David grasped her hand and pulled her to her feet,

leaving a mess of polystyrene behind. 'Come on, then,' he urged. 'A week isn't much time, and the clock is running. Let's go home, love.'

KATE CHARLES

Appointed to Die

A clerical mystery

Death at the Deanery – sudden and unnatural death. Someone should have seen it coming.

Even before Stuart Latimer arrives as the new Dean of Malbury Cathedral shock waves reverberate around the tightly knit Cathedral Close, heralding sweeping changes in a community that is not open to change. And the reality is worse than the expectation. The Dean's naked ambition and ruthless behaviour alienate everyone in the Chapter: the Canons, gentle John Kingsley, vague Rupert Greenwood, pompous Philip Thetford, and Subdean Arthur Bridges-ffrench, a traditionalist who resists change most strongly of all.

Financial jiggery-pokery, clandestine meetings, malicious gossip, and several people who see more than they ought to: a potent mix. But who could foresee that the mistrust and even hatred within the Cathedral Close would spill over into violence and death? Canon Kingsley's daughter Lucy draws in her lover David Middleton-Brown, against his better judgement, and together they probe the surprising secrets of a self-contained world where nothing is what it seems.

FICTION/CRIME   0 7472 4199 6

AN ECCLESIASTICAL WHODUNNIT

CLERICAL ERRORS

D. M. GREENWOOD

In the shadow of honey-coloured Medewich Cathedral, amidst the perfect lawns of the Cathedral Close, the diocesan office of St Manicus should have been a peaceful if not an especially exciting place for nineteen-year-old Julia Smith to start her first job. Yet she has been in its precincts for less than an hour when she stumbles on a horror of Biblical proportions - a severed head in the Cathedral font.

And she has worked for the suave Canon Wheeler for less than a day when she realises that the Dean and Chapter is as riven by rivalry, ambition and petty jealousy as the court of any Renaissance prelate. In this jungle of intrigue a young deaconess, Theodora Braithwaite, stands out as a lone pillar of common sense. Taciturn but kindly, she takes Julia under her wing, and with the assistance of Ian Caretaker - a young man who hates Canon Wheeler as much as he loves the Church - they attempt to unravel the truth behind the death of a well-meaning man, the Reverend Paul Gray, late incumbent of Markham cum Cumbermound.

FICTION/CRIME   0 7472 3582 1

A selection of bestsellers from Headline

MONSIEUR PAMPLEMOUSSE ON LOCATION	Michael Bond	£4.50 ☐
THE CAT WHO WENT INTO THE CLOSET	Lilian Jackson Braun	£4.50 ☐
MURDER WEARS A COWL	P C Doherty	£4.50 ☐
CURTAINS FOR THE CARDINAL	Elizabeth Eyre	£4.99 ☐
ROUGH RIDE	John Francome	£4.99 ☐
MURDER AMONG US	Ann Granger	£4.99 ☐
DEADLY ERRAND	Christine Green	£4.99 ☐
IDOL BONES	D M Greenwood	£4.50 ☐
THE END OF THE PIER	Martha Grimes	£4.50 ☐
COPY KAT	Karen Kijewski	£4.99 ☐
CLOSE UP ON DEATH	Maureen O'Brien	£5.99 ☐
THE LATE LADY	Staynes & Storey	£4.50 ☐
SWEET DEATH COME SOFTLY	Barbara Whitehead	£4.99 ☐

All Headline books are available at your local bookshop or newsagent, or can be ordered direct from the publisher. Just tick the titles you want and fill in the form below. Prices and availability subject to change without notice.

Headline Book Publishing PLC, Cash Sales Department, Bookpoint, 39 Milton Park, Abingdon, OXON, OX14 4TD, UK. If you have a credit card you may order by telephone – 0235 831700.

Please enclose a cheque or postal order made payable to Bookpoint Ltd to the value of the cover price and allow the following for postage and packing:
UK & BFPO: £1.00 for the first book, 50p for the second book and 30p for each additional book ordered up to a maximum charge of £3.00.
OVERSEAS & EIRE: £2.00 for the first book, £1.00 for the second book and 50p for each additional book.

Name ....

Address ....

....

....

If you would prefer to pay by credit card, please complete:
Please debit my Visa/Access/Diner's Card/American Express (delete as applicable) card no:

Signature .... Expiry Date ....